GRAVE
EXPECTATIONS

GRAVE
EXPECTATIONS

ALICE BELL

CORVUS

First published in the Great Britain in 2023 by Corvus,
an imprint of Atlantic Books Ltd.

Copyright © Alice Bell, 2023

10 9 8 7 6 5 4 3 2 1

A CIP catalogue record for this book is available from the British Library.

Hardback ISBN: 978 1 83895 839 8
Trade Paperback ISBN: 978 1 83895 840 4
E-book ISBN: 978 1 83895 841 1

Printed and bound by CPI (UK) Ltd, Croydon CR0 4YY

Corvus
An imprint of Atlantic Books Ltd
Ormond House
26–27 Boswell Street
London
WC1N 3JZ

www.atlantic-books.co.uk

For Colm. hello Colm! iluyu!

and for Jay
ave atque vale

The Wellington-Forge Family Tree

Annotated Edition provided by Alex, the cool one

Nana Forge — m — **Pappa Forge**

(née Heal)

11/10 great-grandmother ever, does not mind you smoking weed in front of her

Didn't know him but everyone says he was cool, and he married Nana so must have had good taste

Clementine Wellington-Forge ——— m ——

(née Forge)

Granny is a good cook but tbh she has some bad vibes, and she definitely does mind you smoking weed

Figgy Wellington-Forge

Auntie F basically lives on Harrods wallpaper swatches and invites to prosecco brunch in SoHo

Basher Wellington-Forge

Best uncle. Terrible hair. Lets me live with him, which is cool. Needs to loosen up though.

Montgomery Wellington-Forge — m — **Tuppence Wellington-Forge**

(née Taylor)

He's my dad and even I can see he's pretty fucked up. Even for a London lawyer.

I wish mum believed she deserves to be happy

Alex Wellington-Forge

Cooler, smarter, better looking than you. The great hope for the future. The one and only.

Hugh Wellington-Forge
(née Wellington)

Gun to my head I think the only thing I know about grandad is that likes brie and rugby

Tristan Wellington-Forge

Cruel thing to say about your own uncle but T is basically a standard embarrassing manchild

PART I

You think you will die, but you just keep living, day after day after terrible day.

Charles Dickens, *Great Expectations*

1

A Dead Girl

The train was two carriages long in its entirety, with rattling single-glazed windows, and it wound its way contentedly along the country line at whatever speed it felt like. It stopped at every tumbledown station it passed through, and this one was so small – a half-length platform of pebble-dashed concrete, covered in ivy at one end and collapsing at the other – that Claire almost didn't realize it was her stop. In the end it was Sophie who roused her from staring, unseeing, out of the window.

'Hey,' she said, waving a hand in front of Claire's face. 'I think this is it.'

'Oh, shit!'

Claire grabbed the bags and clattered out onto the platform just as the engine revved up once more. They turned and watched the train chunter off into the gathering darkness, then took stock. The letters on the sign were starting to peel off, but this was Wilbourne Major all right.

'*Ohmigod*,' Soph commented, as Claire shrugged on her coat. 'This place really is in the middle of nowhere.'

Claire turned round to look at her. Soph was in her usual bright turquoise velour tracksuit – Claire had almost forgotten what she looked like in anything else – the matching jacket and bottoms separated by a sliver of almost luminous midriff. Her chestnut curls were swept back into a high ponytail, and she had a few sparkly mini hair-claws in the shape of butterflies decorating the sides of her head. In fact it looked as if a giant butterfly had landed in the October gloom. Claire was struck, as she was more and more now that she was entering her thirties, by the strong protective urge she felt towards Sophie.

'Aren't we getting picked up? Where the *fuck* is the car?' Soph swore a lot – like, a lot a lot.

'Dunno.' Claire checked her phone. 'I haven't got any signal, of course. Figgy said she'd be here, though.'

'Let's go this way...' Sophie walked off the platform and through the hedge behind it. It turned out that the car park joined almost directly onto the platform, and there was indeed a car waiting on the far side of it. It was a very shiny black Audi.

'*Oof*,' said Sophie, as they walked towards it. 'How rich are they, again? Maybe this weekend won't be a total write-off.'

'I know, right?'

'Didn't you say everyone who has an Audi is a dick, though?'

'Yeah, they totally are. If you ever see someone driving like an arsehole, it's, like, always an Audi.'

'Isn't that like saying everyone who's rich is an arsehole?'

'I'm comfortable with that generalization,' Claire replied, picking at the loose threads in her coat. 'But shh. That's Figgy.'

'Sure, don't want to offend your rich arsehole friend. LOL.' Sophie pronounced it *el oh el*.

Figgy Wellington-Forge opened the driver's door and unfolded from the car like a sexy deckchair. She was very tall and was wearing a blue-and-white striped, figure-hugging woollen one-piece, as if she was off to an Alpine après-ski and not standing in mizzling rain in an English car park. She seemed exactly the same as she had been back in her university days with Claire.

'*Dah*-ling!' she cried, striding forward and bestowing Claire with four (four!) air-kisses. 'So good to see you.' Figgy was one of those people who stretched their vowels to breaking point, so what she actually said was: 'Seeeeeooo good to seeeyeeew!'

Claire slung the battered rucksack and holdall into the back seat, and Soph slid silently in after them. She sat in the middle because she liked to see the road. Claire sat in the front and then leaned back to fuss with the position of her rucksack, as a pretext to shoot Sophie a warning glance.

'Right!' Figgy exclaimed brightly. 'If we get a bit of a wiggle on, we should get to the house in good time for dinner. Mummy is doing shepherd's pie.'

Claire considered this. She'd had worse Friday nights than someone's mum making her shepherd's pie. It was getting truly dark now. When Claire looked in the rear-view mirror all she saw was the occasional oncoming headlight sparkling off Soph's lip gloss and her wide, dark eyes. Like most teenagers, Sophie's emotions passed across her face as quickly and obviously as clouds in front of the sun, but sometimes she switched off entirely and became totally impassive. It was quite scary.

Figgy shivered and put the heaters on full blast, then broke the silence that Claire suddenly realized had gone on for some time. 'So! How was your journey? God. It. Is. A. *Nightmare* getting down here, isn't it?'

Claire opened her mouth to agree – the trip from London had in fact taken the entire afternoon and a good portion of the evening – but Figgy didn't wait for an answer. She carried on chatting almost non-stop, while driving with the speed and abandon of someone who thinks they are a very good driver.

The car barrelled through the village of Wilbourne Major along back roads to Wilbourne Duces (an even smaller village that seemed more like a collection of houses around a pub and a postbox), and out into narrow lanes that twisted through fields. Claire found an opening eventually.

'Who's going to be here for the weekend, then? If you don't mind me asking,' she said.

'*Well*,' replied Figgy, intermittently taking her hands off the wheel to count off on her fingers, 'it's going to be almost all the family. There's Nana, obviously. She'll be hard to miss, she's the old lady in the wheelchair. Eighty-four on Sunday! Then there's Mummy and Daddy – Clementine and Hugh to you, I suppose. My sister-in-law Tuppence is here, too. She's married to my oldest bro, and brought their kid Alex along. Oh, and Basher's here, of course. He's the middle brother and he used to be a proper police detective, but he *totally* quit after the party last year. Bit of a sore spot with the 'rents, so maybe don't ask about it. Actually a huge sore spot. Massive drama.'

'Sorry, did you say "Basher"?'

'Ye-e-e-s! Sebastian, really, but nobody calls him that. I'm sure you met him. He came to a party at halls once.' Claire vaguely remembered a grave, blond young man with grey eyes eating all the Chilli Heatwave Doritos at a weekend pre-game before what was definitely not a pub crawl for Figgy's birthday (because pub crawls were unsanctioned by the uni, ever since a first-year chem student got alcohol poisoning).

'That's a load of people,' said Soph, who always kept track better than Claire. She often had to give Claire name prompts. 'Especially if more are turning up for the main party tomorrow.'

'It sounds like heaps, but it's actually less than last year,' said Figgy. 'Is it a problem?'

'Nah,' said Claire. 'I've, um, had bigger groups.' This was in fact untrue, but there was no reason to tell the truth.

'Gosh, it's so amazing you could come, you know – you really saved my bacon. Usually we take turns to arrange entertainment for the family get-togethers, and I *totally* forgot it was my go this time. But when I ran into you, I was just like: Oh. My. God! Perfect for Halloween, you know? You look fabulous, by the way,' Figgy added, lyingly.

Claire was in the middle of what was turning out to be an indefinitely long lean patch. She was wearing battered trainers with holes in the heels, a pair of black jeans that were so worn through they were grey, and a fifteen-year-old wool coat over her one nice winter jumper, in deference to the fact they were visiting a rich family. Her dyed black hair was showing about three inches of mousy roots, in contrast to Figgy's perfect white-blonde French plait. Figgy wasn't totally unkind. This hadn't stopped Claire asking for a fee about 150 per cent higher than her usual rate, to which Figgy had readily agreed. So readily that Claire realized she should have plumped for 200 per cent.

'Yeah,' she said, offering a smile. 'It should be good. It's a big old house, right?'

'Mmm! It has *wings*. Grade Two listed, because of the library. Of course, really it all belongs to Nana. She keeps joking that she's going to change her will and have Mummy and Daddy out on their ear. They've properly rowed about it a few times, so I hope it doesn't kick off in front of you. That would be so embarrassing! It's just, you know, such an expensive old place to run, and I think Nana is worried that Mummy and Daddy are struggling. But honestly, Mummy would rather sell a kidney than that house.'

There was a pause as Figgy changed up a gear, releasing the clutch so abruptly that Claire jerked forward about six inches and heard one of the bags in the back fall off the seat.

'Whoops! Anyway, you don't need to worry about all that. It's a lovely place, really. I think the house is a couple of hundred years old or something. And the land used to have a monastery, so there are some ruined bits of wall and things that are much older. That's why the house is still officially called The Cloisters.'

'There'd better not be any grim dead monks hanging about,' interjected Sophie from the back.

'There's supposedly *heaps* of ghosts,' said Figgy happily. 'Including this very creepy monk. Every time there's a death, he's meant to appear to the next member of the family who's going to pop their clogs! Although nobody has ever actually seen him – at least not for hundreds of years. Monty made Tristan dress as the monk and hide in my wardrobe once, though, the beast.'

She gave no explanation of who either Tristan or Monty was. Claire imagined some boisterous cousins who visited every summer to have adventures, like the extremely smug children from *The Famous Five*. Boys in knee-shorts and long socks who said 'Rather!' and drank loads of ginger beer and lemonade to wash down doorstep-sized ham sandwiches.

Figgy suddenly swerved right, onto a neat dirt road that sloped downwards. Unidentifiable trees knotted their arms together overhead. The car began scrunching over gravel, and Claire got a glimpse of an imposing grey stone portico, before Figgy swung around the side of the building and came to a stop at the back. There were lights on here – Figgy explained that the family spent most of their time in and around the old kitchen.

'All these bits used to be for, you know, looking after the house,' she said as she got out of the car. 'Pantries, and rooms for some of the important servants, that sort of thing. It's been converted into the family home, so the rest of the place can be used for' – Figgy waved her hands vaguely – 'weddings and corporate away-days and shooting parties, and so on.'

She led them through a heavy green wooden door, which opened directly into a large room with a flagstoned floor and whitewashed walls. Claire was immediately disorientated by the bright light, the explosion of savoury smells and an assault of loud hooting from the family. It was a kind of wordless, elongated vowel noise in place of an actual greeting, to herald their arrival.

A shorter, squatter, older version of Figgy bustled over, though where Figgy's skin was a delicate white porcelain colour with perfect blush cheeks, this woman was more bronzed, as if she spent most weekends gardening. She had a perfect feathery blonde bob and a deep pink cardigan with a string of neat pearls hanging around her neck, but she also had a powerful welly-boots aura. This was not just a mum. This was an M&S mum.

'Hellooooo, dahlings! I'm afraid we couldn't wait to eat, but there's plenty left,' said – presumably – Clementine, giving out air-kisses that left a strong rose-scented perfume in their wake. 'I'll make up some plates. Come in, come in! Say hello. Hugh was just going into the other room to watch the rugger.' Here Clementine gave an exaggerated eyeroll, as if to intimate that they were all girls here – ha, men and their balls!

'That woman never met a Laura Ashley print she didn't like,' said Sophie, talking quietly in Claire's ear. 'I bet she has a knitting circle of dearest friends and hates every one of them. I bet she has a plan to kill each of them and get away with it.'

Sophie had a habit of being unkind about people when she first met them (and also after she'd first met them), but in this case Claire had to admit she was right. Clementine had an intensity to her kindness that hinted at a blanket intensity to all her actions.

They paused to look around. The room they were in was clearly the old kitchen, but had been converted to an all-purpose family room. It had a high ceiling hung with bunches of dried flowers and herbs, and was bright and warm. In front of the door where they'd come in were a couple of creaking armchairs, and a much-loved sofa faced a smouldering fire. A sturdy wooden table ran off to the left, taking up almost the whole length of the rest of the room, towards a large blue Aga at the far end. The table still held the remnants of a family meal, as well as a few remnants of family, who were getting up to be introduced.

In contrast to his wife's crisp consonants, patriarch Hugh's voice was a kind of Canary Wharf foghorn. It went well with his vigorous handshake and his job 'in finance'. He had a ruddy complexion, the pinkish-red inflammation of a white man who drank a lot of red wine and ate a lot of red meat. His watery blue eyes squinted out of a once-handsome face that was losing its definition at the edges, like a soft cheese.

'Hugh looks like a man who never misses an episode of *Question Time*,' murmured Sophie, cocking an eyebrow.

Claire bit on the inside of her cheek, and managed to give a non-committal 'mhmm' in response to Hugh's greeting. He was folding up a broadsheet paper. There was a story with the headline 'I Don't Care What the Wokerati Say, I Won't Stop Putting Mayonnaise in My Welsh Rarebit', and she looked at this in disbelief and confusion for long enough that Hugh noticed.

'Ridiculous, isn't it? Can't do or say anything these days. Corporate political correctness is running amok everywhere, and you can't even bloody eat food how you want!' he said, misreading her expression. 'Now people are complaining that if you make rarebit with mayo, it's cultural appropriation! Can you believe it?'

Claire considered the best way to answer this.

'No,' she said. 'I cannot believe people are doing that.' She was aware that: a) she would probably fall into this newspaper's definition of wokerati; and b) if she was able to conceal this from Hugh like a ratfuck coward, she might be able to get a bonus for good behaviour on top of her already-inflated fee.

'"Putting some mayo in your Welsh rarebit" sounds like a sex thing anyway,' commented Soph. 'Newspaper columnists are all perverts.'

Claire bit the inside of her other cheek. Fortunately, this conversation was rescued by the introduction of a third new family member. Hugh gave an awkward side-arm hug to the newcomer, a woman in her forties. 'This lovely creature is Tuppence. M'boy Monty, my eldest, had the good sense to tie her down!'

Everything about Tuppence was meek: meek ponytail, a swathe of meek pashminas and layered cottons in various browns, and a meek, limp handshake. Even the cold she appeared to have was meek. She kept mopping her nose with tissues that were overflowing from her sleeves, rather than blowing it once, to have done with it.

But when she said, 'It really is nice to meet you!' Claire decided Tuppence was her favourite person in the world. 'My husband can't be here this weekend,' she said, answering a question that Claire had not in fact asked. 'He and Tristan are working on an important case at their firm.'

'Er, sorry – who is Tristan?'

Figgy elbowed in and took Claire's coat. 'Sorry, should have said, darling. Tris is my youngest bro, youngest of the four of us. He's an absolute brat, honestly.'

'They're both lawyers at Monty's firm in London,' said Tuppence. 'But we'll have to make do without them this time, I suppose.'

'Interesting,' whispered Sophie, close to Claire's ear. 'Tuppence actually sounds quite pleased to be rid of Monty. This family is definitely going to turn out to be a mess, I love it. LOL.'

'Most families are a mess,' replied Claire, with an apologetic grimace. 'Uh, I mean... um, organizing events for families, you know – a nightmare.'

To Claire's surprise, Tuppence covered her mouth at this and looked at the ceiling. 'As long as we don't put mayonnaise in the rarebit,' she said, as she looked back at Claire. Claire couldn't have sworn to it, but she thought Tuppence might have winked.

That seemed to be all of the family present in the kitchen. Of Nana, Tuppence's child or the improbable Basher, there was currently no sign. Clementine reappeared, putting down a loaded plate and leading Claire to sit at the table. Sophie stuck her tongue out at the back of Clem's head and declared that she was going to look around – which meant roaming the house to nose through as much of people's private lives as possible.

'So, Claire!' said Hugh, who had conjured a bottle of wine from nowhere. 'Last name Voyant, yes? HA!'

Claire loaded an exploratory forkful of pie, as Figgy sat down next to her. 'Nope. Hendricks. Good one, though.' This was her polite stock response to a joke she had heard about a million, billion times.

Hugh was struggling manfully with the corkscrew, and Clementine took the bottle without speaking and opened it for him. Her expression was dispassionate.

'Terribly exciting, though,' said Clementine, giving a jovial little shrug. 'Very unusual kind of entertainment to do, you know. I was really interested when Figgy said she'd hired you.'

14

'Mhmm. This pie is really great, thank you,' said Claire, shovelling it down. She was quite hungry because she'd only had a thing of Super Noodles for lunch before she got on the train. In contrast, Figgy was taking small and delicate mouthfuls and savouring each, as if she were a judge on *Masterchef.*

'Claire and I were at university together, d'you remember me saying, Mummy?' said Figgy. 'And I ran into her and, when she told me her job, I thought it would be so quirky and spooky. I was only saying to Claire in the car, it's perfect for Halloween. Didn't I say that, Claire?'

'Yes, you did. And yeah, this is usually quite a good time of year for me.'

Claire noticed that everyone in the room was sort of hanging around, watching her. It was a strange feeling. She didn't think they were trying to be rude, but it seemed a bit like they were privy to a rare zoological exhibit. Just as she thought of them as common-or-garden posh dullards, Claire realized that they saw her as the lesser-known drab weirdo. It wasn't that people didn't think she was weird quite often, but they were usually more subtle about it; or, having hired her, were more engaged with the weirdness. And she had seen enough horror films to know that a bunch of upper-class people inviting you to their family home for Halloween weekend, and then examining you like some sort of game bird, was a potential recipe for disaster. She looked around, but Sophie was still off exploring.

Perhaps realizing that everyone was staring at Claire in silence, Clementine abruptly announced that there wasn't a pudding, but there was fruit, which made Hugh grumble under his breath. He sidled off to watch the rugby. Figgy finished eating and started helping her mother to tidy up, which made Claire feel awkward. She concentrated on her plate instead. Her wine glass kept magically refilling as she ate, and soon she was feeling quite hot and sick from all the carbs and alcohol that she had hoofed into her stomach.

As if sensing this, too, Clementine led her away to a neat twin bedroom. Clementine's powers of observation and/or telepathy were unnerving, but the fact that it was a twin room pleased Claire, because it meant there was enough room for Sophie to keep herself entertained. All the furnishings were cream or white, and the walls and roof were a bit higgledy-piggledy. The walls didn't join up where you'd expect them to – like something a child had tried to make out of Play-Doh. There was a little en suite shower and toilet, though, which was probably more complex than a Play-Doh house would allow. It was very nice. A lot nicer than her flat in London.

Claire opened the window to cool down and suppress her nausea. She was leaning out, collecting deep lungfuls of clean country air, when she realized it wasn't as clean as she'd expected. The dense and delicious smell of weed was wafting through the autumn night. Then she caught the sound of quiet talking and, remarkably, Sophie laughing.

It took her a few minutes of self-consciously creeping around cold corridors in the dark, but eventually Claire found a heavy curtain that was concealing a set of French doors. On the other side of these was a discreet patio, with a couple of tables and chairs and one of those big garden wood-burner things.

Sophie was staring into the flames. Next to her, a teenager with blue hair was clutching an asymmetrical black cardigan around themself and holding about two-thirds of a massive joint.

'All right?' said the teenager, jerking their head up in greeting. They were a good few inches taller than Sophie, looked maybe a couple of years older – enough to legally buy a pint, at least – and appeared to have shaved stripes into one of their eyebrows. 'I'm Alex.'

'Huh, I assumed you were younger. Figgy made it sound as if you're, like, twelve. Are you -andra or -ander?'

'Neither. Does it matter?'

'Nope,' said Claire.

'Cool. Don't tell Granny Clem about the weed.'

Claire thought about this. 'Er. I won't if I can have some.'

'Mutually assured destruction,' said Alex, whilst breathing out another thick herbal cloud. 'I like it.' They passed her the joint and moved away from Sophie to get closer to the fire. Claire took the joint, but exclaimed, 'Fucking Christ!' and nearly dropped it when someone else entirely said, 'You must be Claire.'

Claire leaned over to peer at the other side of the wood-burner. There was a very old lady sitting in a wheelchair, wrapped (as is traditional for little old ladies in wheelchairs) in a couple of tartan blankets. Her eyes were twinkling and she looked very much like she was about to laugh. Leaning on a table near her was a man Claire just

17

about recognized as the Dorito-eater from Figgy's party years ago. He had shaved all his messy blond hair off, which made him look gaunt and tired.

'That's Basher and Nana,' said Sophie. 'They're all right. I like them.'

'I'm right, aren't I?' Nana said. 'You're Claire. Figgy's friend from university.'

'Yeah, that's me,' said Claire. She took a modest hit from the joint and passed it back to Alex. It felt weird smoking weed in front of someone else's granny – great-granny, even. 'Um. Basher and I have actually met before.'

'Hmm,' said Basher. 'I think I remember.'

'Wait, you're the medium?' said Alex, suddenly interested. 'Cool. That's cool. So you can talk to ghosts then.'

'Yup.'

'You really expect us to believe that?' asked Basher.

'Erm, no. Not really. Most people don't, obviously,' said Claire.

Nana laughed and her eyes twinkled again. 'Very good answer. She's got you pegged, Bash, dear.'

'You don't *look* like a medium,' said Alex, passing the joint again.

Emboldened by the positive reception, Claire took a healthier pull this time and spent a few moments looking up at the sky. It had become a very clear night, and this far from a city she could see all the stars scattered everywhere, like broken glass in a pub car park.

'I dunno,' she said after a bit. 'What are mediums supposed to look like?'

'Yeah, all right, fair enough. Do you have a – a what-chamacallit. A spirit guide?'

'Yup, I do.'

Basher snorted at this.

'I do, though!' Claire protested.

'Yes,' Basher said. 'I expect he's some Native American chieftain. Or a poor Victorian shoeshine boy?'

'No, *actually*,' said Claire, who was feeling the effects of what really was very good-quality weed. 'Ah – nah, I don't know if I should tell you.'

'You know you have to now!' cried Alex.

'Yeah, g'wan. It'll freak 'em out,' said Sophie.

'Okay, okay. She's a girl in fact.'

'Ah yes,' said Basher. 'With long dark hair, and she is going to crawl out of the TV?'

'That's a whole other thing. That's a movie – that's not real. Duh,' Claire replied.

'Of course, I apologize. So what is your ghost's tragic back-story? A Georgian waif who died at Christmas? A poor misfortunate who pined to death in the fifties?'

'Don't be boring, Uncle B,' said Alex. 'You sound like Dad when you get all smug.'

'She's not a Victorian waif,' said Claire, who was starting to get a bit annoyed by Basher and was keen to prove him wrong. 'She's from the noughties. She died when she was seventeen.'

'Ah, very convenient,' said Basher. 'No historical research required with a ghost from your own generation.'

'Well, joke's on you, because I studied history, so if I

wanted to make up a period-accurate ghost I could. But I don't need to,' said Claire. She was trying to freak them out a bit, but it wasn't really working.

Sophie rolled her eyes.

Claire looked up at the diamond sky again and started laughing. 'It's funny – she's not anything. She's just normal really.'

'Am *not*, weirdo,' said Sophie. 'I'm exceptional.'

'She's annoying,' Claire corrected. She looked over the flames at her friend, bright-eyed and smirking, standing in the clothes she had been murdered in. 'Her name's Sophie and she's been eavesdropping on you for, like, half an hour already.'

2

A Quick Bit of Seance

The truth was that Claire was not a very good medium. Her figure was not suited to maxi-dresses, incense made her sneeze and she couldn't be arsed with smoky eyeshadow. She also wasn't good at coming up with significant but vague things to say about the after-life, like 'Ah, the energies from the Other Side are strong here.' The only part she was good at was that she could genuinely see and talk to dead people, but as it turned out, that bit was the least important.

When Claire had turned to freelance mediuming on a full-time basis she'd swiftly discovered that nobody ever wants a real seance. Attempts to do genuine ones usually ended in disappointment and bad reviews on Tripadvisor. Really, punters just wanted something they could tell their friends about.

They did not actually want to talk to their dearly departed grandad who, even if he was still hanging around, would be more likely to ask about Tottenham's form, and complain that they never visited enough when he was alive, than say that he loved them and was happy where he was, in heaven with Jesus and all the angels. In fact the two were mutually exclusive: a ghost could not be both in heaven (or whatever came after dying) and able to have a chat on Earth.

Claire didn't have an especially scientific mind, but as far as she could tell some people simply stayed hanging around after they died, and that was that. It was usually someone who had regrets, either about how they had lived or how they died. Maybe they didn't get to say goodbye to their loved ones, or their cupcake business didn't get as much recognition as they felt it deserved, or one of their family managed to get the standing lamp they'd said they absolutely couldn't have. If they resolved that – if they real-ized their family loved them anyway, that their cupcakes weren't actually that great, or that the standing lamp was fugly – then they would disappear. If not, they just hung around, making the air cold and sometimes moaning at other ghosts (particularly the case in churchyards, where there were usually a few ghosts corralled together, nurturing petty ghost grievances that were the dead person equivalent of a neighbour not returning a borrowed casserole dish, but sharpened to acuteness over hundreds of years). Unless they made an effort to keep their shit literally together, older ghosts could get fuzzy, and eventually became nothing more than a little cloud of misty unhappiness.

That was how it was; that was what Claire had observed. In the extremely online debates about whether a hot dog was a sandwich, Claire would be the sort of person to say that a sandwich was what got put in front of you when you asked for one in a greasy spoon. Evidence suggested that a ghost was a person capable of annoying nobody except, specifically, Claire, and this rendered the metaphysics of the situation more or less a moot point for her.

Over the years, Sophie and Claire had, using a lot of trial and error, developed what were fairly good versions of fake seances, with a bit of real communication with the dead thrown in – which Claire editorialized and expanded upon, if the ghosts weren't saying anything that interesting or nice. Technically, Claire didn't need Sophie's help to talk to ghosts, but the process (which involved Sophie yelling loudly to attract as many spirits as possible) went more smoothly when they worked together. Claire had an advantage over her spiritualist ancestors: cold-reading was pretty easy when everyone shared everything online, plus Sophie was able to have a good nose around their hosts' houses without anyone knowing.

Their seances were sufficiently skilful now that Claire had a client bench deep enough at least to eat and pay the rent. But she did feel aggrieved that her ability to see and talk to dead people – which was actually a pretty bloody impressive thing to do, when you thought about it – was basically good for nothing. By rights she should be mega-rich and have a syndicated television show. But she wasn't and she didn't, and even if someone offered her a TV gig, she would get scared and turn it down, partly for reasons she didn't like to talk about which had left her afraid of public exposure, but also because she didn't have the natural confidence around people that Sophie did. Sometimes, in very quiet moments at two o'clock in the morning, Claire wondered if it would have been better if *she* had died and become the ghost. Sophie would probably have had a recurring guest spot on *This Morning* by now. All Claire had was this gig at Figgy's parents' weird old house.

And she was possibly jeopardizing even that by chuckling like a gibbon after describing how a girl had died at seventeen and was now her invisible companion.

'Sorry, sorry,' she said, getting herself under control. 'It's just funny that you're saying she doesn't exist, when she's right there.'

Alex, Basher and Nana looked, variously, alarmed, incredulous and sympathetic.

'Seventeen! That's no age,' said Nana. 'I'm sorry to hear that, Sophie dear.' She looked towards where she assumed Sophie was standing, and Sophie obligingly moved so that she wasn't wrong. 'Did you two know each other when you were alive?'

'No-o-o. No. Nope,' said Claire. She had learned from experience that people didn't respond well to her spirit guide being her best friend from school, a real person whose memory Claire was – to the outside observer – exploiting for money. 'We would have been born around the same time, but that's it. Never knew her. She just, uh, turned up one day. It was when I was a teenager, too, so

24

we suspect it was something to do with hormones and, er, moon energies.'

Sophie grimaced. 'You know, I still hate it that that line actually works on people.'

'A bit like the X-Men,' said Alex, snickering. 'In the films a lot of them got powers around the age of sexual maturity. Is seeing ghosts also a metaphor, do you think?'

'I think I understand that. I got a lot of stretchmarks when I turned sixteen. I grew about a foot overnight, I remember,' said Nana.

'Oh, come on, Nana. You don't seriously believe any of this is true?' said Basher, who seemed to be getting annoyed. He would be the useful sceptic, Claire could already tell. 'Not the stretchmarks. The talking to ghosts.'

'Well, I'm very nearly dead, dear, and you're talking to me,' Nana said.

'Before you arrived,' Sophie told Claire, 'they were talking about how the family should just sell the house to a hotel chain that's sniffing around. Du-something. Du Lotte Hotels, I think.' Claire repeated this.

'That doesn't prove anything!' said Basher, his eyes flashing in the firelight. 'You probably heard that yourself. And by the way, it's bloody rude to listen in to private conversations.'

Sophie moved around to blow on his neck idly and make him shiver, and giggled when he did.

'That's her. She's blowing on your neck.'

'Give over. It's cold out here – I am cold.'

Sophie next started tickling the side of Nana's face. Nana raised a hand to her cheek.

'Yeah, that's her,' said Claire, before Nana could ask. 'She's tickling your face.' Claire elaborated, explaining: Sophie wasn't a poltergeist, she couldn't pick things up or rifle through your knicker drawer, but if you'd left your knicker drawer open or a private letter out somewhere, she'd have a proper good look. She'd been naturally nosy even before she'd died; being invisible only made it easier. If she blew on your face, it felt like you were looking into a freezer; and if she tickled your cheek, you might think a cold spider was walking across it. But that was all she could do, unless she was getting help from Claire.

'That's jolly interesting, isn't it?' said Nana. 'Do you know, I'm quite looking forward to dying now. I'm sure ghosts don't get swollen feet.'

'First of all,' said Basher, 'can we stop talking as if you're going to shuffle off your mortal coil tomorrow morning? And, second, have we just accepted the existence of ghosts now? Is that all it took?'

Alex shrugged and carefully put out the joint. 'We should do a seance. Can we do a seance? I've never done one before, I wanna do one.'

'Doing one tomorrow night. S'what I'm here for. What *we're* here for. When all the other guests have arrived. Midnight seance: bell, book and candle, the whole thing. Well spooky. Proper seance business.'

'I mean we should do one *tonight*. Now.'

Claire looked over at Sophie.

26

'*I* don't care if we do one now,' Sophie said. 'Figgy was right: there are a load of deados hanging around, for me to drum up for conversation. An old lady was having a blazing row with a little Frenchman in one of the rooms in the big house. Also a pervy old gardener, like, you know, a really shit version of Sean Bean in that TV series about a woman shagging her gamekeeper. On the other hand, they seem quite boring, they might not turn up, and you're pissed and also high, so I dunno if you'll be much use at cold-reading, if the ghosts are rubbish. It's a gamble. But one I'm willing for you to take. LOL.'

Alex misinterpreted the long pause while Claire listened to Soph, because they tipped their head on one side and said, 'I'll pay you extra, if that's what you're worried about. Half fee on top again, right? Exclusive preview for the family, which all our horrible godparents and Grandad Hugh's mates from work don't get when they turn up tomorrow.'

Claire had *not* been worried about getting paid extra, and then worried that she hadn't worried about it, because that meant she really was quite high.

'That means,' added Basher with a slight smile, 'Alex is going to persuade someone else to pay you extra.'

'Potato, pot*ah*to's rich lawyer dad,' said Alex, flapping their hand impatiently.

Claire opened her mouth to object, then shut it again, and Alex took advantage of this indecision. They bundled her back inside and into the kitchen, and before long had convinced Clementine and Figgy that they could have what Clementine called 'a quick bit of seance' before bed, as long as Nana didn't get too worked up. They went to crowbar Hugh from his game ('For heaven's sake, it's a recording, Hugh! You can just pause it!') and Claire went to her room to try and prepare as best she could.

She filled the sink with cold water and stuck her face into it, while Sophie lay on one of the beds and watched.

'You're such a train wreck. You haven't done one of these while you're pissed since like, what... 2013? This is going to go terribly – it's going to be amazing.'

'"Bit of seance",' Claire muttered. 'It's not a sugar-free fizzy drink. You can't do a... a fucking "seance lite". Christ, I hate rich people.'

'You know, I'm not even sure they're that rich, really,' said Soph, thinking out loud. 'I mean obviously they *are*, in a relative sense, but if you look around at this place, you start to notice all the bits where it's falling apart.' She pointed out cracks in the plaster around the window, and patches of rot in the wooden frame itself.

Sophie was much better at noticing things. All she did now was watch, of course, but she had watched when she was alive, too. She had noticed, for example, the introverted, mousy girl nervously waiting alone at the bus stop on the first day of Big School at the turn of the millennium, and although Soph had been alone as well, she had not been nervous. It was an emotion that was beyond her, even aged eleven. She had gone up to Claire and said, 'Hello. Let's be friends.' And so they were. Claire had never been sure why she'd been chosen, but it had happened. And Sophie was pretty, and knew how to plait her hair and do make-up, and already shaved her legs, and pretended not to try in class, even though she secretly did. Her association threw a shield around Claire, who suspected she would otherwise have been consigned to the weirdo kids who wore bow ties and wrote poetry at lunchtime.

In return, Claire helped Sophie with homework – which was the sort of thing Sophie never had the patience for – and made her laugh, and bared her secret innermost thoughts and listened to Sophie's, and drank blue WKD in a field until they were sick, and swung on children's swings on frosty nights until they went so high that Claire was afraid of what would happen if they fell.

Soph was never afraid. She would always have kept going.

As they got older, Sophie decided her favourite drink was Bacardi, and that was what she was like, too: strong, sweet, clear, overwhelming. (Claire was rosé wine, something a bit childish masquerading as almost adult.)

When Sophie vanished, Claire had lost touch with who she was as a person. The disappearance had given her, by association, a layer of grim, Gothic mystique. The missing girl's best friend! The *enfant tragique*! But after a while everyone had tired of that and had dropped Claire, for her rapidly increasing strangeness: the talking to herself, the covering her ears to block out inaudible sounds, the wearing of layers and layers of clothes even indoors, and then the eventual embracing of the cold. Because Sophie had come back. Like she had chosen Claire all over again. Sophie was the first friend Claire had, and the first ghost she saw. After she returned, Claire saw dead people everywhere.

Secretly she had been relieved at Sophie's return – even in her ghostly state. But lately, although she'd never share the thought, Claire had begun to wonder how much she and Sophie really had in common, apart from the fact that they'd been friends for so long. Perhaps, under normal circumstances, their friendship would not have survived the test of adulthood. Luckily – or, technically unluckily, she supposed – any testing was now moot. They were stuck together. Almost literally, because unlike most ghosts who were tethered to a place, Sophie was tethered to Claire, and when they got far enough apart Claire could feel it like tension on a lead.

Worse, perhaps, was that Sophie was stuck as a person, too: she had the lifetime of experience of an adult, but assessed it like a teen. She was quick to anger, quick to invent and point out injustices, as swift and as casual in her insults as she had been when part of a tribe of adolescents, picking sides and drawing battle lines at house-parties and pubs. More and more, Claire worried that she herself was the same. Perhaps she had never got rid of her worst, most immature impulses because they were given voice and form every day. They were there when she woke up and when she got into bed, and they watched her while she dreamed.

*

Left alone in her guest bedroom, Claire changed into what she thought of as her work clothes: a sober black dress and, retrieved reverentially from a plastic baggy that years ago had held a small quantity of terrible cheap cocaine that was later snorted off a toilet in a student union bar, one of Sophie's real-life butterfly hair-claws. Claire carefully fixed it into her own hair, pinning back the wonky bit of her fringe left from where she'd tried to trim it herself. Then she gathered her equipment: a big brass hand-bell, a heavy silver candlestick with impressive wax dribbles, a plastic Bic lighter and a large, old Bible.

The main house would normally have been hosting guests or some kind of event, but was kept free on birthday weekends so that the Wellington-Forges could pretend it was still all theirs. That they had the run of the whole place and bossed servants about, like their ancestors used to. The bit of seance was going to be held in the library, an impressive room with floor-to-ceiling shelves on one wall, full of leather-bound books with gold-printed spines: bottle-green, wine-red, earthy brown tomes. Opposite these was a bank of huge leaded-glass windows.

The clouds peeled back from the moon outside, and the room was filled with little diamonds of black and white. Claire felt her skin tingle, like she was being watched. She breathed in and, instead of the dry air of a room full of books, she tasted mud in the back of her throat. Her heart rate spiked in sudden panic and she was struck with a wave of fear and nausea – a nausea distinct from the churning red wine sickness she already felt. Sharp pain flashed behind her eyes and she groped for the back of a chair to lean on.

There was a sudden rattle as Figgy started to pull the curtains shut, and Clementine switched a lamp on. The moment was over, and nobody seemed to have noticed. Claire looked at Sophie, who nodded grimly.

'I felt it too,' she said. 'I'll keep an eye out for any buzz kills.' Some spirits stayed bitter. The mean ones did try to ruin things sometimes.

The family were arranged around a large round table. Nana patted a seat between her and Basher. Claire went over, placed the candle and book in front of her, then bent to put the bell under the table in a slow, exaggerated fashion.

'Hold on,' said Basher, on cue. 'I read about this. Houdini showed how you can just ring the bell with your foot and we wouldn't know.'

Claire tried not to smile. She could always count on one person knowing about Houdini. 'Of course,' she said and put the bell in the middle of the table. She nodded to herself, turned the lamp off and then regretted the order in which she'd done things, as she blundered back to the table in darkness to light the candle.

The room narrowed to a point as the darkness became darker. As if they knew what was expected of them, every-one took the hands of the people on either side of them.

Sophie knelt in the centre of the table, her pale face illuminated from below by the flame. She crawled forward until she was on top of it, and the candle burned inside her. Everyone else saw the candle begin to burn blue at the edges and throw strange, refracted shadows that danced on the ceiling and walls where they had no business being. Claire saw her friend glowing like a paper lantern. She saw the pink hair-claw that she now wore mirrored in Sophie's hair, the ghost of a hair-clip. It was here, but also there. It was in two places at once. This always made her feel weird.

Claire leaned forward and bowed her head, and Sophie reached out and put her hand on top of it. It was like someone had plonked a bag of frozen peas on the crown of Claire's head, and she couldn't help shivering. She felt the *zip* of the connection between them, like she was a battery pack and Sophie was an iPhone that had just been plugged in. She fought the urge to yawn.

'Line!' said Soph.

'Mmm? Wzt?'

'It's your line, weirdo. "Sophie, spirit guide, lost souls of this place, yadda-yadda, and so on." You are useless.'

Claire stifled a burp. 'S-Sophie. My spirit guide. Please – ugh – please connect us to the lost souls of this place. Help us speak with them. Is there anybody there?'

Sophie reached in front of her and, by using Claire's strength, was able to lift the bell about half an inch. She began ringing it gently, but rhythmically. Claire was pleased to hear several gasps from around the table. They would have been less impressed by the mystic forces at work if they could hear Sophie's yelling: 'COME ON THEN! BRING OUT YER DEAD! LET'S GO! TALKING TO THE LIVING, RIGHT HERE! ROLL UP, ROLL UP – I'VE NOT GOT ALL FUCKING NIGHT.'

A few foggy shapes began to seep through the walls – the really old dead, who couldn't remember who or what they were any more. Only one ghost who turned up still looked like a person: an elderly white man with a green flat cap, a big white moustache and yellow corduroy trousers. He was leaning on a pitchfork.

'Here,' he said, in a strong Cornish accent. 'Can us really talk to them? Ask about the girl who visited last year. Where's she to? She had a cracking pair of—'

'Ohmigod, shutthefuckup, you old perv! I think he's your lot tonight, to be honest,' Sophie told Claire, apologetically. 'Go with an old standby. I haven't discovered anything properly juicy yet.'

They fumbled through a few cold-reads, based on family photos that Sophie described, and the people round the table were more or less impressed by the whole thing (mostly less, if Claire was being honest with herself). Sophie kept laughing and suggesting she reveal that Tuppence was going to cheat on Monty and abscond to the Lake District with her lover and all the family's money. Getting desperate, Claire tried intimating that Clementine's father gave the family their blessing to sell the house, which went down extremely poorly. Basher's hand tightened angrily in her own. But at that point the old gardener, who was still hanging around, got bored. He hobbled forward and grabbed Sophie's ankle with an experimental air. Claire felt another *zip* as the drain on her doubled, and then a ghostly argument rang out across the silent room, for everyone to hear.

'How does this work? Tell them we don't like all the young lads who comes here and has big parties and pisses in the rose garden. Ruins the soil.'

'*Ohmigod*, let go, that is *so* rude!'

Claire craned to try and see what was happening, because no ghost had done this to Sophie before. None of the family around the table had leapt from their seat in alarm, so she was fairly sure the ghosts weren't visible to anyone else, but the old man was definitely pulling energy from her through Sophie, because she could feel herself getting more tired by the second.

Claire could just about see that Hugh and Clementine, off to her left, were looking around to try to locate the source of the voices. Normally dead people sounded sort of two-dimensional – not without emotion, but flat, appearing in Claire's ears without bumping into any air in between. It was hard to tell, but now it was as if someone had turned on an invisible speaker above the table, so that Sophie's and the gardener's voices were being pumped into the room, echoing off the walls, crossing over one another and wavering in volume.

'Also, please tell Her Majesty congratulations on the birth of her son. I would have written, but I couldn't, on account of being dead.'

'Okay, well, you could mean literally, like, three differ-ent people by that, so I don't know—'

'You button up, young lady. Trouble is that young people like you got no respect for their elders, so you just let me talk—'

'Claire, this grotey old perv won't let go of my *foot*.'

Nana started laughing.

'Well! Is that Miss Janey?' asked the gardener, ignoring Sophie's attempts to kick him off her. 'You know, I always took an interest in you – a very particular interest. Bright as a button you were.'

'Hello, Ted! I'm glad you still seem to be in good form. For a dead man,' said Nana.

'Ar, good form, Miss Janey, good form.' Ted was starting to look alarmingly *solid*.

Claire felt light-headed. Basher was leaning forward.

'And may I say you looked beautiful on your wedding day. You were a fine girl and, if I may add, meaning no disrespect, you grew up into *a very fine young woman*—'

Sophie shrieking 'Ohmi*god*, put a fucking cork in it, Ted!' was the last thing the party heard, before Claire jerked her head back from Sophie's reach. It was like unplugging a really strange and specific radio. But *she* could still see and hear the ghosts. Sophie was kicking at Ted while he cackled heartily.

'The, uh, the circle is broken, or whatever,' said Claire vaguely. She blew out the candle. The darkness was reassuringly normal and gave her a few moments of cover to slump back in the chair. She would say it felt as if she'd just run a marathon – if she had ever done any recreational running whatsoever.

Around her she could hear the Wellington-Forges reacting. Figgy was doing happy piglet squeals, enjoying being scared in a safe way. Hugh kept rumbling, 'Very good. Bloody good, I thought.' Nana was humming. Clementine immediately began bustling, and soon had the lights on again. This revealed that Alex was on their hands and knees under the table, and Basher was pulling large books off a shelf at random.

Alex poked their head out and looked up at Claire, unabashed. 'No wires,' they said, with a grin.

'That does not rule out wireless technology,' said Basher. He continued feeling along the shelves and checking books.

'Ah,' said Claire. 'You're, er, looking for a speaker.' At least she tried to say this, but the word 'speaker' disappeared into a yawn.

'You should go to bed,' said Sophie. 'This idiot properly wiped you out. Could have hurt you. D'you hear me? Look at her.' She glared at Ted, who took his cap off and wrung it in his hands in such a cartoonishly subservient way that it looped round into sarcasm. He walked out into the garden through the wall.

'Well now, that was fun!' said Clementine. 'But you look tired, darling. Don't let us keep you up before the big day tomorrow! And you too, Mum,' she added, turning to Nana.

'Yes, I do think it's time for me to turn in,' agreed Nana. 'I'll be up past my bedtime tomorrow, too!'

They all started to troop out of the room. Claire thought she was last out and pulled the door almost to behind her, but then Soph gave her a nudge. 'Here, look,' she said and pointed back into the library. Claire peered around the door.

Basher had lingered and was standing by the table. He looked around and, satisfied that nobody was watching, waved a hand cautiously through the air where Ted the gardener had been standing during the seance. Then he sighed and seemed to sort of pull himself together. Claire hurried away before he spotted her.

Nana insisted that Claire escort her to bed, although Basher caught up and followed them suspiciously.

'Ted was the gardener here when I was little,' Nana said. 'He died in the middle of turning over potatoes. How extraordinary!'

Claire helped her into bed, while Sophie sat on the end of it, looking at her. Nana had hair like very fine silvery cobwebs, and her skin had shrunk close to her bones, which felt light and breakable like fine china. Claire looked at the veins on the backs of her hands and saw that Nana had very bad arthritis, too. She must be in quite a lot of pain all the time, but didn't show any sign of it. And her eyes, stormy and grey, flashed quick with intelligence. Nothing got past Nana.

'I'm so pleased we'll be doing another one of those tomorrow, dear. That was fantastic! Don't you think so, Basher?'

'Hmm. Yes, fantastic. Unbelievable, one might say,' said Basher, hardly dripping with sincerity. 'But you should get some sleep now, Nana. You have your party tomorrow.'

'Yes, yes. Because, apparently, I *won't* sleep when I'm dead! Ha-ha!'

'I don't think Nana will become a ghost,' said Sophie. 'She's too content. She seems quite ready to go. Whenever it happens.'

Claire relayed this, and Nana agreed.

'I do wish, though,' she said, 'that I had sold this place when I had the chance. I kept trying to arrange it, and Clemmy kept putting me off. "The estate agent people couldn't come today" – that sort of thing. It's a millstone in this day and age, you know, a big place like this. Well, I still have time to get it done. I'm going to really push for it. It's still my house, after all.'

Basher carefully tucked his nana in and she snuggled down into the pillows. As she was leaving, Nana grabbed Claire's hand. 'You're a nice girl, Claire. Let's talk more tomorrow.'

Basher helped Claire find her way back to her room, which she was happy about because the corridors all looked the same to her. At one point she tried to open the wrong door, and Basher steered her away, one hand on her elbow. His fingers were long and fine, and his grip was firm but careful – gentle.

'Um. Thank you,' she said.

'Don't mention it. This is not the most normal of houses. But great for Hide and Seek.'

'Were you good at it?'

'Very,' he said, with a smile. Claire imagined he was. Basher was thoughtful and sceptical and thorough. The sort of kid who'd search one room at a time, pulling all the cushions off the sofa before moving on to the kitchen.

He stopped and opened a door to reveal Claire and Sophie's room.

'Thank you again,' said Claire. 'Er. Goodnight. See you tomorrow.'

But Basher lingered in the doorway. 'Listen,' he said, suddenly very serious. 'I cannot explain how you did that right now, but it doesn't mean that I *will* not. And I want you to know that I don't really care if you play cruel tricks on the rest of my family, but do not do it to her.'

'Who?' asked Claire, all innocence.

'You have no poker face, weirdo,' said Sophie, who was leaning against the wall to watch. 'You know exactly who he's talking about.'

'Nana. It's her birthday.'

'I know it's her birthday – that's the whole reason I'm here.'

'You know what I mean. Don't tell Nana she's talking to her parents or her sister, or anything like that.'

'I wouldn't do that. I'm not actually a horrible person,' Claire protested.

'You told her you were passing on a message from her dead husband, though.'

'Er. I mean, yes, I did, but it wasn't a—'

'And it sounded a lot like you were riffing on something Figgy might have told you.'

'Rumbled,' said Sophie, who had a faint smile on her face.

'Well, I... Look, um.' Basher raised an eyebrow and Claire floundered. He was right was the frustrating thing, but she *could* talk to dead people, and it wasn't as if her bit of ad-libbing was really that bad, because Nana wanted to sell the house. Claire felt like she was getting a telling-off from a smug uncle, which seemed very unfair when Basher was in fact a couple of years younger than she was.

'It is her birthday,' he said again, embarrassingly earnest. 'She is old. Leave Nana alone.'

Claire held up both her hands. 'All right, all right – you got me. Don't arrest me. Oh, wait, you can't.' She was snapping back at him like a sulky child, and regretted it straight away.

Basher looked genuinely hurt. He stared at Claire, chewing on the inside of his lip for a few seconds. 'Fuck you,' he said. 'Absolutely fuck yourself.'

He almost slammed the door, but at the last second stopped short. It shut in Claire's face with a sharp click.

In the end, Basher needn't have worried. There was no chance Nana would become upset by Claire's messages from the Other Side. She wouldn't fret any more about selling the house. She wouldn't even get another chat with Ted.

The next morning, Nana was dead.

3

The Body in the Library

Claire was sitting on a wooden bench facing the garden, wearing all her warmest clothes at once. It was mid-morning, but the day was sufficiently grey and grim that the sun hadn't managed to wake up properly. There was still a mist low on the fields in the distance, and everything was damp. She was smoking a cigarette – one of her last – without enthusiasm, and generally trying to stay out of the way. At some point she had acquired a slice of toast. She munched on it rhythmically, between drags on the cigarette, like a cow chewing cud. Ted the ex-gardener was sitting next to her. He seemed to have developed an attachment to her and Sophie.

'I don't know,' he said, jutting his lip out. 'Don't seem right. Don't seem like her time.'

'That's not a thing, Ted. People die when they die.'

But although she was trying to avoid thinking about it, Claire had to admit it felt a bit neat. Old, infirm ladies die in their sleep all the time – it's an occupational hazard of being elderly, exacerbated by how many naps old people take. And yet...

Nana had apparently been found by her daughter, peaceful and cold in bed, when Clementine went to wake her up with a cup of tea. After that, everything became a weird flurry of inaction: people either being busily upset or sitting around not knowing what to do. Claire had sat with Figgy for a bit, making a cursory attempt to comfort her, but it had mostly been excruciatingly long silences until Figgy asked to be left alone. Once rebuffed, Claire extricated herself quietly. She was clearly not supposed to be here, but felt too awkward to approach someone to ask how to leave. Or how she was going to get paid, which was worse. And she still had no phone signal. Couldn't even download her podcasts.

Soph had been roaming around the place most of the morning. There had been little tugs on the connection between them every so often, but now Claire felt it slacken. Sure enough, Sophie walked out of the back door and came over to her.

'Can't find her in there,' she said. 'I'm pretty sure she's gone.'

'G'morning, Miss—'

'Fuck off, Ted.'

'Ted thinks Nana might have been done in before her time,' said Claire gloomily. 'I bet loads of rich people have smothered their grannies. Who would check?'

Ted nodded sagely.

Claire decided to get some blood back into her chilled limbs, so they walked around the outside of the house. The old servants' area, where the family now lived, was a sort of annexe on one side, like a cluster of different-sized barnacles on the bum of a majestic cruise liner. If you looked at the house from the back, it was on the left side, and was partially obscured by a tall box hedge. This was mirrored on the right-hand side, where another hedge stood in front of what Ted said was the rose garden – his pride and joy, when he was alive. He kept up an unceasing monologue of complaints about every gardener who had dared to step foot on the property since him.

The layout meant that, when standing in the gardens and looking back, the big, imposing grey block of a house was symmetrical, with a grand doorway flanked by identical rows of windows on either side. Sophie pointed out the library windows (bottom right), the old dining room that doubled as a kind of ballroom (bottom left), and described the rest of the house as 'just loads of fucking, different-coloured sitting rooms and four-poster beds'. From the back door, a wide patio and shallow stone steps led down to some depressed-looking empty flower beds and more box hedges, these ones about knee-high. There was a big lawn beyond that, stretching off to some trees in the distance.

Claire lit a fresh cigarette and strode down the steps and towards the treeline. 'The thing is,' she said. 'The thing *is*... that it does make sense, doesn't it? Old lady – legal owner of an estate that will pass to her family

– dies immediately after she tells a stranger that she's going to sell to the luxury hotel chain sniffing around, thus doing the family out of—'

'Out of a massive, mouldy old drain on the bank balance?' interrupted Sophie. 'For God's sake, Claire.'

'Yeah, but it's not necessarily about that, is it? It's about, you know, honour and... and tradition. Posh people are all mental about that stuff,' Claire replied.

Ted agreed enthusiastically.

Claire had always secretly thought she'd be quite good at solving crimes. She listened to three different true-crime podcasts, and her favourite TV show was *Murder Profile*, an American police procedural about a murderer-catchin' team made up of people who were all FBI agents and expert psychologists, as well as unbelievably attractive. Sophie found it incredibly boring because every episode had a very similar pattern; you could tell who the murderer was based on who appeared on screen when. But that was why Claire liked it. It was comforting to think that people were predictable even when they were creepy killers. It was, she argued, just like their seances. Patterns of behaviour. And death.

Claire warmed to her subject and started waving her arms around, describing and inventing ways in which everyone in the house could conceivably be a suspect, after the seance: Clementine would apparently sell her organs before she was forced to sell the house, so offing her mum wasn't much of a step; Hugh was probably having an affair with his secretary and, if Nana had found out, he would have needed to kill her before she revealed all; Figgy might be in for a chunk of inheritance in Nana's will, and there was no way that general fanny-ing around in Carnaby Street generated enough income to pay for fashion-onesies and expensive hair salons. Plus Basher had witnessed the conversation at bedtime when Nana had talked about making another push to sell the house, so he could be in it with Clementine. 'Or *he* could have done it alone! You never know. Basher seems quite normal, but scratch the surface of an old family and inbreeding starts pouring out! Plus, as a former copper, he'd know exactly how to—'

But at that moment the ground vanished from beneath Claire's feet. As she fell she let out a kind of strangled squawk, like a surprised chicken. She found herself lying flat on her face and rolled over to look up at the two ghosts, who appeared to be standing on top of a wall that hadn't been there a second ago.

'Ha-ha,' said Ted placidly.

'Piss off,' she said, as soon as she got her breath back. He gave her a look that was old-fashioned, even on a man who'd been dead for decades.

'No,' he said, very patiently, as if talking to a child. '*This* is a ha-ha. Stops sheep and that coming into the garden, but don't spoil the view with a bloody great wall. S'called a ha-ha cos you're surprised when you fall in it.'

'Then it should be called a "bleeding hell" or an "ah shit!", shouldn't it?' Claire stood up and mourned the loss of her precious cigarette. Ted and Sophie weren't on a wall.

They stood on solid ground, but Claire had fallen into a sort of trench about six feet deep (or tall, depending on your point of view) that ran the width of the lawn as far as she could see on either side. The vertical face of the trench was a rough brick wall, and from the bottom of this the ground sloped upwards again, until the lawn continued at almost the same height as before. It was nearly impossible to see the ha-ha until you were right on top of it. Or in it.

Ted pointed further down the trench. There were some bricks set sideways in the wall to use as a kind of ladder. Claire stumped along towards them and eyed the occasional slippery grey rock that poked mutinously out of the nettles at the bottom of the ditch. She could have landed on one of those. Trust the rich to build an architectural death-trap into their lawns, just so they wouldn't have to look at poor people or animals. In fact lawns themselves were simply a grim colonial hangover. *Ooh, look at me, I'm so rich I don't even need to put all this space that I own to any practical use – now how many Irish peasants did we starve today?*

A couple of sheep were looking at Claire with ovine disinterest, as if idiot townies fell into their field all the time. One of them went: *MURRRRRRRM.*

Claire stuck her tongue out at it. The sheep were probably only there for show anyway. Behind them, mist was still clearing from between the trunks of bare trees, the drifts of dead leaves and scrubby brambles.

There was also, it took Claire a moment to realize, a figure standing right in front of the copse. At this distance

47

it was hard to make out amid the trees, especially because it was so straight and still, and the same indistinct, wintery colour as the bark. But once she saw it, she could not unsee it: a hooded, imposing person, staring at her from the black void of their cowl.

As she watched, they raised a long, imperious arm and pointed straight at her. Then, with the same unstoppable yet excruciating slowness of the *Titanic* scraping the side of the iceberg, they pointed off to the side, further back into the hidden depths of the grounds. Claire felt her brain fighting the urge to put a horror movie dolly zoom over the scene, like on the beach in *Jaws*. She shivered.

It was a ghost, of course. Sophie was resolutely unspooked and yawned with great theatricality.

'I suppose it's a choice, isn't it? But it's not very original,' she said.

'That's Brother Simeon,' said Ted, equally unmoved. 'Gloomy old bugger. He's probably the oldest of us still hanging around. He's a family legend, on account of having frightened some people to death a few hundred years back. Used to try and comfort people after funerals, right? Being a monk and all. But some bloody great dead monk turns up after your son dies – that'll give some people a bad turn.'

'Ohhh, yeah. Figgy mentioned it,' said Claire. She was impressed, though. You didn't meet many ghosts who could actually incorporate and appear to the living. She and Sophie still hadn't exactly figured out how that worked, either, but it did happen, and it definitely took a lot of effort. Claire's theory was that the living person needed to sort of *expect* to see them, too, which was why, since fewer people actively believed that ghosts were real in the twenty-first century, people saw them less and less. A monk wandering around a place reputed to be haunted by a monk would just about do it, though.

Brother Simeon still had his arm raised.

'What's he pointing at?' Claire asked Ted.

'The old ruins. S'where The Cloisters gets its name from. He wanders about them most of the time, not talking to any of us. Stuck up, if you ask me.'

Claire surveyed Brother Simeon critically, then cupped her hands around her mouth. 'Oi! What. Do. You. Want?' she called.

But Simeon merely started to glide, with much ominous presentiment, back to his haunt. The effect was only slightly spoiled when he floated through the sheep.

Claire shrugged – suit yourself, mate – and turned to haul herself back onto the top lawn. As she threw her arms onto the grass, she caught sight of someone else walking towards the rose garden. She could barely make them out, and she realized it was another ghost. The place was lousy with them, it seemed.

In contrast to the living, ghosts were harder to see in daylight. She squinted. 'If the silent sheep-botherer was the local mad monk, then who's *that*?' she asked.

Sophie turned to look, too, and after a couple of seconds she exclaimed, 'No way!' and started marching quickly back to the house.

'Sophie! SOPH! Wait for me!'

Claire had to jog to catch up, and by the time they made it around the side of the house to the rose garden, she was out of breath and had a stitch in her side. It was all right for the dead.

The rose garden was, like much of the estate, a bit of a sorry sight in autumn. It was a walled garden designed to be a suntrap, but roses aren't evergreen and the plants had been pruned back for winter, so it was basically a garden of dead sticks. There was a mildewy wooden pergola that probably trailed flowers at other times of the year, with a heavy stone bench under it.

'What? What's the matter?' Claire gasped, bending over and knackered out. When she looked up she gasped again and started off a coughing fit in her shock. Nana was sitting on the bench. She smiled and patted the space next to her.

'I knew it! I knew you'd have unfinished business! Ted said – wait, where's Ted gone? Anyway Ted said, he reckoned – *thought* that—'

Nana raised a faintly see-through hand, calmingly. She looked healthier. Her face was fuller, and she had clearly been right about her sore feet. 'I'm sure you think you know what happened, dear, but you're not right about everything. I wasn't suffocated. Nobody put poison in the glass of water by my bed. I just died, like most old people do.'

'But you were going to sell the house! Hugh is probably having an affair!'

Nana looked a bit confused by this. 'I don't know about that. Although I suppose if Hugh were having an affair, I wouldn't be wholly surprised. But I do have what I think you would call some unfinished business.'

'Ooh, fun!' said Sophie. 'What is it?'

'Well, I'm afraid you're right, in a way. I think that my family did kill someone – but someone else.'

Claire tried to formulate a response to this, but her brain seemed to have short-circuited. Theorizing that Nana had been murdered had been, you know, sort of fun. A game. It wasn't real. But this wasn't fun. This was weird. It went against the usual social norms, even for dead people.

She scratched the back of her head, looked up at the sky and then at the ground, trying to find a way to reboot.

'I... sorry... Sorry, what the *fuck*?'

Nana sighed. 'You know, I thought we had done all right with them. It's very disappointing.'

'What do you mean, Nana?' asked Sophie, who had caught up much more quickly.

'Look into the library, dear.'

Nana pointed to a nearby window in the imposing grey wall of the house, so Claire ambled over. This was the short end of the library, furnished with an end-table and a couple of armchairs. It was hard to see anything beyond that; nobody had opened the curtains at the front of the house since the night before, and the room was so long that the far end of it was in almost total darkness. But she could see something moving around, stumbling a bit as they came closer. They seemed to be clutching their head in their hands and wheeled here and there, criss-crossing the floor with no real purpose, like a wounded animal trying to outrun the pain.

Claire's scalp began to tingle. Just like the night before, she felt nausea rise in her like a wave. Her pulse leapt and she tasted dirt and mould. She wanted, more than anything, to look away, but she couldn't.

It was a ghost, and they were thin. Very thin. Too thin. As the figure loomed towards the light of the window she finally saw: they were bones.

It was a skeleton. But they were still... juicy. Claire could make out patches of flesh melded to the arms and legs, and sagging across the jutting ribs. The crown of their skull glistened and the tips of their fingers clicked as they clawed at it. Straggling fibres of long hair came away as they did so, dropping like wet string.

Claire gagged. She started to shake uncontrollably, panicking but rooted to the spot, deathly afraid, but also unbearably sad. Pain crackled through her head and then returned to stay, sharp and increasing, like someone was worming a needle around behind her eyes. Her legs began to shake. She was about ten seconds away from a dead faint.

The skeleton in the library paused in their terrible, questing walk. They turned, their jaw gaping over-wide in a wordless, tongueless scream, and suddenly Claire was looking straight into the empty void of their eye sockets. They swallowed her whole.

When Sophie had disappeared all those years ago, Claire had of course been sad, but when you're young and healthy, death is something that happens to other people. And now Claire was not a stranger to death. She lived in its chill, looked into its many faces every day. She walked by taxi drivers on Oxford Street who were now far beyond the effects of the massive heart attack that had killed them in their sleep; by victims of violent crime who bore, philosophically, the bloody wounds that lingered into forever. She saw the sad, grey ghosts on the Thames, who waded in and out of the water at Battersea, never far beyond the reach of the river. Ever since Sophie had come back, Claire had been able to see them all, and she wasn't afraid because it was normal now. It was a mundane tragedy. A stubbed toe, a bitten tongue. The sleeping bag in the shop doorway that you walk past every day.

The death staring at her from the library was horror. Agony. Trapped, alone, in your own pain. For all time, where time meant nothing. Claire felt herself disappearing into that misery, and experienced terror. Undiluted fear.

She was afraid, so afraid. For the first time in her entire life, she was completely and totally afraid to die. The effort to turn away was almost beyond her.

Somehow, eyes watering, heart pounding, she managed to jerk herself backwards and away from the window. She fell, shaking, retching into the dead flower beds. Sophie was black-eyed, nervous, fluttering back and forth like a caged bird. She made motions as if she was about to walk into the library, then stepped back again.

'I died and I was about to leave, but then I found that poor person,' said Nana calmly, as Claire sat down next to her and started to get her trembling limbs under control. 'They don't know who they are, dear. They can't remember. They've lost themselves. I think they were murdered and thrown in an anonymous hole somewhere on this property. And I think – in fact, I am quite sure – that they were killed by someone in the family.'

'Um. Okay,' said Claire. 'That's... that feels like quite a bold take, if I'm honest, Nana. There are loads of ghosts in this house. A lot of people have died here. Including, you know...' Here she gestured awkwardly at Nana herself.

'Well, yes, but this person feels different, don't they?' Nana replied, and Claire nodded involuntarily; they did feel wronged, pained, lost. 'And they look... I don't know quite what you'd say, but they look like they're still—'

'Fresh,' completed Soph, who was still looking through the window. 'I think she's right. They're not very old, but they've lost who they are. They're barely aware of anything. It almost looks like they can't *think* even, and that only happens to, you know, violent deaths and unmarked burials, and things like that. I mean, isn't that why you never want to go near Marble Arch?'

Claire did a full body cringe. The Marble Arch corner of Hyde Park was near the site of Tyburn Tree, where public hangings had taken place for hundreds of years. Claire knew this partly because there was a little stone marker in the ground, partly because she was generally interested in history, and mostly because dozens of previously hanged ghosts wandered around there, joining the crowds at Speakers' Corner and yelling, shouting, trying to touch the living. But that wasn't the worst bit.

While they were generally the same age and personality as when they'd died, there was some elasticity to ghosts, especially how they looked. Some were wearing what they were buried in, rather than what they'd died in, some kept their gaping wounds and others were perfectly whole, but a very few were walking corpses. Sometimes people who died in violent or otherwise traumatic circumstances completely forgot who they were and so, in the absence of any other influence, they looked like what their body did. People would enjoy Marble Arch much less if they could see how many yellowing skeletons were sitting on the benches beside them.

And if the ghosts realized Claire could see them, they mobbed her, asking if she knew what was happening. Sometimes, if they couldn't speak any more, they simply screamed and shoved her. She never had any reply to give, so she avoided that whole area as much as possible. Newgate Street was also out, for similar reasons. And those skeletons were dry and dusty. The one in the library belonged to someone who was still... decomposing.

'They're not starting to go fuzzy, like old ghosts, either,' Sophie went on. 'They... feel new. Ish. About a year, I'd say.'

'That's why I think it was my family,' said Nana. 'Because not many events happen here in the autumn, you see. But there was a private party for my birthday this time last year, and there were a number of guests invited by the family, none of whom had met each other, or the family at large, before that weekend. And they all left suddenly, after a row. I never heard from any of them again, and I wonder if they did all manage to leave in the end… I think you should start there.'

'What d'you mean "you"? Do you mean *me*?' asked Claire. She was growing alarmed. 'What am I starting with?'

'You're the only one I can think of to help that poor soul, dear. Well, the pair of you. I must say, Sophie, it's a pleasure to be able to see you. You will help them, won't you? You'll find out who they are and set it right?'

'I mean… what? I can't…' Claire sputtered. 'We have to leave, Nana – they're organizing *your* funeral!'

'It'll be fine, my love,' said Nana, who was growing younger by the second. Her hair was falling in lustrous blonde waves down to her shoulders, her skin was fresh and wrinkle-free, and she gave a dazzling smile, with bright white teeth. 'Basher and Alex will help you, I expect. I'm fairly confident that those two are all right, you know. Say to Basher "Opal Fruits". And tell him… Say that I kept my word about the pink shepherdess incident. Until now. Right! Unfinished business over. Off I go.' And, just like that, she stood up. And was gone.

'Fuck,' said Claire. And then, 'Fuck. Shit. Fuckshit. What do we do now? Can we call the police?'

'Oh yeah, that'd be brilliant,' said Sophie, holding an invisible phone to her ear. "Hello, the cops? Yeah, I think this posh family murdered someone, because their dead nan told me so. No, I don't know who, or when, or how, or why. Also, please don't run my name through your files because we all know what will happen then." *Ohmigod.* You're so lucky I'm around to do the thinking for both of us.'

Claire swallowed. 'But I dunno, like... There isn't anything else to do, in that case. So, let's go?' She flapped her hands, frustrated and wanting to go home and eat chips.

'That doesn't feel right, either. That person needs help.'

'They've already been fucking murdered, so what are we supposed to do at this point? There's no way I can convince the family to let me stay here, when Nana has just died—'

'Oh, don't be so defeatist,' said Alex's voice. 'Just say that her ghost told you she buried a load of treasure in the garden. They'd be all over that.'

Claire looked round. She kept spinning stupidly on the spot, like a video game character when you've forgotten all the controls and are trying to figure them out.

'Look up.' Alex was leaning out of a second-floor window. They appeared to be smoking a joint again. 'I'll come down.'

'This is great,' said Sophie. 'Nana said Alex would help!'

It took a while for Alex to reappear, having sauntered outside and around the garden with the same urgency one would employ in getting a beer out of the cooler at a beach barbecue. Then Claire had to wait while they retrieved the stub of their joint from behind one ear – they had, Alex explained, put it out while they went through the house, in case Granny Clem saw – and relit it.

'So,' they said. 'What was all that about then? Who were you arguing with?'

'Er. Sophie. We, um, were talking to Nana,' said Claire.

Alex's eyebrow shot up. It was the one with the slits shaved into it, Claire noticed.

'Um. She's gone now. To be honest, Nana said... She said some stuff.'

'Interesting,' said Alex. They appeared to think of something and walked a little way out of the rose garden. 'Looks like we're alone,' they said, coming back. 'Spill 'em. Your guts, I mean.' They sat on the bench and patted the spot behind them, in such a mirror of Nana's gesture that Claire was quite taken aback.

So, with a lot of prodding and encouragement from Sophie, Claire told Alex what had happened, as honestly as possible – I met your nana's ghost, there is a terrifying skeleton haunting the library, and Nana is convinced that someone in the family murked a guest from last year's party – and hoped she wasn't going to get summarily thrown out.

Alex was quiet for a very long time. At one point they got up and, hands cupped around their face, peered through the window into the library. 'Yeah,' they said eventually, taking a heavy drag. 'That sounds about right.'

'What... really?'

'Yeah. I'm a practical person. Either you were actually talking to a ghost right now, or you're such a committed liar that you sometimes talk to yourself when you're alone in random places, to keep up appearances – and you obviously can't even commit to a hairstyle with any conviction.' They blew out a large plume of smoke as Claire baulked at such a casual death blow. 'And I do smoke a lot of weed, which helps me deal with unusual family news. I'm surprised it's taken this long for a potential murder to come up, to be honest. My dad in particular is a giant dickhole. And at what point does consistently voting for policies that defund social safety-nets and disproportionately punish the poor, disabled and queer not become a form of indirect murder?'

'Er... I don't know: at what point?'

'It was rhetorical, but, since you asked, I would say the answer is "very early on". Let's go and find Uncle Bash.'

Uncle Bash was holed up in his own guest bedroom near the kitchen. He and Alex made quite a strange pair, in comparison to the rest of the family. The others cut about in expensive shirts and neat cardigans and ironed trousers, but today Basher was in a faded and paint-spattered hoodie and Alex was in bright orange dungarees under a black faux-fur coat that crackled with static. It was like finding a gloomy pigeon and an angry raven hiding out amid a flock of fancy hens.

In any event, Basher was much harder to convince of the whole ghosts-and-familial-murder thing than Alex.

He still refused to entertain the idea that Sophie existed; even when she used Claire's energy to pull a lace doily a couple of inches along the top of the dresser, he said things like 'magnets' and 'fishing wire'.

'All right, this is a good one,' said Claire, after about forty-five minutes of attempting to persuade him. 'This one usually works. D'you have a pen? And a bit of paper or something?'

Basher produced a biro and a scrap of paper from the front pocket of his hoodie.

'Okay. Okay. I'm going to close my eyes. Alex can put their hands in front of my eyes even. And you write down whatever you want. Anything at all. I don't care. Doesn't matter. Literally anything. And then leave it face up on the table, so Soph can see. She can tell me what it says, and I won't even have to open my eyes.' Claire closed them, and after a moment felt Alex's hands cover them. She couldn't tell if their hands were very warm or if it had been too long since she'd touched a living person.

She could hear Basher sighing his assent. Then Sophie's reportage: 'He's scribbling to get the pen to work... Now he's licking the end of it. Okay... He's written, "Shall I compare thee to a summer's day? Thou art more lovely and more..." It looks like he's written "temperature"? His handwriting is terrible. God, what a loser.'

'"Temperate", not "temperature",' corrected Claire. 'Sophie says you've written the first two lines of Sonnet 18. Er... and that you're a loser with bad handwriting.'

Alex burst out laughing.

'You're a loser too, for knowing what sonnet that is,' said Sophie.

'I want another go,' said Basher. 'Keep your eyes closed.'

'He's doing the thing people do when they think they can win at this,' said Soph gleefully.

'She says you haven't written anything – you just pretended.'

'Now he's written PISS OFF, in big capital letters. I told you I liked these two, didn't I?'

Basher was still not convinced.

'Wait!' Claire cried, suddenly remembering. 'Nana said to tell you she always kept her word about, um... something. God, I can't remember. Nana was talking a lot and getting younger, and disappearing at the same time. It was a lot to take in.'

Soph wasn't helpful; she'd been paying too much attention to the skeleton at the time.

'Oh!' said Claire triumphantly. 'Oh, "Opal Fruits". That was something.'

At this, Basher narrowed his eyes. 'Opal Fruits were my favourite sweet when I was little. Nana took me to the beach once and I was scared I'd lose her, and she said if she sent anyone to find me, "Opal Fruits" was the codeword to know they were a friend, so I should trust them. But that is not actually proof that she spoke to you after she died, or that you have a dead best friend, is it? Just that you're very persuasive and people tell you things. You should think about joining the police.'

'I would literally, genuinely, prefer to also be dead,' said Claire, giving voice to the contradiction at the heart of her murder mystery obsession.

'Yes, *thank you*. It is a solid job with good career prospects. And a lot of camaraderie, not that you asked.' Basher flopped down to sit on the bed and stared at the floor. He seemed quite bitter, but Claire couldn't exactly tell what he was bitter about. He was very defensive about a job he had left some time ago.

'There are more things in heaven and earth, Horatio...' he murmured to himself.

'All right, well, we can sort out things viz. Uncle B believing in the paranormal later,' said Alex, with sudden briskness. 'I have other concerns.' They stomped over to the window, opened it and smoked a normal cigarette out of it, with brutal efficiency. Claire started to get nicotine pangs.

'Look, Uncle B, just give us your professional opinion – *ex*-professional opinion – on the case.'

'The case? The *case*? There isn't a case!' he replied, with an explosion of exasperation. 'Even if I accept that there has legitimately been a murder, which for the record I do not, where would you even start? Normally with a murder you have a body, which you use to work out who has died and how they were killed, yes? This isn't a whodunnit, it's a... a who*dead*it. And a *how*deadit. And a *when*deadit,' he finished somewhat lamely.

'Well, there's a finite pool of suspects, isn't there? No offence to you and your family, but the ghost is definitely a fairly recent one and it's haunting this house's library, so the killer is one of you. And there's also a finite pool of potential victims,' said Claire, who, if she was being honest, probably agreed with Basher more than she wanted to admit. But, crucially, she also did not particularly like Basher, so she was ready to solve the murder out of spite. 'Nana said she thought it was probably one of the guests at last year's party.'

'Good point,' said Alex. 'You two – three – make a list of everyone who was here last year. I'll go and sort it, so that Claire can stay.'

Under such direct instruction from a supremely self-possessed teenager, two hapless living millennials and one dead one couldn't help but do as they were told. Basher hunted around in a still-packed travel bag and produced a notebook. He seemed to be acting on instinct, in the absence of something else to do. He wrote a mercifully short list in what was indeed very messy handwriting:

- *Kevin*
- *Mattie*
- *Sami*
- *Michael*

'Okay, that's not too bad,' said Sophie. 'Let's work down the list, then... Who's Kevin?'

There followed about thirty seconds of silence, at the end of which Claire finally realized that Basher could not hear Sophie. 'All right, we're going to have to come up with some kind of system,' said Claire. 'I'm not used to you trying to have conversations with other people, Soph.'

'Are you talking to me?' said Basher.

'Jesus, it's like the Three fucking Stooges or something. Look, Sophie, if you *don't* want me to repeat you, tell me. Otherwise I'm going to parrot everything you say. All right? Clear? Basher, Sophie says could we please start with Kevin?'

'This is ridiculous. I do sort of commend you for taking your bit so seriously. But fine, the sooner we get this over with, the sooner I can get back to... oh, I don't know, mourning my nana.' He rubbed his face. His voice was not unlike his father's in its richness, but calmer and more even, as if he'd once been told that he was loud and had never forgotten it. 'Kevin was Figgy's boyfriend; they'd been together for about ten months, and she brought him down to meet us all for the first time. I felt a bit sorry for him. It was a trial-by-fire situation.'

Basher described Kevin as a wealthy mummy's boy who'd found himself on holiday in South America and had become a grubby Trustafarian type, who pretended he wanted to give up all his family money and become a monk, whilst simultaneously using said money to fund his extravagant international lifestyle.

'Mum absolutely hated him,' Basher summarized. 'Monty and Tris were pretty mean as well. I think it was a hostile environment for him. He and Figgy argued, broke up and Kevin left.' Basher shrugged, as if it was cut and dried.

'Nana said there was an argument. Was that it?'

'Sort of. It would be more accurate to say there were several cluster arguments that ended up coalescing into one giant, purple-spots-behind-the-eyes migraine of an argument.'

'Um. Like you quitting?' Claire asked, after a brief hesitation. Real detectives suspected everyone, right? Or they risked ending up in a Netflix documentary in twenty-five years' time, trying to explain why they didn't investigate the husband when, in hindsight, it was really obvious that he'd chopped up his wife's body and buried her under his new patio. *Yeah, yeah, Detective Handlebar McStetson, we've all heard 'people own massive knives for lots of reasons' before, but you still biffed it.*

Sophie had obviously had the same thought – well, not like exactly the same, but similar – because Claire could see her watching Basher carefully.

'Yes, that was one of them. Before you ask, it is none of your business. I don't want to talk about it.' He rubbed his eyes and looked tired again. 'Anyway. Suffice it to say that Mum and Dad were really upset when I told them I was packing the job in.'

'What d'you do now then?'

'Things. I've not really settled on anything. Copywriting, shifts in bars sometimes. Mostly I do cases as a private investigator, but it's all finding stolen bikes or trailing cheating boyfriends. Nothing exciting. Alex lives with me in Brighton, in a flat I bought when I was still gainfully employed.'

'Having a long, dark winter of the soul is affordable if you're from a family with money and property, huh?' said Claire, before she could stop herself.

'I would be affronted, but you are entirely correct.'

'What about this Kevin anyway?' asked Sophie. 'Let's get back to the murder. Is he definitely still alive?'

'I do not know. It's not like we kept in touch. Tris might know, I think he was friends with Kevin first – he may even have introduced him to Figgy. I cannot even remember his last name, I'm afraid.'

'Hmm. Okay. What about Mattie then? Who's he?'

'*She* is Mathilda. Mattie worked here for years, ever since I can remember. She started out helping at weekends and, over time, became the estate manager. She did most of the accounts and organizational things and was probably the most reliable adult around the place. I don't think Mum and Dad manage without her, to be honest.'

'What do you mean she "was"? What happened?' Claire asked.

At that moment Alex crashed back into the room, a small electrical storm that had managed to source a large paper flipchart from regions unknown.

'Right, Claire can stay. I told Grandad that we'd been talking and you were helping me realize that maybe I want to go to university and study PPE after all,' they said.

Sophie gave a loud bark of laughter. Alex swept the top of Basher's dresser clear and balanced their flipchart on top of it, snatched the list of victims and copied it out carefully in large letters.

'Where did you get to?' they asked.

'Basher told us about Kevin, and started introducing Mattie.'

'Is that all? Blimey.' Alex chewed the end of the biro and looked critically at the flipchart. They wrote 'POTENTIAL VICTIMS' as a heading, but started too enthusiastically, so it ended up looking like **P O T E N T**IALVICTIMS. They surveyed their work. 'Okay, maybe this isn't working. I know what we need to do,' they said.

'What?'

'A flashback. To Nana's birthday dinner a year ago. That would give you a better handle on things.'

'To do that, we are going to have to explain the entertainment last year,' said Basher. He was, for once, actually smiling.

'Oh *God*,' groaned Alex, 'there was entertainment. I think my brain had blocked that from my memory in self-defence.'

'We take it in turns to sort out some kind of act or band, or something. It was Mum's turn, and she did what we all do, which is book something shoddy and ill-advised at the last minute,' explained Basher. 'Present company, et cetera, and so on.'

'I guess it took the better part of a decade for the brief mainstream vogue of "fun" a cappella groups to filter through to her,' Alex continued. 'But she also tried to get a kind of Nana-friendly one, so' – and here they shuddered – 'so imagine, if you will, an a cappella group themed around the forties and fifties, mashed up with the hits of today. Except it was the hits of yesterday, because they were all sad thirty-year-olds like you two, wearing poodle skirts. Vera Lynn ft. Pitbull ft. Ludacris. It was a black hole formed of everything wrong with your generation. I could feel myself becoming an objectively worse person just by being there.'

'It was pretty bad,' admitted Basher. 'They were booked for the bigger party the next day, but for some reason Mum got them to perform the night before as well – sort of like your seance last night, but actually *during* dinner. It was... awkward, especially since everyone was already really tense anyway. Made all the bickering feel like part of a special musical episode on a TV show. They had some terrible name as well. You know, a pun.'

'It was The Clefs of Dover,' moaned Alex, pretending to half fall backwards against the wall, dangling their arms pathetically.

'After what happened, Mum told them the party the next day was cancelled, and I think they were offered rooms, but they elected to leave pretty quickly that night. For which I cannot blame them,' said Basher.

'God, it was like staring directly at the surface of the *sun*,' said Alex. They produced another regular cigarette, opened the window and sparked up, this time noticing the heat of Claire's stare. They were kind enough to share drags with her.

Thus, in between exhales out of the window, and with some clarification from Basher, Alex described that fateful evening.

4

Dinner and a Show

It was a dark and stormy night, both literally and in spirit. Most of the time the family just stayed in their part of the house, because most of the time there were a load of bankers or office admins charging around the grounds doing team-building exercises, or wedding guests being sick in the gardens and falling down the ha-ha. But for Nana's birthday and Christmas – also an intense and uncomfortable weekend affair – dinner was always in the proper dining room.

It was a weird choice, to be honest, because it was a massive room for only a dozen people. They could comfortably fit fifty in there for functions, so they always ended up all sitting down one end of the long table, and it looked and felt absurd. Whenever they ate in there the cutlery scrapes were really loud, like nails on a chalk-board, and combined with Tristan talking with his mouth full. Plus it was miles from the kitchen, so at least three people had to help carry things through and by the time everything was plated up, it had all gone a bit cold.

Anyway, that night dinner was roast beef with all the trimmings, which was Nana's favourite. There was a strawberry sponge cake with fresh cream. It was going to be lovely. Well, on paper, and if it had been a different family.

The weekend had already been more than usually complicated. Normally outside guests weren't invited to the family dinner. This time, however, there were several: Figgy had brought her well-meaning but annoying and somewhat noisome boyfriend Kevin; Sami, Basher's partner, had come along for moral support, but was seriously regretting it; and Tris and Monty had turned up with an accountant working with their firm, whose name was Michael. The last was a complete surprise.

Tensions were high going in, because of Clementine's constant needling of Kevin about his job, his future, his hair, and the way she kept smelling an odd smell whenever he was in the room, but couldn't quite place it. Monty was also doing this, but in a manner that wasn't so much needling as openly stabbing; and Tristan, who was often the family's equivalent of the shitty ratfink kid who stood behind the bully going 'yeah!', joined in because he copied whatever Monty did. The great irony, of course, was that this behaviour really only inspired a large amount of disdain from Monty, who would have been more impressed if Tristan struck out on his own. But Clem and Hugh were so absurdly protective of Tristan that Monty had got him a job at his firm to keep the peace. Tristan was just happy to slouch into whatever version of life other people made for him.

So by the time dinner rolled round, Kevin had endured thirty-six hours of basically undisguised insult; Figgy was embarrassed, but *by* him and not by her family's treatment *of* him; and they'd already had one argument about it themselves.

This dinner was the extravagant top hat on a day that had started out by pulling on the grim socks of a son revealing that he had quit the job his parents hated him having in the first place – seen by Clementine as a grievous insult to injury that caused a shouting match over breakfast. When Basher had first joined the police, his mother had been subjected to a deluge of jokes on the theme of 'PC Plod' (it was the sort of area where that passed for top bants). Clementine had, otherwise, produced two lawyers and a daughter who once had lunch with a Middleton, or at least had been in a room around midday at the same time as one, so a lower-waged son who didn't shop at John Lewis was a chink in the armour that Clementine's peers were quick to exploit.

At least when Basher became a detective it was good for casually bringing up at the checkout, when you ran into another mum whose son did something less noble and brave, like working in advertising. Morse was a detective, and it was good enough for him. The revelation that Basher did not feel noble and brave about his job, but in fact felt a bit of a shithouse and was having a personal and existential crisis – and didn't even do cryptic crosswords – was profoundly destabilizing for Clem and Hugh. At the same time, this was being revealed in front of *outsiders*, one of whom had arrived with Basher. Sami was supposed to be providing Basher with moral support, but she was already looking quite demoralized herself. The rest of the family had not really known how to treat her so far, and it was clear that Sami had taken on probably the most excruciating weekend of her life. At any rate, there had been tears in the scrambled egg.

It was also obvious that Mattie, who was usually such a brick, was being deeply weird with Clementine and Hugh. That weekend she had been either absent or hard to find for long periods of time, or locked away in the office.

Possibly even weirder was that Michael the accountant had, by dinnertime, disappeared entirely, after being driven into the village by Kevin and not returning. Monty was angry about this. Kevin claimed that he'd dropped him out past the station and Michael had said he quite wanted the walk back.

With hindsight, this was deeply suspicious and absurd, but by this point Kevin was so miserable around anyone other than Figgy that he couldn't be caught alone, and had avoided being interrogated further by Monty. In any case, Clementine was now also annoyed that they would have too many potatoes instead of too few, even though she had only acquired more potatoes specifically because Michael was to be joining them for dinner.

So, the events of the dinner played out like this:

Rain was sluicing down the windows in rivers. There was instantly an issue because at the time Alex was vegetarian and Clementine pretended to have forgotten this.

In fact she had been reminded several times in the run-up, and even the day before. She offered, by way of replacement for the portion of meat, a literal block of Cheddar from the deli over in town. Just a big lump of cheese.

'It's really very nice, darling,' she said. 'Quite as rich and lovely as beef, I'm sure.'

Alex elected to eat merely the vegetables and the other sides, and felt the cheese thing was a pretty passive-aggressive dig and that they were being deliberately excluded, especially when their dad started on about not knowing why they couldn't eat meat this one time, for God's sake.

'It's your great-grandmother's birthday, and the bloody thing is already dead anyway,' he said, throwing his phone down on the table with some force.

'Now, Monty darling. No phones at table!' said Clem, tapping his hand like a playful coquette.

'I don't mind at all, dear, of course,' said Nana to Alex, as the dishes of peas, carrots, cheesy leeks and cauliflower were passed down. 'It's just lovely to see you here at all. And I understand why you do it. It's marvellous all the things you can eat instead now. In my day it would have been quite impossible.'

'It's still your day now, Nana,' said Basher. 'And it definitely is today.'

'Here, here!' said Hugh automatically. He slapped the table a couple of times and it shook all the cutlery and glasses, making a jangling metallic sound.

'Yes, of course, Basher,' said Clementine, who had placed the impressive roast topside of beef in front of

Hugh. She pulled her chair in as Hugh started to carve. 'And everyone is quite free to make their own personal choices, aren't they?'

'Mum...' said Basher, in a warning tone.

'Well, they are!' said Clementine, defensive and innocent. 'People can make whatever choices they like, about what they eat or where they work or who they go out with.'

Kevin, whose body language was already screaming that he would rather be anywhere else in the entire world, pulled his chair closer to the table and glanced quickly in Monty's direction. He was prepared for a flanking attack.

'Look, can we just eat, please?' said Figgy, cutting Monty off at the pass.

They all turned to watch Hugh carving a row of thick slices, one after the other. He performed very well under the pressure of an audience.

The beef was, to give it its due, perfect. Juicy, exactly the right shade of pink inside, and with a crisp herby crust on the outside. Clementine could certainly cook very well, and everyone made the expected noises of approval.

'That looks lovely, Clementine,' said Sami. She had spent the weekend being polite to a fault, so as not to further tarnish Basher by association. Even for Sami's iron-clad self-control, the Wellington-Forges had been an unusual challenge.

'Thank you, poppet,' said Clementine. 'Do have some horseradish sauce, too.'

One advantage of a large dinner is that it occupies your mouth for quite a long time. This meant the family was given a good excuse not to speak while they hoofed down many pounds of protein and carbs, and vegetables covered in different forms of protein and carbs.

Tristan was obviously unable to read the room, though, so he kept making abortive attempts to start conversations that, if you didn't know Tris, you would assume were calculated to cause the most conflict. In fact, he was simply one of nature's oblivious blunderers.

'So, Basher, old chap,' he said jovially, 'what are you going to do for work now then? Any ideas?'

'Nope,' said Basher. 'None at all.' He shovelled a load of potato into his mouth in a carefree way.

'Well, that's good!' said Clementine. 'And I'm sure you'll be out on the street with nowhere to live soon.'

'Don't be silly, Mum, of course I won't. I have my flat.'

'And how are you supposed to pay the mortgage now? You'll end up back here, and it'll be *my* fault somehow!'

'Bash will be able to get quite a lot of consulting work, if he wants, Mrs Wellington-Forge,' Sami added quickly.

'You see? Please stop, Mum. I'm an adult.'

They lapsed into silence again.

'Could someone pass the gravy?' asked Tuppence.

'There's none left,' said Monty, in the middle of the act of pouring the last of it over his beef.

'Oh, well, not to worry,' she said, getting up. 'I'll make some more quickly. Do you have any Bisto, Clementine?'

Clementine explained that even though she knew Tuppence relied on the instant stuff, she herself always

76

made gravy from scratch, but there might be some at the back of the cupboard somewhere.

Tristan cleared his throat and said, 'Good turnout for the birthday this year, eh, Nana?'

Nana twinkled at him. 'Yes, dear. It's lovely to see your shining, happy faces around this table, I must say.' Sometimes it seemed like she entertained herself by disguising sarcasm behind sweet-old-ladies-say-the-funniest-things-isms. It was hard to tell.

'Shame Mattie isn't here, though,' Tristan went on. 'Where *is* Mattie, Dad?'

Hugh said 'fired' at the same time as Clementine said 'sick'.

'Well, I mean,' said Hugh slowly, looking towards Clem for any obvious signs he was saying the wrong thing, 'she isn't here tonight because she's sick. But also we had to let her go.'

'What? Mattie? Why? When?' asked Basher.

'Well, it was a mutual decision,' said Clementine, taking a prim bite from a bit of carrot. 'We need to cut some costs, and Mattie wants to spend more time on watercolouring.'

'How odd,' said Nana, who had lost her twinkly, jovial air and replaced it with an expression of concern. 'You always used to say you couldn't run the place without her.'

'Anyway, Mum, Mattie has never done watercolouring in her fucking *life*,' said Basher, who was starting to do what he did in times of stress around his mother and revert to being a teenager. Sami laid a restraining hand on his arm.

77

'Don't swear, dear,' said Clem. There was a hint of a snap. 'For your information, Mattie has done a lot of seascapes of the Cornish coast.'

'As if you'd know, dahling brother – you barely ever come here,' said Figgy. 'Mattie could have had a whole seasonal collection in a gallery in town, for all *you'd* know.'

'Just because you're wholly unsatisfied with your life, *dah*ling, there's no need to take it out on me.'

'What's that supposed to mean?'

'We all know what that means,' said Monty.

'She's talking about Kevin,' chortled Tristan, at a normal volume.

'Oh, okay. Cheers then,' said Kevin.

'Anyway, at least I still have a job,' Figgy went on. She did not respond to the dig about her relationship but, crucially, did not deny it, either.

'Oh, please, showing your married mates different wallpaper swatches every three months and spending lunchtimes wanking around Soho doesn't count as a job.'

'Well, you'll need a new job soon, because I happen to know that Mummy and Daddy are cutting you off!'

'What?' Basher asked, turning to Clementine.

'Well, dear,' said Clementine, 'since you clearly don't value our opinions or feelings and are determined to be an independent man, that's what you'll be. But it's not a fitting subject for the dinner table.'

'Oh my God, you are absolutely unbelievable. Does my happiness come into it at all? What I want?'

'You do not know what you want,' said Clementine firmly, boring a hole into Basher with her stare.

Nana waited for a gap and sighed, loudly, which shut everyone up again, out of guilt. There was another long pause for eating.

'Not hard up, though, are you, Mum?' asked Tristan after a while, wheeling back towards yet another poor conversational choice and careening into it with the grace of a wacky clown-car with the doors falling off. 'Are you still thinking of selling up to those hotel types, Nana?'

Clementine slammed her fork down. 'Nana was never thinking of selling up, Tristan. It's off the table.'

'Oh, I'd like to keep it on the table, I'm afraid,' said Nana calmly. 'This one in particular is my birthday table, after all.'

'Well, we can talk about it tomorrow, when we're not in front of guests. Okay?'

'Yah, you should ask Michael for advice, Mum,' said Tristan, again lifting the fragile rabbit that was the evening in his big, clumsy hands for one last inadvertent throt-tling. 'He's a total genius at money stuff and the firm's accounts, and so on. I say, Monty, where *is* Michael? And what are we going to do about the thing he was talking about, with the irreg—'

'For Christ's sake, Tristan! What did Mum just say? Can you honestly not shut up for five fucking minutes?'

'I wasn't talking about the hotel types, I was talking about work—'

'Jesus, Tristan, I told you to stop, so stop! This is exactly why you're not allowed in any of the meetings any more.'

'All right, chaps, let's calm down a bit,' said Hugh.

'Yeah, Granny, please collect your large failsons,' added Alex helpfully. 'They're embarrassing the family in front of outsiders.'

Tristan was making the sort of face some young men do when they look like they want to cry, but direct it all inwards through a heroic effort at repression. It's the face of someone suffering from a cross between constipation and acute sunburn as they try to blow up a balloon.

'Yes, that is quite enough,' said Clementine. She put down her cutlery and clapped her hands together twice, like a nursery-school teacher calling the children to attention for storytime. 'We haven't even got to the cake yet! We don't want to make our guests feel uncomfortable.'

'You don't,' said a voice, 'want to make your guests feel uncomfortable? You *don't*. Want to make your *guests*. Feel *uncomfortable*.'

Every head swivelled. It was Kevin.

The air seemed to crystallize. Alex turned to look back at Basher and Sami whilst doing a comical gaping-mouth Muppet grin and could have sworn they were all moving in slow motion; Basher was starting to lean back in his chair as if he was accelerating in a fast car; and Sami was wide-eyed and shaking her head.

It was the moment before a natural disaster. A huge wave of insurmountable awkwardness – a sweeping, crushing tide of *Schadenfreude*, second-hand embarrassment and terrible arguing so acute as to be unbearable – was poised over them all. Alex imagined it suspended outside the dining-room windows, and in half a second it would sweep through them and lacerate them all with shards of glass.

It *almost* didn't happen.

Nana looked defeated. Clementine's knuckles were white. Figgy's mouth was half agape. Monty was reaching for his phone, so he could pretend to be disinterested in whatever happened next. Hugh didn't know where to look for guidance and was defaulting to his wine glass. And Kevin was giving off the same vibes as someone in a zombie movie who has definitely been bitten and is trying to conceal it from the rest of the group: red-eyed, pale-lipped, slightly green tinge to the skin. There was a moment when Alex thought Kevin was going to manage to swallow his next sentence.

But then:

'I'm sorry, Kevin, I'm not sure what you mean?' said Clem, with one of her bright, brittle smiles.

Three things happened at once. The first was that Kevin shouted, 'You're going to pretend to care about making us uncomfortable, when you've been making me miserable on purpose the whole weekend? Not good vibes!'

The second was that Basher pushed his chair back and jerked his head at Sami, whilst also making a move towards Nana.

The third was that Alex decided to make like a tree and fuck off, except they did it by *shoving* their chair

81

backwards and sprinting towards the door with exaggerated limb-flailing.

Basher and Sami were slower, but Nana decided that she did actually want to leave as well, and asked Basher to take her to the kitchen for a cup of tea. They were coming round the head of the table with Nana in her wheelchair as Clementine said, 'Hugh! Are you going to let him speak to me like that?'

'Oh, er, sorry, Clem. Yes, Kevin old chap, that's not on, is it?' He stood up and grabbed the first items on hand, to gesture with for added emphasis, which meant he was waving around a carving knife and a half-full glass of red wine, which he was spilling over his chinos.

This caused Basher to stop and try and retrieve the knife from his father, and a small scuffle broke out.

As this was playing out, Figgy started shouting at Kevin in the approximate tones of someone who has turned up to ruin a wedding on an episode of *EastEnders*. It was rapidly devolving into full-on yelling on both sides and was the kind of argument where previous, very specific incidents were going to be brought up as ammunition. Indeed it was when Kevin said, 'Oh, wow, so this is going to be like that tea shop in Bath all over again, is it?' that Alex turned their head to look, yet continued in their forward momentum towards the dining-room door.

That is why they did not see it opening, as Tuppence finally returned to the room carrying a large jug of gravy.

At the last second Alex noticed their mum and managed to half turn away, whilst also throwing themselves forward to try and get under the arm carrying the gravy. The result was that they barrelled into Tuppence's stomach and severely winded her.

Tuppence, of course, threw her hands forward without thinking, which meant that she chucked almost an entire jug of Bisto into the air.

It arced gracefully in a single shining sheet until its path was interrupted by Basher, Hugh and Clementine. All three of them were struggling over the carving knife and the glass of wine, and being suddenly doused in ribbons of slimy, hot meat-gunge did not improve the situation.

Either from all the added lubrication or from surprise at suddenly being more gravy than man, Hugh relinquished his grip on both glass and knife. The one smashed on the floor and stained the carpet, and the other flew into the air and landed point-down in the (antique) table with a cartoonish thud. It stood there, upright and wobbling, increasing the chaos tenfold with every wibble back and forth.

Alex started ministering to their mum and apologizing non-stop; Clementine was shrieking tearfully at Hugh about the table, while on her knees trying to mop up the red wine; Monty had seized the cover provided by everything going on to start hoarsely having a massive fucking go at Tristan; and Figgy was shouting at Kevin about the way he had looked at a woman in a bar in Islington one time.

Nana and Sami, who had narrowly avoided the engravying, both got a serious case of the giggles. Sami was snorting and chewing on her sleeve, and Nana had silent tears rolling down her cheeks.

Without warning, Clementine spun round to turn on them.

'Oh, I'm very fucking glad this is funny!' she hissed, hauling herself back up to her feet. 'I'm glad someone is enjoying this. This was supposed to be your birthday dinner, Mummy! And *you're* not even part of the family – how *dare* you?'

'Steady on, poppet,' rumbled Hugh. He was licking gravy off his hand in a kind of philosophical way.

'Oh, don't *you* dare start!' Clem shouted, wheeling back again. 'I'm working my fingers to the bone, keeping this place going, and what help are you? Don't think I haven't noticed money going missing. Or Mattie sneaking away in the middle of the day. What sort of grubby rendezvous are you having, eh?'

It's worth remembering at this point that, from the start of the evening, and indeed throughout the proceedings, about half a dozen thirty-year-olds in faux-retro fifties cardigans and Brylcreemed hair had been standing awkwardly to one side, singing.

They had, in complete fairness to them, carried on gamely in what must have been supremely weird circumstances, encouraged by stern looks from the woman with the tuning fork who was the lead White Clef. They'd only faltered a couple of times, notably during 'The Lambeth Walk' versus 'Walking on a Dream' by Empire of the Sun. The songs weren't natural partners at the best of times.

84

Although at this late stage they could barely be heard over everything, fully half of The Clefs of Dover were still struggling through a mashup of 'Boogie Woogie Bugle Boy' and 'Down With the Trumpets' (called, on their set list, 'Boogie Woogie Trumpet Bois').

Figgy let out a howl, grabbed a handful of cauliflower cheese from her plate and threw it at Kevin.

He ducked.

It hit the lead Clef squarely in the cleavage.

From then on, the evening broke apart a bit.

5

A Pint with the Lads

'Wow,' said Claire.

'Yeah. I mean, fucking hell,' added Sophie.

'I know it sounds weird, but honestly it's not that weird for *us*,' said Alex. They had closed the window and crawled over to the bed on all fours. Instead of sitting on it next to Basher, they lay full length on the floor with their head propped against it. 'A blowout like that happens pretty much every Christmas. It was just... extra blowout this time. It's not suspicious to us. It's Wednesday. Well, Saturday in this case. But I suppose at what point do you have to recognize your own dysfunction?'

'It is quite a lot of dysfunction,' said Basher, almost under his breath.

'We should debrief,' said Soph. 'Like, go over the evidence. Find clues.'

'Er. Soph wants to start looking for clues and stuff. But maybe we shouldn't do it here?'

'There isn't any evidence to find,' said Basher. 'There's no proof anything happened!'

Alex tapped the biro on their chin. 'Maybe. But if we talk about it enough, we'll find some. *Or,*' they added, catching Basher's expression, 'exhaust the possibility, and I'll get bored and stop talking about it. Anyway, Claire has a point about finding a secure location to talk. I bet you need a drink, don't you? I do.'

'You have me there, I admit. Fine, we can go to the pub. At least there, nobody – living or otherwise – can bother my parents. While they're *grieving,*' Basher added pointedly.

So they went to the pub. Claire was simply happy to leave the house and its unbearable atmosphere. The local turned out to be the one in Wilbourne Duces that Figgy had driven past the night before, red-brick but with a thatched roof and thick crown-glass panes in some of the windows. Claire knew, before they went inside, that it would have loads of horse brasses on the walls. There was a spaniel sitting outside, in such a grotesquely charming pose that it might as well have been an agency dog that was getting a decent day rate to flop on the steps. 'Yeah,' Claire imagined the dog saying, whilst smoking during a union-enforced break, 'this is a pretty good gig. I've got a spot as a patient on *Casualty* coming up, though.'

Where there would normally be a pub sign depicting a tree with a crown, or two men trying to strangle a swan or something, instead there hung a single plank painted red. This was because the pub was called the Red Line. Claire had been told this during the drive over, but had assumed Basher said the 'Red Lion', which she didn't think was an unfair assumption to make.

'Apparently,' Basher explained as they went inside, 'it was supposed to be called The Red Lion, but the very first sign-maker misheard, and so the Red Line it was for evermore. I do have reason to doubt this story, which is that it was definitely called The Red Lion up until it came under new management in the early noughties. It's a good story, though, and they do a decent shepherd's pie.'

'Ohmigod, is shepherd's pie the only thing people eat around here?' said Sophie. 'We should sit by a radiator or something. These two'll get cold, otherwise.'

They'd arrived for the lunchtime rush, but since it was in a village pub in the middle of nowhere, it wasn't hard to get a table of their choosing in a corner. It did indeed become a bit chilly, the longer Sophie sat there. Claire found that running an investigation from a pub came with a couple of distinct advantages, one being that you could work with a cheeky glass of wine.

The other was that the Red Line came with free Wi-Fi for patrons. Not only was the Wellington-Forges' home a dead spot for phones, but they were internet-free, apart from a wired connection in the estate office. It made the house a popular venue for a certain kind of wedding or corporate team-building event that used words like 'unplugged', but for everyone else it was really annoying. Alex noted that it made it very difficult to keep up with their social media pages, where they were building a decent following for their art and their costuming. They were now busily tapping away on an impossibly slim laptop.

'I know that story reveals that your family is even more

unsettling than the cousin-fuckers on *Downton Abbey*, but it does give us at least one interesting clue for murder,' said Soph.

'What d'you mean?' asked Claire. She had been so focused on the shouting and food-fight bits of the story that she'd almost forgotten to pay attention to the potential crime bit.

'Financial, obviously!' When Claire still looked blank, Sophie threw up her hands. 'Ohmigod, could you even tie your shoelaces without me? Clementine said something to Hugh about money going missing, first of all. And secondly, Tristan almost spilled the beans on something to do with irregularities that Michael found at the legal... the law... the lawyer-place. Where they build lawyers.'

'Legal firm?'

'Yeah. Michael's an accountant – he wouldn't have found irregularities in the ham sandwiches, would he?'

'That's actually a very good point,' said Alex.

'Er, can I add a "thirdly"?' said Claire. 'How fucking long did it take your mum to make instant gravy?'

'Yeah, now you mention it, she was gone for, like, forty-five minutes. Mum couldn't have killed anyone, though – she's not the type.'

'Everyone's the type,' said Claire very seriously. 'But it doesn't help much right now anyway. It's all, you know, hearsay.'

Basher looked up from ignoring the conversation, and concentrating on the menu, long enough to make a 'yeah, not bad' face.

'Can we tell if any of the potential victims are dead without digging up a body?' Soph asked. 'Wouldn't they have been reported missing?'

'Maybe. But Kevin might not be the easiest one to start with, actually,' Alex said, opening up Instagram, Facebook and a host of other social networking sites that Claire had heard of, but was not familiar with. 'Are you sure you can't remember his last name, Uncle B?'

'Neither can you,' pointed out Basher. 'Also, I would like it noted that I am not getting involved. I am here as a chaperone to make sure you don't do anything properly illegal whilst playing detective with a strange ghost-whisperer we don't know. Are you hungry? I'm hungry. They have pheasant stew on today.'

'Ah! I think this is him. Uncle Tris is following him on Insta,' said Alex, having been stymied by the lack of a last name for approximately twenty seconds. 'Hmm. It's an account specifically for a big trip he's doing around South America at the moment. His handle is 'NoPerryJustKevinGoesLarge. God, your generation is embarrassing. I think I would rather die than be one of you. Genuinely, Uncle B, I would kill myself, if I were you.'

'So that's three pheasant stews, O grateful one?' Basher said as he stood up, ignoring their dig. He went to order at the bar, shoulders hunched and hands in pockets.

Alex spun their laptop round to show Kevin's Instagram to Claire and Sophie. It was a lot of pictures of Kevin doing stuff like hiking through jungles, holding up a fish next to the local man who had clearly caught

90

the fish himself, and smiling at children in traditional Peruvian clothes. Basher's description of Kevin had been accurate. He was white, good-looking and had several vaguely Celtic tattoos and lots of blue glass-bead jewellery. He probably had a COEXIST patch on his backpack.

'Last post was about three weeks ago. We can mark him down as a "probably not dead", I think,' said Alex, who had switched to working on a spreadsheet. They had indeed listed Kevin as Probably Not Dead.

'Sami isn't dead, either,' said Basher, returning to the table.

'I mean, you would say that,' said Claire. 'Surely if Sami was the victim, you'd be the most obvious suspect.'

'Sorry, you're right – I forgot that, out of all of us, you have the most crime-solving expertise.'

'I have *some*. Seances aren't easy, you know, there's a lot of investigation involved. Sort of. And I've watched all of *Murder Profile* at least three times,' she added, sounding as if she was joking, but secretly being serious. Basher snorted. Claire realized she was trying to impress him and made a mental note to catch herself next time.

'Don't be shitty, Uncle B,' said Alex, without looking up. 'Sami is actually alive – I've seen her since the party last year, too. A lot. We babysit for her.' They wrote Definitely Not Dead next to Sami.

'Yeah, unless you're both in on it,' said Claire.

'It would be good to talk to Sami, though,' said Sophie. 'Like, interviewing witnesses, yeah? Even the ones who haven't been murdered might remember things. We should, you know, reconstruct the weekend.'

Claire nodded without repeating aloud what Sophie had said, and made a further mental note to follow up on the Sami thing herself. If she'd learned anything from TV, it was that the person you least suspect is the person you should most suspect, and in this case that meant Basher and Alex. Even from a non pop-cultural angle, Basher at least made a good suspect. He had the know-how to commit and cover up a murder. She would simply need to figure out the motive – even if the victim wasn't Sami. Plus, it was probably a good idea to keep a healthy emotional distance from Basher and Alex, because eventually they would both decide they didn't want to talk to her ever again.

The pheasant stew arrived in large, steaming bowls. It was very hearty. There were dumplings and everything. Claire hadn't eaten any kind of game before. She discovered that pheasant tasted luxurious and meaty. Like chicken, but if hens voted Tory.

'Did anything else happen that weekend?' she asked, mouth full. 'You know, around the dinner?'

Alex and Basher paused and looked at each other, as if silently discussing how much dirty laundry they should air. Finally Alex shrugged.

'Not really. It was like this weekend, but with more shouting and less elderly-relative death. It was all those arguments, and then the non-family people left early and without properly saying goodbye, and the bigger gathering the next day was cancelled, out of embarrassment. You know, Uncle Bash argued with Granny and Grandad – Hugh and Clem, that is, not Nana – but Granny also argued with Figgy, and Figgy argued with Kevin. Oh, and Uncle Tris ruined a suit by falling over in it. I think that's less an event and more a metaphor for Uncle T's entire life, though. Like, at what point do you not realize that you are a walking stereotype? And the Mattie-quitting thing, but that happened sort of offscreen, from our point of view. I did see her a couple of times that weekend, though, and it looked like she had been crying.'

'Oh yeah. Um, what's the deal with all that then?'

'Mum would never admit it, but she can't properly run that place without Mattie. Like I said, Mattie was basically the estate manager, but Mum always said "housekeeper",' Basher explained, stabbing gloomily – which was how he did everything, Claire noticed – at a dumpling. 'It sounds ridiculous. I think Mum thought it was more proper for a big family to have a housekeeper. And in the summer Mattie's husband worked on the gardens a bit, so Mum could say the housekeeper was married to the groundskeeper. Very BBC costume drama, you know? Mattie had been working at the house for about twenty years, but packed it all in that weekend. Just quit. Or maybe got fired? Never got to the bottom of that really.'

Claire didn't point out that Basher's policy of non-involvement in the case wasn't standing up to much scrutiny. He obviously missed his job, or at least having some kind of defined purpose, even if he'd become disenchanted with being a policeman. Sophie was looking at him, an inscrutable expression on her face.

'My theory is that Granny shit-canned Mattie out of nowhere, because she thought she was having an affair with Grandad,' added Alex. They made a face at the thought of this.

'Yes, but you think that because it would be the most drama, not because you have evidence for it. I don't really believe that Dad would cheat on Mum,' said Basher. 'And Mattie was part of the family. She was always so nice to us. Like having an aunt. Loves kippers, as well. Was always making kedgeree. She lives around here somewhere. I was in the same school year as her son. In fact...' Basher said, craning his neck to look through the bar, 'I think that's her husband Alf over there.'

He pointed to a dour-looking man in a wax jacket and flat cap, the picture of a miserable country bloke. Alf was drinking a pint of ale, obviously, and was making a concerted effort not to look at anyone.

Sophie immediately said they should go over and talk to him, but before anyone could make a move in that direction, the door crashed open and in strode patriarch Hugh, flanked by two tall men in fashionable business suits. Hugh, in contrast, looked like he was dressed for some sort of obscure countryside Olympics. A tweed waistcoat and jacket strained over his tummy, which within seconds he was supplementing with a lager, and he wore matching three-quarter-length trousers that tucked into long maroon socks with fluffy garter-ties. Hugh, it was fair to say, did not have the legs for the ensemble. He noticed them at their table and shambled over.

'Been shooting then, Dad?' asked Basher.

'About to... about to. It was all arranged anyway, and I thought: why let the day go to waste? Nana would have wanted life to go on, you know, Basher,' he said, with an abrupt approximation of respectful sadness. 'Anyway, look at what the cat dragged in from London, eh? Chaps, meet Claire. This is m'dear little boy Monty,' he said, clapping a forty-something man on the shoulder proudly.

Monty was still handsome, with salt-and-pepper hair not unlike George Clooney's and a crisp white shirt and expensive watch, also not unlike George Clooney's. His eyes were as blue as his father's, but much more focused, and there was a smug twist to his mouth that Claire did not like. Alex seemed to have inherited more from their mother, thank goodness.

'Montgomery Wellington-Forge,' said Monty. 'Of Parker, Parker and Renwick. Figgy tells me we should be very pleased to meet you.'

Claire immediately filed this comment away for future petty seething, while Soph made a scoffing noise.

Monty was wearing a jewelled tie-pin that stood out against the relative sobriety of his suit: a silvery bar with three diamonds studded in it. The sort of thing you wear when you want to appear tasteful, but still want people to know that you have way more money than they have, or ever will. It glinted in the light.

Sophie was looking at it, too. 'There is absolutely no way he has enough money to spend on that, as the family in general can't afford to repaint their windows. Are you kidding me?'

Tristan, the youngest Wellington-Forge sibling, was pushed forward in his turn. He had a very square jaw, the same familial blue eyes and a messy blond pompadour that was, on closer inspection, actually rock-hard and frozen in place with product. Combined with the jaw, it gave the impression of a Lego-man from a Build Your Own Junior Lawyer playset.

'Yeah, hi. Tris,' he said, shaking Claire's hand and maintaining the grip for about five seconds longer than was comfortable. 'So. This is pretty weird, huh? You being here still. With old Nana dead in the back bedroom. Pretty awks. *Awkwarino*. Awkward city.'

He laughed nervously and sat down in Sophie's seat. She did not move, and the magic-eye picture effect of two people being in one place immediately began to make Claire's eyes water. Tristan would be feeling like he was sitting in an ice-bath, but, she was interested to see, he was trying his absolute best not to betray this fact by shivering or looking uncomfortable in any way. It was a losing battle.

'I'm not staying long,' Claire said. 'Er... my condolences, of course.'

'Yes, well, very sad, but it was a bit overdue, I suppose,' said Monty, who had not looked up from sending emails on his phone. 'I hear you're helping Alex sort their life out.

'I don't suppose you can get them to move back in with their parents, where they ought to be.'

'Alex is nineteen, Claire, so they can actually live wherever they would like,' said Basher mildly, though he had flinched almost imperceptibly when Monty spoke.

'That's nonsense, and you know it. My child has been bloody kidnapped!' snapped Monty.

'Excuse me, can we not talk about me like I'm not here,' said Alex, trying to cut in between them, but they were interrupted by Hugh, who was not paying attention, saying, 'Jolly good, jolly good. Are you all right, Tris?'

'Your mother is worried sick all the time,' said Monty, cutting back across Hugh to acknowledge Alex.

'I'm totally fine, Dad,' whined Tristan as he squirmed in his seat.

'You look a bit cold, mate – we can switch places, you know.'

'Alex is perfectly safe with me, and I resent the suggestion that they are not.'

'He's always been a bit sensitive, ha-ha-ha, eh, Claire? Come on, Tris, I'll switch with you if you're chilly.'

'Still actually here – hello, has own opinions on their own life.'

'I'm not cold, Dad, I'm *fine*—'

At this point Tristan physically squirmed away from the jovial teasing of his father and/or the freezing-ghost aura, and tripped over a chair leg trying to stand up. He managed not to fall over completely, but staggered awkwardly, and two iPhones, his keys and a load of pens showered from his coat pockets.

'If you've broken another work phone, the firm isn't going to pay for it,' said Monty, without looking round. 'You're a bloody disgrace.'

'Er, no harm done, Monty. Sorry.' Tris scrambled to pick everything up, turning a bit pink.

Claire felt sorry for him. It was as if her mind had retconned Tristan staggering around, juggling all his possessions, going 'Wh-wh-wh-*whoooooah!*' until he sat in some jelly, even though that had not happened at all.

Hugh cleared his throat. 'Don't worry, Tris, Mum and I will get you a new one if anything is broken. Anyway, just seen Alf at the bar, chaps. I need to find out if he's going to be at the shoot this afternoon.'

Claire and Sophie exchanged a glance, and Sophie got up to follow Hugh as the three brothers began to exchange tense pleasantries.

'We're down here to see Mum,' said Monty. 'Brought the will down, and so on. But we'll probably have to leave again tomorrow.'

'Yeah, work is bloody *mental*, eh? Eh, Monty?'

Claire noted with some interest that Nana's will had apparently been drawn up by her own grandson, but she was distracted by Sophie, who was furiously waving her arms across the room. 'Look!' Sophie shouted. 'Look!'

Hugh and Alf were having a discussion in lowered voices, but it was obviously a *heated* discussion. Claire leaned back casually, so that she could see what happened next. Hugh, in what he clearly thought was a discreet way, reached into his pocket and pulled out a big folded wodge of cash. He passed it to Alf under the bar. Claire quickly returned to poking at her stew, as Hugh barked an awkward, too-loud fake laugh and returned to the table.

Sophie came back, too, and recounted what she'd overheard, talking in Claire's ear so that she could be heard over everyone else.

'Hugh said he wanted the "usual arrangement today", or something like that, and then that Alf guy said he wanted more, because people were watching and it was getting harder to avoid questions,' she told Claire, with conspiratorial glee. 'They weren't even talking that quietly.'

Claire choked on a hard bit of potato and Hugh slapped her genially on the back. She often found it weird, and inconvenient, to have to smile nicely at people while Sophie casually discussed secrets she had uncovered about them. Claire had to remember what she wasn't supposed to know, as well as acting like she didn't know it, and this was especially difficult in circumstances such as murder and investigatoring.

'Anyway,' Sophie went on, 'Hugh said it was the usual this time and he'd see about next time, but he wasn't happy about it. We need to talk to Alf, like, one hundred per cent. What if Alf hid the body and is being paid off?'

This was a good point. Alf was now industriously rolling cigarettes. He slipped one behind his ear, downed the last few dregs of his pint and headed outside. Claire waited for a few seconds, then waved her own lighter at the table apologetically and followed him.

Alf was holding the lead of the day rate glamour-spaniel and sucking aggressively on his rollie. He had acquired a cadre of similar men, all in various combinations of flat cap and wax jacket, and each in charge of a pink-tongued, shiny-coated dog. In a happy coincidence Claire discovered, checking for the fourth time since her last fag that morning, that her box of Marlboro Lights was empty. She approached the group cautiously.

'Er... sorry, mate. I'm out. Don't s'pose I could steal a fag off you?'

The men all stopped chatting and their heads swivelled. Alf looked at her with distaste. He was slightly unshaven and had the jowls of a very sad basset hound. Eventually he tutted and rolled his eyes, clearly unimpressed by a townie who couldn't even keep up her own supply of cigarettes, and fished out a roll-up for her, out of pity.

'Thanks, mate. So, er, you all mates with Hugh and the Wellington-Forges? I'm staying with them.'

'You're saying "mate" way too much for someone who never says "mate",' said Sophie.

Alf exchanged looks with the group. They seemed to come to a silent consensus to tolerate her, because he nodded curtly.

'I know 'em,' he said.

'Your wife, Mattie – someone said she used to work for them?'

'She did. Not any more.' There was no advance on the conversation.

Claire decided to try a different tack, and knelt down to say hello to the dog, which was very friendly. Especially in comparison to its owner.

'Nice dog you have. Beautiful! Hugh said you go on the, er, shoots?'

'We go picking up. Dipper never misses a bird.' There was some quiet pride there.

'Great. Yeah. Never been myself, but uh, I hear Hugh loves it. I guess he pays you to pick up for him?'

Soph whistled. 'Oooh, bold play from the rookie detective.'

To the surprise of both of them, there were a few snickers from the men. 'Yeah, Alf picks up for him all right,' said one.

'Always bags a bunch of birds, does Hugh,' said another.

'Mind you, there's a lot of that going around in that family, eh, Alf?'

'What d'you mean?' said Alf, eyes narrowing.

'Ah, nothing, don't get your arse in your hand.'

There was obviously some shared secret between them, but Claire couldn't think of a way to keep the conversation going. 'I, uh, I saw Hugh give you some money just now, that's all.'

'LOL! A bad follow-up, though; the opponent won't let her get away with that,' interjected Sophie, clearly enjoying herself far too much.

'Don't see how that's any of your business,' said Alf, turning to her as his eyes narrowed, if that were possible, even further.

'So, er, he *wasn't* paying you for picking up?'

'But the rookie hits back: fifteen all!' Sophie yelled.

'Stop fucking mixing metaphors – you're getting me confused!' Claire snapped back.

'What?' asked Alf, who was clearly thrown by this. The men shuffled their feet and gave Claire the disconcerted look that everyone gave her when she forgot to not talk to Sophie out loud.

'Not you. Ugh, bollocks! Sorry. Listen – just, how's your wife? Is she all right?'

'What? What do you mean by that? What have you heard? Who are you?' Alf was becoming not angry, but upset and embarrassed. Claire was surprised to see that his eyes were beginning to fill up a bit. She took a step away from him, as one of the men put an arm around his shoulders. 'Did one of you say something?' Alf asked, wheeling to look at them.

'No one said anything – I haven't heard anything about anyone. I'm sorry.' Claire felt guilty. She didn't yet have the hardened emotional carapace of a seasoned detective. Feelings had to be hurt in pursuit of the truth!

'Piss off and mind your own business,' Alf hissed, stomping away down the road. The other men, and their mismatched pack of dogs, headed off after him, giving Claire sour looks and insulting her loudly enough that she could hear every word.

She looked after them, still smoking Alf's cigarette. Sophie came and stood next to her. They stood in silence for a couple of minutes. Then 'Fumbled that one, didn't you?' said Soph, sucking air through her teeth.

6

Little Bones Go Snicker-Snack

The four of them had returned to the house. It wasn't too far a walk, really, although it was further than Claire would have liked and down a rough public right-of-way cut through the fields, in order to make a path as-the-crow-flies from the pub.

With Hugh off to his shoot and Monty and Tris having their own lunch at the pub, Alex told Claire that there was an opportunity to do a bit of snooping. 'If our lead is finances,' they said, 'we should have a rummage around the office, look through the business accounts, that sort of thing.'

But Basher was still not on board. He had ridiculous concerns about 'warrants' and 'chains of evidence', which were never mentioned on *Murder Profile* but which, Claire had to acknowledge, were quite important in real life.

'I'll keep him busy,' Alex whispered, letting Basher get a few steps ahead of them as the group walked across the gravel drive towards the house. 'You should be the one to look in the office, because it's the only place with a working computer. If you get caught, you can claim ignorance and say you didn't know you weren't allowed, and you wanted to check your email. Just don't let Uncle B catch you, okay? He is the CEO of overreacting, sometimes.' They patted Claire on the back to reassure her and called Basher back.

'So listen, Uncle B,' Alex said. 'I know you've gone all super-pig about it – all right, all right, it was a joke, calm down – but surely there's no harm in having a look around the general rooms and the big house? If we find anything, then we can leave it exactly where it is and not touch it; and if we don't find anything, then you can say you were right all along. And you love that.'

'Hmm,' said Basher. This was not a no. 'I suppose you can explore, if I supervise. Our fingerprints and hair are already all over most of the house anyway. But Claire can't touch anything. That would cross-contaminate.'

'Cross-contaminate *what*? How?' said Sophie. 'We haven't even been here before today. Ohmigod, he just doesn't like you.'

Claire might have imagined it, but she thought she saw Basher's cheeks colour a little when she relayed this.

'That's exactly why you would contaminate evidence – in the highly unlikely event of evidence ever being collected. And I am not trying to be mean. But you are not... you're a stranger. This is family,' he said.

'It doesn't matter,' replied Alex cheerfully. 'Claire can stay in the kitchen with Granny, right, C?'

'No, no,' said Basher. He clearly felt bad about the suggestion that he didn't like Claire. Which he probably didn't, but it might be weird to hear that said out loud to someone's face. 'I would not wish that on anyone. Look, would you stay in bits of the house where you've already been? Please? The library or your room, and so on. Please?'

Claire watched them walk away. She felt guilty that she was about to betray this trust. She had not yet mentioned that she and Sophie had seen Hugh paying off Alf. It was the only proper lead so far, a concrete thing suggesting that Hugh might have killed Mattie and covered it up – either by paying Alf to do the dirty work, or by paying Alf to keep quiet about something he saw. But it was a difficult thing to bring up. The enormity, the sheer ridiculousness of what they were doing, had become real to Claire, and she was trying to sit on that realization, like a large and uncomfortable egg, until she decided what to do with it. It was one thing to think you'd met a dead murder victim, and quite another to say to someone, 'Hey, I think your dad/grandad might have killed a woman and is paying her husband to keep quiet about her disappearance.'

'You should say something sooner rather than later,' Soph said. And she was probably right. But for now Claire was nervously chewing her thumb and looking at the door to the estate office.

Figgy was reportedly inconsolable and crying in her bedroom. Clementine was in the kitchen down the hallway. Dinner was going to be chicken soup, she'd told them all, and she was preparing the vegetables. Claire could hear the rhythmic chopping. But she didn't want to push her luck. She didn't really know how long it took to search a room. Was searching very labour-intensive? What about a 'fingertip search', compared to a general poking around?

She glanced again at the big oak door in front of her. It looked noisy. She opened it very, very slowly, as if she were unwrapping a sweet in the cinema or a sanitary towel in a public toilet. To her surprise, while it was heavy, the door opened quietly. She slipped inside, leaving it slightly ajar.

'Can you keep watch?' she asked Sophie.

'Ohmigod! No way. I want to see what they have in here, too.'

It was a small, oppressive room with no windows. There were a couple of filing cabinets, shelves full of storage binders, and a desk with a small office computer. There was also, as promised, a blinking router.

Claire gave a cursory rummage through the binders, but they were all physical receipts and she had no real idea what she was looking for. Then she tried the filing cabinets. 'You're looking under N for Nana, aren't you?' asked Soph.

'No,' said Claire indignantly, flicking quickly to M. At Sophie's suggestion, she checked under D for Du Lotte Hotels, the company that wanted to buy the building, and found a posh brochure dated the previous year, advertising winter breaks at a much nicer-looking estate than

The Cloisters. There was a business card for Mary Tyler, Head of New Developments, tucked into it. Someone had written, *'We can definitely help each other. Let's talk more!'* in biro and had added a mobile phone number. She showed Sophie.

'Ugh, those police shows have given you literally no common sense,' Sophie said. 'Sounds like someone from Du Lotte was in contact with a member of the family – or someone who was here last autumn, right?'

'Okay. So clearly selling the house was an issue around this time last year as well. But Nana wasn't involved in the day-to-day running of this place, was she? She didn't use this office. So someone else was doing some insider trading? They were sufficiently invested in the house being sold that they kept this contact info...'

'Yeah, maybe.'

'I bet it was Mattie. She used this office the most. What if they caught her – you know, passing info to the enemy?'

'Bit of a reach maybe, but I can see it,' said Sophie.

Claire was pleased with this success, but dithered about keeping the evidence, because she thought Basher would be cross. Sophie pointed out that she had already touched everything anyway, so in the end Claire took the business card and put back the brochure. Sophie rubbed her hands together: now, she indicated, they were cooking with some kind of flammable accelerant.

Next Claire went over to switch on the computer and establish her alibi for being in there. It was password-protected, obviously. She was already starting to get nervous, imagining that she could hear Basher's footsteps approaching every second.

'Try "password",' said Sophie. 'I bet you anything. There's no way Hugh would remember something more complicated.'

'Oh, come on, there's no way th— Oh, it worked.' Sophie was, Claire had to admit, still much better at this than she was.

'Fucking legend. Is there anything marked "our bad killing and how we done it"?'

Claire snorted, but she did have a look through the files in the vain hope that there was something obviously murdery. It seemed to be mostly more financial records and booking information, and she was not clever enough to understand if any of that was incriminating – although she harboured a vague suspicion that all rich people's finances were incriminating somehow. It did look as if the diary had started to thin out over the past year, or at least wasn't being kept as up to date. Perhaps Mattie had been more integral to the business than anyone – apart from Basher maybe – had realized.

Claire opened the email application and it automatically loaded the in-box. There wasn't anything suspicious in the recent emails, either, so she went back to around the same time last year. The Monday after the party weekend there was an email from Monty, from his firm's work address, that didn't have a subject line.

'Look!' she whispered. Sophie leaned over as Claire opened it. Her heart was genuinely racing. All it said was:

It's all under control. I told you not to use this
address. I'll call later.

Below it was the message to which it was replying:

We got an email from hmrc.they must have been
tipped off.if they investigate they will find out. w.hat
should I do now? dad

'Ohmigod. Fuuuucking hell,' said Sophie.

'It's not looking great for Hugh, is it?'

'No, I mean old people emailing. Surely he has to type
in his job?'

'He probably has a secretary or something,' said
Claire. She forwarded the email to herself, trying not
to think about how disappointed Basher would be, and
closed down the computer.

'You're going to be like that when you're old,' said
Soph, picking invisible spectral lint off her sleeve.

'You're six months older than me!'

'I am not! I haven't been since 2007. We've been
through this. I am for ever young and in my prime, while
you waste your life and become older and more decrepit
with every passing year.' Sophie's tone was breezy, but
she was avoiding eye contact. 'Talking about it gives me a
headache,' she said quickly.

'You can't get headaches,' said Claire absent-mindedly,
rattling one of the drawers on the desk.

'How would you know?'

110

'You don't have a head.'

'Do so,' said Sophie. She turned away and added, 'I'm just not sure where it is.'

Claire pressed her lips together. Even if nobody knew the specifics of what had happened to Sophie, everyone knew what the answer *probably* was, based on what usually happened to girls who went missing without a trace. It was on the long list of Stuff That Is Easier If We Just Don't Bring It Up, and Claire always got worried when Sophie showed signs of introspection. Who knew what she thought about at night, alone, unable to sleep, staring into the dark. Did she try to remember, or try to forget?

Claire attempted to concentrate on the task at hand. She pulled open a drawer and drew out a sheaf of letters, and a small, slim, bright blue notebook with what looked like a perfectly round blue eye on the front. She was about to open the plasticky cover, which felt like one of those waterproof ones you buy to protect the real cover, when suddenly she heard footsteps in the corridor outside. Instant panic – if Basher caught her with her hand in the cookie jar, he'd be very cross, and she did not like raised voices. She put the book back in the drawer and tried to shuffle the letters into the right order before stuffing them in as well. Before she had time to close the drawer, the door to the office swept open.

'Basher, sorry, I—' she started to say.

Clementine was standing there, staring at her. She paused, looking surprised, and then her features arranged themselves to convey a special kind of menacing kindness – politeness wielded like an ice-pick.

'Hello, sweetheart. Are you lost?' she asked.

'Uuuuuhhh,' replied Claire, who'd had just enough time to arrange herself with forced nonchalance in the office chair.

'Ohmigod, you sound like a confused cow. Say yes, for God's sake,' said Sophie.

'Hhhyes,' Claire finished finally. 'Sorry. I was. Um. Going to check my emails – someone said there was a computer in here, but of course the computer is password-protected, ha-ha. And then, um... my, um... sleeve got caught on the desk,' she babbled, trying to close the drawer as casually as possible.

'Of course. But I'm afraid there are lots of private documents in here,' said Clementine. She put her arm around Claire's shoulders to ferry her towards the door. 'Who was it who said you could come in here?'

'Aahhhmmm,' said Claire, who realized her voice had risen to an absurd pitch, 'I'm not *quite* sure.'

'Jesus *Christ*,' said Sophie. 'Sometimes I think that you're actually the dead one, I swear.'

'Of course you're not, dear,' said Clementine, with the sweetness of a sour lolly. 'Why don't you come and help me with the soup? I'm sure it will come to you.' She produced a key and locked the office door, before pulling Claire down the hall and depositing her at the kitchen table. 'You can finish peeling these potatoes for me,' she said.

112

Claire noted that it was not delivered as a question, and picked up the peeler.

Clementine resumed stripping the carcass of a roast chicken. She didn't look at Claire, but kept her eyes on the meat and bones as she pulled one from the other. Her fingers became covered with grease, but they didn't slip at all. Sometimes she would pick up a kitchen knife that had been worn to a thin strip by repeated sharpenings. The occasional *crack* as she drove it through a joint punctuated her speaking.

'Chicken soup is so comforting, isn't it? So restorative. I'm sure it'll cheer Figgy up.'

Crack.

'Of course, you don't have children, do you? I always think you can't understand until you do. Not really.'

Crack.

'You'd do anything for your children. Protect them from anything. From anyone.'

Cra-ack.

An entire drumstick was torn from the bird. The knife was raised and driven into the flesh again, and Claire found she was focusing on the only bit of nonsense she remembered from studying 'Jabberwocky' at school: 'One, two! And through and through / The vorpal blade went snicker-snack!' Round and round in her head it went, over and over again. *One, two! And through and through!*

Clementine dropped more cleaned bones onto the plate with little clatters. Then she picked up a wing and pulled it in two.

Snap-crick-crack. Snicker-snack!

She turned the bird over. Claire stared with ferocious intensity at the potatoes, and considered the combat potential of a vegetable peeler versus a knife. Sweat was breaking out on her forehead.

'Do you know what these bits are called, just here?' said Clementine, pointing out two little bits of dark meat near the leg.

Claire's top lip was also very sweaty. *One, two!*

'They're called the oysters. They're the most flavour-ful, best bit of meat. But you have to really dig them out.'

'*Ohmigod*. I think she's actually going to eat you,' said Sophie, visibly disturbed. 'Any second she's going to leap across the table and dig out *your* oysters.'

Claire did not find this helpful. *And through and through!*

Clementine drove a manicured nail into the offending bit of meat and began to winkle it out.

Claire watched with a growing dread. Clementine's fingers were slipping on the handle of the peeler, and Claire would give anything in the world for something to stop her getting the oysters out; something terrible was going to happen once she got the oysters out – please God, stop the oysters... *The vorpal blade went snicker-snack!*

Suddenly Basher and Alex exploded into the room. Claire yelped and jumped up, at the same time as Sophie exclaimed, 'Oh, thank fuck!'

Walking into the atmosphere in the kitchen must have

been like being hit in the face with a very awkward plank. Alex flinched.

'Everything all right?' said Basher, stepping forward to steal a bit of the chicken.

'Yes, darling, Claire was just helping me with the soup,' said Clementine brightly. 'Where have you two been? Would you like a cup of tea?'

The air returned to Claire's lungs. She breathed back out very slowly.

They all helped chop the remaining vegetables and put them in a large pot for later. Claire struggled. She stared at her hands and peeled potatoes, while Basher and Alex chatted with Clem. Her fingers trembled as the tide of adrenaline in her blood suddenly receded. She glanced up and caught Alex looking at her weirdly, so she looked down again.

'You been hanging out in the kitchen a while, Claire?' they said.

'Oh, Claire has been very helpful,' said Clementine. She tipped a handful of grains into the stock on the stove and smiled again. She maintained unblinking eye contact with Claire. 'A very busy little bee, aren't you, dear?'

'This woman is seriously fucked up,' said Sophie.

Claire finished the last potato with a sense of great relief. 'I'm just going to... um... please excuse me.' She ran back to her room, closed the door behind her and collapsed on her bed like a little girl hiding from a bully.

In a few moments Sophie walked in through the door. She mostly used doors like a normal person, unlike a lot of ghosts, even waiting for Claire to open them and go through first. It was either out of habit or wishful thinking. Sophie sat down on the other bed and whistled through her teeth, but otherwise didn't say anything.

After a while there was a knock on the door, followed by a tentative 'Hello?' in Basher's voice. Claire was lying with the pillow over her face, so she yelled an indistinct 'Come in.'

'Hello,' said Basher. 'What have you been up to, then? I take it, from Mum's behaviour, that you did not stick to our agreement.' He sounded more resigned than angry.

'Alex told us to look around the office, and then your mum did a one-woman performance of *The Texas Chicken Massacre* at me,' Claire replied, in a muffled voice. She pulled back half the pillow to see his reaction. It was surprisingly mild.

'I cannot say I approve at all, but I am quite tired, so please imagine that I shouted at you for looking through personal family documents and don't ever do it again, yes? Arguably, watching Mum debone a chicken carcass is punishment enough.' Basher paused and then, with a bit of a guilty tone, added, 'I suppose you didn't find anything, did you?'

'Yes. Well. Maybe. I don't know,' said Claire. 'Did you?'

'No. But the house is too big anyway. It's mostly dust sheets. And it's a whole year later. And I still do not think anything happened. But... well, I can see that you and Alex really are taking this seriously. I am not making fun of you by being sceptical.'

'Yeah, I know.' Claire sat up.

Basher was leaning against the dresser and the evening sun was cutting across his face. It made his grey eyes almost luminous and the soft blond stubble around his mouth stand out.

'What's that Alf guy like?' she asked, shaking off thoughts of Basher's face.

Basher shrugged. 'He's all right. He's a local old boy, hangs around with other local old boys, goes on shoots, takes good care of his dogs. Bit grumpy, but they all are. Indulges Dad, who is an abjectly terrible shot. Wouldn't have thought he was of any interest.'

'When did you last see Mattie?'

'Last year. What? I don't come here often,' he went on, rubbing his face. Claire noticed he did that a lot, enough for it to be a habit. 'Claire, Mattie is probably fine. If she had gone missing, someone would have noticed. I am sure she got a much better job somewhere else. "Nothing will come of nothing",' he added, a little sadly.

'Tell him – go on. About Alf,' said Sophie, who was now picking at her nails.

'Soph... listened to your dad talking to Alf in the pub. And I saw him hand over a load of money. I asked him – Alf – about it.'

'Ah, the direct approach. And?'

'He told me to piss off.'

'You shock me. When you say "a load of money", what do you mean?'

'It was a bunch of twenties folded in half. Like you see

117

drug dealers passing around on TV, in the detective shows Claire watches,' said Sophie. 'Except neither of them was wearing a cool leather jacket.'

'Hmm. I'm pretty sure Alf isn't the type to have a sideline in gak. And my dad isn't the type to take it.' He paused. 'Now, if you'd said *Tris*...'

'Well, what *was* the money for then, if not to keep Alf quiet about something? Plus, I found this business card from Du Lotte, which makes it look like someone was in cahoots with them. Clearly Nana wasn't the only one interested in the house sale – so who else was?' She passed the business card to Basher, who frowned and turned it over in his hands. '*And* I saw an email from your dad to Monty from last year saying, like, HMRC had been tipped off and were going to investigate the family finances, tax owed and that sort of thing, so what should he do? And Monty was like "Don't contact me at this address". What if that's something to do with Michael?'

Basher scratched his chin. His fingers rasped a little across the stubble. 'Ye-e-e-s, well, reading people's private correspondence is getting into dicey territory, legally speaking...' he said. But he sounded and looked worried.

'It was an accident,' said Sophie tartly. 'Claire was trying to read her own email and your dad's just opened, right? Anyway she's not a police officer, so no harm, no foul.'

'Hmm. I'll be honest. When I asked, I wasn't expecting that you'd uncovered evidence of actual wrongdoing.' Basher started to pace back and forth, as much as was possible, and kept pushing the sleeves of his hoodie up to his elbows and then pulling them back down again. He suddenly wheeled back to face her. 'We're getting back to the point where I find it hard to trust you, I'm afraid. It feels more likely you've made this up. You could have written on this card yourself, and everything else is just your testimony.'

Claire shrugged. She was used to mistrust. 'You can go and look at the emails yourself. Anyway, why would I bother making it up?'

'To get me on board with this *investigation*,' said Basher, dropping heavy air-quotes around the word.

'I thought you weren't making fun of me?'

'This is not me making fun of you, this is me being catty.'

'Bit full of yourself. Anyway, if I wanted that, I'd have made up an email saying, "Dear son, hope nobody finds out how we totally killed someone!"'

'All right – maybe you want to blackmail my parents for money.'

'In which case, why did I tell you about it?'

Basher looked at the ceiling. He was weighing up the logic of her arguments, which Claire thought was pretty bang on, in fairness. She pressed home her advantage. 'Look, I know you don't believe I can see dead people, but you don't have to think I'm the worst person in the entire world. Something weird *is* going on here, and I can tell you want to find out what.'

'No comment,' he replied, flashing a shy smile. '*But* as you pointed out, that email is not evidence of murder, is it? At the end of the day, you've caught my dad emailing his son and paying for something cash in hand.'

'I dunno. It seemed more shady than that. And your mum is very aggressive about the correct way to strip a chicken.'

'Even so. That would not, as we used to say, hold up in court. Although... *arguably* Monty could say that email is confidential, under legal-advice privilege, since he is the family lawyer and Dad asked him what to do. So why wouldn't he want the email to go to his Parker, Parker and Renwick address? Unless the firm itself was exposed somehow...' He put his hand over his mouth and lapsed into silence, eyes unfocused, deep in thought. 'Bollocks! I'm going to have to get a bit involved, aren't I? This isn't playtime for teenagers any more.'

'Hmf. See? Shady,' said Claire.

'Just don't call the police yet, please. Creative accounting and tax-free business aren't in the same league as murder. This is probably all some huge misunderstanding, so I would like to learn more before you waste police resources. In the meantime, I will continue to assume you are being genuine. It is nice to be nice.'

'Honestly, weirdo, you should be relieved he doesn't want to involve the police,' said Sophie. She was picking at her nails again. 'You know. Because of Essex.'

'Er, yeah, okay,' Claire said to Basher, without repeating Sophie's comments this time. 'We'll see what we can find out for ourselves, first. That seems fair. What's their last name, by the way? Mattie and Alf, I mean,' Claire asked.

'I don't know,' Basher said and had the decency to look embarrassed. 'She was always just Mattie to me.'

Claire flopped back onto the bed. 'God, what is it with you lot and surnames?'

'All right, calm down. Easy enough to find out.'

'That's not the point – you should know already. You know, you're not so different from the rest of your family,' she snapped, with sudden bitterness. She wasn't entirely sure where it came from.

'Right, okay. Pleasure talking, as ever,' Basher said. And he left.

Claire lay in silence and stared at the ceiling. Out of nowhere her eyes started prickling, so then she felt annoyed and sad at the same time.

'You totally deserved that,' said Sophie. 'He was actually being quite nice.'

'Piss off.' Claire put the pillow back over her head. It was all quite confusing and upsetting. Was the theory that Hugh had killed Mattie? Or that Hugh and Monty killed Mattie together and were hiding it from Clementine? In which case, emailing about it on a shared business address was a bit stupid. But then Hugh did have that sort of energy... But Mattie couldn't force them to sell the house, so why would they need to kill her in the first place? But if it wasn't that, what *was* Hugh giving out shady backhanders for? But, but, but... The possibilities were endless.

Clementine had been very angry to catch Claire in the office, so maybe she was in on it as well. Maybe it hadn't been to do with the house at all, and instead Mattie really had been having an affair with Hugh, and Clementine had caught them at it and stabbed Mattie to death in an instant rage? Then Hugh would be shamed into helping her cover it up.

Claire yelled into the pillow and immediately regretted it, because the cover got into her mouth and made her tongue all dry and fluffy.

'Maybe we should just go,' she said, suddenly feeling very tired.

'What?' Sophie exclaimed. 'You're giving up already? It's been less than a fucking day! What about Nana? You promised! What if she gets un-unfinished businessed and comes back?'

'I can't, Sophie. This is already too weird, and I'm tired,' said Claire. 'Also, I don't want to be turned into soup.'

'*Ohmigod.* When the going gets tough, the tough piss off back to London, eh? Come on, this is the only interesting thing that's happened in the last… three years, at least. Could be worse. *You're* not dead or anything.'

'You never complain.'

Sophie sighed and flopped weightless on the bed, on top of and/or through Claire's feet. Claire wiggled her toes as they became frigid, like standing in an icy stream while wearing welly boots. She pulled her knees up out of the way.

'I miss KFC,' said Sophie eventually, staring at nothing.

'Not nice expensive restaurant food, or home-made cake or anything?'

'Or creepy chicken soup? Nah. Mum was a shit cook. I miss KFC chicken. And McDonald's. Remember going to see *Finding Nemo* at the shopping centre and getting a burger afterwards?'

'Yeah. You snogged Martin Yates during the film and said he'd been drinking Fanta, and it got Fanta all on your face.'

'Yeah. *Finding Dory* wasn't anywhere near as good as *Finding Nemo*.' They'd gone to see that at the cinema too, but it hadn't been the same – not only because Soph had been dead for almost a decade by that point.

'Yeah.'

'Is KFC shit now?'

'I could lie, but no. It's still great. If you can forget that the chickens live miserable, painful lives, which, when I'm hungover, I choose to do.'

'I don't mind being like this exactly,' said Soph suddenly. 'It's just that it gets boring sometimes. You're the only person who ever talks to me normally, but Alex actually believes I exist and says stuff to me. And Basher does too, as long as he isn't thinking about it.'

'You're the only person who ever talks to *me*,' said Claire, feeling a bit like a teenager who thinks her best friend is being stolen.

'*I'm* fucking *dead*, whereas you're too boring and weird for everyone else. I don't have a choice.'

'You are literally the thing that makes me weird, though, if we're honest.'

Soph looked a bit sad, which was alarming in itself, because she normally wavered between impassivity and happy flippancy. Claire was so used to her being around that they didn't talk much these days about the fact that she was dead. She'd first turned up just a week after she'd gone missing, suddenly standing next to Claire at her own candlelight vigil, her shining eyes reflecting the flames. It had been a shock. Soph had always liked to make an entrance. But now it was simply how things were.

And yet sometimes, like now, they skirted around huge and improbable questions – like what would happen to Sophie when Claire eventually kicked the proverbial bucket, or how Sophie had died in the first place. In fact Claire was one of only three people who even knew for sure that Sophie was dead. Technically speaking, to the world at large Sophie was still a missing person. And maybe it was nice for the girls they'd gone to school with to be able to move on and forget, and in another five years say something like, 'I think a girl I was at school with ran away from home actually' at a dinner party. And maybe it was nice for Soph's family to cling to the possibility that she was still alive. But Claire didn't have either of those options. She knew Sophie was dead and had been dead for years, and in fact was often reminded of this by the second person who knew: Sophie herself.

The third person who knew what had happened to Sophie was whoever had killed her.

To Claire, Sophie was still vibrant and present, and she laughed and tossed her hair and complained about every-thing and nothing just as she always had, but to the rest of the world she had become a footnote. A sad, unsolved mystery from decades earlier, a girl who disappeared one weekend and whose ghost couldn't even remember what happened to her, and who occasionally had threads posted about her on very specific bits of Reddit.

And she could never eat fast food again.

'Can we please stay and figure this out? You're the one who's supposed to like detective stuff,' said Soph, after a long silence.

'Yeah, okay. We'll stay a bit longer. But we have to start doing it in a way that makes sense or I'll properly throw a wobbler. All we did today was go to the pub, and I feel like I'm on the verge of a breakdown.'

'Okay.'

'Also, you need to stop saying so much while I am doing interrogations. It really throws me off.'

'I won't stop saying *everything*,' Soph replied, raising an eyebrow. 'We're like good cop, shit cop. If I didn't give you ideas, it'd just be shit cop.'

Claire didn't think this was entirely fair; it was not, after all, Sophie who had the bedrock of knowledge from repeat-watching fifteen series of *Murder Profile*. She wanted to object, but decided to have a prohibitively hot shower to try and pep herself up a bit instead. She sat down in the bottom of the bathtub and played the game where if you angle your arm right, it looks like you can control water.

She sat in there for almost forty-five minutes and thought about Sophie. Maybe her life, her death and their life/death together was something they should talk about.

In fact it was almost 100 per cent certainly something they should talk about. But since they were both each other's sole moral support, and had been for years, neither of them had the emotional maturity to do so properly. It'd be like the blind leading the blind, if everyone involved was also a weird cross between a thirty-plus-year-old and a teenage girl.

In the early days Sophie had tried to remember what had happened. The entire day of her disappearance was a blank for her, but there were odd things. As a ghost she had, for example, a new, intense but inexplicable hatred of the scent of thyme. In the beginning she and Claire had hypothesized, come up with theories, even called the murderer 'The Third Man' and imagined that he sounded like Orson Welles and made a joke of it. But there was nothing to follow up on. It stopped being funny the more years passed, the longer Sophie couldn't remember, the older she didn't get. Eventually they stopped talking about it at all.

It wasn't as if there were relationship therapists who specialized in counselling for you and your dead best friend (though there were, they had discovered, when Claire had mentioned Sophie's appearance to her parents early on, therapists who specialized in it as an adjacent issue, but that had not been helpful). So. Probably best to not go round, or through, but to head in a different direction and avoid the whole thing entirely. Yes. Good.

Claire mentally updated her own version of the list that so far comprised their entire investigation:

Victims

- *Kevin, Figgy's ex – Probably Not Dead*
- *Mattie the housekeeper – Possibly Dead*
- *Michael the accountant – also Possibly Dead and needs investigatoring*
- *Sami – Possibly Dead: not taking anyone's word for it yet*

It seemed to be a definite fact that someone on the inside had been passing info to the predatory hotel chain, and someone (maybe the same someone) had passed info to the tax office on some shady finances the family were involved in. Either of these represented a decent motive for murder, but the someone in question could have been any of the four potential victims.

Claire almost added a sub-category of Suspicious Persons, but decided this was futile, given that it would include basically everyone she had met so far. She did, however, put Clementine in a special column in part of her brain marked 'What the Fuck?', alongside such characters as 'old manager who made me try and get condoms from the NHS walk-in centre because she didn't want to pay for them and she'd heard teenagers could get them for free' and 'man who stroked the back of my neck at the zebra crossing that one time'.

Organizing her thoughts went some way to making her feel less anxious, so she was a lot happier after she dried off and got dressed again, pulling a fresh T-shirt and pants out of her bag. The plastic baggy holding Sophie's pink hair-clip fell onto the floor and she tipped the clip out onto her palm. It was technically a piece of evidence; the police had found a couple of the hair-clips that Sophie had been wearing in the search for her, but since they were generic hair accessories and there wasn't any trace evidence on them, after a while they'd been returned to Soph's mum. Claire had stolen one from her house when she was about twenty-one, on the urging of some dark impulse (Soph telling her to do it), and she felt bad about it. But it was a physical connection to Sophie. It was here, and it was still on Sophie. A dead object. Claire didn't think about how this meant that Sophie must have been wearing it when she died.

Instead of putting it back in its bag, she rolled it between her fingers and rubbed her thumb against it, like a worry bead. She put it in her pocket. It made her feel a bit better.

'It's good that chickens don't get unfinished business,' she said when she eventually came back into the room. 'Or *I'd* never eat KFC, either.'

But Sophie wasn't there.

Claire stuck her head out into the corridor, but there was no sign of Sophie. She took a few experimental steps towards the kitchen and felt a little jangle on the invisible line in the opposite direction. It took her past the office into the main house.

She slipped as quietly as possible through the corridors, because she was pre-guilty about being somewhere she shouldn't. She was aware this was exactly the wrong attitude to have, though. Behaving like you belong everywhere was, after all, how families like the Wellington-Forges moved through life – but Claire didn't have it in her. Sophie did. She had been able to go wherever she liked even before she was able to go, ghostly, wherever she liked.

Claire shuffled down a long corridor and passed a big, dark-wood door that she opened to peep through. It was a dining room, as large and imposing as the library, and it seemed even bigger because the long dining-room table only took up a comparative sliver at the centre of the room. It was an island in an ocean of varnished wooden floor. Claire's feet echoed very loudly as she crossed it. She looked at the ceiling and spun round, keeping her eyes fixed on the chandelier. There was a lot of impressive moulding and gold paint, but on second glance you could see the cracks in the facade. The room didn't smell of polish, it smelled of dust. The paint on the moulding was starting to peel and the chandelier was catching cobwebs. She looked down at the table and saw a deep scratch in it that had been repaired with wood putty. She ran her thumb over it to feel the slight break in the smooth surface.

She kept going and realized that Sophie was back in the library just before she got there herself. It looked very different at this time of day. The sun was setting, so the bars of light thrown across the room were bright gold instead of the silver-grey cast by the moon the night before. Claire could still feel the wrongness, the tinny taste of sadness, which was even more pronounced now that she knew it was there, and why. But the room was definitely empty, apart from Sophie stepping impatiently from foot to foot in the middle of the room.

'Ohmigod, finally,' said Sophie.

'What are you doing here?' hissed Claire.

'I saw them!'

'Who?'

'*Them*. The fucking skeleton! I got bored waiting for you and went out into the corridor and they were at the other end. They looked at me and then turned round and staggered off here again. It felt like... I dunno, they didn't exactly beckon, but I think somehow they know we're here. I think they're trying to help.'

'Well, where are they now?'

'They came over to these shelves here,' said Sophie, pointing at a section of the library near the fireplace. 'They were sort of scratching, like trying to get through the books, and then they fell forward, into the shelf. And they were gone.'

Claire was secretly pleased. She wasn't sure she was up to another face-to-skull meeting. Although the library was at least a long way from Clementine and the kitchen.

'Hello?' she ventured, for the look of the thing. But anyone who might have been listening stayed as silent as the – a-ha-ha – grave.

Sophie was looking at the books on the shelves. 'It's all classics. Shakespeare and Dickens, and big old encyclopaedias and what-have-you. I bet nobody has ever read any of them.'

'Smells nice, though,' said Claire, inhaling the deep, musty scent of old leather and paper.

'Maybe there's a secret passage,' said Sophie. 'Quick! Pull out some of the books – maybe one is a lever. Like on TV.'

That seemed a bit unlikely to Claire, but she knew from long experience that it was better to comply with Sophie's requests, unless you really enjoyed constant humming or singing, or loud shouting while you tried to speak to anyone else. She began pulling out some of the books.

'Ooh! This one – do this one!' Sophie was pointing at a slim volume on the bottom shelf. It was conspicuously blue, in a row of red volumes.

Claire crouched down and tipped her head to one side to read the spine. '*The Old Man and the Sea*,' she said. 'All right, here goes.'

She reached out and hooked the top of the book with a finger. There was a slight resistance as she tugged it. Her heart jumped and she locked eyes with Sophie. She pulled again, harder. The book slid out, top first.

Nothing happened. Claire pulled again and *The Old Man and the Sea* came out all the way. It was a normal book.

'This is stupid. Can't you just look through the books?' Claire asked.

'Oh, yeah. Sorry. I'm so used to you having to turn on the TV for me that sometimes I still forget I can do stuff you can't.' Soph leaned forward and stuck her head and shoulders through the shelves. 'There's definitely something back here,' she called, slightly muffled. 'It's dark but... there's a space. Like a cupboard. Maybe it's a pope-hole?'

'A what? Ohh, I see. It's "priest-hole", but well remembered. It's weird, I wouldn't have thought this building was old enough to have one.'

Priest-holes were little hideaways built into posh Catholic houses during the 1500s and 1600s, when Catholicism was outlawed. If anyone came to check that you weren't doing any naughty Masses, you could bundle yer priest into the secret cupboard in the staircase. *No, sir, only good clean Protestants here!* Priest-holes were one of Claire's favourite oddities of history. It seemed such a high-effort, impractical solution to a problem that it circled right back round to practical. And, of course, it was evidence that laws really only apply to poor people. For rich people, most laws are just minor inconveniences. If they wanted to keep going to Mass, they could simply build a secret church in their own house.

Claire looked down and saw an ornate section of carved leaf on the bottom of the shelf, right where it met the stone of the fireplace. It was clearly not a solid part of the shelving. She pushed it in, and there was a click and the shelf popped out. She pulled it open: over and through Sophie.

'Well, you were sort of right, I suppose. But I mean, it's a bit obvious, isn't it?' she said, unimpressed.

'It's not going to fox your average Popefinder-General for long, nah,' agreed Sophie.

132

The space behind the not-particularly-secret door was about the same size as a small wardrobe. Claire got in. It smelled a bit musty, and had the odd, empty aroma of a room that is cold all the time. There were cobwebs on the walls, but they were old and abandoned – no flies in here. There were smears of dried mud on the wall, too, down near the floor. Claire picked at a flaky bit sticking out, and it turned out to be an ancient dead leaf. She bent down and saw there was actually quite a *lot* of mud, on the wall and on the floor too, and some faint water stains. She pointed it out to Sophie, but as soon as Sophie stepped inside the space she did a kind of full-body spasm, like she had cringed with every muscle at once.

'Eesh,' she said, after recovering, 'can't you feel that? The body was in here. For definite.'

Claire shut her eyes, but she didn't feel a thing. 'How do you know?'

'I dunno. I just do.'

'Ah, like one of those specially trained dogs, is it?'

'Well, it's not like I had loads of experience being dead before I died. I don't know how it works. But they walked into the shelves here, and their body was definitely kept in here at some point. I think that's why they're still hanging around in the library.'

Claire brushed the mud some more. It was very dry, so it had been there a while, but she didn't know if you could, like, forensically date a dirt smear. It made sense, though.

'I believe you. But *why*? The mud would have had to come from outside. Why would you kill someone outside, drag them *inside* and then move them again? If you're already outside, might as well chuck 'em in a ditch or cover 'em with leaves or something.'

'Hmm. Maybe. Claustrophobic yet?'

'It's quite roomy, actually,' Claire said. 'Compares favourably with our flat.'

'Bet it starts to feel poky with the door shut, though,' said Sophie.

Claire reached out and pulled the door to, leaving it cracked a little. Yeah, probably wouldn't be heaps of fun to be stuck in here for a couple of days, while a bunch of humourless Protestants with a hard-on for persecuting Catholics tore up the floorboards outside.

Something sparkled and caught her eye. The concentrated line of light from the door was falling on something shiny, stuck between the floorboards. Claire crouched down and worked it loose; it was a little fake crystal button, the sort you might find on the cardigan of a nice mum.

Just as she stood to examine it more closely, there was a creak as someone pushed the door closed and the locking mechanism clicked into place. She was plunged into total darkness.

Claire sighed, and waited.

There was a blast of cold as Sophie came in. One advantage of having an invisible friend is that it's quite hard for anyone to punk you. 'It's Tristan and Monty, obviously. You all right?'

'Mmm.' Claire knocked on the door. 'Hell-oo? Could you, um… let me out please? I can't see anything.'

There was no response, apart from some obvious snickering. 'Look, I, erm… I know it's you, Tristan. If you let me out now, it'll save a lot of time, won't it? Please?'

'Maybe you should pretend to be scared instead. It's what they want,' Sophie suggested.

'I have some self-respect, thank you,' muttered Claire.

'Coulda fooled me. Have you considered that you might have been trapped in a box by some vicious killers?'

Claire had not. She pressed an ear to the door, but couldn't hear anything. Logically she knew that eventually someone else would come back into the library, but at a more emotional level she knew in that moment that the entire family were cold-blooded murderers and they would enjoy hearing her pathetic scratches on the door as she starved to death while they ate dinner.

She smacked on the door with the flat of her hand. 'Hello?'

Silence.

She hammered with a bit more urgency. 'I would like to come out now, please. Come on!'

After a few more seconds there was a click-clack and the shelf popped open. Monty was standing a little behind Tristan, still typing away on his phone as if he was above it all, but with a thin-lipped little smile. Claire was 100 per cent sure that Monty had told Tristan to do it, like the school bully giving himself plausible deniability. He turned sideways, and the diamonds on his tie-pin flashed in the sunlight, so brightly it made Claire wince and look away. He couldn't have done that on purpose, could he? Surely nobody was able to weaponize jewellery.

Tristan, meanwhile, was doubled over with exaggerated laughter. 'Oh my God – your face! God, you were so scared! "I can't see anything",' he said, choking back tears. 'Oh my God, you're so freaked out: look at you! Ha-ha-ha. Oh, blimey. Don't worry, it opens from the inside too. You were totally safe the whole time.'

Claire stared at him. 'Yes,' she said. 'Yes, sure – you really got me there. Top. Top banter. Bants. Whatever.'

Monty was looking at her curiously, as if he were a scientist and a single-celled life form with no intelligence had just waved up at him through his magnifying glass. Claire didn't like it.

'You like exploring our house by yourself, don't you?' he said suddenly.

'I think Clem has been telling tales after cookery class,' said Sophie, who was trying to get a look at Monty's phone.

'Yep, well. I'm a student, I mean I was; I was a history student. Not any more, obviously. But I like... old... things.'

Monty raised an eyebrow. 'Is that so? So what can you tell me about our priest-hole then?'

'Ohmigod, this guy is gatekeeping *history*,' said Soph.

Claire drew in a deep breath. 'Actually I don't think it's real. I think it was put in later as a curiosity, because the house isn't old enough, it's really badly hidden and it's way too big,' she said, in one nervous breath out again.

'Oh, wow!' exclaimed Tris. 'Monters, she's bang on. You're bang on.'

'Shut the fuck up, Tris.'

Tristan flinched a little, like he'd been slapped.

'Anyway,' said Claire, who once again felt like her skull was shrinking at the profoundly weird, confrontational awfulness of this family. 'I am going to go. Back to my room now. Thank you. Goodbye.'

She sidled out of the room. Something about Monty made her feel like she was in the wrong, or on the back foot. She suspected he'd learned it from his mother.

But in her hand she clutched her sparkly little trophy, like an Olympic gold medal. If she found out who this belonged to, then maybe she would find the murderer.

7

Soup for the Soul

Quite a lot had already happened that day, so they had returned to their bedroom to catalogue their new evidence. Claire and Sophie sat and stared at the button. It was on the bedside table under the reading lamp, which Claire had turned on. The button looked like it was being interrogated in an interview room. Claire stared it down. She felt sure it knew something. It was definitely a clue. A Clue.

'We don't know if it's a clue, weirdo,' said Sophie. 'It's probably Clementine's. She could have dropped it there yesterday while cleaning, for all we know.'

'Maybe. But it didn't look like anyone had cleaned in there for ages. It was still muddy, remember? Ugh, what kind of person builds a fake priest-hole into their house?' Claire continued to glare at the button. If this was *Murder Profile*, it would have an initial carved into it or something. Or represent the killer's mother or possibly sister (who died tragically young).

'All right, what do we know so far?' asked Claire.

'Fuck all. LOL.'

'No, seriously, come on. Your memory is better than mine. I want to write some of this down.'

'Ugh, okay. So we know that someone died here, in distress, about a year ago. Let's assume it was one of our two suspected victims from Nana's birthday party – excluding Kevin, for reasons of Instagram.'

'Three victims. I don't think we should trust Basher and Alex completely, so I'm keeping Sami on the list. Basher is an ex-cop, and he's still really sore on that subject.'

'Okay. So, it's Mattie the housekeeper, Michael the accountant or Sami, Basher's ex. We don't know how they were killed, but we do know their body was stored in the priest-hole in the library for some time.'

'Right,' said Claire. She was scribbling bullet points on an envelope she'd found in her bag. 'And that they might have been muddy when they went in there. And at some point someone was in that priest-hole in clothes with buttons like this.'

'But it might not have been at the same time, or related to the murder. Not everything is a clue.'

'Lots of things are a clue. Like all the money stuff – the HMRC stuff, and someone having dirty dealings with the hotel chain.'

'None of that implicates anyone definitively, though,' said Sophie. 'The tax thing is more likely to have been Michael, but he wouldn't have been involved with Du Lotte. That's more of a Mattie move, surely? It doesn't make sense for them to have been done by the same person, but it's also a big coincidence if they weren't. It's very annoying.'

'I know, but I think getting all my thoughts in order is helping,' said Claire. 'I think there's definitely a financial element to this crime.' She started writing more, making links between different potential killers and victims.

Sophie got bored almost immediately. She got up, stretched and went to look out of the window.

'Hey, stop looking at that, weirdo,' she said suddenly, and beckoned Claire to the window. 'Ted's skulking around down there... What is he doing?'

Soph leaned over and called down to him. 'Ho! Ted! What're you up to, eh?'

'I'm sampling the pain and emotion of the human condition, Miss Sophie, such as is now beyond my reach, and has been for many a year,' came the faint, haughty response.

'You're doing *what?*'

'I'm listening to Miss Figgy having a good old cry.'

'Oh. I'd forgotten about her.'

While in keeping with Ted's vaguely voyeuristic attitude in general, this sort of thing wasn't an unknown phenomenon among the dead. A lot of ghosts were drawn to humans experiencing strong emotions, of all kinds. Claire got the impression that a ghost's emotions gradually slipped away, the longer they were dead, until feelings were memories of feelings. Eventually, unless they put in the effort, they became vague foggy wraiths, floating aimlessly, lost.

And so a lot of them were drawn to fits of emotion in the living, treating sadness or elation like the aftershave of a middle-aged man in an enclosed space: a thing that could be soaked in, experienced vicariously, even if you weren't wearing it yourself. And, indeed, whether you wanted to or not.

Sophie wasn't like that – at least not yet. She was going through a phase of wanting to watch exclusively romantic comedies, but that could have been for unrelated reasons (like, for example, being tired of repeat viewings of *Murder Profile*). In fact Soph was presently flapping her arms and making big eyes at Claire.

'Come on. Let's go and talk to Figgy. Now's our chance!'

'Why am I the one who has to do everything? I'm not even bloody related to her. Can't we make Basher or Alex do it?'

'That's exactly why you have to do it. The others would be, you know, compromised as witnesses if they had to give evidence.'

'Whatever,' Claire grumbled. 'The things I do for you.'

'This isn't for me, weirdo. This is for Nana. And justice. And the American way.'

'Oh, fuck off.'

Claire's reluctance was mainly because she didn't particularly like Figgy, as Sophie well knew. It didn't stem *just* from Claire's innate prejudice against people of Figgy's make and model – which had mostly developed after university anyway – but from the fact that Figgy had always been kind of a self-involved dick. They'd not been

141

close friends, but they'd been in the same halls of residence in first year and had friends in common, so they ended up orbiting each other quite a lot.

Claire remembered her as very similar to how she was now, only slightly less grown. If Figgy in the present was a horse, past Figgy was a foal. A bit gangly, but still a long-legged, sleek creature that could be described, by some, as elegant or even majestic. She studied PPE, but without any evident interest in any of the letters, and was always exactly the right amount of fun and drank exactly enough.

Claire drank a lot when she was at university. Sophie's existence gave her a profound sense of otherness, but also a kind of selfish bravado. Nothing would happen to her, probably, and even if it did she had a witness who could tell her everything that had occurred. So, ignoring Sophie's protestations, Claire tried to reinvent herself and leave behind the strange, pale girl who had to have loads of therapy after her best friend disappeared. Who lost most of her other friends. Who started talking to herself, or to thin air. She would be the fun one.

She poured burning hot spirits down her throat and threw them up again before the end of the night. She fell asleep nestled in the cold hollow next to the toilet. She had one-night stands that she regretted almost before she'd even had them. Claire still associated university less with her classes and more with the taste of sambuca and the dizzy embarrassment of retching in an alley at 7 a.m., as middle-aged women in sensible jeans did the school run mere feet away. It was, in the end, a failure, because Sophie was always still there. And, really, Claire didn't want her gone. Sophie teased Claire when she was falling over drunk, but pressed her cold hands to Claire's face when she cried in confusion at 3 a.m. Sophie stood in the hallway yelling if Claire ever brought someone back to her room, but Sophie was the one who was always there in the morning.

Next to people like Figgy, who seemed so poised at the age of nineteen, Claire felt like a hot, lumpen fool full of bile. Everyone at uni had quite liked Figgy, because she made you feel very important. Even Claire, the first time they'd met (at a party, at Claire's house). Figgy had been luminously happy to be introduced. But this facade began to fall away the next time they met and the time after that, and every time after that, because each time Figgy would reintroduce herself as if they had never met before. And this cast other things, like Figgy casually opening *your* fridge and getting out *your* bottle of white wine, in a different light. Once, Claire had told her that her dress looked nice, and Figgy had thanked her. Then, ten minutes later, someone else had said her dress looked nice, and Figgy had said, 'Oh my *goodness*, thank you – do you know you're the first person to have said so?' Claire wasn't sure if Figgy had a problem with her specifically or was a bellend in general, but either way she wasn't impressed.

Figgy had even reintroduced herself when she, and a group of old uni friends, had spotted Claire in the queue at a Pret a Manger a few weeks ago. It had prompted Sophie to yell, 'God, not this awful bitch again!' and Claire spent the whole conversation with an openly mutinous expression – at least until Figgy mentioned offering her a job...

'We can't just... turn up, can we?' Claire said to Sophie now. 'I need to have a reason to show up at Figgy's room, I can't arrive going, "I know your entire family are here, but I thought *I* would be best at comforting you in your grief." That's not normal.'

'I dunno – posh people have weird ideas about normal behaviour, don't they?'

Claire thought about it, and then very tentatively made her way back to the kitchen. Basher and Alex were sitting on one side of the table, with Hugh and Clem on the other. They were eating soup.

'Hello,' said Basher. He raised an eyebrow. 'We were just wondering if you were hungry.'

'Um. Yes. But I thought, if you hadn't taken any to Figgy yet...' Claire trailed off, unsure of herself.

'Not bad, weirdo,' said Soph. 'Good impulse.'

'Oh, that's a great idea!' Alex leapt up from the table. 'Here, I'll get a tray...'

Soon Claire and Sophie were following Alex back through the house. They stalked the halls with a tray loaded with bowls of chicken soup, like a high-fashion goth version of Meals on Wheels. It was a great opportunity, they pointed out, 'to strike Kevin off the list for good'. They were clearly still as enthusiastic about the project as Sophie.

They knocked cautiously on Figgy's bedroom door and entered in response to a quavering 'Yes...?'

It was obviously Figgy's room through childhood and teenagedom, and now occasionally adulthood, when she came home. It was a decent size and, unlike Claire's B&B-esque room, showed some personality. The walls were lilac, and there were shelves of trophies for different sports, rosettes for events that Claire suspected involved horses, and several teddies staring at her with blank black eyes.

Figgy was lying full-length across her double bed, one foot tucked under the opposite knee, one arm cast across her face, and a tissue clutched to her breast in the other hand. Claire felt slightly resentful: Figgy was justifiably in mourning and could not be grudged this, and yet if you had told her that Figgy had carefully arranged herself thus before her visitors entered, she would not have called you a liar. It was unfair for someone to be annoying whilst living through legitimate sadness, because Claire wasn't allowed to be annoyed by it, which was even more annoying, and it locked her in an ouroboros of being a shitty person.

'Oh, darlings,' said Figgy, with a weak sniffle. 'It's too awful. Too, too awful.'

'I know,' said Alex, not unkindly. Claire distanced herself from her uncharitable thoughts, and reminded herself again that their nana had actually died an actual day ago, and they were all actually related. Sophie was right; this was all probably way less taxing for Claire than it was for anyone else.

Figgy sat up to take her bowl of soup on the tray and tucked her feet under herself. Alex took a seat at a small desk. The desk chair had once had part of a cheap feather boa glued around the backrest for decoration, and the remains flopped limply off one side. Claire, after an awkward look around, knelt on the floor.

They all sat in silence, slurping their soup. Life here, reflected Claire, seemed to revolve around meals. Pies, soups, stews. The only other activities people got to do were ultimately for sourcing food. Where are we going? Off to have lunch. When will we be back? In time for tea. All hearty, home-cooked stuff. It was probably quite annoying for Sophie and her KFC cravings.

Also, it was all very good. Maybe Clementine's recipes were a closely guarded secret, or maybe they were a stolen secret. Maybe she had a folder of pages torn out of *Good Housekeeping*, but told everyone they were all old family recipes handed down over generations. Maybe that's what she was hiding in the office. Perhaps she would go on a murderous rampage to protect them.

'I feel a bit better after that,' said Figgy eventually, as her spoon scraped the bottom of the bowl.

'Yeah, I'm pretty sure if I had to live on my own I would die,' said Alex. 'Like, I would either starve to death or die from overdosing on pasta and mini-doughnuts. Those are literally the only two options.'

'You should get one of those delivery boxes – the ones that send you all the ingredients and instructions,' said

Figgy. 'I had a fully organic one from Abel & Cole. And another that sends me fresh flowers every month.'

'Yeah, I'll get on that right after I start shopping exclusively at Harrods and buy a three-bed flat in Soho,' said Alex, who did not miss a beat from taking a photo of their long nails. They were bright pink with shimmery stripes of gold glitter on each ring fingernail, and Alex had correctly spotted that they looked good against the backdrop of a lilac wall.

Figgy made a non-committal scolding noise, and asked Claire what she thought about the soup.

'Oh, yeah, er, it's really good,' she said, taken off-guard. Soph rolled her eyes at her again and went to peer at the trophies and bookshelves.

'Hmm... Showjumping and gymkhana stuff, nothing really interesting there.' She ran a finger slowly and critically along the spines of the books. '*The Seven Habits of Highly Effective Dickheads*... a lot of stuff on the "Men Are from One Planet, Women Are from a Second, Different Planet" theme... a few romances, but modern girls having it all, rather than bodice-rippers. Those ones are all really worn, so she likes them. But there's one here about meditation – ooh, and a copy of *Chicken Soup for the Soul* – and the spines aren't even cracked.'

Claire processed this information: self-help, romantic troubles, insecurity, pretending to like new age shit. The latter felt firmly in Kevin territory.

'Have you read *Chicken Soup for the Soul*?' asked Claire.

'I have a copy here, but I haven't read it,' said Figgy. 'It... well, it was a present from Kevin, my ex. He gave it to me last year.'

Alex gave Claire an undisguised look of astonishment; without knowing that Sophie was the mastermind, it must have looked like Claire had made a frankly amazing shot.

'Oh, sorry,' said Claire. 'I didn't mean to rake anything up. I just thought, I think I read a post by, er... er, Gwyneth Paltrow? It's supposed to be very uplifting in... in sad and stressful times.'

It was not, at least in Claire's mind, totally implausible that Gwyneth Paltrow would post about *Chicken Soup for the Soul*, presumably as part of a long ramble on Instagram where she also talked about steam-cleaning her fanny to get rid of bad auras (Special Fanny Steam Water only $700, plus international shipping). Figgy did not appear to notice anything untoward about it, either, because she nodded.

'Yes, you're right, darling. Maybe I'll read some tonight. Just, gosh, I don't know if I can start thinking about Kevin right now, too! A loss is a loss, my therapist says, and a break-up can hurt as much as any other.'

'That actually sounds quite sensible,' said Sophie thoughtfully. 'It would be something she learned from someone else.'

'Did you really like him, Aunt F?' asked Alex.

'I did. I thought I did. Kevin was this amazing free spirit, you know? Sometimes he would turn to me and say something like, "Figgy, let's go to *Barcelona* and eat chicken croquettes in the shadow of the *Sagrada Família*",' she said, getting a dreamy look in her eyes. Figgy hit the accents on 'Barcelona' and 'Sagrada Família' like a 2 a.m. pisshead swinging enthusiastically for a bouncer, and it made Soph laugh.

'Go on,' she encouraged Claire. 'See if you can get her to say "chorizo" next. Ten points.'

Claire pressed her lips together to stop herself laughing. She realized that Figgy really hadn't changed since university.

Alex had, without Claire noticing, produced a small embroidery hoop from somewhere in the depths of their jacket, and was working on a circle of mixed autumn leaves and fruits surrounding the word 'OOOF', in exquisite cursive script. They said, in a carefully neutral tone, that they remembered Kevin having a lot of opinions about various religions and global cultures. 'And also,' they added, in a slightly less neutral tone, 'gender. He used the phrase "sacred feminine" several times.'

'Oh yes,' said Figgy, absent-mindedly, still in Barcelona. 'Yes, he's brilliant. And so switched on about social issues, you know? But it would never have worked between us long-term. Mummy was right.'

Claire murmured 'star-crossed lovers' sympathetically, and Figgy nodded with approval. 'What happened?' Claire asked, pushing on.

'Well, we'd been together for a few months, and I got on really well with his folks – Sue and Jeremy, lovely little cottage in South Withemswall – so I decided to bring him to Nana's party to properly get to know everyone. But Monty was being so rude, asking about Kevin's job prospects. He couldn't understand that someone like Kevin doesn't *care* about job prospects. He cares about what's really *important* in life. He calls them M&Ms – memories and moments.'

'Yeah, I remember him using that phrase at lunch on the Saturday, too' said Alex. 'I think he made an impression.'

'He did on Mummy, anyway. At least according to Kevin. He said she pulled him aside after that and told him outright he wasn't good enough for me. I was quite shocked, I told him I couldn't *believe* she would do a thing like that.'

'I can,' said Claire out loud, at exactly the same time as Sophie. 'Er, I mean... Clementine, your mum, she's very protective of you all, isn't she?'

'Yes, but I'm totally my own person, and she respects that,' said Figgy. 'So then things were a bit sour between me and Kevin for the whole day, and after dinner, when we'd all had a bit of wine and... Well, Kevin said he wasn't going to stick around if my family were going to treat him like that, and I'd better decide if I was going to choose them or him.'

Claire asked what she had done, with appropriately bated breath.

'I chose my family, of course!' said Figgy. 'Kevin was so... He was different, you see. I think Mummy was surprised. But I do miss him.'

150

'Did you ever see him again?'

'Oh no. I stormed off to, well, this room. All tears at bedtime, I was *quite* emotional. Kevin went to the garden to try to centre himself, but I don't think he came back to bed even. The next morning he was gone. Someone said he'd headed off early to the station.'

Alex made significant eye contact with Claire. 'I didn't see him either,' they said.

'Well, he does text me every so often still, so we chat, but he's moving around a lot,' said Figgy.

'Oh!' blurted out Claire. 'You do?'

'Not often,' said Figgy defensively. 'Kevin's in South America now. It was just hard to cut him out. He's so open – not like anyone else I know. But he broke up with me via text, did I tell you that?' She scrolled back on her phone and passed it over:

17.37 Sorry Figgy Pud, this is all really unfun. Ur fam are fucking mean & pretty bad vibes

17.37 i dont like whats been happening. have to get out of here tbh.

17.37 we can talk properly when im home

Claire agreed that Kevin was clearly a massive prick, which is what you're supposed to do in these situations. She quickly scrolled to the most recent messages. One from Kevin said, '*goin 2 colombia next. still no plans 2 come bak sry bby.*' Then there was a big list of messages from Figgy asking how he was, and if he was safe and okay, and what he was up to that night, and if he'd met anyone nice, dot-dot-dot, pregnant question mark. Then an hour later Kevin responded '*ttyl*'.

'Oh, Aunty F,' said Alex, glancing at the messages and grimacing. 'You should really disconnect entirely if you want to move on. Self-care, you know? At what point do you become responsible for your own happiness? As soon as possible, if you ask me.' They bit off the thread they were using and then looked at it. 'Shouldn't have done that – that's screwed it right up,' they burbled to themself.

'You're right, Alex, I'll delete all of it!' cried Figgy suddenly.

'Oh no, fuck, don't do that,' said Claire, panicking as she saw critical and important evidence being flushed down the digi-drain. Figgy looked at her weirdly. 'I mean, er... if you don't know where you've come from, you can't know where you're going.'

They left Figgy nodding sagely and thanking them for visiting, with the mournful largesse of Queen Victoria in her widow's garb.

'Okay, let's go back to the kitchen,' said Alex. 'It's the only properly warm room in this ancient, single-glazed nightmare of a building.'

Claire hesitated. 'Er, I sort of would rather. Not go back there. Or something. I don't know.'

'What? Why?'

'Normally I would be making fun of her for this, but actually I agree with her,' Sophie said, and Claire

152

repeated this backup of her position. 'She has fair reasons to feel safer alone.'

Alex rolled their eyes. 'Right, so obviously for some big weird reason you're keeping private, you are terrified of going anywhere near anyone else right now, is that it?' They were towing Claire down the hall with one hand, and fishing a cigarette out of another internal pocket with the other.

'I told Basher, Clementine got *really intense* about that soup, okay?'

'Whatever. You can stay in your room if you really want, nobody will care. But I've worked up a plan for the next few days, and we can fill Basher in now.'

'I just want to point out again,' said Sophie, who was trailing along behind them, 'that you are an adult who is being adulted by a teenager. And it's not even me. Claire, you're like thirty.'

This Claire did not repeat, although it did remind her of something she'd wanted to ask about.

'Weird question maybe, but how old is your dad, Alex?'

'Oh. Hmm.' Alex stopped walking to think. 'I want to saaaaay... forty-two? Forty-three? Somewhere around there, anyway. Why?'

'Well, it's a big age gap between him and the others. I thought it might be, you know, relevant if it turned out he was, er, adopted or something like that.'

'Oh, it's far more standard kitchen sink than that. Granny and Grandad got married young, and Granny was eighteen and pregnant. Gasp! Unthinkable!' Here Alex feigned a look of horror. 'Then there was a break for about a decade while they all grew up a bit, and Grandad got a stable job and a decent income and all that lark. And between you and me, I don't think Granny was keen on having another baby any time soon, either. She doesn't like to talk about it – it's not very picture-perfect-family-values of her. But yeah, after Dad it goes Aunt F, Uncle B and poor old Tris on the end. He's properly the baby. Mothered and smothered. So, interesting thought, but no. Dad's meanness is all natural.'

Alex pulled Claire along again, swung round some more corners and pushed her into what turned out to be Basher's room. Basher was looking fretfully through his bag.

'Hey, Uncle B,' said Alex. 'We should probably leave tomorrow, huh?'

Basher sat back on his knees and shoved his hands into their resting position in the front pocket of his hoodie. 'Yes, I agree,' he said. 'We should get out of Mum and Dad's hair while they arrange the funeral. The others are probably shoving off, too. We can drop Claire at the station on our way.'

'And Sophie,' said Alex. 'And no. They are coming with us, obviously.'

'Oh, *obviously*.'

'Well? We have a sofa.'

'Ohmigod! What about the investigation, though?' said Soph, immediately on the verge of being outraged and lining up the ammunition needed to fight this particular battle a second time.

'What do you mean? This *is* the investigation,' Alex replied.

'Now I am also confused,' said Claire. 'Don't we have to stay in the village and uncover all the clues?'

The pitying silence with which Alex met this statement was one of the most humiliating things Claire had ever experienced. 'God,' they said, after a moment. 'No wonder you lot totally failed at solving any global problems, cursing my generation to save the world. *Obviously* we won't stay here. There is no phone signal, internet, or even any actual people. There are no clues. What kind of murder-solving outfit do you think this is? How am I going to clear my family's good name, and be the star of a limited-series documentary, if we don't go about this the right way?'

Claire wondered if Alex was taking this as seriously as Basher thought they were.

'There are some clues,' said Claire sulkily.

'Well,' said Basher, 'I must agree with Alex. Assuming there was a crime – and, by the way, I have to say again that we only have the faintest second-hand suggestion of *financial* crime – the majority of witnesses aren't based here, and since we have no idea where the actual crime scene might be, the chance of uncovering physical evidence is very slim. And, as noted, the resources here are... poor. They'd be poor even with any added official police resources.'

Basher started ticking off things on his fingers, getting quietly excited, despite himself. 'You work it like a cold case, right? The coldest, technically. Establish a timeline, establish persons present, interview witnesses, identify potential corroborating evidence... Identifying the victim would be favourite, of course, but we're coming at that arse-backwards by working out who it is *not*.'

'But look,' Sophie continued, gamely trying to be helpful, 'we still have loads of gaps. Like, what about the entertainment? We haven't even thought about the tragic a cappella group yet. That's like... half a dozen potential victims?'

There was silence after Claire relayed this, as everyone thought about how the whole thing might be more hard work than they'd anticipated.

'But they sound like they'll be pretty easy to track down,' said Claire. 'I'll... er... I'll call them, if you like?' She found she was anxious to contribute more practical help to the operation. Also she had noticed that when Basher was thinking of practical things and steps and the progress of the investigation, he got excited and forgot that his official position was still anti-investigation. He had, for example, ceased to object about Claire and Sophie staying with him and Alex.

'Right, okay, so what we do is,' said Alex, ignoring Claire and stabbing the air with their unlit cigarette, 'we go back to Brighton and talk to Sami, right? Then we go up to London to Claire's and talk to Tris and that accountant guy. And if there's time we also go to Camden.'

'Camden sucks,' said Claire automatically, at the same time as Basher said, 'Camden is awful' and Soph said, 'Camden is fucking great.' Claire met Basher's eyes and they smiled at one another. This pleased her, in the way a child is pleased when they do something to gain adult approval.

Alex waved their hands in the air, batting away this millennial nonsense. 'Sure, fine. And then we put together everything we know and come back for Nana's funeral, where we will be able to—'

'Do a round-up and confront the killer?' finished Claire.

'*No*, Claire,' said Sophie.

'Jesus, Claire, it's a funeral,' said Basher.

'It's what Nana would have wanted,' said Alex, with blank-faced solemnity. 'But nah, I was going to say "poke around the house and grounds again".'

'But shouldn't we interview your family as well, though?' asked Claire. 'They're all suspects!'

'No, no way,' said Basher. 'I'm vetoing that, at least until after the funeral, and at least until you've actually proven that someone is missing. Come on. I'm agreeing you can come to Brighton with us, so compromise with me here.'

'Okay, I suppose that makes sense,' Claire replied, after considering all the angles. Mostly she was keen to leave the house, and the watchful, baleful eye of Clementine.

'I'm on board,' Sophie added.

'Right. I am accepting this plan,' said Basher, 'firstly because the Brighton mainline train can get Claire to London in an hour, if it comes to it. But mostly because it turns out I did not bring my full box of meds, so we do need to get home.'

Alex was concerned. Basher conceded that immediately following your grandmother's death was not an ideal time to discover you had run out of antidepressants.

'I will be fine,' he said. 'I am but mad north-north-west. And I have only missed a day, so nothing to panic about. Probably have a good old despairing and listless stare at the ceiling when I get home, though.'

'I made you that pill organizer and everything,' Alex scolded him.

'It doesn't travel well. It has loads of little dicks on it.'

'Sorry, next time I'll do you one with one of those hamburger cats on, or the physical embodiment of always fucking going on about how you're the last generation to understand why a pencil and a cassette tape are connected. Or whatever it is you people like. Honestly. At what point are you not embarrassed to exist?'

Sophie pointed out that they still needed to properly record a timeline of the events of the suspicious weekend.

'We can do that in the car tomorrow,' said Alex. 'To prevent ourselves from being overheard.' They wiggled their eyebrows conspiratorially, then paused before crashing out of the room again. 'I'm going for a fag,' they said over their shoulder. 'By the way, Uncle

B – Kevin isn't dead, we can definitely cross him off the list.'

Basher sighed and went to stare out of the window. He did that for quite a long time, so eventually Sophie said that Claire should probably go and pack.

PART II

Take nothing on its looks; take everything on evidence. There's no better rule.

Charles Dickens, *Great Expectations*

8

The Time Is Out of Joint

At about 7.45 a.m. the next day, Claire was wedged in the front seat of Basher's car. It was a discreet and battered Peugeot 306 for improved private investigatoring, he had explained, as she'd sat down in it at bang on seven – although Basher had refused to start the car until Claire put her seatbelt on. It'd almost felt like they were escaping like thieves in the night before anyone else noticed. The only person who was there to see them leave was Ted, who was quite sad about it. He'd hooted and waved his cap as if he were seeing off a ship.

Claire viewed most times of day before 11 a.m. as uncivilized, but she had ultimately been glad to leave because, as they'd exited through the kitchen door, she'd come face-to-face with several brace of dead pheasants hanging on a nail on the wall outside. Their eyes were closed and they could almost have been asleep, except that they were strung together by their necks, which lolled uselessly. Some of them – the hens – were speckled brown, but the males had bright green heads and fussy white collars, and long striped tail feathers.

Their features were so soft and lovely, but they looked cold and wet, and Claire had fought an impulse to stroke them and warm them up. Hugh had bragged the day before about how he'd hit, just, loads. Beaten his PB. The chaps had all been really impressed. Then Claire had imagined Clementine gutting, plucking and cooking them, and had scrabbled quickly across the yard.

There was a tacit understanding that none of the living people in the car was really a morning person, and they were not going to make moves towards conversation for a while. Claire spent some time groggily considering The Case. At some point she had slotted in the ominous capital letters, but wasn't sure when. She started scribbling things down on the crumpled bits of paper she found at the bottom of her rucksack: empty Virgin Media envelopes, bus tickets, old napkins in various colours.

Now, in the light of day, things weren't making much more sense than they had the night before. And unfortunately Soph *was* a morning person – and a midday, evening and midnight person – so she was very bored during the drive and kept interrupting Claire's investigative thoughts. She sat behind Claire sighing, huffing and tutting, as well as intermittently humming the same mis-remembered snatch of 'Wannabe' by The Spice Girls. It was this last bit that finally made Claire snap after forty-five minutes.

'You're getting the words wrong! Fucking hell, shut up,' she bawled suddenly, making Basher start. 'Why would it be "Ham your shoddy clown and wipe it up and down"? *Why?*'

'Ohmigod, what is wrong with you this morning? I thought you'd be happy to get out of that house,' said Sophie, pleased to have caused a reaction at last.

They were now barrelling into the New Forest, and although this morning was another cold one, it was bright and brittle and cloud-free. Claire's head rattled uncomfortably against the window and it was making her feel sick, but it was the only angle where the sun didn't get her in the eyes. She was feeling sorry for herself and overwhelmed.

Once, in a spirit of short-lived culinary experimentation that had included attempts to make her own sourdough bread, Claire had tried out baked stuffed apples. When she had pulled the little treasures from the oven, she had been appalled by their appearance, simultaneously wrinkled and wizened, but also horribly full on the insides and oozing out of hitherto unknown orifices. She'd been so put off that she binned the tray and had eaten a whole thing of Mr Kipling mini-pies instead.

Right now, her head felt like one of those apples. It was so full of facts and contradictions and awful things that had happened over the last couple of days that she thought grey matter was going to start leaking out of her ears. She explained this, because she was quite pleased with the metaphor, but it only made Alex and Sophie laugh at her. Basher, who was whistling through his teeth and tapping the steering wheel, said that baked apples are actually quite easy to make, and she must have got the recipe wrong somehow.

'Look, there's a garage coming up in a minute,' he said, relenting at Claire's forlorn expression. 'We can take a break for coffee and terrible pastries. And Topic bars.'

'Why Topic bars?'

'When I used to go anywhere with Nana and Papa – my grandad, the nibling's great-grandad—'

'He died before I was born,' said Alex, who was occupying the two seats in the back that Soph wasn't, by spreading out: a) most of their body; and b) a huge canvas tote bag and the contents thereof, which were many, varied and confusing. They were working on a different embroidery hoop today. It was an image of Baby Yoda, but as if he were a saint on a Catholic votive candle.

'Papa would stop at a garage or whatever and go in to pay for the petrol and get chocolate bars. I hate Topics, but they're Nana's favourite, and I'd sit in the car with her and chant, *'Pick Topic pick Topic pick Topic'* over and over again. I just liked saying the words.'

Basher smiled as they pulled into a standard-issue Shell garage. Claire noticed that Basher and Alex both had red eyes today.

They piled out of the car and inhaled the weird, drill-up-your-nose smell of the forecourt. Claire and Sophie nodded hello at a ghost in oily overalls who was hanging around the pumps, and followed Alex (who was dressing down today, in bootcut jeans and a crisp white T, but under the same signature, crackling black hell-coat) into the shop to load up on supplies. Claire was pleased with her haul:

Item: *tea, one large, grim cardboard cup of*
Item: *saus. roll, two, grey*
Item: *peperami, one, impulse purchase*
Item: *cheese-and-onion crisps, sharing-size bag of*
Item: *sunglasses, one pair, round, silver-framed*

The actual sunshade bit on the lenses of that last item was so graduated that it might as well have been transparent, but needs must when the devil pisses sunshine into your eyeholes.

After some consideration of her bank balance, Claire also got twenty Marlboro Lite and a sharing bag of Starburst. They sat down at a plastic table around the corner to break their fast in style. Basher joined them and accepted a Starbust with the shy smile that Claire was growing to recognize.

She put on her sunglasses.

'You look like a Minion,' said Sophie immediately.

'*You* look like a Minion,' said Claire.

'Ohmigod, I do not, weirdo. I look like a rock star who died tragically before her time,' said Sophie. 'As in, pre-rock star. I definitely would have been a rock star if I'd have had the chance.'

There, variously bickering, flicking fag ash around, collecting sweet wrappers on the table in drifts, yelling, nearly spilling tea on the laptop and insisting on making pen-and-paper notes as well, because it just felt better, they established their timeline.

First thing on the Monday after the party, a truckload of office workers from a nationwide pasta shipping company had turned up, so the timeframe for the murder was quite tight. The most exact timings they had could be locked in by the time-stamps on photos Alex had on their phone. They also knew what times to place people at meals (before they scattered off the timeline again, like so many inconvenient cockroaches into unknown areas under the bath) since Clementine had strict and unwavering deadlines. Breakfast was on the table at 8.30 a.m., lunch at 1 p.m. and dinner at 6.30 in the evening. But apart from that, it was mostly guesswork, without anyone else to corroborate it. Which was, Claire supposed, the point of going to find other people to corroborate it.

Eventually they came up with a serviceable, if messy, list of key events:

Friday 25 October

Clementine, Hugh, Nana assumed all to be at the house. Also assumed Mattie arrived at 10 a.m., via bike, as usual. Monty and Tris reported to have arrived 'about half twelve' with Michael, in Monty's car.

4.17 p.m.	*Alex and Tuppence arrive, also by car*
5 p.m.	*Mattie leaves to go home after work*
6.40–7 p.m.-ish	*Figgy and Kevin arrive by car*
9.01 p.m.	*Basher and Sami arrive, also by car*
1 or 2 a.m.	*Monty, Tris and Michael still up working – heard arguing*

Saturday the 26th

9 a.m.-ish	*Basher explains he quit his job. Breakfast is ruined.*
10 a.m.	*Mattie arrives (dropped off by Alf)*
10.04 a.m.	*Alex gets a lift to the village with Alf*
2 p.m.-ish	*Clementine warns off Kevin*
2.30 p.m.	*Michael asks to go somewhere he can make a phone call*
3.45 p.m.-ish	*Figgy and Kevin argue*
6.30–8.30 p.m.-ish	*Most disastrous birthday dinner in history. Sunday party with wider family guests is cancelled.*

Sunday the 27th

8 a.m.	*Hugh and Tris out on a shoot all day*
10 a.m.	*Mattie doesn't come to work*
1.30 p.m.-ish	*Alex leaves with Basher and Sami*

Monday the 28th

8.30 a.m.	*TOI Food Inc. corporate retreat (3 days)*

Claire cast a critical eye over the list. She'd wanted them to note down more detail, like what was eaten by everyone at every meal, because she had learned from every book or TV murder mystery that this could be crucial information. 'Say that at dinner one night you'd had, like, a really hot sauce,' she pointed out. 'That could have concealed the taste of poison.'

'Ye-e-e-s, probably it could. Although it could not, I fear, have concealed the symptoms of being poisoned,' said Basher. 'They're usually too noisy. Also, we did not have anything with a really hot sauce.'

'Yeah, well. The point is you *might* have had.'

Soph was also looking at the list, and had more pressing concerns.

'*Grave* concerns?' asked Alex, wiggling their brows again (evidently their go-to punchline for a joke).

'That is very insensitive,' said Soph. She yawned lazily, which Claire was almost 100 per cent sure was an affectation, since Sophie did not get tired or need to breathe. 'Tell them I said that coldly.'

'You do everything coldly,' replied Claire. Alex snickered. Nevertheless, Sophie asked them to fill in, in more detail, what they had seen *after* the fateful dinner on Saturday night, since previously they had been derailed by talking about family dysfunction and going to the pub. The answer was: not much.

'I went and had a cup of tea with Sami and Nana, in Nana's room,' said Basher. 'We had a bit of the cake, as well. Nana fell asleep around half ten, and Sami and I both went back to our rooms after that. Sami was in the same room as you were, facing the garden, so she might have heard something.'

'I was hanging out with Mum in the kitchen for a bit. I *think* Granny and Grandad were there too – no, actually, Grandad was watching football or rugby or something,' said Alex. 'Then, after a bit, I went up to my room. I was having a secret spliff, tee-emm, out of the window and I heard Granny having a go at Uncle T for ruining his suit – he got it all covered in mud. So that's how I know he fell over. But I don't know what time that was. Sorry.'

'It's really annoying that you two left so early on Sunday, because you didn't see Hugh and Tristan come back from their shoot, and you didn't see loads of people leave. Sunday is *very* thin. In fact...' Claire narrowed her eyes. 'I don't think you saw any of our potential victims leave at all.'

Basher pulled the analogue paper list towards him, while Sophie leaned over to look at Alex's screen. Basher frowned. 'No, you're right. There are a lot of '-ish' times as well.'

'When was the last time you saw Mattie?' Claire asked. 'You didn't see her leave on Saturday, and she didn't come in on Sunday?'

'No. Alex?' asked Basher.

Alex shook their head. 'I saw her on Saturday when she arrived, but not when she left.'

'And does she normally work at weekends?'

'Yes,' said Basher. 'Weekends are busier than weekdays for events, right? Mattie's normal days off are Monday and Tuesday. That weekend, I think she didn't strictly need to be there; she was just in the office doing paper-work and admin.'

'We know what happens to people who go in there,' said Sophie darkly.

'So,' said Claire slowly, immensely pleased because she was pretty sure she was forming a full piece of useful data in real time, 'even if something happened to Mattie that weekend, you wouldn't have thought it was weird if—'

'If nobody in the family heard from Mattie on Monday or Tuesday,' finished Basher. 'It gives you nearly two full days of grace, if you'd murdered her.'

'But the most sus person there, based on circumstantial evidence, is Grandad,' said Alex, 'and he was out at the shoot all day Sunday, so he couldn't have been burying a body or anything.'

'Ahh,' said Soph, 'but was he? You two weren't at the shoot cos you'd left by the time he and Tris supposedly came back, and you haven't checked with anyone else who was at this supposed shoot to confirm Hugh's alibi. Who's to say? We have reason to believe the body was hidden in the priest-hole at some point. Maybe that's why it was stashed there – playing for time until the murderer could bury it secretly.'

Basher, as seemed to happen whenever he did some investigative work, was warming up to it and putting himself in a good mood. This was the case even if, or possibly especially because, he was investigating his own family.

'We know Kevin spirited himself away sometime between Saturday night and Sunday breakfast,' he went on. 'That's a massive window. Say, ten hours.'

'Yes, *but*, Uncle B, we already ruled out Kevin. At what point mustn't we definitively let Kevin go? It sounds like Kevin has let Kevin go even. And, soon, Aunt F should, as well.'

Michael the accountant could not clearly be placed leaving, either. In fact he was something of an enigma all round. If nothing else, one's accountant seemed like quite a weird choice of house-guest for your nan's birthday. Apparently he had been a somewhat unexpected one.

Monty and Tristan, Basher explained, had phoned with only a couple of hours' notice to say that they were bringing Michael down, because they needed him for the urgent work they were handling that weekend. Alex specifically remembered Clementine's potato-based concerns around the dinner. Apart from the meals, the three had spent most of their time either in the office or in Tristan's room working – which was where Basher heard them arguing on the Friday night when he got up for a slash.

Basher described Michael as taller and better-looking than Monty, which was an extra source of tension, but he seemed more devoted to good accountancy than anything else, with nothing in his life except work. It, or things related to it, were the only things he talked about.

'I expect,' said Basher, 'that Michael has loads of people mooning after him all the time, competing to somehow be the last one in the office working late with him, but he doesn't even notice because they're not quarterly figures.'

Alex produced a picture with Michael in the background. He was indeed a tall and very good-looking Black man, with a large, strong jaw, a shaved head and excellent shoulders. His suit was clearly less expensive than the ones Monty wore, but was doing more for him, which did seem like the sort of thing Monty would dislike.

'It was really late – or, well, early,' said Basher, 'and they were still at it in Tris's room, but arguing, not working. But the weird thing was they were arguing about breakfast.'

'Breakfast?'

'Yeah. I couldn't make it out exactly and I didn't think much of it at the time, but I definitely remember thinking it was strange. I could hear Tris doing his wheedling "Oh, come on, mate" voice, and Monty doing his more normal angry bellend voice – sorry, Alex.'

Alex made an 'eh' noise and wobbled their hand in the air.

'And then I heard Michael say something about breakfast. "I'm serious", he said, about… sausage? I wish I could remember. I suppose I should have paid more attention, but I had my own things to deal with. I just assumed it was business stuff about one of their clients, I suppose. Or that Michael really was that serious about hollandaise.'

That added more weight to the idea that some financial irregularities had been discovered. Claire pointed out the time on Saturday when Michael asked to go somewhere to make a phone call. 'Was that when Kevin drove him to the station? Maybe we could, you know, trace the call.' She ignored Basher almost-but-not-quite-managing to stop himself rolling his eyes.

'It was then,' said Alex. 'I went for a walk and then hung around at the pub. I saw them drive past The Line towards the station as I was packing up to come back.'

'Hmm,' said Basher, staring at the timetable of events with the expression of someone wiggling a loose tooth or squeezing a blackhead.

'That doesn't make sense,' Sophie yelled suddenly. 'You didn't have a signal at the station, Claire, so they wouldn't, either. Why would they go there?'

'You get a signal once you drive another lick *past* the station in that direction, up the hill,' Basher explained. 'Or past the cenotaph, away in the other direction. It's about, what – a forty-minute drive, in either case.'

Claire got her phone out. She could tell what time her phone signal had returned because she'd got new texts and missed calls since their trip to the pub Wi-Fi, which were all marked 7.42 a.m. that day. She thought about this.

'But *that* doesn't make sense, either. Look,' she said, grabbing the paper from Basher and nearly tearing it, 'if it was definitely Kevin who drove him, then there's no way he could have driven for that long, waited for Michael to have a chat and then been back in time for an argument with Figgy at a quarter to four.'

'But it definitely was Kevin with Michael,' protested Alex. 'I saw them in the car, and I remember checking the time. It was like, five to three.'

'Ish?'

'Ish.'

'So then he didn't argue with Figgy.'

'But *I* was there for their afternoon spat,' said Basher. 'I was being depressed at Sami in the garden, so I didn't hear them, but I saw Kevin and Figgy having a little hissing match on the terrace.'

'So then one of you has the timings wrong. Must have. Either Kevin and Michael drove past the pub earlier than Alex thought, or the argument Basher saw happened later than it did. Or...'

'Or Kevin didn't do the full drive with Michael, like he said he did,' finished Sophie, who had caught on.

'But,' said Alex, 'we all agree that Kevin is alive, right?'

'Right,' replied Claire. 'But I'm not saying Kevin's dead. I'm saying Kevin is very much alive, but Michael might not be. There's at least one other reason Kevin might have disappeared after that night.'

Alex's mouth formed into a small, perfect O.

'The time,' said Claire, tapping the paper and locking eyes with Basher in triumph, 'is bloody well out of bastarding joint!'

'*Ohmigod! Claire!*' squealed Sophie. 'I'm so proud of you! You did a clue!'

9

Home Is Where Your Dildo Is

Basher and Alex lived in a terraced flat on the top of a windy hill in Brighton. The buildings were white, tall and narrow, with dark doors and steps, and window frames that stretched from floor to ceiling. Without embellishments by the occupants, they would look like a row of very serious, teetering seagulls.

The occupants, however, had embellished aplenty. Every third or fourth flat had some kind of banner or flag or poster displaying various affiliations, or else could not be seen because there were too many plants on the outside sill. Basher's flat, which was on the second floor, was next to one that had a massive rainbow Pride blanket pinned up instead of a curtain, and below one that had an Algerian flag and a 'SAVE THE NHS' poster.

Claire huffed and puffed and coughed up a mere two flights of stairs so much that she had to rest once she got to the door, and Alex glanced at her with some alarm. When they got inside, Basher hurried to the toilet and produced a sparkly purple pill organizer. The days of the week were, indeed, marked by letters formed from small but impressively detailed model penises. They were of many shapes, colours and sizes.

'Off for a stare, Uncle Bash?' Alex asked. 'I'll put the kettle on anyway.'

'Yes. Be all right if I can get a nap in, I think,' he said. He yawned by way of proof, and vanished into his bedroom.

Alex gave Sophie and Claire the short tour. The living room faced the street, and was large enough to hold a corner sofa in front of a coffee table and TV, *and* a table and chairs for dinnertime. There were books everywhere, mostly with charity shop stickers still on them, which Claire attributed to Basher. The kitchen was stuck onto one side of the living room, and the toilet – which was covered from floor to ceiling in small white square tiles, and made Claire feel vaguely like she was inside a tooth – was behind the living room and at the top of a narrow hallway; Basher's bedroom door was at the other end, with a third in between. They were not allowed in Basher's room, not even a brief look for completeness. Claire found this suspicious. What could he have to hide? Evidence that he had murdered his partner, perchance?

Claire caught herself there. It was very unlikely he had, for instance, a year-old body in there. It would smell. Also, if she did really think Basher was a potential murderer, then it was very silly of her to have come here.

It was a nice flat, even though the enormously high ceilings were festooned in cobwebs that neither permanent occupant had the motivation to hoick down. Claire was a card-carrying member of Generation Rent, and that card was an overdrawn one. She swallowed some resentment.

Alex opened the third door with a saved-the-best-till-last flourish. The first thing at Claire's direct eye level was a shelf of bright purple dildos in different shapes.

'Ohmigod. I mean, I guess your decorating has a clear *theme...*' said Sophie, snorting with laughter.

'Eh, they're for a thing,' said Alex, pathologically unembarrassed. 'Just not sure what, yet. A friend works making them, and there was a flaw in the curing of these or something. They're too wobbly. So she gave them to me. I thought maybe, like, unicorn horns, but dicks?' They chucked a distinctly thick dildo at Claire, who caught it.

'*Way* too on-the-nose,' said Claire. She flicked it and it *boinged*.

'Yeah, you're right,' said Alex. 'Someone would definitely buy that, though, is the thing...'

'What about mounting them on, like, a plaque, with "Home Is Where Your Dildo Is" painted on it?' pitched Sophie.

Alex was delighted by this suggestion. 'They *do* say that, don't they?'

The rest of Alex's room was as messy as the inside of their pockets undoubtedly were. There was what Claire assumed was a bed, buried under a heap of clothes. There was also a work desk that appeared to be doing similar double duty as a wardrobe.

Apart from that, every available surface was covered with *stuff*. Embroidery thread, fabric, empty bottles, plant pots, paint pots, interesting rocks, marbles, two halves of different picture frames stuck together, a bit of modelling foam half sanded into the shape of something else, the ammunition for a hot-glue gun but without a glue gun in sight, many jars of sequins and buttons. It was a very eclectic assault on the senses.

'So, yes, this is *my* room, and as you can see it is amazing. Don't worry, I definitely know where everything is. Just don't... don't walk around too much.'

Claire looked down and was unable to see carpet.

'What's this all for?' asked Sophie, who was unburdened by physical feet and was having a good nose around.

'I make kitschy *stuff* to sell online,' said Alex. They sat down on the edge of their bed. 'It's going... well, not amazingly, if we're honest. Also,' they added, after a pause, 'I'm still in the "making friends" stage here, really. Brighton is cool, but I've not been living here long. My school friends are all at uni. I'm actually – like, I sell things I make, and Mum sends me money, but I work at the library. Bash's council connections, I guess.'

It was the first time Claire had heard them say anything remotely age-appropriate. Sophie looked shocked as well. She went and sat next to Alex.

'I know who I am,' Alex added, 'but it's much harder to figure out what I want to *do*. Or how to do it.'

'I don't think most people ever know how to do anything really,' said Sophie. 'The trick about life – speaking as an outside observer – is realizing that everyone is making it up as they go, all the time. Even David Attenborough and people like that.'

'Hmm.' Alex hefted a dildo thoughtfully in one hand. 'What did you want to be when you grew up?'

'Famous,' said Sophie. 'On the bright side, I suppose I sort of was, for a bit.'

'That's a very bleak sort of bright side.'

'You learn to take wins where you can get 'em.'

Claire felt as if she was eavesdropping, even though she was an integral part of the conversation. 'That's great, though,' she said, to cover her embarrassment. 'Libraries are fucking awesome.'

They left Alex to change their clothes, and Claire went for a wee in the big tooth-room. The toilet had long ago been established as a restricted zone where Soph could not follow, along with whenever Claire had a man over, or whenever she went to the doctor.

Claire realized she was still holding the dildo, which was surprisingly weighty, and put it on the side of the bath. An ancient kettle shuddered and roared like some latter-day species of sex toy – a terrifying, steam-powered nineteenth-century one, loud enough that Claire could hear it all this way from the kitchen. Hysterical paroxysms for women: satisfaction guaranteed.

Chance, considered Claire, with some detachment, *would be a fine bloody thing*, although truthfully she had always regarded the sex part of relationships with apathy at best. This was another source of annoyance to Sophie, who regarded it as 'a massive fucking waste' and, when they were arguing, cited it as yet another reason it was monstrously unfair that she was the dead one.

For reasons she could not entirely explain to herself or Sophie, who thought it was very funny, Claire stowed the wibbly dildo in her rucksack. It was one of those ubiquitous Vans rucksacks with the white-and-black chequered front, but because she had had it since school, the white squares were almost grey. Some of them had long ago been coloured in with different highlighter pens or biro.

In the kitchen, the kettle had finished boiling, but whichever Wellington-Forge had turned it on had vanished back to their room. Claire decided to be a good house-guest and make the tea herself.

Sophie noticed her hesitating with the spoon. 'Hmm. Well, Bash is a splash of milk, no sugar – that's obvious. Heaven forbid he should allow himself to enjoy anything. But there *is* sugar next to the tea caddy, so that means...?'

'Alex probably takes some.'

'Right!'

'You don't have to be so patronizing about it.'

Claire took her shoes off and crept stealthily down the hall to Basher's room. She hesitated, then pushed an ear towards the door. She could hear a faint, gentle snore every few seconds. She thought again about the peach fuzziness of his stubble.

Sophie's face hove into her view from the side, with glacial slowness and a similar accompanying blast of frigid air. Her eyes were narrowed. 'And what exactly the fuck are you doing now?' she hissed. 'Ohmigod. Please. No. Stop!'

In the end Claire put the tea down in front of Basher's door and hurried off, as Soph carried on berating her.

'You're worse than those proper weirdos who go on relationship subreddits.'

'Shut up.'

'"I [30F] am a big creepy loser who listens to my new friend [28M] breathing through the door, how can I take things to the next level?"'

'I know.'

'If you do that again, I swear I'll find a way to tell him. I thought you didn't even like Basher,' said Sophie.

'I don't, he's annoying. What kind of real person casually drops Shakespeare quotes into everyday conversation? Nobody. It's something you have to try, like, really hard to do.'

'And yet you fancy him?'

'I dunno. A bit? Maybe?'

'Probably because he's the only man you've spent more than an hour with in one go for, like, a whole year. You can't actually fancy someone you don't like.'

'That is *one hundred per cent* untrue – of course you can.'

'Okay, yeah, but you can't form a proper long-term relationship with someone you don't like.'

'A lifetime of watching reruns of sitcoms from the noughties has taught me that heterosexual couples aren't s'posed to like each other or have anything in common,' said Claire. 'It's probably a Pavlovian response, if anything.'

'Ohmigod. As arguments for the Defence go, "I was trained to fancy people I don't like by Ross from *Friends*" is pretty weak,' Soph replied, raising an eyebrow. 'Anyway I *do* like him, and Alex, and if you ruin this by being creepy, I'll never speak to you again.'

'I *know*, I know, fuck off, I won't.'

But Claire was appropriately shamed. She didn't want to ruin any burgeoning friendships, because those can be hard to come by, when you have the habit of occasionally saying things to thin air; and they become mostly non-existent when you disclose that your actual job is being a medium. Or, rather, the people who did want to be Claire's friend at that point were all really intense and offputting, and did stuff like trying to cultivate psychic connections with ravens, while Claire did, at a basic level, view herself and Sophie as pretty normal. Like, apart from the obvious.

The rest of their trip back through the New Forest had gone well. Basher and Alex had shared stories about Nana, catharting quite merrily. Claire had been the intermediary in a long conversation between Soph and Alex about embroidery, which Sophie claimed to find very interesting. The bonus was that Claire relaying questions about specific colour choices or stitches that Alex was doing – but which Claire, in the front seat, couldn't be seeing herself – seemed to erase any remaining doubts Alex had about Sophie's existence, and even, she hoped, a couple of Basher's.

And when they got on the motorway proper, Basher had put on the radio and 'Mr Brightside' was playing, so he and Claire ended up sing-yelling it in a pretty good imitation of the pissed-up top table at every wedding that either of them had ever been to in their adult lives. Alex filmed it, to make fun of them on social media later. It had all been quite nice.

'Just don't ruin this by being all weird, you big weirdo,' said Sophie now. Her tone wasn't totally unkind. 'I wonder when we'll get to meet this Sami person,' she added. 'It's, like, we're really making progress now, so I don't want to stop.'

'Living people need to sleep, though, Soph.'

'I *know*. It's just so fucking boring. You have no idea how bad it is having to hang around doing *nothing*.'

Claire wasn't sure what Sophie did when Claire was unconscious. She knew that Sophie didn't disappear, but could walk a little way from her, and did. But sometimes she didn't. Claire would wake in the night and see the faintly luminous outline of a figure in the corner of the room, or by the door. At this point it would take a lot to make her afraid of the dark.

'I leave the TV on for you, you're fine. It's like leaving a dog home alone, but way less cute and likeable.'

'*Ohmigod*. Such a bitch.'

Claire threw a cushion through Soph in a lazy, automatic way, and then remembered they weren't her cushions and picked it up again.

Alex, who had a peculiar knack for bursting into rooms at the most convenient time, came back in with their blue hair in a messy bun on top of their head, wearing yellow jeans and a crisp white shirt with rolled-up sleeves. They looked a bit like an iced-gem biscuit, but, like, were totally pulling it off.

Alex was not only confident enough to wear all these things, but also clearly knew that confidence was the best way to look good doing it. They were also physically gifted – while only a little taller than Claire and Soph, their shoulders, hips and feet were all perfectly balanced against one another, and Alex had the same bone structure as the rest of their family. It's usually an insincere compliment to say that someone would look good wearing anything, but in Alex's case it was probably true. Claire was quite jealous, and said so out loud.

'Me, too,' added Sophie. 'You should dress Claire, Alex. Her wardrobe hasn't expanded much over the last – what – three years?'

'I can't afford to expand fuck all,' said Claire, looking down at the same grey jeans and jumper that she'd worn to arrive at – and depart – the Wellington-Forges.

'That doesn't have to be true,' said Alex. 'I get most of my clothes from charity shops.'

Claire could not fathom this attitude. She didn't approve of people having loads of money, but she also thought rather perversely that if your family *did* have money, and several houses, you could at least have the decency to behave like it. Alex didn't have to pay rent, was still financially supported by their parents and could clearly afford to shop at, for example, Zara and John Lewis, but appeared to be cosplaying at having a stretched budget; Claire could not really afford her rent *or* to buy new clothes. Surely Alex could subsidize one of them for her? Even a new pair of shoes? It seemed only fair. Then Claire would have new shoes, and Alex would have a reason for buying second-hand ones. Everyone wins.

She sighed heavily. She remembered being nineteen. Alex was very sincere, and burning with confidence and righteousness like a bin fire at a student protest, but they clearly weren't an idiot.

'You all right?' asked Alex. They looked concerned; they had the same lively grey eyes as Basher and Nana, so it almost seemed like the three of them were a little family unto themselves.

'Yeah,' replied Claire. 'I'm all right. Just sometimes how fucking weird this all is sort of, like, hits me, you know? And it's not even my family, so I dunno how you're coping.'

'I'm okay,' said Alex. They hauled one of the windows open and started smoking. They actually looked quite precarious, because it was a sash window that opened directly upwards and had a low sill and no safety railing. 'I think the murder thing is distracting me from Nana dying, and Nana dying is distracting me from the murder thing. They've cancelled each other out, so I'm basically normal.'

'Better brace for whenever one of them gets resolved,' said Sophie. She went to sit on Alex's feet, like she did with Claire. She seemed to be enjoying making her presence felt by people who sort of knew she was there, and what was happening when she did it.

Alex pulled their socks off. They nodded and agreed that they would most likely be in an absolute state after the funeral, but they weren't thinking about that now. 'I mean,' they said, 'it's odd to realize that even without the murder thing, I don't think that, as a family, we really like each other very much.'

'Yeah but that's true of a lot of families. Most, probably,' said Claire, thinking about how often she spoke to her own parents, which was: not often. Her dad lived in Norwich with a nice woman who had strong opinions about rooms needing to have a feature wall in a pattern or a bright colour, and he called her on Christmas, birthdays and other special occasions. Her mum still lived in London and worked in a sensible bookshop, and they avoided one another so that the subject of Claire's profession never had to come up in conversation.

She shared this with Alex. 'It's, like, I was in therapy for so long, over saying Sophie existed. They almost had me convinced that she didn't. And now, doing what I do... It's like all of it was a waste of time and money, and they might as well not have spent it, and maybe Mum and Dad would have stayed together.'

'I think it's like, to her, if you tried hard enough, you'd be normal,' said Soph. 'But from our point of view, there's not actually anything wrong with you.'

Alex said 'Ooof' with some solemnity. 'With us,' they went on, 'it felt like Nana was the one thing that kept us all together. She was the one who loved us and wanted to know what we were all up to, and wanted us to be together and talk to each other. And she wanted to know everything, and try everything. I dunno how our family ever produced her. She very nearly got me to shave her eyebrows like mine, once. Now that she's gone, I don't know what else there is for the family. Except that house.'

'Was last year what made you come and move down here?' Sophie asked.

'Yeah,' said Alex. 'I love Mum, and Dad even, because, you know: he's my dad. But it's like, at what point do you start thinking about your own happiness? I would have left home to go to university anyway, which is what they wanted me to do. And that dinner... Nana's last-ever birthday dinner and it was a waking nightmare, set to Vera Lynn crossed with Maroon 5.'

Claire snorted through her nose with enough force to get snot on her own top lip. She rummaged in her rucksack for a tissue, or acceptable tissue-like matter, and along with a slightly grubby napkin she found the various crumpled and piecemeal lists of Suspicious Things about the Case that she'd been working on in private. She looked at them and pursed her lips. No wonder detectives went through so many notebooks, she thought. There were so many bastard things they had to remember.

'We should make ourselves useful,' she said, 'and try to tick something off the list. Let's call those singers. The World's Most Brexit A Cappella Group.'

'LOL. The Clefs of Dover,' said Sophie. 'Good idea. I bet you don't get many results when you google *that* hot mess.'

Alex was up for it, and The Clefs had indeed cornered the internet search results in their very extreme niche. As Soph pointed out, 'It's a USP – but how many people are buying that P?'

It turned out that The Clefs had a lot of photos and a whole YouTube channel, so the three of them spent quite a while being mean about them and falling about laughing. It wasn't that they were bad singers exactly, but the task they were bending their voices to was utterly, utterly terrible. You could engage the greatest soprano in the world for a concert, but if you asked her to perform mashups of wartime hits and noughties pop songs, then that's what you'd get.

Their expressions were so uniformly earnest. Claire found the second-hand embarrassment so great that she kept trying to skip through the videos or turn them off as soon as they started playing, but Sophie wouldn't let her.

'Don't look away,' she screeched. 'Fear is the little death! Fear is the mind-killer! Permit the a cappella to pass over you and through you.'

'God, Alex, you're right,' said Claire, ignoring her. 'It *is* like looking directly at the sun. Why has nobody ever told them to stop?'

'That guy's dad definitely has,' said Alex, pointing at one, 'but he's all "The Clef's are my life, Dad!" and is convinced they'll be finalists on *Britain's Got Talent* one day.'

'They probably will,' said Claire, suddenly sobered by a vision of Glenn Miller versus Amy Winehouse getting performed in front of a glassy-eyed Prince William. 'Anyway, there's nothing on their Twitter or any blog posts about being a Clef short or anything, either.'

'I bet if one of them had been murdered by a weird family in a remote country estate, they'd be straight on to Netflix for a documentary,' said Sophie.

There was a number on their website, so Claire called it before she had time to decide it was a bad idea.

'Whoa!' Sophie exclaimed. 'We've not even discussed a game plan! What are you going to say? You can't just ask, "Excuse me, did you happen to see a murder a year ago?"'

Claire didn't respond. She put the phone on speaker and set it on the table between them.

'Claire...' said Sophie, sounding concerned. 'Claire, you do know you can't say that, don't you? Please don't say that.'

She ignored this, too. For one thing, it sounded like the sort of comment Alex *would* say.

Someone picked up the phone and said, 'Hello-oooo!' in a very sing-song voice.

'Oh, er, hello. Is that... I'm looking for...' Claire sighed. 'I'm after The Clefs of Dover.'

'Oh yes, that's me! Well, us! Ha-ha-ha!' The laugh clearly thought of itself as being like the tinkling of silver bells, but perhaps came a little closer to brassy than the owner would like. Claire imagined this was the chief Clef, the one who'd been cauliflower-cheesed. 'Would you like to book us? Our rates are—'

'Um. Sorry. No. My name's Claire, and I wanted to ask about a gig you did this time last year.'

'Oh yeah?' The Clef sounded a lot less enthusiastic. The sing-song tinkle had vanished almost entirely.

'Yeah, it's the Wellington-Forges at The Cloisters? Big weird family in a big weird house in the country? I just did a, um, a gig, I guess, for them and I'm having trouble getting paid. Someone mentioned you were there last year, and I wondered how you got on and if you had any trouble.'

Sophie looked at her in amazement. There was a crackle of static on the phone; the Clef had exhaled down the line.

'Yeah, that was *weird*, all right. I won't go into it, but that family has issues.' Alex made an it's-a-fair-cop-face, as the lead Clef went on. 'You're lucky if getting paid is the worst story you have. But as it happens, yeah, we got the runaround a bit. The guy kept saying he would get the money to us soon, offering to send a cheque. Pshh. Eventually paid us through their company instead of personally, after almost nine months.'

'Oh, wow, that's ages.'

'Yeah, I guess they wanted to try and write it off as a business expense, too, the cheeky gits. It was a pain actually, the more I think about it. Had to threaten the small claims court in the end. Total bullshit obviously, but it shook something loose. Gemma handled most of that. You should give her a ring – see if she can remember anything else.' The Clef passed on a phone number, which Alex noted down.

'That's great, thank you,' said Claire, though she was disappointed that gentle shaking of the clue-tree hadn't yielded any murder-solution fruit. Alex was paddling their hand to encourage her to keep going. 'So what was so weird about your gig, if you don't mind me asking? You all made it out okay? Ha-ha?'

'Very subtle, weirdo,' said Soph.

'Ugh! I mean, yeah, we were physically all fine, just mentally scarred. It's in the middle of nowhere, obviously – I mean, *you* know – so they told us we could stay over, which was a bit *The Hills Have Eyes*, but we charged extra for the time involved, so no biggie. Then, when we arrived, the atmos was so awkward, like they all hated each other. And the actual gig was just us singing while they ate dinner and bitched out loud. And *then* an honest-to-God food fight broke out!'

'Whoa, no waaaaaay,' said Claire, in a totally surprised tone. Alex struggled not to laugh out loud.

'Yes. I got food in my bra! Oh, that reminds me: the youngest son? Total creep. Stared at my boobs the entire time. He got punched by one of the others and I wasn't sorry about it.'

'Whoa, someone got *punched*? Who punched him?'

'I don't know – his dad, I guess? Or one of his brothers? One of the family anyway. I didn't see him get hit,' she conceded. 'But that must have been what it was. They all stormed off in different directions after dinner. A bit later we'd cleaned up and had finished loading our car, and a bunch of the men came past, propping each other up. And the dad was like, "The boys have been at a bit of horseplay", and one of the others was like, "Oh, I can't believe you hit me, Tarquin or Mumford, or whoever."' There was a pause. 'So anyway, what is it you do?'

'Oh. I'm a medium. I did a seance.'

'Huh. Nice. Very post-postmodern? I guess? How did it go?'

'Bad,' said Claire, after thinking about it.

'What happened?'

'Their nana died.'

Silence.

'Are you still there?' asked Claire, after a while.

'Yeah.'

'Okay, well. Thanks for the advice. Bye.'

She hung up and looked at Sophie, who tipped her head on one side, curls tumbling everywhere, and laughed. 'Ohmigod, don't look at me like that. You did really well. Proper private detective improvising.'

'Fucking too right,' replied Claire, satisfied by this – enough to convey Sophie's compliment to Alex.

'Yeah, the payment line was great,' Alex agreed.

'It, er, was actually based in truth. I have not been paid as yet, although I know it's only been a couple of days. Felt like a bit of a weird time to ask, to be honest.'

'Yeah, fair enough,' said Alex.

Claire called secondary Clef, Gemma, who corroborated the night's events, as well as the fact that all of The Clefs made it out alive.

'Not much going on with The Clefs, it sounds like,' said Alex. 'Good to cross them off the list.'

'I don't know about that,' said Sophie thoughtfully. 'That thing about the brothers fighting. Sounds... weird.'

'Maybe that's how Tristan ruined his suit?' suggested Claire. She suddenly felt very tired and wanted a lie-down. The throw on the sofa was quite fluffy and the cushions were nice and soft. 'I still think maybe Kevin killed Michael when he drove him out of town. I mean, that's *well* sus, isn't it?' she said, making an effort not to yawn.

Sophie pointed out that if Michael had been killed away from the house, he wouldn't be haunting it; he'd probably be wandering around a field and not bothering anyone, except the occasional psychically sensitive pigeon. Claire's argument was that if he'd been *buried* at the house, then that's where he'd be hanging about – hence the terrifying library skeleton. But she had to admit there would be no need for Kevin to drag the body all the way back there.

'I've been thinking about it anyway,' said Sophie, 'and, based on that picture you showed us, there's no way our victim can be Michael.'

'What makes you so sure?'

'If you didn't notice, then I'm not going to tell you,' said Sophie. She pouted and stuck her tongue out.

'Oh my God, you're the worst.'

Alex crawled over to lie on the floor, propping themself awkwardly against the sofa, and asked what some of the rules for ghosts and hauntings were, but Claire and Soph didn't really have any hard-or-fast answers for them. Where you died, where your body ended up or where you lived most of your life were your three best bets for where you might spend your ghostly existence, but there were exceptions. Notably Sophie. Claire didn't count on any of those three points, and yet here Sophie was.

Claire suddenly remembered her adventure in the priest-hole and told Alex about it. She fished the button out of the bottom of her backpack, but Alex shrugged. They didn't recognize it specifically; it could belong to Tuppence or Mattie or Clem, or to a guest. There was no telling how long it had been there, after all.

Solving crime was more frustrating than Claire had anticipated, although the team on *Murder Profile* did always have at least one stumbling block per episode. Maybe if she waited long enough, one day she'd figure it out. But she'd have to theorize a lot first. Preferably out loud. That always worked on *MP*.

She leaned back onto a pile of turmeric-yellow cushions and sighed. 'The killer clearly had an adolescent mindset,' she said experimentally.

Sophie stared at her and called her a weirdo. Claire did

not relate this to Alex, because they said, 'Bit weird, mate' at almost the same time.

Claire idly looked up The White Clefs of Dover on Twitter.

OMG #clefheads. Buckle up, because I have a story for you! It starts with us being booked for a gig in the middle of nowhere, and ends with a medium killing an old lady at a seance! Strap in (1/?)

The next thing Claire knew, she was being nudged awake. She had fallen asleep somewhere around tweet number six of The Clefs' Twitter thread ('btw, Marie Claire doesn't have any tips for getting cauliflower cheese out of underwiring!'). During her nap she'd scrunched herself down so that her head was thrown back and she had probably been, at best, breathing *very* heavily in her sleep.

'You were snoring,' said Sophie's voice.

Basher was kicking Claire's feet. Her mouth tasted like she'd been sucking an old washing-up sponge, or possibly a sock. Outside, the seagulls still screamed.

'Hello,' said Basher. Claire looked at him and felt very sleepy and confused. He had changed into a cleaner, slightly less worn hoodie of light blue, and he had wet hair, so Claire surmised that he had showered. In her half-awake state, she was quietly pleased at this observation. She was definitely getting better at detectoring.

'Herk—' she croaked.

Basher, who was holding two mugs of tea, offered one to her. She tried again.

'Hello. What's happening?'

'Lunch.'

'Oh. What's for lunch?'

'A police interview.'

10

This Is the Police

Claire had been to Brighton before, but when she was quite small. She remembered a beach that was uncomfortable to sit on, and an aquarium with a depressed octopus that wouldn't come out of its pipe. These things did, Basher assured them, still exist. Although they'd probably gone through several new octopuses since then – but Basher said the current one did seem pretty depressed whenever he saw it, which was quite often. He had an annual pass to the aquarium, because he liked going there on weekdays sometimes to sit in the underwater tunnel that went through the big tank (which apparently all aquariums are legally mandated to have) and eat some sandwiches and read a book.

But Claire did not remember anything else about Brighton and, not having been there since Soph had attached herself like a spiritual mollusc or carbuncle, they both looked around with interest as they left the flat.

It was sunny, but blustery. Clouds were chasing each other across the sky so quickly that the street was flickering dark-bright-dark very quickly, like a child clicking the sun's light switch on and off to be annoying. You could see the sea from the front door of Basher and Alex's building, if you looked down the hill to the right, but it was a narrow strip of iron-grey with a lot of houses and shops in between them, and it was dotted with white bits where the wind was catching the spray. At this distance the sea wasn't the stirring, poetic sight Claire had expected. It reminded her of the bonnet of a car spackled with birdshit, in fact. She decided not to say this, and instead plumped for the traditional, if vague, 'Oh look, the sea!' because she thought that was what you were supposed to say when you saw the sea.

'Yes,' said Basher, without looking. 'The sea. I am afraid we're going this way, though.'

The four of them went left, up the hill to the other end of the street, and then set off roughly parallel to the sea, so they kept getting glimpses of it. Sophie pointed out some kind of attraction that must have been on the beach front – a giant metal pole with a big glass-and-metal doughnut-shaped thing going slowly down it. Claire thought it looked like a ring toss in slow motion, but Soph said it was 'well Freudian'.

They walked into town, past nice front gardens with gnomes and rambling roses, and side streets that had houses painted in different colours, and residential streets with those weird trees that look like angry fists because, for some reason, the council wouldn't let them grow branches. Claire noticed that a lot of the electric feeder-pillar cabinets in the street were covered in graffiti of cartoon characters saying something encouraging.

Alex peeled off, explaining that they wanted to explore the mounted dildo art idea and had got a hot lead from a Facebook group on a number of broken Big Mouth Billy Bass.

From a casual self-conducted survey of the pedestrians they walked past, Claire observed that the Brighton demographic was split pretty equally between nice old people who had been living there for decades, aggressively teenage teenagers, families with very young children, queer people with cool hair and big shoes, and people working at, or visiting, tattoo parlours.

Basher led them into a cluster of almost totally pedestrianized shopping streets where all these people mingled together, bumping into each other and peering in the windows of independent stationery shops selling paper as thick as leather, or jewellery shops with costume brooches that looked like you could eat them, or innumerable cafés selling small-batch roasted coffee. Claire wondered how one town could sustain them all. Maybe Brightonians worked on a rota system: you do Tea for Two on Saturday, and I'll do Proper Coffee next week.

The buildings still weren't as tall as Claire was used to. Seeing that much sky at once was a bit weird and made her feel small, although not as much as the unfeeling country skies at the Wellington-Forges' estate. She knew other people felt lonely in London, but she liked it. Rather than making her feel claustrophobic or self-conscious, all the people crushed into London made her feel the opposite: relaxed and confident. There were so many other people to look at that it was unlikely anyone would pay attention to her, even if they bothered to stop worrying whether or not someone was looking at *them* (which most people didn't). She liked the Tube especially. It felt very safe, and warm. The Tube was so hot in the summer that Claire, constantly followed by her own talkative and perambulatory air-conditioning unit, reliably did feel a comfortable temperature on the Central Line at rush hour. Wandering around the weird bits of the Underground felt like what she imagined being in the womb was like.

The streets were narrower now in this bit of Brighton. There was a market on one, and Sophie diverted them by running off to have a look. She leaned over a table with a red crushed-velvet cloth, on which was dumped a mountain of unsorted silver: jewellery, charms, trinkets, scraps. Her nose was about half an inch from the heap. She was like a magpie. She liked pretty, shiny things.

Claire and Basher started poking through a bookstall nearby. He glanced at his watch, but didn't seem rushed. It struck Claire that having an actual watch and not checking the time on his phone, like everyone else these days, was the sort of deliberate choice Basher would make. She also noticed that he had nice hands. He was looking at some slightly mouldering old copies of Shakespeare's tragedies.

202

'You bloody *love* Shakespeare, don't you?'

'I do. There's something about his work that people can understand, especially when it's being performed. He has this amazing emotional clarity. Like when you see a video of a toddler listening to the *Moonlight Sonata* and they just *know*. And yet he invented so much at the same time. The inside of Shakespeare's head must have been amazing. But probably a nightmare to experience.'

'I think that probably applies to everyone in the world, in some ways,' said Claire. 'But I do agree with you about Shakespeare. I once saw a production of *Much Ado About Nothing* that was for, like, schools, and they changed the line 'I had rather be a canker in a hedge than a rose in his grace' to 'I had rather be a boil on a maiden's cheek than a rose in his grace' and I've never forgotten it, because of how pointless and stupid that change is.'

Basher laughed. 'Wow!'

'I know. Completely dicks the balance of the figurative language, for no reason whatsoever.'

'You did Literature too, hmm?'

'Actually I didn't. I did History. I suppose the difference now is small. Few practical applications, made fun of by STEM grads, no proper job. But I dated a guy who studied English Lit and I wanted him to like me, so for a few weeks I studied Shakespeare, too...'

Claire paused, realizing she had probably revealed too much about how strange and intense she could be, or at least had been when she was twenty. She pretended to be very interested in the other books, and thumbed through a modern romance novel. It had one of the two covers that romance novels were currently allowed to have: a cartoony rendering of modern woman in sunglasses, with the title in curly Comic Sans adjacent font; the other kind was a woman with her back to the camera in a sunhat, looking out to sea, with the title in a font meant to resemble handwriting. The implication, in either case, was usually that the woman in question was in desperate need of a man, or had one who it would turn out she did not need at all.

She bought the book. It was fifty pence and was called *The Misadventures of Lilly Addison* and, in Claire's experience, books like this were usually very good.

'Although you did,' she added, as they moved on to a table full of old *The Beano* and *The Dandy* annuals, 'have a quote-unquote proper job, I mean.'

'A lot of people would argue that I did not,' Basher replied, raising an eyebrow. His hands were back in his front pocket. 'I suppose, traditionally, the younger sons should join the clergy, shouldn't they?'

'Um. Or the military, I think. Or become lawyers.'

'Ah, well. The others have that covered. I think I only really joined the force because Mum and Dad were getting at me about, as you said, my lack of other specific prospects, and the police were desperate for bodies at the time, so you could sort of fast-track a career out of it. I didn't have a thirst for justice or anything; it just seemed easier than having to listen to Mum. I wanted to... I wanted to belong somewhere.'

'Didn't fancy getting well into *Call of Duty*?'

'I'm not really the type.'

Claire did not say that Basher didn't really seem the type to be a cop, either. 'Were you good at it?'

'Again, depends on who you ask. I am good at figuring things out, I suppose. But that is not necessarily one of your key performance indicators, as a police officer. Anyway, it turned out that Mum was even more incensed at me being unemployed than she was at me having the kind of job that anyone can do. She was just starting to imagine that I might be Police Commissioner one day, which she would find acceptable, when I packed it all in. An unforgivable betrayal, twice over.'

The next table was an assortment of bric-a-brac. There was a statuette of a cute shepherd boy in a green smock, carrying a lamb, and Claire suddenly remembered something.

'The pink shepherdess!' she cried, almost shouting. 'Nana said to tell you she kept her word about it. What does that mean?'

Basher kept looking at the table. He was otherwise incredibly still, until he reached out and, very carefully, picked up the shepherd boy. The boy had a yellow mop of curls and was frozen in the act of laughing. Basher stared into his face.

'Nana had a case of Royal Doulton figurines,' he said eventually. 'You know, the ceramic ones of women in ballgowns and children sitting on logs? I really liked them, and she let me take them out and look at them when I was little. And I dropped the pink shepherdess. Smashed it into many irreparable pieces. Nana told Mum that she broke it when she was cleaning, and we promised we'd never tell anyone. Although now, I suppose, we both have,' he said, smiling to himself, and to the shepherd boy. Basher paused again then, the smile slipping from his face. He chewed his lip and hesitated. 'Is Nana still... around?'

Claire hesitated too, wondering what it was he actually wanted to hear. 'No. She was too content with herself. Her unfinished business was asking me to figure out what happened a year ago, so I'm afraid we can't talk to her again. Er...'

Basher put the shepherd boy down slowly, but kept his hand on it. He still didn't look at her.

Claire unexpectedly felt a lump form in her throat and she coughed awkwardly. 'Um. Unless we don't figure it out, cos then maybe Nana will come back to haunt me,' she added. She felt the moment pass, the weight lift a little. 'I dunno – it's never happened before.'

Basher turned his clear grey eyes on her suddenly. 'Maybe you're not so bad, Claire,' he said.

She blushed and looked away.

He bought the green shepherd boy and carried the bag awkwardly for the rest of the day.

They moved along to another stall, this one selling comics and old annuals in individual plastic bags. Claire was surprised that such bags were allowed in a place like Brighton, where every coffee cup was reusable or biodegradable, or both. Individual plastic bags were the sort of thing that killed dolphins and ducks, but dolphins and ducks were both sexually deviant creatures, in Claire's opinion, so she didn't feel particularly aggrieved about the comics.

Sophie had wandered over now and was complaining that she was bored again. Claire blew her nose, which was both running and blocked at the same time, and looked sideways at Basher. He seemed relaxed. Like he was enjoying himself. She didn't want to ruin that, but she also thought: *What would the* Murder Profile *team do?* So she asked him about the breakfast where he had announced that he was leaving the police.

Basher rolled his neck, sighed and took a great interest in the annuals. 'Did you know,' he said, 'that the *Bash Street Kids* comic strip was originally created as *When the Bell Rings?*'

'Don't let him distract you with all his facts,' said Soph.

Claire hesitated. 'I'm not asking for The Case. I'm asking as – I dunno. A mate.'

Basher took a deep breath. 'It was terrible. It was... it was a big deal, for everyone. My job was the only thing I felt Mum and Dad could be proud of me for, if I put enough effort in. But I was miserable doing it. I got worn out. There's something rotten in the state of... here. I thought it would be noble, which sounds stupid now, but... the police catch baddies. You could make any parent proud, being a hero. Except it is mostly not doing that, even after detective training.'

Claire made a note to look up how it all worked, because she had assumed that being a detective was another rank, possibly somewhere above sergeant, but definitely below captain, because your captain was always on your ass about something. As in: 'Hello, I'm Detective Hendricks, we have to catch this serial killer soon, because the captain is on my ass about all the murders!' It was possible that *Murder Profile* was not as accurate as she had suspected. Also, it was set in America.

Basher was now flipping through copies of *The Dandy*. 'When you try to be in the in-group, you start to notice who is kept out. At least I did. But I was about the only one. And it felt as if no matter how hard I tried, I couldn't change anything. Including how Mum and Dad felt about me. I had quit before I told them, you see, but it felt like something I had to tell them in person. Like a break-up. I was dreading it. So I asked Sami to come, to *make* me.'

'I read once that if you tell someone you're going to do something, it makes you more likely to do it,' said Claire wisely. She had never told anyone she wanted to stop smoking.

'Yes, I suppose so. And I couldn't keep pretending that I was still a copper. That is a BBC2 daytime series waiting to happen. I know I'm making it sound like a massive issue, but... I was already the disappointment anyway. Mum has this weird way of... Well, I think everyone has different hang-ups about their parents, don't they?'

It wasn't rhetorical. He wanted reassurance.

'Oh, yeah. Definitely. Me and my mum don't even talk very much.'

'Neither do me and mine,' said Sophie, completely deadpan. This was true on two levels, because Sophie never asked to visit her mum. She hated the idea. It was convenient, because Sophie's mum definitely didn't want to see Claire – especially after the Essex incident put their names in the paper again.

'Sami had a go at me before breakfast about it, so that was another argument to add to the heap. She could not see why I wasn't just getting it over with. I had dragged her all the way there...' Basher went on. 'I remember sitting at the breakfast table. I was looking at the little bits of chives in my scrambled egg and instead of saying, "Could you pass the salt, please", I said, "I handed my notice in two months ago." And Mum burst into tears. She said, "How could you do this to me?', which really irritated me. Everything is about *her*, even when it really isn't. I started shouting and said she was a horrible witch who was hell-bent on controlling all of us. She said I had broken her heart, that I was ungrateful, that I'd wasted my life and everything they'd given me.'

Basher sighed heavily. 'I think that might be why I am keeping a step ahead of this – whatever this investigation is. Because while there isn't any evidence someone was killed, secretly I think... I think Mum *would* kill for one of us. Mum loves us. Very much. So much. But in a way that, I think, hurts us.' He smiled suddenly, fast and heart-breaking. 'I mean, just look at Tris.'

Soph laughed. Boys will be boys, and some boys clearly couldn't even do their own laundry.

Claire found that she had the first few lines of the chorus to 'Love Hurts' stuck in her head. She'd always assumed, when people said 'Love hurts', that they meant loving someone or something and not being able to have it, or losing it. She hadn't thought they meant that *being* loved could hurt you. Claire had a sudden urge to be open with Basher and tell him the truth about who Sophie was, and what had happened in Essex. Maybe he'd understand. He was an empathetic person, wasn't he?

She was about to open her mouth, when he did. 'We should head over, or we'll be late,' he said.

The moment was gone. Claire shoved her hand in her pocket and pulled out Sophie's pink butterfly hair-clip, which she hadn't yet tucked back away for its special seance purposes. She was finding that she liked fiddling with it – like clicking the top of a pen.

'Hey!' said Sophie. 'Careful with that. It's mine. It's... there's only one of that.'

'I know. I'm careful.'

'If you lose it—'

'I'm not going to lose it.'

They walked to a vegetarian restaurant on the next road over. It had a living wall of plants by the door and a cabinet of cakes that were many-layered and each about a foot tall.

When she arrived about ten minutes late, Sami turned out to be both very much not murdered and a smiley British Indian woman, with a gap between her front teeth that only made her smile nicer. Her black hair was tied back into a loose bun, but it looked like it was cut so that she could easily pin it back into a style of shining professionalism. Her eyes were kind, but also lively and quick, taking in everything. She noted, for example, the brief wince that Claire made as she looked at the prices on the menu.

'I assume you'll be treating us to lunch, *Sebastian*, since you're clearly about to ask me a favour,' she said, grinning. 'He is, isn't he?'

'I don't know,' said Claire, who realized too late that she hadn't asked anywhere near the number of questions about Sami that an inquisitive detective should.

When Basher and Alex had described Sami as Basher's partner, Claire had assumed it was as in 'girlfriend', which she was now realizing was incorrect. Sophie pointed out that Sami was wearing a ring, and her clothes were covered in small sticky thumbprints and bits of food, the everyday accessories of parents of a toddler. Sami was actually Detective Sergeant Sami Wilson, Basher's old *police* partner, which now seemed very obvious. After the successful Case of the Man Who Had a Shower Recently, Claire demoted herself down to a mere amateur detective for making an assumption.

'Oh, wait, um… Can I see your ID, you know?' Claire asked.

Sami smiled indulgently and produced her warrant card – she even had it in one of those flippy-open holders, like on the TV.

'Thanks. Always wanted to see one,' Claire said. In fact it confirmed Sami's identity. So now she could be almost 100 per cent sure that Basher was trustworthy, or at least had not killed his former partner. Which was a great relief.

'It is for a bit of a favour that I asked you here, I'm afraid,' said Basher. 'And a... well, a slightly strange one.'

'You going to ask me how I am, first?'

'How are you?'

'All right. You?'

'Nana died.'

The smile instantly dropped from Sami's face. 'Oh god, Bash. I'm sorry. Of course I'll help. Whatever you need.'

Basher hesitated. 'Well, it's not... If I am being totally honest, it is not directly about that. That's just the head-line of what has been happening to me lately.'

'I see,' said Sami, the smile cautiously creeping back, like a cat coming out from under a sofa. 'So that was to make me feel like an arsehole for demanding lunch. I activated your trap-card. You can definitely pay now.'

'Yes, yes, all right. It is tangentially related, though. Nana only died a couple of days ago, but she told Claire something...' Basher paused. He seemed to be thinking of the best way to proceed. How to frame what The Case actually was.

'Don't say anything,' Sophie advised. Claire nodded.

'You remember her birthday last year? Well, Nana told Claire that she thought someone was killed that weekend. I er... I think she might have seen a body.'

Sami was shocked. She half laughed. 'What... really?'

'Yes. Seriously.'

212

Basher outlined what had happened, although he made it seem like the conversation had taken place before Nana had died.

'Are you asking me to try and open a case?' asked Sami. 'Because—'

'No! No, of course not. There's nothing to report to anyone. There are no signs of a body *now*. Or anything, really. But Nana trusted Claire, and I trust Nana.'

'And I trust you, I suppose,' said Sami. She rolled her eyes and sighed. 'So what do you actually want?'

'I want to check out the other guests who were there that weekend. They have been quite hard to track down.'

'Oh, is that *all*,' said Sami, 'just a casual invasion of privacy, based on hearsay?'

'I do not mean address and blood type, plus inside leg; merely, you know, check there aren't any open Missing Persons cases or reports from concerned relatives. And then nobody has to think about it ever again.' Basher spread his hands appealingly. 'I want to rest easy, knowing that my family did not kill anyone.'

'I don't think he'll ever be able to do that,' said Sophie tartly.

Sami raised her eyebrows and said Basher would definitely owe her more than a lunch after this, but her manner became a bit more businesslike. 'Was Nana making sense? She wasn't confused?'

There was a long pause while Claire worked out that Sami was talking to her. 'Oh, uh, yeah. She was fine. Sharp as the proverbial tack.'

'Did she say where she saw the body?'

'Um… in the library. But I think it was more like, you know, remains. She couldn't tell who it was.'

'Why did she tell you this?'

'I dunno, really. I think she liked us – er, me. I think she liked *me*.'

Sami looked quite hard at Claire for a few seconds. 'All right,' she said eventually. She opened a notepad, although not, Claire saw, an official police one. 'Give me their names, Basher. I'm not promising *anything*, mind you,' she added, pointing her pen at him sternly. She slid both the notepad and the pen over to him.

'I wouldn't ask you to,' said Basher. 'Thanks, Sami.'

'Yeah, yeah,' she replied. Basher wrote down three names and pushed the pad back. Sami started adding her own notes . 'Oh, I hope you don't think I'm being rude, Claire, but why were you there?'

'Oh, I was the entertainment. Er, this year's Clefs of Dover.'

Sami laughed at this.

'Don't tell her what you do,' said Sophie quickly. 'Make something up. Anything.'

'What do you do?' Sami asked, on cue.

Claire was again unable to think on her feet. 'I'm actually a medium,' she confessed. 'I was going to do a seance. You know, sort of spooky, for Halloween.'

Sami nodded. She did not ask anything else, or look up from writing, or make any comment at all. This was strange. People usually at least went, 'Cool!' in a polite and insincere way, such as they might respond to someone saying, 'I'm a taxidermist' or 'I make small sculptures out of boiled eggs'.

Then the notebook was put away, and Sami went back to not seeming at all like a police officer. Claire ordered the soup of the day, which turned out to be some kind of spicy sweet potato thing. She asked Sami if she remembered anything from that weekend.

'Well, I don't think I'll ever forget that dinner,' she said. 'It was intense.' She gave a brief summary of her memories of the dinner, which were basically in line with Alex's, but more concentrated at her end of the table.

'Yes, my family are quite odd,' said Basher. His air was a bit apologetic.

'Actually,' said Sami, 'apart from the food-hurling, I'd say they were fairly typical of families of their type. If that's any consolation.'

The expression on Basher's face indicated that it was not.

'Did anything else weird happen that weekend?' Claire asked. 'Did you hear anything after dinner?'

Sami shook her head. 'I sleep with headphones in. And the dinner does overshadow most of my other memories, to be honest. I remember seeing Figgy and her boyfriend – whatshisname, the awful one – arguing before that. You were sitting in the garden doing your sad act, remember, Bash? It was just before four o'clock.'

'Told you!' Basher said to Claire, with a note of triumph. 'Timeline wobbles. The weekend does not all match up,' he added to Sami, by way of explanation.

215

'Still doesn't match up,' Claire mumbled into her spoon.

'There was one thing, actually,' Sami said suddenly.

'Was it to do with Michael? The accountant guy?'

'Ohmigod, I told you, it's so not him,' said Sophie.

'No, not him – he spent the whole time avoiding me, if anything,' Sami went on. 'No, it was the housekeeper. Mattie. She pulled me aside on the Saturday and asked if we could have a private chat. But then your mum came down the hall and she clammed up. Never saw her alone again. Or at all.'

'You never mentioned that,' said Basher.

'I assumed it was about you, or something. Mattie was a bit nervous, but not sweating bullets or anything. You should ask Alex's mum about her, actually. Whenever anyone made a round of tea, Tuppence would always take a cup to Mattie in the office. Probably chatted a bit.'

After they'd finished lunch, Sami had to get home to help her husband with their two- and four-year-olds, describing the former as a 'fucking tyrant', but she thanked them for giving her a reason to get out and about by herself. Sophie asked Basher, via Claire, if they could go and see the depressed octopus.

Brighton aquarium purported to be the oldest aquarium in the world that was still operating. It was underground, and gave off quite Victorian Gothic vibes inside. It was as if Dracula had suffered in the economic crash and had to sell his holiday dungeon, and the Sea Life people had snapped it up.

It was dark and quiet. At the end of one long, low room there was a circular tank of jellyfish. They were zooming around it in a spiral in an unseen current. It looked like someone had put a bunch of carrier bags into a washing machine.

'I feel sick,' said Soph.

'You don't have a stomach,' said Claire automatically.

'They do actually!' said a dead teenager in an aquarium polo shirt, who had clearly been waiting hours for this very moment and appeared so suddenly he made Claire go 'Argh'. He went on, 'It's a very simplified one, very different from the stomach you have.'

'She was talking about me, not about the jellyfish,' said Sophie. The boy shrugged and walked off and into one of the tanks, where he stood, distorted by the thick glass and water, looking at the huge fish swimming around and through him with interest. 'God, that looks quite creepy,' said Sophie. 'I might try it.'

Claire scuttled over to the tank on the opposite wall, which turned out to be the depressed octopus's. Mission accomplished! It was squished inside a pipe, styled to look like a water valve, which was the only thing in the tank. Claire imagined there was a nicer half of the tank kept secret from the public that had enrichment toys in it, where the octopus could play football, or whatever octopuses did on their downtime.

The only things visible were some anaemic tentacles poking out, and the suggestion of a baleful yellow eye in the darkness.

'Fucking hell,' said Soph.

Two other employees were talking quietly nearby. 'She's not doing well today, no,' said one. Claire realized he meant the octopus. 'Probably only a few months left, they say.'

'Ohmigod. Most depressing octopus ever. Ten out of ten.'

Basher had ambled over to stand next to them. All three – *four* – stayed there in silence for a bit.

'You know,' said Sophie conversationally, 'I couldn't read Basher's writing, but Sami added a name to the list. She has very neat handwriting. She wrote your name down. She's going to look you up. She's going to find out.'

Claire stood rooted to the spot, maintaining eye contact with the sickly octopus.

'Big,' she said eventually, 'mood.'

11

The Sesh

The flat didn't have a third bedroom, or one of those inflatable mattresses that are only really used at Christmas, and which slowly deflate over the course of the night so that in the morning the occupant is sleeping on the floor anyway. Instead, Alex added some pillows and a blanket to the sofa. Claire and Sophie slept the sleep of the dead – i.e. they did not, instead flipping between analysing clues and watching reels of the worst-case scenarios of Sami looking up Claire's name playing out behind her eyes.

Eventually the sun came up again, which made it Monday. This would have been a complication, except that nobody currently in the flat had what would traditionally be thought of as a real job. Accordingly, when Claire woke up from a fitful doze, it was after eleven. She found Alex carefully clearing space on the cluttered coffee table so they could put down a mug of tea. Claire sat up to drink it, with something of the air of a stray cat sniffing at a kind stranger's hand. Basher walked in from the kitchen, and Claire scrabbled to get under the blankets again, because she didn't have any jeans on. Soph laughed, but Basher hadn't even glanced at her. His nose was in an open recipe book, and he was tapping a biro on his chin.

'We could make some stuffed apples properly,' he said. 'They make a nice cold-weather dessert with cream. But that would need a lighter main. Maybe salmon... Well, whatever the case, we shall need to go into town to get some supplies.'

'What about the murder investigation?' asked Sophie. Claire echoed this. Surely there were pressing things to be done.

'Uncle Bash says it'll take a few days to hear back from Sami anyway. So we might as well have a nice time,' said Alex. They sat on the floor and patted the space in front of them. 'Here, c'mere, S. I want to see if I can feel it if we do pat-a-cake.'

Basher sat by the coffee table and produced a notepad, on which he started to write a careful list of things he needed to buy, with amounts in brackets.

Claire started to say 'Um...' but Basher waved a hand towards the kitchen without looking up. 'There is bread for toast, and cereal in the cupboard above the kettle,' he said. 'And I have hung a clean towel on the back of the bathroom door.'

Claire had a shower and put the same jumper on for the fourth day in a row. She stopped at the doorway to the living room and looked in. The room was full of weak autumn light. Basher now seemed to be making a duplicate of his shopping list in an app on his phone. Alex had their hands up for Sophie to hit at them, and they were both giggling. Claire stood there watching for a long time, until Basher looked up and said, 'Oh, are we all ready to go then?'

They walked into town in a different direction from before, and ended up at a covered market. They bought some thin fillets of salmon at the fishmonger's, where Claire eyed the blank fishy faces staring up at her from a bed of ice with extreme suspicion, in case one of them moved. She had not yet seen an animal ghost, but shops like that seemed the most likely place.

At the greengrocer's Alex talked to Sophie out loud, as if they could hear her, and without any worry about what other people might think. 'We need at least four of these, S, but probably six, to be safe. What about this one? Or this?' They held huge green apples into the air for invisible approval. Basher called Claire over to ask if she preferred green beans or sugar-snap peas, sultanas or raisins.

Basher turned out to be a very enthusiastic cook. It was oddly exhilarating watching him – an intentionally drab person – light up from the inside to the out as he mixed together double cream and raisins and rum, rubbed rich butter into flour, and used twice as much garlic and chilli as the recipe suggested to stir-fry green beans to go with the salmon. He only put up a cursory objection to Alex insisting that he plated up a portion of everything for Sophie as well. They pretended to be a fancy maître d', tea towel over their forearm, as they put down the huge stuffed apple, swimming in cream, in front of where Sophie was sitting. She beamed. It was delicious.

That night Claire dreamed that she woke up the next day in a bed. In her dream, Basher came in and said they didn't have anything to do today, either. She went and sat on the sofa and he brought her a bowl of chicken soup.

She was almost surprised when she woke up on the sofa and saw that, while there wasn't any soup, Alex had again left a cup of tea on the coffee table for her. She was even more surprised when, just after she had finished a plate of what Basher told her was butternut-squash risotto for lunch, the ancient buzzer screamed like a modem shagging a blender, and a crackling robot version of Tristan's voice announced that he was outside. This was an unexpected development, especially on a weekday. Alex seemed suspicious.

'I'm suspicious,' they said, buzzing Tristan in. 'Dad wouldn't simply let him have an afternoon off work. I bet he's here as an undercover agent.'

'Bet they're right,' said Soph. 'We're lucky Tristan isn't the sharpest tool in the proverbial. He'll be even less subtle than you would.'

Tristan entered in a suit and slightly loosened tie, accessorized with a home-made wool scarf that he was obviously under maternal orders to wear when it was cold. After saying hello, he flopped down on the sofa and, as if he had overheard Sophie and specifically wanted to prove her right, said, 'So, Claire. Bloody hell! Ghosts and stuff. How long have you been doing that? Ever met any murder victims or anything cool?' He did not seem surprised to see her, or to consider that maybe he should have pretended to be surprised to see her. Claire wondered how Tristan had known she was there.

She smiled and was vague, although she always was when people asked her for exactitudes on her job. 'Only been doing the medium thing full-time for a few years really, but I've been able to see and talk to ghosts since I was a teenager.'

'Oh yah, cool, like the X-Men,' he said, with much enthusiasm.

'Yes,' replied Claire, calibrating her tone to better suit, for example, a Labrador who was not following proceedings exactly, but could stay on task with encouragement, 'like the X-Men.'

Basher walked in and displayed no visible surprise at Tristan's appearance, although Claire noticed a fractional pause in his stride towards the kitchen.

'Good afternoon, Tris,' he said mildly. 'To what do we owe the pleasure? Can I get you a cup of tea? Coffee?'

'Mate, I can answer *both* of those questions by taking you down the pub. It's been so long since we had a proper sesh, you know?'

'On a Tuesday? Just like that? Why?'

Tris appeared to fumble when called upon to improvise. Claire had some sympathy. 'Why not?' he said eventually.

'Because I am nearly thirty and if I get tanked on a Tuesday I had better not have any other plans until Friday?'

'Speak for yourself,' said Alex. 'I'll come out with you, Uncle T. Life is short.'

'Yeah, exactly!' said Tris, grasping with visible relief at this lifesaver. 'I've been thinking about, er, life. Because of Nana. *Carpe diem* and all that.'

'Interesting,' said Basher, calling through from the kitchen. 'And it's only you, is it?'

'Like, who else would it be? Figgy is staying with the 'rents, by the way. Bit of a state still.'

Claire absorbed this information and silently looked over at Sophie, who shrugged. 'I mean, did any of us really think Figgy had the mental fortitude to do and/or cover up a murder?'

And when she thought about it, no, Claire really couldn't believe that Figgy was involved. She was too surface-level. And, she realized, watching Tristan's fore-head wrinkle in time with every thought that formed behind it, so was Tristan, but this pub sesh might provide an opportunity to get more information. She could play good cop, and lull Tristan into a false sense of security by slamming a Jägerbomb with him.

Basher re-entered from the kitchen carefully eating a Custard Cream, one corner at a time, and stared at his brother. Then he tossed one at Tristan, who caught it and grinned. It seemed to be some kind of obscure, silent peace ritual, because then Basher said, 'Yes, all right then. Coming, Claire?'

'Er, yeah, okay. Bit early to get started, though, isn't it?'

'It's the sesh, mate! The *sesh*,' said Tristan, awkwardly punching her on the shoulder. 'Afternoon pre-game, yah?'

They all put on jackets and jumpers, which they would regret putting on once they got hot on the walk, and headed out.

'Most perverted way to eat a Custard Cream I have ever seen,' said Sophie, watching the back of Basher's head. He was talking to Tristan. 'Bet he's into some weird sex stuff. One hundred per cent freak.'

'Like you'd know!' muttered Claire, blushing, as Basher dropped back to talk to her, letting Alex and Tristan lead the way.

'I, er, think I might know why Tristan is here,' he said. He looked a bit sheepish. 'He told me Monty says hello, and to remember to tidy my room. Which is Monty having a dig. You remember the big flipchart that Alex put up in my room?'

'The one with a heading saying "Potential Victims" on it? And a list of their names?'

'That's the one. The thing is that I *didn't* remember it...'

Sophie groaned. 'Oh *no-o-o*, that house of chicken-fucker psychos found a giant flashing neon sign saying, "You are suspected of doing a bad murder."'

'That's not great, is it?' said Claire.

'No. And it is also not good that Tris has been sent here.'

'I dunno, I think we're lucky that your mum doesn't have a strong hand of cards to play,' said Claire, watching as Tristan almost walked into a lamp post because he was looking at one of his phones, and being pulled out of the way by Alex at the last moment.

'True,' replied Basher, half smiling, 'but that's not what I meant. If nothing happened, the list would just have confused Mum and Dad. But it seems it didn't. Tristan's appearance smacks of guilt. So I am not thrilled at this turn of events, you see.'

Claire saw. 'I'm sure it'll be all right, one way or another,' she said after a pause. 'Things usually are, aren't they?'

'"Everything's for the best, in the best of all possible worlds",' Basher said and smiled at her very nicely. Sophie cleared her throat sarcastically, and Claire's tummy swooped. She tried to ignore both.

They arrived at a pub that was covered with shiny green ceramic tiles on the outside, which gave Claire the impression that it was either upside down or inside out. The interior was full of hanging plants in copper bowls and exposed light bulbs, and very few people. There was a pause as Alex tried, unsuccessfully, to get Tris to open a tab on his company credit card. They almost managed it, but ultimately Tristan's abiding fear of Monty's wrath outweighed his desire to be liked – although he got the first round in, as a compromise. At Alex's urging, this included two bottles of wine and a tray of sticky layered shots, as well as Tristan's pint and a fizzing whiskey ginger for Basher. He drew circles on the sweating glass with his finger, while Claire surveyed the shots with rising alarm.

'Seems a lot for this early on a Tuesday...'

'Well, if you're going to do something wrong, do it right,' said Alex, cheerful and unrepentant.

'Oh, to be young again,' murmured Basher.

Sophie cupped her chin in her hand and sighed. 'I hate it when you get hammered. You have no idea how boring drunk people are, when you're sober. You all just yell and repeat yourselves and fall over.'

Tristan raised his glass and gave a 'Chin-chin!', so Claire gave a half-shrug and took a gulp of wine. What seemed like a very short time later, she noticed that she was feeling much more relaxed, and the entire glass of wine was empty. The outing suddenly didn't seem like such a bad idea.

When it became clear that Tristan wasn't going to *immediately* admit that he or members of his family had killed someone, Sophie got bored and fidgety. She started wandering around the bar and eavesdropping on the staff and the scant few other customers. Alex had obviously been thinking along the same lines as Claire, because they were palming most of the shots off on Tristan. He was getting louder, and his pale cheeks bloomed with two little ruddy-pink patches – the ghost of Hugh yet to come. As he mixed more sticky, brightly coloured drinks with cold fizzing lager, it was as if Tristan, too, began to effervesce. He talked a lot about lads from the office who all had nicknames that were their last names suffixed with -y or -ers or -o (as in: Smithy, Campers and Gibbo), and then, gradually, began to complain about the workload and about how strict Monty was.

The problem, Claire thought, as she noticed that her brain and her body were about a second out of sync – her thoughts a toddler wearing those elasticated reins, and her skull the lumpen parent holding it back – was that the rest of them weren't drinking *no* drinks at the same time as they were funnelling them into Tristan.

'Hey,' she said suddenly, 'hey, who's going to be the... you know – designated driver?'

Tristan frowned. 'We're not driving anywhere,' he said, quite reasonably.

'Yeah, but I mean, like, who's *in charge*,' said Claire, trying to look significantly at Alex, who was developing a definite list to one side.

'It's fine, C, I am totally in control. One. Hundred. Percentiles,' they said, angled at about one o'clock.

Claire looked to her left. Basher was smiling a lot and had bought a sharing packet of Doritos from behind the bar.

'I remember them. Remember you eating them, I mean. At a party at our uni,' she said.

'What uni? Oh, Figgy's? Yes, I visited,' Basher replied. He squinted at her. 'Your hair was different.'

Claire said, 'So was yours' and that made Basher laugh again. She was okay with that.

Alex went and ordered more drinks. Claire realized *she* was going to have to be the adult, which didn't seem like a recipe for success. But she was still sober enough to realize that, which meant it was probably fine, right? In fact she was pretty sure she was sober enough that she could safely have another drink. She continued thinking this for some time, until suddenly she noticed it was dark and she was in the queue for a karaoke bar near the seafront.

Basher was next to her. He kept singing the first lines of the chorus of 'Sweet Caroline' at an enthusiastic volume.

'Sweeeet Caroline!'

Claire blinked slowly. She was supposed to do something here. 'WHOA-OH-*OOOHHH!*' she offered.

Basher threw a delighted arm over her shoulder. 'Not so bad. Not so bad at all, hmm?' he said.

Claire, against all probability, giggled.

'You're wrecked,' said Sophie.

'M'not,' said Claire, before remembering she wasn't supposed to talk to Soph out loud. There were people around who weren't in the know. Claire tried to tap her nose and missed. She focused on Tristan, who was standing nearby. He was smoking with deep concentration, his eyes almost closed. He was wobbling slightly. This reminded Claire of the purple dildo and made her laugh a lot.

'We should. We should get you a purple suit, Tristan. Hey, Tristan. Hey, Tris! You should get a purple suit.'

Tristan smiled happily at her. He was all right, Tristan. Just stupid. But lots of people were stupid. Like the man said – the seven-words-on-TV man. Think of how stupid the average person is. He had a good point. You can't put people in prison for being stupid. The prisons aren't big enough.

Alex staggered back over.

'Here,' they slurred. 'Couple of my mates are' – they paused to stifle a burp – 'my mates are in a room. C'mon.'

'I thought you didn't have many mates,' said Claire.

Alex stopped and stared at her imperiously, if without focus, for a few seconds. 'I have at least two,' they said eventually and led them all inside.

'Wow. Drunk Alex is a... is a... is an *arsehole*,' said Claire. Basher heard this and laughed, and half picked Claire up in a squeeze. 'Drunk Basher is a hugger,' she added.

'Yes! Yes, yes, I'm a hugger. Big hugs,' he replied, turning to hug his brother as well.

'George Carlin!' Claire suddenly yelled triumphantly.

'Wh... what?'

'S'nothing. Never mind.'

They trooped into a dark, hot, upholstered box with a screen at one end and a bench running around three of the walls, while Sophie muttered expletives and *ohmigods* under her breath. The chill of her presence did immediately make the karaoke booth a less oppressive place. There were vague humanoid shapes already taking up most of the space in it, two of which hugged Alex and nearly fell over. Everyone else was singing 'Come On Eileen'. Someone tried to introduce themselves, but Claire only heard *WOMP-WOMP-WOMP-WOMP*. She started singing instead and was immediately enveloped into the group. She couldn't see any of the others. Except sometimes someone with blue hair or grey eyes would scream lyrics happily in her face. Sophie alternated between standing next to Alex and singing, if it was a song she liked, and sitting in the corner and sulking. All the beer was in plastic bottles and got hot too quickly. It tasted awful. After 'Don't Stop Me Now' was over, Claire went outside to be sick. It was the most fun she'd ever had in her life.

She was sick behind a car over the road. She was pleased to see it was an Audi. Ha-ha. Take that! She leaned back to look up at the sky and nearly fell over a bin, so she sat down on the kerb. It was cold. Her breath caught in her throat. But it was nice cold.

'I'm the king of the world,' she yelled at nobody in particular, still looking upwards. 'I'm never going to die!'

Claire saw that a bouncer outside the bar was looking at her with quiet amusement. He offered a light to a man who stumbled outside, and Claire realized the man was Tristan. She waved at him and he came over. He, too, sat down very heavily on the kerb. They looked at each other muzzily.

'So what—'

'Did you—'

Claire realized they were both making a last-ditch attempt to intro... interior... in terror... interrogate each other. She laughed.

'S'okay, Tris,' she said, graciously. 'You go first.'

Tristan opened his mouth, then paused, and looked confused again. 'Oh. I forgot.' He giggled to himself. 'Oh my *God,* that is *so* un*fair*! Never mind, old chap, never mind. Dad'll sort it.'

'Hey, Tristan,' Claire said, as he started to slump against her side. 'Tristan, what happened that night?'

'What night?'

'*You* know. That night last year. The party.'

'Oh yah. We're s'posed to talk about that. Well, I'm not, but you are.' His expression suddenly crumpled and he looked forlorn. 'Terrible. Horrible business. Wish I hadn't been there.' He sniffed like he was about to cry and turned into her shoulder.

'Hey. S'okay, man,' she said. 'S'not your fault.'

Tristan sat up and rubbed his nose, making a very snotty noise. 'That's right. That's right. I just do what I'm told, don't I?'

Claire felt her head going a bit dizzy. She shook herself and noticed that Sophie had wandered out, probably looking for her, and was walking over to listen. Claire pulled herself together as much as was possible and tried again.

'What happened to your... your suit?'

'Purple one?'

'No, you... do you have a purple one? No, the muddy one.'

'Mate. Can't blame me for falling over. It was all rainy and slippery.'

'Why were you outside if it was so wet?'

'Mum was livid – she said it'd never get properly clean. Can't blame a man. If someone shoves him, you know?'

'Aaah-*HA!*' Claire shouted, pointing a finger at him. 'Gotchu there. Who shoved? You said before that you fell, but you just said you got shoved. Caught you!'

'No one shoved me.'

'But you *said.*'

'Well, what's the difference anyhow?' he said defensively.

'Pretty big difference actually,' said Claire. She noted that Sophie was watching with a similar expression to the bouncer. Detached, but amused.

'You're pretty,' said Tristan out of nowhere. He lunged at her with amorous intent. Claire went, 'Eugh, fuck off' and put a hand across his entire face to push him away. He flopped happily onto the pavement.

'See,' said Claire, looking at Sophie and pointing at the prone Tristan. 'That was a—' She stopped, leaned to the other side and was sick again. '*That* was a shove.'

12

Working from Home

Basher's prediction was correct, in that when they all woke up on Wednesday morning, he and Claire were monstrously hungover. Tristan, who had slept in Basher's room, had gone to the train station before Claire had even approached consciousness, and she couldn't imagine what that journey would feel like. Alex confidently declared that they were minutes from death, was very noisily sick in the bathroom and then was absolutely fine to do their shift at the library. Then Basher also went out, because he had a lunchtime shift at a pub.

'I'm going to walk along the beach first,' he said, as he was going. 'With any luck I shall be found frozen to death on the waterline before I am called upon to do anything.'

Claire asked if he wouldn't prefer to cancel his shift, but Basher said he preferred to be doing something, so that he couldn't dwell on... anything, including the most immediate feeling that his frontal lobe was gently dissolving – and could Claire please not go into his room while he was gone, thank you; there's a spare key in the kitchen drawer with all the batteries in it. It was only after everyone else had left that the paracetamol started to kick in and Claire, staring balefully at herself in the mirror as she brushed her teeth, remembered that she had uncovered some important new Clues regarding The Case the night before.

Sophie didn't mind when they were left alone in someone else's house. She was always able to behave, within the specific limitations of her condition, exactly as she wanted. And did. She wasn't used to a flat with such huge windows and when Claire went into the front room, Sophie was sitting cross-legged on the coffee table in beams of sunshine, looking curiously at her own self becoming see-through. It made her look a bit like a faded photocopy of herself. Like the missing posters of her that had gone up on lamp posts and telephone poles around town.

Claire, on the other hand, did not like being left alone in other people's houses; no matter how much the occupant would impress upon her that she really could make herself at home, she always felt like this was not really the case.

Say if she got hungry and she decided to make a sandwich: she couldn't shake the feeling that someone would leap out from behind a corner and have a go at her, for using too much butter. If you are somewhere you can't make yourself lunch without being concerned the entire time that you might be using the Special Ham – and that later there would be an awkward conversation, where Basher asked where his ham was, and then said it was totally fine that she'd eaten the ham, but several times and with a *tone* – then you aren't anywhere that is home to you.

But what made it more obviously a lie was that in her own home Claire could sit around in her pants or without a bra on, gnawing on a hunk of cheese like an animal, because there were too many steps involved in making an actual meal (and also cheese is nice). Clearly this sort of thing is not allowed in someone else's house. For this reason, Claire did make a sandwich, because she was hungry, but almost immediately retrieved the spare key and told Sophie they were going out.

Sophie shrugged. 'Where to?'

'The aquarium,' said Claire decisively, naming one of about three places in Brighton that she could remember how to get to.

They walked down to the sea and along the front, past the remains of another pier that had burned down decades before and were now barely keeping together out at sea – a collection of ribs sticking out of the water. The beach was home to a small but not statistically insignificant collection of ghosts, mostly sad people in swimming suits from different decades, or sailory types in woolly jumpers. These lads strolled around in twos or threes, discussing whether or not it looked like a storm was coming in.

When Claire and Sophie arrived at the aquarium, however, Claire ran into a problem that hadn't presented itself when she went there with Basher, which was that it cost £30 to get in. She hovered in the entrance nervously, trying not to catch the eye of the woman behind the till, and was about to turn round and go home when she distinctly heard someone go, 'Pssst!'

'Er...' She looked around.

'Pssst!'

'Oh! It's the water-boy from the other day,' said Soph. 'Look, he's hiding round the corner. For some reason.'

Claire looked. Sophie was right; the teenage jellyfish enthusiast was peering round the wall that led to the aquarium proper, on the other side of the ticket barrier.

'Pretend to be looking in your bag for your pass,' he hissed, once he saw that he had Claire's attention. 'Then get a card out. Any card – doesn't matter.'

She did as she was told, feeling a bit stupid. She even said, 'Ah, there it is!' as she got out an old train ticket, in case the living employee was bothered.

The water-boy dropped to the ground and commando-crawled to the ticket barriers. He got into a crouch and beckoned Claire over. 'Pretend to swipe it,' he said in a stage whisper. As Claire did so, the boy stuck his hand into the guts of the machine and the light on it blinked green. She pushed through the gate.

'Thank you,' she said.

'Anything for a lady,' he replied. He puffed up his chest a bit. 'I'm not supposed to, but my manager told me we can use discretion to bring in special guests sometimes.'

'Yeah, thanks,' said Soph, looking at him out of the corner of her eye. 'What was all that spy stuff about, though? You know they can't see you?'

He deflated a little. 'I suppose some habits... well – you know.'

They walked on. After a bit the boy jogged to catch up.

'My name's Elton,' he said. Claire was incredulous, but Elton was obviously used to this. 'My mum was a big fan of his,' he explained.

'Didn't ask,' said Sophie. She sniffed.

Elton grinned. He was evidently a man who wasn't going to let a rare opportunity pass by when it turned up dead in front of him. Claire noticed that, if you looked closely, the polo shirt he was wearing wasn't the same shade of blue as the ones the living aquarium employees had on. Elton himself was tall but a bit gangly with it, wore his hair in boy-band curtains and had unfortunately brought a couple of spots on his chin into the afterlife.

Claire went to the depressed octopus's tank and looked in at the sad eye in the pipe, but kept one ear on the conversation happening next to her.

'I died in a car crash in 1992 when I was eighteen,' Elton explained. 'But I'm, like, fully over it now. I was going to be a marine biologist and now I'm continuing my studies on a – you know – ad hoc basis. What about you?'

'None of your beeswax,' said Soph. 'But I was seventeen, in case you wanted to know.'

This part-schoolyard bickering, part-banter continued as they walked around the rest of the aquarium. Eventually they came to a dark room, where a motion-sensitive camera demonstrated luminescence in sea algae by lighting up a section of floor when you walked across it. There were wave sounds playing over a speaker.

'Here, look,' said Elton. He grabbed Sophie's hand and pulled her along under the camera, and after a delay of a few seconds the lights worked, blooming under their feet. 'Cool, huh? Some things can tell we're still here. Sort of.'

A couple of tourists who'd been trying the lights out nearby decided that it must be broken and walked away.

'My name's Sophie,' said Sophie. She kept looking down at her feet. They were bathed in pale blue lights.

'Nice to meet you, Sophie,' said Elton. 'We could, you know, meet up at the café sometime next week? If you wanted?'

Sophie abruptly dropped his hand. She seemed to be speechless for a moment. This eventuality had not occurred to her.

'I don't think I'll be here then,' she managed. 'C'mon, let's get out of here, Claire. We should get back.'

They tramped back up the hill and into the flat, Sophie resolutely refusing to talk about Elton the entire time.

By the time they arrived it was after four, and Basher and Alex were both home.

Alex said they had spoken to Tristan and he claimed not to remember anything from the night before, which reminded Claire that she did recall some things – and that Sophie could fill in the bits she didn't. So she recounted what Tristan had said about being shoved.

'Yes, I've been thinking,' said Alex, after seeing off a pint of Berocca, 'about the murder.' They were lying in their habitual position: full-length on the floor, neck crooked up against the sofa, legs at weird angles. 'I have some new ideas. Like, we can send a DM to Kevin. I already called Dad's firm, so we can also go up there and look for clues about Michael – that needs to happen. And I know Mattie isn't answering her phone, but didn't you say you were at school with her kid, Uncle B?'

'Mmm,' said Bash, who was slumped on the other end of the sofa with a tea towel on his face. 'So? Ugh. Oh God, I feel dreadful. Weep for Adonais – he is dead!'

'So, look him up on Facebook! I bet you're friends on there, so you can check that nobody you went to school with is much more happy and successful than you are. That's what Facebook is for, right? At what point do we not simply admit that most police work could be done via webcam?'

Basher waved them away and said he would message the man now.

'*I* was thinking,' said Soph, warming to the theme, 'of what we were saying about the body the other day – how it must be at The Cloisters somewhere. Well, *where*? It's not in the library.'

Claire was frankly disgusted that Alex was able to move, let alone think, and resented the fact that Soph was acting as an accomplice, but she still emptied out her Case Notes and started arranging them in some sort of order.

The body couldn't be in the house, she reasoned, or at least was unlikely to be, because there had been a whole year's worth of corporate retreats and weddings kicking about there. Someone would have noticed the smell, so inside the house wasn't a safe place. Unless they'd misjudged everything and they were actually in a horror movie situation, and Hugh and Clem were running a meat farm so that the rich could eat pies made of people instead of chicken, the body was probably somewhere in the grounds. The trouble was that a large expanse of the place was a lawn, and you can only blame moles for so much.

'Well, look, Tristan definitely knows something,' said Claire. 'He said he was pushed over, right? And the Clef told us that they saw the brothers "propping each other up" after a fight. What if they saw some combination of lads carrying a body into the house? Then they stashed it in the library until you two and Sami were out of the way. Then, according to our timeline, they only had an afternoon to put the vic in its final resting place before a bunch of Hooray Henries turn up for business-approved bonding during the week, right?'

'That's pretty good,' said Alex. 'So the vic must have been Michael or Kevin, right? The Clef said they were propping up another man.'

'*Unless* they dressed Mattie in Tristan's suit in the garden as a disguise, and that's how it got all muddy,' said Claire. 'You know, rolling the body around, trying to stuff the arms in and all that.'

'You *just* said Tristan let slip that he was pushed,' said Sophie. 'So that has to be the way his suit got muddy. Someone pushed Tristan over.'

'Oh yeah. Wow, this is a tough one, isn't it? I wish we'd had a proper look round before we left,' Claire added, with the air of a seasoned investigator. 'For signs of, er... turned earth. Or things like that.'

'Ah yes, things of that nature. May I remind you that you were very eager to leave, to avoid running into my small, inoffensive mother?' said Basher. He rolled his eyes, but with a smile – like you do with friends.

'I didn't look round the grounds, either. Grass is boring,' said Soph.

Alex googled things like 'How to get blueprints, UK' until they declared that someone should call the local council for Wilbourne Major. Basher was the last to touch his nose.

The lady at the council told Basher that they didn't have anything, because the house was well old and hadn't had any planning permission applications for donkeys', but he should try giving Liz and Joe from the Wilbourne Historical Society a call, because they had all sorts of stuff.

Joe from WHS (Liz was at home, on account of her feet) was very accommodating; he was pleased that anyone was as interested in any bit of Wilbourne's history as he was in all of it. In fact, he said, he *did* have some blueprints for The Cloisters, but they were really very old and might not be much use – but he was happy to send some scans over.

Joe's scans took a while to turn up in Alex's email, because they turned out to be photos he'd taken on a digital camera – most likely whilst standing over the table on a chair, though he had included thoughtful close-ups of some sections. Claire got a bit of a lump in her throat and hoped that Joe had children and grandchildren who appreciated him. The blueprints seemed to be genuine antiques, which Joe almost definitely shouldn't have had, and had probably acquired without asking. They were on thin yellowing paper, looked like they were hand-drawn and showed the house from before the wing existed that the family lived in, so it was a big box with the servants' rooms all in the attic. The grounds were more extensive than Claire had thought.

'Used to have a stable, look,' said Sophie, pointing.

'Cor, that'd be a fucking great place to hide a body,' cooed Claire. 'No horses any more, so nobody goes there – out of view. Classic body stash, right there.'

'Except it doesn't exist in this century,' said Basher.

'A minor detail. Which bits do still exist? Here, look, that must be the ha-ha.'

A curving line bisected the blank expanse of paper that was the lawn. Then there was more lawn, and an area marked as a copse – a lazy kind of kite shape that had some small, inky cloud forms within it. Those, Claire supposed, were the trees she'd seen off in the distance. But tucked behind the top wedge of the copse was a little void of lawn, with a huddle of three buildings in it.

'What does that say? Rains? Ruins?' asked Soph, squinting with her nose almost touching the screen.

'Ruins... Oh!' Claire exclaimed. 'They must be bits of the monastery. Now *that* is a good place for a shallow grave. Away from the house, shielded by the trees there – must be why we didn't see it from the lawn? I bet you that's where the body is.'

'Very ITV teatime,' agreed Soph. 'If the body actually turns out to be there, you'll spaff your pants.'

'C makes a convincing case, Uncle B,' said Alex. 'We should have a look when we're back for the funeral.'

'I'm looking forward to how awkward that's going to be for you, by the way,' said Basher, grinning at Claire. 'I want you to know that.'

'Yeah, yeah, fuck off,' she replied, although quite amicably, and ignoring the faint crackling of an animal impulse somewhere at the back of her brain.

'You should bring the dildo, too, definitely,' said Soph, giggling.

'Wh – oh!' When she'd emptied her bag of her Case Notes, Claire had also displaced the purple dildo. She was surprised to discover that she had been squashing it in her hand like one of those grip-strengthener things.

'You've been doing that the whole time,' said Alex. 'I didn't like to say anything.'

'LOL,' said Soph. 'It's probably the coolest thing you've ever done in your life, you little perv.'

Claire put on *Murder Profile*, which she thought would provide a helpful ambience. She was trying to convince Alex and Basher of its quality, but she was afraid that watching it with them was ruining it for her. Basher pointed out all the practical and legal flaws, and Alex got extremely cross about copaganda. Like, Claire knew they weren't wrong, but that was misunderstanding the appeal of *Murder Profile*. When stern but sexy team leader Smitty responded to a suspect asking for a lawyer by shouting, 'You don't want a lawyer, you want to still be alive in half an hour', was that a violation of rights? Yes. Did it make it harder to see Smitty and the team as the good guys? Also yes. But did it get results? No, because that wasn't actually the murderer, it was a red herring. After a while Claire muted the TV with some savagery and complained that they just didn't get it, but Alex unmuted it and started recording bits of it on their phone, so they could make fun of it in social media posts later.

Basher leaned back, closed his eyes and pinched the bridge of his nose. Claire noticed that he had shaved off all his peach-fuzz beard, which made her a bit sad. She looked at the corners of his lips. His mouth seemed very grave, but the corner looked like he was always close to smiling, or at least smirking a little.

She wondered about him, this quietly sad man who memorized Shakespeare and random facts about fifties comic strips. Who clearly cherished calm and solitude, but had taken in a loud, chaotic teenager who seemed almost his opposite.

'It's like he tries to fade into the background, isn't it?' said Soph, who was watching Claire watching Basher. His hoodie today was the same colour as a sun-faded Royal Mail van. It would have been called Pale Brick or

Dead Salmon on a paint colour chart. 'I wonder if he was always like that, or if he used to be like Alex. Ohmigod, maybe he used to go to all-night ragers and, like, shopped at Cyberdog.'

'How are you?' Claire asked him, on impulse.

'Yeah, have you spoken to your parents or anything?' said Sophie.

'No, not yet. There was a passive-aggressive text from Mum after we left without saying a proper goodbye, though,' said Basher, still keeping his eyes closed. 'And I'm as okay as I ever was. Did Mum or Dad or Figgy or anyone pay you yet, by the way?'

Claire was surprised he'd thought of it. 'No, actually. I wasn't planning to bring it up for a while. For obvious reasons.'

Basher flapped a hand and opened one eye long enough to send a text. 'You have friends in high places now. There. Got on to the patriarchal unit. He'll sort it out soon enough, I expect.'

'Thank you.'

'He's changing the subject. Like, this guy does not want to talk about himself or his feelings *at all*.' Soph leaned forward to wave a cold hand over Basher's face and he shivered. 'How are you really?' she persisted. 'Like, it has been a time of change. And great stress. I know how you're feeling.'

Claire snorted at this, even as she relayed it. In her view, Soph hadn't experienced any change since 2007. Although, in fairness, the change in '07 had been significant.

'I'm fine, really. Mum and Dad are organizing the funeral stuff. It's all fine.'

Claire looked at Soph, who shrugged. Claire thought back to when she met Basher at the house and had mentally compared him to a pigeon. She dug around in her rucksack and retrieved the sharing bag of Starburst that she'd bought at the garage after their flight from The Cloisters. There was still a handful of sweets in it. She nudged Basher and shook the bag in an encouraging way, then stayed very still.

He took one. Excellent.

'How are you feeling about The Case?' she asked.

He shrugged, almost the mirror of Sophie. 'Fine,' he said again. 'I'm still mostly expecting that we'll prove everyone is alive, and nobody is dead.' He looked down and started rubbing the inside of his left palm with his right thumb. 'I hope all that happens is that my dad has to pay a very big tax penalty.' He stopped and looked at Claire, and smiled. 'But in the meantime this has been... I hesitate to say fun exactly, but... not unenjoyable. You are very odd, but I think you know that.'

'Thank you. I, er, like you, too.'

She exchanged a glance with Sophie that communicated the truth they both knew: that therein lay the problem. It had already been days since they'd started hanging out with Basher and Alex, so there wasn't much time left to run out on the clock before something went wrong and they got kicked out. No matter if it was to a gangly fish-worrier or to Alex, Sophie couldn't get too attached because she already knew she wouldn't be staying in Brighton much longer. Quite apart from the sword of Essex hanging over their heads, sending one of Basher and Alex's family down for murder probably wasn't a stable basis for friendship.

Basher's deep, quiet voice broke into her thoughts. 'Huh. Mattie's son David has replied to me,' he said. He sounded genuinely intrigued, as if he hadn't expected anything to come of sending the message at all. 'David said he doesn't want to talk about it and that "you lot have done enough". That's... pointed.'

'Whoa,' said Alex. They sat up. 'That's pretty major, Uncle B. He doesn't say she's alive.'

'He has not said she was mysteriously killed or otherwise spirited into the night, either,' said Basher. 'It is normal to not state the dead-versus-alive status of your parent in small talk.'

'Ask if she's alive, though,' prompted Alex.

'I categorically will *not* do that.'

'It could be just because your family are mostly not very nice and fired Mattie, and accused her of having an affair with your dad,' said Sophie. Basher agreed that this was a solid point and he was pleased to see that someone else was finally thinking sensibly.

'Well, we did maybe dismiss Mattie too quickly before,' said Claire. 'I think we should look into her more.'

'We spoke to her husband. He seemed... sad. Embarrassed,' said Claire. 'Not a killer.'

'Well, as long as he didn't *seem* like a killer, there you are then,' said Basher.

'Yeah, but that guy was definitely hiding something. Maybe they had an argument when he was picking her up or dropping her off at work,' said Sophie, 'and he snapped and hid her body on the property, in a panic.'

'Ooh, okay,' said Alex, getting involved. 'Like, he discovered... she really was having an affair with Grandad!'

'*Sordid* affair.'

'Much as I would like this to be true, for reasons of not being related to a killer, and much as the stats *are* on your side, and much as I appreciate the enthusiasm,' said Basher, in the moderating tone that Claire had come to recognize as the one he used whenever he was about to throw a girder in front of a train of thought, 'we have raised and discounted this idea a ludicrous number of times by this point. And, according to our timeline, Alf would have had to drop Mattie off at work on Saturday morning, give Alex a lift back to the pub and then come back later on in the day, to kill his wife and remove or her hide her body – all without any one of us seeing him there at any time. I think you're going to have to work up some other theories.'

'I am an ideas woman, Basher,' said Claire.

'Yes, I have noticed,' replied Bash, smiling. 'Sadly, to bring a case home we tend to need things like logic and observable facts and rational conclusions, as well.'

'Oh, Claire! What was that business card we found in the office? Remember? What if that was Mattie selling out to Du Lotte?'

Claire had no earthly idea what Soph was talking about. There were several busy minutes while she relayed

249

Sophie's explanation and then, remembering finding the hotel chain business card in the filing cabinet, she exclaimed, 'Oh!' to herself and started talking over Sophie. Which, to outside observers, was just a woman arguing with herself. In any case, after Alex and Basher had untangled the information, it turned out that Basher couldn't remember where he'd put the card, and that neither of them could remember what the Du Lotte Hotels employee was called, so then they had to endure the agony of navigating a corporate website. But eventually they located Mary Tyler and her phone number.

Claire rang it immediately, which made Basher a bit cross. When Mary Tyler answered, she and Alex and Sophie shrieked like naughty kids making prank calls at a sleepover, and Claire threw the phone at Basher.

'Hello? Hello? Is everything all right?' came the confused voice over the speakerphone.

'Hum. Yes, hello. This is Basher – Sebastian Wellington-Forge. I understand you had an arrangement with Mattie Briggs regarding The Cloisters, my family's home?'

'That depends,' said Mary. Her voice suddenly took on the delicate tones of one who was handling a wild animal and wanted to avoid the teeth. 'Would you like to... come to a similar arrangement?'

Alex, Claire and Sophie were all staring at the phone with eyes like saucers. Somehow, inexplicably, a real clue was happening.

'That depends,' said Basher, matching Mary's tone, 'on the terms of the arrangement.'

Mary sighed very heavily. 'Look, this has been dragging on for fucking ages and, frankly, I'm not sure if that
old pile is even worth it, so I'll stop the cloak-and-dagger
shit and cut to it. The arrangement was: Mattie told us
about tyres to kick that brought down the value of the
house, and hence the offer we made. Secret dry rot in
the attic, and so on. And in exchange we... showed our
appreciation. To a modest extent. But she ran out of useful
info before she dropped off the map last year, so I don't
know if there's any more you can do for me.'

'Sorry, just a second. So Mattie wasn't trying to force
a sale?' asked Basher. 'She didn't get any extra for a sale
going through?'

'Of course not. And there's no way she could force a
sale anyway. Her name isn't on any of the paperwork. But
after talking to Mattie we were able to make an offer that
was still attractive to your grandmother, but was equally
attractive to our bottom line.'

'And you paid her for this?'

'Now I didn't say that. Call it a cash gift. And not
even very much, by the way. I gather Mattie was saving
up for something, though. Not that it matters to me now
anyway.'

'What do you mean?'

'Well, as I'm sure you know, we were very close to
making a deal with your grandmother, but we were
recently informed that the estate has now passed to... ah
yes, here we are. Clementine, daughter of the deceased.
My condolences, by the way. But Clementine has let us

know, in no uncertain terms, that a sale will no longer be considered. Under any circumstances. I'm surprised you don't know this already.'

'I am clearly a bit out of the loop,' said Basher.

'I'll say.'

'But, sorry, to circle back – you've not heard from Mattie again?'

'No. She stopped calling around this time last year. I remember because the same awful pumpkin decorations were up in the office. But look, I'm a very busy woman, Sebastian, and I don't want to keep dicking around with this, so how about you call me if your family actually wants to talk, hmm?' Mary Tyler hung up abruptly. Claire imagined her crossing her Louboutins on top of her desk and smoking from a sexy cigarette-holder.

'Wow! I've got to say, I'm fuckin' on Team Mattie for our victim now,' said Sophie. 'Affair with Hugh or not, I bet if Clementine found out that Mattie was passing info to Du Lotte, she'd lose it. I'm saying it was Mrs Wellington-Forge, in the office, with the chicken knife.'

'*Please* stop saying things like that. Let's not jump to any conclusions. I know we have a lot of circumstantial evidence now, but...' said Basher. He was starting to look seriously worried. 'I'll... Look, if I don't hear back from Sami soon, I'll message David, Mattie's son, again, all right? Does that satisfy everyone?'

'Don't worry, Uncle B, we have another potential victim still,' said Alex. They were sorting through Claire's disorganized Case File. The notes had probably made sense to her when she'd written them. 'Look at this obviously crucial theory C worked up. I have a feeling it'll crack The Case wide open.' Alex held up a scrap of paper that said 'K + M TRAFFICKING'.

'Oh, she wrote *that* one after waking herself up in the middle of the night with a really loud snore,' said Soph.

'I don't snore. Did I say what it meant?' asked Claire.

'You said, "Cocaine, Soph, loads of fucking cocaine, it makes sense!" and then fell back asleep,' said Sophie. 'Weirdo. I think your theory was that Michael found out that Monty and Kevin were smuggling loads of coke together, based on the fact that Kevin travels a lot, and Monty and Tris are clearly the type to take titanic amounts of cocaine.'

'Heroic quantities,' agreed Alex. 'Kevin posted another photo on Insta this morning, by the way. "Few cheeky shots in the local bar! #blessed #nomeasures #EyeballPaul". I am glad he is living his best life. Oops, better take this...' Their phone started ringing, so they retreated to their room.

Basher was still leafing through Claire's notes, squinting at her handwriting.

'I still think it would be more helpful if we could, like, interview some of your family,' Claire said. She poked Basher's shoulder to get his attention. 'Even Figgy.'

'Still no,' said Basher, without looking up. 'I am only just about not cross with you for last night. It's lucky Tris won't have the faintest idea what happened. Your notes really are atrocious. You have not properly organized any of your ideas. Have you even considered motives?'

'Yes,' said Claire. She was defensive about her detective work, but also thought it was unfair to blame her for last night when Basher, too, had drunk enough to floor a rugby team. 'As we have already discussed, maybe Kevin was secretly a drug kingpin and murdered Michael, then ran to South America.'

'That is one way to flee a crime scene,' conceded Basher. 'But things are not usually that exotic in real life, I'm afraid.'

'There isn't anything else about Michael that you can remember?'

'Only the breakfast thing. "I'm serious about breakfast, Monty" – that's what he said; or something like that anyway. I wish I could remember. But he mostly kept himself to himself. Sensible man.'

'Like me, right?' said Sophie.

'Yes, of course. My compatriot in reason.'

The Entente Sensible was weakened by the reappearance of Alex, who looked positively incandescent with excitement. They clearly had something thrilling to say, but couldn't choose between saying it immediately and withholding it, for the drama.

'He's alive!' they exclaimed, sort of plumping for both at once.

'Who is?' asked Basher, trying to still sound disinterested.

'Michael!'

'How does your mum know Michael's alive?'

'That wasn't my mum, stupid. She's fine, by the way,

although it's been weirdly difficult to get hold of her. No, Helen told me.'

'Who the fuck is Helen?' asked Sophie.

'The office manager at Dad's firm. Remember I said I called Dad's office, about visiting? Helen called me back just now to arrange it – but *she let slip* that Michael was still on secondment there until a couple of weeks ago, when he left without any warning! And apparently he left a load of stuff behind. Let's go and look through it all.'

'*Ohmigod*, yes! Industrial espionage. Let's do it,' said Soph. The dead girl looked suddenly very lively and excitable.

'I… I guess I could try and get in touch with him? Michael's never met me, so he won't be suspicious,' said Claire. 'And there's all the stuff he left in the office, right?'

'All right, that is enough,' said Basher, abruptly standing up. 'I can allow Alex to suggest a lot of wild ideas, but as a notionally responsible uncle, I have to draw the line at things like actual crime. I may not be a police officer any more, but pawing through personal belongings, or any business files that you can find in a privately owned office, sounds suspiciously felonious to me. And if Michael is alive, there's no need to investigate his disappearance, is there? The plan is… the plan is that we wait for Sami to get back to me, before we do anything stupid. Right? Yes?'

He stalked into the kitchen and there were sounds of him rooting around in the fridge. Claire heard him say, 'I thought I had some ham in here…' before Basher turned on the roaring kettle.

He reappeared suddenly and pointed a butter knife at them, for emphasis, as he spoke. 'Do not – and I cannot stress this enough – get on a train to London, try to interview Michael or break into Monty's office. I am very serious about this.'

13

The Gang Gets on a Train to London

'Here,' said Alex, sliding a little plastic packet across the table. Claire picked it up. It had a blocky Bluetooth earpiece in it, of the kind beloved by middle-aged men driving Land Rovers around the M25.

'Thank you,' she said. She was confused, although she didn't say it. Like most normal people, Claire viewed phone calls the same way she viewed flavoured gin: with suspicion, and as a last resort only. The whole point of texting was not having to call people. Soph had liked calls, though, and she used to call Claire and immediately hang up, so Claire had to phone back and Sophie didn't use up any credit.

'I thought if you wore it, people would think you were on the phone with someone. Rather than talking to yourself. You know, with the "Sophie says" stuff all the time,'

Alex explained.

'Oh. That's... actually a very good idea.' Claire struggled to tear the vacuform prison open.

'Alex talks to me out loud,' said Sophie. 'They don't get embarrassed.'

Claire did not repeat this.

'You can pay me back whenever,' said Alex.

Claire chose to strategically ignore this. In fairness, Alex had been letting her bum cigarettes off them for days.

It was Friday. The three of them – Claire, Sophie and Alex – were seated on a mainline train that was still on the platform at Brighton, owing to a points failure. There were often points failures on the Brighton mainline, but today's were a special annoyance because the line had been out of use for almost all of September for essential maintenance, notably to the points.

Claire found that, while to start with she'd seen Alex as a raven or a crow, as time went on she was increasingly comparing Alex to sweets. They were in cream jeans and a pink blouse, so it looked as if an incredibly cool drumstick lolly was wedged in one corner, against the train window, in order to make full use of the socket. Sophie was next to them.

They were going to London for exactly the reasons Basher had told them they were not allowed to. More pressing for Claire was that this whole thing was originally meant to be a weekend job, over by Sunday. A surprise murder investigation had now dragged it out for five more days, so Claire was at the 'wearing a used pair of pants inside out' stage of travel discomfort. She had also been hauling around a massive Bible, bell and a candlestick wherever she went, which was quite inconvenient.

It had taken a day for the three of them to decide on their forbidden plan and then carry it out. Luckily, Basher would be at work for most of today, so it would take ages for him to realize they were gone. After all, as Alex had reasoned, they were both adults who could make their own decisions and were doing nothing wrong by going to London (which did not exactly chime with going in secret, but let's not think about that too closely).

Thursday, as the day before their daring heist, had accordingly been spent on fun. They'd passed the time walking to Hove and looking for new clothes for Claire, who had loved the outfits Alex picked out, but then felt self-conscious in them and had returned to the comfort of her faded jeans.

There had, however, been one anxiety-inducing incident when they went to the pier in the evening, with Sami and her husband and children. Sami had confirmed that no, there were no Missing Persons reports on anyone involved, but that was not the source of the anxiety. The weather had been blustery and clear, and the lights of the boardwalk reflected off the water. The sea air blew through Claire to her very core, carrying the smell of candy floss and hot, fresh doughnuts. Sophie ran back and forth after Sami's kids, watching them, and watching chips and waffles being fried. Halloween decorations were still up everywhere.

Claire had gone out for a cigarette, coughing into

the wind as it snatched the smoke away, while everyone else was in the arcade yelling at the 2p fall coin-pusher machines. Sami came out and stood next to her. She looked out across the waves and did not turn her head to look at Claire.

'I looked you up,' she said.

Claire's chest burned. She began to shiver as adrenaline suddenly coursed through her. She looked around, but Soph was nowhere to be seen. Claire said, 'Er...' and Sami didn't say anything for a long time.

'You know,' she replied suddenly. 'I get pretty sick of Basher's shit sometimes.'

'Er... what d'you mean?'

'Oh, you know. This constant fucking "Woe is me, misery, misery" shit, but at the same time as "Basher knows best". I would have thought it was pretty difficult to have an inferiority complex at the same time as a superiority complex, but then he is also an over-achiever... Did he tell you why he quit his job?'

'Uh, yeah. He said, like, he couldn't be part of the system any more and—'

'Thought so. See, that's what *I* said.' Sami didn't sound angry. She sounded very tired. '*I* wanted to quit, and *I* hated being part of that system, but apparently I said it often enough that he thought it was his idea. And I *can't* quit because I have two kids and a mortgage, and Brighton won't support as many private detectives or security consultants as it does drag brunches. Basher didn't even *ask* me if I wanted to leave, too. If his leaving

260

would affect my plans. Didn't even say he was going.' She leaned on the railing, the wind whipping her hair across her face. 'I won't tell Basher and Alex about you yet,' she said, after another long wait. 'But you should. I'll give you another day or so, but you need to say something.'

'Thank you,' said Claire. But she said it so quietly, as Sami walked away, that she thought it might have disappeared into the air, along with her fag smoke.

She hadn't told Sophie about the conversation. She wasn't sure why, except that Sophie was happy at the moment, and Claire knew, deep down, that she wasn't going to say anything to Basher and Alex anyway, because if you didn't think about something, it was sort of like it wasn't happening.

She sighed heavily now, remembering it all, and had a coughing fit. It sounded like she was hacking up both of her own lungs, and possibly someone else's as well. Alex reached over with their long, graceful arms to alternate rubbing her on the back with smacking her between her shoulder blades, like a parent attending to a toddler who'd tried to swallow an entire Twix in one go.

'God, are you still feeling rough from the other night, C? I thought Uncle B was exaggerating about how bad hangovers are, when you're ancient,' they observed. 'I suppose being a smoker doesn't help. Maybe I should quit. Maybe *you* should quit. And go home and get into bed.'

Claire considered this. She and Sophie lived in a poky flat above a twenty-four-hour newsagent, and whenever it rained (so approximately eight to ten months of every year) the roof started leaking near the foot of her bed. This meant the flat was also damp, but Sophie kept telling her that it was black mould and not damp, and that pretty soon they would *both* be dead, and Claire would be found frozen in bed like Jack Nicholson at the end of *The Shining*, half eaten by cats and/or rats.

'I am not sure,' she replied, when she got her breath back, 'if that would help.'

'Also,' said Sophie, with some indignation, 'I would get really fucking bored.'

Claire looked out of the window.

'When I was little,' she said, 'I used to sit in trains and cars looking out of the window and imagine we were keeping a few feet ahead of a catastrophe – like a tornado or a fucking, giant saw blade. And it was ripping everything up behind us, but we stayed just ahead of it.'

'Really?' said Alex. 'Me too. Huh. Cool.'

'You never told me that,' said Soph. 'You massive weirdo.' She sounded hurt.

'We don't have to tell each other everything, you know,' replied Claire.

It was only about an hour before Claire was looking down at the great grey sweep of the Thames and the Chelsea suspension bridge, which looked so pretty lit up at night. She was of the considered opinion – having never lived anywhere else – that London was the greatest city in the world. She contained multitudes. In the sunshine, she glowed. Even the grime and pigeon shit and piss-soaked alleys glowed. Today was another grey day spattered with rain and whipped by wind, and the whole town felt grey and glowering, like the city was hunched over herself. Waiting. Biding her time. Claire always thought of London as a she. Very Freudian, probably.

She led Alex through Victoria Station with the air of a tour guide at the National Gallery, with Soph mooching along behind with a slight smirk on her face, like a teenager who was bored by the tour guide at the National Gallery.

'Just follow me on the Tube; it's a bit overwhelming at first, but it's actually *reeeally* fucking simple – you only need to not let the crowds get to you. And have your ticket ready, because otherwise everyone will tut at you at the barriers—'

She stopped when she realized that Alex was looking at her strangely.

'Yeah... You realize I grew up here, right, C? Like, I am from London?'

'Er...'

Sophie started laughing. 'Yikes. Felt that one!'

Monty and Tristan's office was near St Paul's, and Soph was a bit sad they didn't get to walk down Fleet Street. She liked the strange, narrow buildings – the pubs that were five storeys tall, but fifteen feet wide.

'The deados down there are fun to talk to as well,' she added, looking wistfully in that direction. '*Ohmigod*, trying to explain this century to a drunk journalist who's been dead, like, hundreds of years? Suddenly things don't seem so bad. They're always like "But what of the Poor Laws!" or "What became of the *Whigs*?" or whatever.'

The office had the sleek, early noughties look of frosted glass and chrome, but someone had made recent efforts to incorporate the current trend for exposed brick, coffee table books about design and funky pot plants. The complimentary fruit juice said, 'We've heard of Silicon Valley'; the small inflatable ball pit in the corner added, 'But we did not really understand what we heard.'

Alex breezed everyone through reception with a cheery wave to the woman behind the counter and into a lift. They had a security pass, so they could visit their dad, although they claimed they never really used it.

'Just leave the talking to me, okay?' they said, tapping away at their phone still. 'Dad and Uncle T probably aren't even here.'

Soph whistled when they stepped out of the lift. The place was full of grey desks staffed by identikit law boys exactly like Tristan, working away on computers and exchanging paper files, and occasionally cracking the air of industrious quiet with a braying laugh.

'Drop an allergy pill, C – this place must really be setting off your eat-the-rich glands.'

'Jesus,' said Claire. 'It's like a *Where's Wally?* book of cunts.' Alex let out a single loud 'HA!' and then clapped their hand over their mouth, as every eye in the room swivelled towards them.

Two of them belonged to a woman in her thirties and were behind some extremely fifties cat's-eye glasses. She bustled over. 'Hi, Alex! We weren't expecting you to bring anyone.' It was a statement, not a question.

'Hi, Helen. I'm in town visiting my friend Claire, and it seemed rude to leave her outside. Just wondering if Dad or Uncle T might be around for lunch later.'

Helen gave a bright smile. 'Oh, *fun*. Come over to my desk and I'll check your dad's schedule.'

'Oh, H, I was meaning to ask,' Alex said, as if it hardly mattered at all, 'do you have a number for that Michael, the accountant guy we talked about the other day? He seemed cool – I wanted to ask him some stuff about doing taxes as a freelancer.'

'Uh, funny you should ask, I was just thinking about the box of his stuff I have in that meeting room. I have *no* idea what to do with it,' Helen replied, pulling up a calendar on her computer. 'He left without saying anything or even packing up his desk, did I tell you that?'

'Wow, *rude*,' said Alex, making eyes at Claire.

'Say you need a slash, genius,' said Sophie.

'Er, Alex, do you know where the toilets are?'

Alex waved vaguely down a corridor and continued to distract Helen with banal chit-chat. Claire and Sophie were able to duck into the conference room quite easily. The room clearly wasn't used much, and there were a few cardboard boxes stacked in different corners.

'It's this one,' said Sophie, tippy-tapping on her feet next to one box, like a cat waiting for food. She couldn't properly look inside until Claire opened it for her.

'How d'you know?' said Claire.

'It says "Michael's stuff" on the top. You are the world's worst fucking detective. I'm serious.'

Michael hadn't actually left that much. There was a stress ball and a fake cactus, a mouse mat and a bunch of notepads – yellow legal paper ones that opened upwards instead of sideways.

'If he was on secondment, this wasn't really *his* office,' said Sophie. 'I bet he didn't bring a lot of desk stuff with him. I wouldn't be arsed, would you?'

Claire shook her head and flipped through a couple of the notepads. They were blank new ones. All unused. 'It's a bust. Again,' she said. She felt like a deflated balloon. 'I'm starting to think maybe nothing did happen after all.'

'Maybe,' said Soph. She shrugged.

'You serious?' hissed Claire. 'You're the one who was all "Do this for me! Do it for Nana!" about it. You convinced me!'

'Sure. It's fun to pretend stuff happens. Sometimes it doesn't.'

'Unbelievable!' Claire slid down onto the floor and found she was blinking very quickly and trying not to cry. Stories in real life are not as neat as they are on television. Living was hard. Sometimes Soph forgot that.

'Hey, don't worry!' said Soph. 'I still think something's up. That ghost in the library was definitely real, anyway.'

Claire nodded. She half-heartedly flipped through the pages of another notepad. A loose sheet fell out of the back of it.

She grabbed it and quickly got to her feet. She glanced at it and saw it was a single printed-off email, which definitely felt like a clue. She stuffed it into her backpack, which was being forced more and more to play the role of Mary Poppins's infinite carpet bag, and then hastily left the room again, anxious not to be caught. She was not, unfortunately, as confident during searches as the *Murder Profile* crew were. Somehow she thought that if she tried the 'I can always come back with a search warrant!' line, it would not be as convincing.

'Come the fuck on,' moaned Sophie, 'you barely did anything there – we can't go yet. Look, this says it's Monty's office. Let's go in.'

Claire hesitated, jiggling her leg like a dog that needs a piss.

'Ohmigod, Claire, you watch that stupid show all the time, but when it actually comes down to it, you won't do any crime-solving at all. Put up or fuck up, come o-o-on.'

Claire relented, looking quickly around and trying the door. To her disappointment, it was open. Soph was delighted, and whooped as Claire slid inside, pointing out that, really, the worst that could happen was that she'd be chucked out – it wasn't like she was in danger of being murdered or anything. Although, er, come to think of it...

Claire's heart started to pound. She genuinely had no excuse or reason to be in there. It was the office at The Cloisters, all over again. She started to have visions of Clem bursting through the door wielding a still-greasy kitchen knife.

Monty's office was quite utilitarian. It had a glass desk, glass shelves and a set of spangly new tumbler glasses next to a decanter. Glass was the overall theme. Claire was tempted to sit in the chair behind the desk and pretend she had an entirely different life. She sometimes secretly wondered if she could ever have been that sort of person: do this, sue that person, rabble-rabble-rabble!

She swiftly decided that there'd be no point trying the computer, since Monty evidently had a firmer grasp of digital security than his dad did, so she started to rifle through the paperwork in his desk organizer.

'Look at this,' said Soph. She was gazing at an open folder on the side table (glass). 'It's Nana's will! She left everything to Bash! But there's a sticky note on it listing, like, possible ways to challenge it. I think they're trying to claw it back from him. Fuck, he probably doesn't even know.'

'Yeah, remember they told Du Lotte that Clementine inherited, too, so they're lying to everyone. God, what a bunch of... of...' Claire, growing more and more angry on Basher's behalf, the longer she thought about it, couldn't find a word that fully expressed her contempt for Basher and Alex's extended family. 'What a bunch of *losers*.'

'Tell 'em how you really feel, C,' said Sophie.

'Well, they are – they're just terrible at being people. Who does that? Who tries to snatch back an inheritance from their own son? I am honestly so surprised Nana wasn't murdered,' said Claire. 'Genuinely seems more likely than natural causes. *Oooh!*'

She had come across a letter notifying Monty that Tuppence had applied for a divorce. This seemed more like salacious gossip than detective work, but it did give Claire no small amount of evil satisfaction. Yeah, Tuppence. Fuck that guy. Sisters are doing it for themselves.

'Huh. You know if I were Monty, I'd give Tuppence the divorce as quickly as possible, *before* I contested the will, because if I managed to get anything out of it, I wouldn't want to then have to share it with my ex,' said Sophie, looking over Claire's shoulder.

'Jesus! We're lucky you aren't Monty. Sometimes the way your mind works is quite frightening. Anyway he won't do that, because he's clearly way too much of a controlling dickhead to not object to the divorce.'

They suddenly heard Alex's voice approaching, saying, 'I thought you'd be pleased to see me, *Dad*!' at high volume – practically shouting, in fact. Claire immediately flew into a high panic. She was trapped like a rat and began uselessly circling the desk. Hiding under it surely wouldn't work, would it? No, stupid idea; it was see-through.

'The window – stand by the window!' hissed Sophie. 'Get as far away from any *stuff* as possible.'

Claire hopped over and managed to be looking out at the view as Monty entered, flanked by Alex, Helen and his usual hype-man, Tristan, who was nervously vibrating as if he'd just done a line, but was also afraid he was about to find out it had been cut with something unpleasant.

'Well,' said Monty, as chilly as Sophie, 'this doesn't seem at all suspicious.'

'He's got us there,' said Sophie, clearly amused. 'How are the gang going to get out of this one? Because I think the answer will be "Flail and say 'er' a lot" like a big fanny. But let's see.'

Claire took a deep, shaky breath in and tried to imagine what Smitty and the *Murder Profile* team would do: act with confidence, lie and probably lightly brutalize the suspect.

'Suspicious in what way exactly?' she said, sounding very calm, despite the fact that she was pretty sure even the soles of her feet were sweating. 'I'm concerned about the matter of my pay for this past weekend, since I still haven't heard from anyone. I thought it was perfectly acceptable to wait in the fuc— Ahem, in the office of a lawyer on business premises. I'm sorry if I am incorrect about that. What else do you imagine I would be doing?'

Claire wasn't sure where it had come from, or why she'd sounded increasingly formal as she spoke, but she was pretty happy with that.

'Wow! Okay. That was great – good for you, weirdo, I take it all back. I think he actually is going to kill you now, but it'll be worth it,' said Sophie.

Monty narrowed his eyes.

'I am sure I don't know,' he said, after a length of time during which Claire was sure the seas froze and melted again, mountains crumbled and stars went supernova in the vastness of space. 'You will be paid. It hasn't even been a week yet. Rest assured, we settle debts with even the most minor of employees. I would like you to leave, please.'

Claire suppressed a shiver, and realized that she definitely didn't have another performance like that in her, and that Monty in terror mode was the next-closest thing she had experienced to Clementine with the kitchen knife.

They trooped out. It felt very much like Claire was leaving the headmaster's office after getting detention, and she felt a flush rising to her cheeks.

'He's not wearing that gaudy tie-pin any more,' commented Sophie. 'Maybe he's having to liquidate some assets...'

'I hear you were asking about Michael, Alex,' said Monty, walking and talking them through the office in a really shit version of *The West Wing*. 'He is not a very good accountant, and we are no longer working with his company. We can put you in touch with a better one. Helen, please compile a list.'

Helen nodded and appeared to start doing so immediately, on a sleek Samsung phone. Sophie was very interested by this. 'Ask if that's the standard company issue,' she said quickly.

Claire did so, and Helen answered in the affirmative, and Monty looked at Claire with even deeper suspicion.

'I thought Michael was quite nice,' said Alex, who was very unperturbed by Monty's potential rage.

'Please, let's keep going, shall we? I'm going to put your strange behaviour down to grief, in this instance,' said Monty.

'So, Alex, yah, we should totally go out, if you're in town tonight,' said Tristan, who clearly now saw himself as the funcle – or, at least, wanted to. 'There's this really cool bar that me and some of the boys go to, that does, like, massive trays of themed shots?'

'Sounds good, Uncle T,' said Alex, in a kind yet massively condescending tone of voice that Tristan seemed not to notice. 'I don't know what my plans are. I'll let you know, okay?'

'Yeah. Cool! So, like, you know if you do shots into your eye, it gets you drunk quicker?'

'You've said that before, Uncle T, and I really don't think it's true.'

'That is an incredibly stupid thing to say to my child, Tristan. Alex, we will speak later,' said Monty as he deposited them back in the lift. 'And you...' the icy-blue eye of Sauron fixed itself on Claire, 'it would not affect my life in any way, whatsoever, if I never saw or heard from you ever again.'

Claire waited until the doors had closed and the lift had started moving before leaning heavily against a wall. 'Jesus. Christ. Fuck. Alex, your dad is terrifying.'

Sophie was crouching on the floor with her hands on the back of her head, as if she was in a plane that was about to crash.

'Fucking hell. That was almost as bad as the chicken thing,' she moaned.

'He gets it from Granny, but I've had a lifetime of practice with it,' said Alex, back to tapping on their phone straight away. 'All bark and no bite,' they added.

'That was my second field operation, though,' added

272

Claire, brightening up a bit. 'How did I do? I think I was better that time.'

'Aw, you did really well,' said Alex, looking up. 'Caught my loud and obvious signal and everything.'

Claire beamed.

14

Summing Up

'What do we do now?' asked Claire, as they huddled on the windy street outside.

'You're asking me? You're the grown up, C,' Alex pointed out. 'Ha! Only joking. Your face! At what point are you going to start being comfortable with any amount of responsibility whatsoever? Don't worry, I've arranged to meet Mum for lunch at the National Theatre. Bit early, but we can mooch over to the South Bank now.'

'Oh, sure, that'll be cheap,' said Soph. 'You enjoying pretending you can afford to grab lunch at the Nash, babes?'

Claire did like the National Theatre, though. A big, raw concrete fuck-off of a building: a pile of rectangles and layers that, when viewed from some angles, looked very persuasively like a dominant cruise ship that was trying to top every boat on the Thames. And inside its echoing heart, words came alive.

She had seen a play there in person once in her life, with her school. She remembered feeling the huge, sucking space in front of her, and how amplified the small, personal sounds of the audience were. How a tiny cough echoed around the vast auditorium, and how she had been frozen in fear, not wanting to make a sound because someone would hear and they would know – they would know it was her who had made it and she'd be told off. And then the stage lights went up and she saw how magic was somehow real. She saw the floor lift up and turn and become a room within a room, and she saw paper animals come alive, and a hole cut in the sky.

How could a building be so ugly and so beautiful at the same time? How could it produce the impossible? How could people be other people?

But as she got older, the National Theatre had started to remind Claire more of the sarcophagus over the Chernobyl reactor, put there to stop the radiation from leaking out too much. She started to suspect that some types of theatre people wanted to stop the magic inside the National getting out, in case ordinary people discovered it worked for them as well. The prohibitive cost of most theatre tickets helped, too, of course.

It started to rain as they arrived, so they huddled at a table inside the little canteen and Claire felt the great weight of the building on top of them, and wondered if they'd be able to make it out and far enough away if it started to collapse.

'It's good we're meeting your mum,' she said to Alex. 'She could be just the neutral witness we need to bust The Case wide open. In *Murder Profile* there's always, like, some urchin hiding up a chimney or in a bookshelf who knows who the killer is the whole time, but only gets found in the last ten minutes.'

The Wellington-Forges at large seemed to treat Tuppence as less like a member of the family and more like a trusted servant, ever present, yet always unseen and unnoticed. It would actually form the basis for a pretty good motive for murder. Except that, based on the TV she watched, the choice of victim didn't make sense: Claire would have expected Tuppence to suddenly snap and rage-kill her husband and in-laws, turning them into mannequins that she arranged around the dinner table – and possibly later into stringed puppets to act out the sort of loving family meal that she had always wanted. Divorce was probably a safer option. Claire wondered if she should tell Alex. It was a bit of a guilty secret to have, but it seemed like the sort of thing that was supposed to come from your parents. If she hadn't been snooping around Monty's office, she wouldn't have known anyway.

'Did you say *in* a bookshelf?' said Sophie, breaking through her thoughts. Luckily Claire didn't need to defend herself, because Alex got a phone call.

'Yello... I'm fine. Yeah. Yeah, I am. Really? Okay.' They held the phone out to Claire. 'It's for you.'

'Er... hello?' said Claire, looking to Sophie for reassurance.

'Don't look at me,' she replied.

'Ahoy!'

'Oh. Hello, Hugh.'

'Yes, indeed. M'boy Basher said you needed paying, and we'd normally do thirty-day terms and so on, but, well, friend of the family and all that. So it should have come through. It's from a company account.'

'Right, well. Er, thank you, Hugh.' He sounded about as awkward as she did. It felt very much like a conversation neither of them wanted to have, which prompted the question: why were they having it?

'Yes and er...' Claire could swear she could hear someone whispering in the background. 'Yes, and we hope you do stay a *friend*,' said Hugh, reading from *The Ladybird Book of First Veiled Threats*.

'Yes. Me, too.'

'Jolly good. So we've sent a little extra to make sure – to *en*sure your discretion.'

'About what?' said Claire quickly.

'Er, everything. Anything. Whatever you feel might need it,' said Hugh, casting a wide and desperate net. Claire could hear his perspiration down the phone.

'Right, yes. Of course.'

'Because m'boy Monty mentioned you'd just been by with Alex. And we felt that maybe you'd got hold of the wrong end of the old stick.'

'Oh, I'm sure I haven't,' said Claire cheerfully. 'Don't worry.'

'Yes and... I am *doing it* – and, needless to say, it would probably be inappropriate for you to come to the funeral. Friends don't always have to see each other, to stay friendly.'

'Of course, Hugh,' said Claire, who was honestly starting to feel sorry for him. 'Don't let it trouble you. Thank you and goodbye. And my condolences again.'

She checked the banking app on her phone as soon as she hung up. She had indeed received a payment from a generic business name that she didn't recognize. She scribbled the name, Arrowhead Beacon, on the back of her train ticket and made a mental note to add it to her Case Notes later. Soph, looking over her shoulder at the amount, whistled.

'That's... way too much. Even with how much you inflated your price for them.'

Alex was looking at her curiously – expecting her to explain the call, she realized. 'It was nothing really,' she said. 'Hugh wanted to make sure the money came through, and asked me not to come to Nana's funeral.'

'Ha! Classic us,' said Alex.

Claire chewed her lip. She didn't feel good keeping more secrets from Basher and Alex, even though it was because neither Soph nor Claire wanted to upset their newest, bestest friends with news about how criminal or awful their family was. She still hadn't decided whether they should say anything about Nana's will or Tuppence's yearning for freedom. She would have felt awkward having lunch with Tuppence even without knowing she was keeping the divorce a secret. Claire was letting her feelings compromise her unimpeachableness as a detective, which was always a bad sign. Next thing you knew, she'd be in danger of forgetting which side she was on.

Tuppence arrived, accompanied by the faint scent of lilies and a general air of capitulation. She looked pleased to see her child, and had pink cheeks and sensible mum-jeans. She was adept at nice mum-pleasantries and talked about how she didn't have much to do at home, but everyone was very busy with the funeral at The Cloisters, and how she didn't like to be a bother, and so on and so forth.

'Oh, I thought you'd stayed down there,' said Alex. 'I keep not getting through when I call you. And I texted you a couple of times, but they didn't send until yesterday. I assumed you didn't have signal.'

'That's odd,' said Tuppence brightly. 'No, just been rattling about at home all alone, I'm afraid.'

Claire cleared her throat. 'Do you remember Nana's birthday last year?' she asked.

Tuppence replied in the affirmative. Her brief description of the dinner tallied pretty closely with everyone else's.

'It sounds like you were gone for a while, making gravy.'

Claire might have imagined it, but she thought Tuppence went the slightest shade pinker. 'Was I?' she said absent-mindedly. 'I suppose I was. I think it must have taken me quite a while to find the instant gravy, you know. Clem does make a big thing out of having it at the back of a shelf.'

'And what time did you go to bed that night?' Claire was getting businesslike. She was quite enjoying herself. Alex was staying uncharacteristically quiet.

'Oh, gosh. I don't remember, I'm afraid. I think we stayed up in the kitchen for a little while, didn't we, Alex? There was some fuss about Tristan ruining a suit, but he didn't come back in through the kitchen, I don't think. I wasn't up too late. I remember I wasn't staying in the same room as Monty because he was always up working. Sorry, not very helpful, I expect.'

Tuppence's genuine desire to be helpful was matched only by how terminally incurious she was. Not only did she not seem to care why Claire was asking this, but she also hadn't observed anything she considered odd during the entire weekend. She was very apologetic about this, as she was about everything.

Sophie clearly found her quite boring. She had propped her head in her hand and was staring right through Tuppence, not really paying attention. Soph sighed and it blew in Tuppence's face, in response to which Tuppence shivered and fished a carefully folded cardigan out of her massive standard-issue mum shoulder bag.

'Chilly in here, isn't it?' she said, shrugging it on.

The cardigan had a transformative effect on Sophie, who immediately sat up and stared. 'Oh no,' she said. 'The buttons. Look at the fucking buttons! They're little crystal ones. Ugh, there's even one missing. Christ, I can't take much more of this.'

'Er... Weird question, Tuppence, but do you go in the library at The Cloisters very often?'

'No, I don't. It's a bit spooky in there, if you ask me.'

'What about the priest-hole?'

'No,' said Tuppence, right away. Almost too quickly, Claire thought. 'I wouldn't have any reason to. It would be a bit silly to go standing around in a little box, wouldn't it?'

'Oh, well. It's nothing really. I just found this in there and it looks like one of yours,' said Claire, producing the treasured button, which had stood up so well to interrogation. But it had finally broken and given up its boss, so she could probably hand it back.

'Oh, how funny,' Tuppence said. Claire wasn't imagining it: Tuppence had definitely gone at least two shades pinker. 'It must have rolled in there or something. I can sew it back on now at least. Thank you.' She took it and wrapped it in a handkerchief, which was exactly the sort of thing she would have on hand, to wrap errant buttons in.

Tuppence pulled her sleeves over her hands and got up to pay. She invited Claire to have dinner over at theirs, and Alex brightened at the suggestion. 'Fancy a trip to our place in Richmond, C?'

'Full offence,' said Claire, while Tuppence was at the till, 'but that is fucking miles away.'

'It's not that far,' said Alex. 'I mean, we came here from Brighton.'

'Yeah, and it'll take almost the same amount of time to get to Richmond! Richmond *is* miles away, even by London-to-Greater-London standards.'

Those standards never really made sense in the context of anywhere else, Claire thought. On a night out in London she had heard people say things like, 'Yeah, Stratford is dead, mate, but a friend of a friend is apparently at a great house-party in Battersea', which in travel terms was almost like someone in London complaining that England was boring, but they'd heard there was a great party currently happening in Dublin.

'Well, look,' Claire said, 'if we're going to Richmond, I definitely need to go back to my flat first and get a clean pair of pants.'

'Fair enough, grubby knickers,' said Alex.

'If Monty catches you at his house, it is one hundred per cent chicken-soup time,' said Soph. 'This is a terrible idea.'

Claire mulled over the potential of being turned into a family meal as they got on the Tube to her flat in Brixton. It was an idea she kept coming back to, so perhaps that really was the key to the whole thing: The Cloisters was actually a front for an elite club of cannibals. It wouldn't be that surprising.

'You know what,' she mumbled, once they had arrived, 'don't come up. It's not very big.'

'Don't be silly, C,' said Alex, pushing their way past.

The sight of Alex standing politely in the kitchen-cum-all-purpose-living-area, which, when you allowed for furniture, was barely large enough for all three of them to fit in at once, without Sophie literally standing in someone, made Claire oscillate between shame and defiance. She shouldn't have let them come up, damn it. But then again, what of it? This was how normal people had to live! London was probably loads of fun if you were rich and came from Richmond, and didn't have to think twice about having extra cheese on your plain pasta as a treat. Fuck them!

She realized she had been standing stock-still, in silence, for some time. Sophie was looking at her. Claire found herself wishing she could curl up under the duvet and sleep for an entire day. She was tired in her very bones, a tiredness she could not shake, and she wanted to be alone to think and exhale.

She couldn't shake the feeling that the answer to The Case – which would, of course, solve all her problems – was staring her in the face; that she'd heard or seen something that was important, and if she got hold of the last piece, they could put it all together. Like getting the centre square on *Catchphrase*. Although Soph was better at that, too.

She escaped to her room, where, instead of collapsing on her bed, she threw the old clothes in her bag onto the washing heap, avoided looking in the mirror and had a quick sink-wash.

When she stepped back into the living area, Alex had already become characteristically at ease and appeared to be looking for teabags. Claire pushed the second-hand Ikea coffee table (which doubled as her dining table and desk) up to the wall to try and make more room, and also so that she could discreetly sweep some old crumbs off it and onto the floor. Unfortunately there was no way to dispel the general gloom, since the only window opened onto an alley and was close to the wall of the building next door. The curtains could never really be opened far enough. Luckily, Alex had already got into the habit of carrying extra jumpers or fuzzy scarves, for times when they would be in enclosed spaces with Sophie.

Alex, after some furious texting and a phone call to their mum, declared they had changed their mind and wanted to go out in Brixton with some friends. Claire hesitated at this, but Alex was something of an unstoppable force.

'It'll be fun! Come on, seize the moment. Live in the now!'

'Some of us don't even live in the anything,' grumbled Sophie. 'I told you, it's rubbish watching you all get drunk.'

'Don't be like that. I'll talk to you, I promise.'

Before Claire could stop them, Alex had rifled through her wardrobe to produce tights and a bright red dress that she hadn't worn in years, held it up against her with a critical eye, declared that it would do and waited while Claire got changed. Suddenly she found herself stumbling from bar to house-party and back again. Claire started the night feeling like a haggard old woman trying to pretend she was young – the sort of person who would force her daughter to take her out and screech, 'They think we're sisters!' at people – and ended it feeling like she was back at university. This was probably not a good thing.

If it hadn't been for Sophie – perennially sober and once again furious, because while Alex sporadically remembered to talk to her, Claire kept forgetting to relay the conversation – Claire would probably have forgotten how to get home.

Alex fell into bed when they got back and looked at their phone. 'Ha-ha-ha,' they mumbled. 'Million missed calls from Uncle B. Ha-ha! Sh'up.'

Claire went to the bathroom and was heartily sick in the toilet. Alex was a bad influence.

She woke up the next morning half curled in the foetal position on the sofa. Consciousness came to her like a brick hitting an egg. Someone was hammering on the door of her flat.

'Oh God. Eurgh,' said Claire. She wasn't used to being hungover, and certainly not twice in quick succession. She couldn't be sure she wasn't actually the butt of a smoked cigarette that had been stubbed out on top of a bin, and then found by a disgruntled fairy godmother and cursed to live as a human. She crawled to the toilet and was sick again, which made her feel a bit better. Sophie watched her without any trace of sympathy.

Alex stumbled in, their hair plastered to their face on one side and sticking straight in the air on the other. Claire realized that they would be fine almost as soon as they had some coffee.

'Soph, please go and see who that is, before I die of noise.'

Sophie went out to listen at the door. She came back into the room and looked at Claire, and Claire knew at once – because she knew Sophie's face like she knew her own

– that Soph was worried. Her eyes did not sparkle. They were as dark and dull as pebbles, as cold as flint buried in a field and left undisturbed by the metal teeth of the plough.

'It's Basher. He's, like, well angry. Furious,' said Soph, in a leaden voice.

Claire's stomach dropped. Sophie was the constant by which she set her own mood. When she said, 'I don't like this, Claire', then Claire did not like it, either.

She opened the door, and Basher brushed past her without a word. 'Hello?' she said. 'What are you doing here? And how did you know where I live?'

'Your address is on the invoice you sent my parents,' Basher replied in a monotone. He didn't turn round. 'Alex? Are you all right?'

Alex was in the kitchen area. They turned and handed Claire a mug of tea. 'Wotcher, Uncle B. Cuppa?'

Claire perched gingerly on the coffee table, cupping her mug in both hands like a shield. Sophie stood in the corner. Alex threw themself down on the sofa, taking up its entire length and groaning theatrically. And Basher was standing in front of them, framed in the gap that marked the border between the watching-television area and the preparing-food area of the room. For the first time Claire saw him as he must have looked as a police detective. Basher did not speak, but began pacing back and forth, breathing hard, like he'd just finished a sprint.

'So-o-o... what are you doing in town, Uncle B?' asked Alex, flashing a winning smile. They were trying to disarm him.

'You know exactly why I am here,' he growled. 'What on earth did you think you were doing? You vanished – without a call, without a text, *nothing*. Disappeared with this... this fucking charlatan that we barely know.'

Claire opened her mouth, then thought better of it. The quick fluttering of butterflies of anxiety began in her chest. She made an effort to control her breathing, but felt nervousness tingling at the back of her throat and behind her ribs.

'We are leaving. Right now. And *you* are not coming with us,' Basher said, turning at last to look at Claire. His brow was heavy and he was unblinking, trembling with rage, his fist clenching and unclenching. 'When it became clear that you had, essentially, kidnapped Alex—'

'Uncle B, that's not what hap—'

'Shut up. I know you think you are an adult and that you understand everything, but you are not, and you do not.'

Basher took a deep breath in, and Claire hoped he wasn't about to say what she had dreaded he would, almost from the start. But she knew that it was coming. She felt the weight, the inevitability, and she had always known it would happen. But still, she let herself hope that he would say something else. He didn't.

'Sami called me, Claire. She told me everything. I cannot believe I ever fell for it. I always suspected that you were a grifter, obviously, but... God, you are so much fucking worse than the normal kind.' He started pacing back and forth.

287

Alex was looking between the two of them in confusion. 'What... what's going on, Uncle B?'

'She's a liar, Alex. She uses dead children – *children* – to make a name for herself. I should never have agreed to any of this. I should have run a mile the second you said your spirit guide was a teenage girl. Jesus!'

Claire felt a block of ice come to rest on her shoulder, as Sophie put a hand there. She stared at the floor.

'We can get through this Claire,' Sophie said, very quietly. 'We've done it before. We'll do it again.'

Basher put his hands to his head, like a goalkeeper who had just let one in during penalties at the final of the World Cup. 'Do you know, I remember it being on the news. *The Star* got a scoop on how the police were working with a medium... but I never put it together.' He resumed his slow pacing. It had to be slow: there wasn't much room for each circuit. If he paced too fast, he'd be spinning on the spot. And as he spun, he told – who? Alex? himself? her? – the story that Claire was never able, or allowed, to forget.

Just over seven years ago the police in Essex made a public appeal in a Missing Persons case. A sixteen-year-old boy had disappeared on his way home from a friend's house. He'd been drinking. He walked into a park and didn't walk out. There were no leads, and nothing was caught on CCTV. And the officer in charge got a little desperate. He was under pressure; it was a pet case for the local press. A medium answered the call. She was able to do uncanny things – such that when she said the missing boy was within sight of a castle, the police took it seriously.

'So off they went to Colchester. Oh, they must have been *so* desperate! I can sympathize, really I can.'

Claire still did not move her head to look at either of them, but she could see out of the corner of her eye that Alex was making the 'O' face that they did when they were surprised. Basher paused, as if daring her to speak, but she concentrated on the feeling of Sophie's hand instead. It was an encouragement to stay quiet; her shoulder was starting to numb, and if this dragged on much longer, it would start burning with cold.

'Of course they found nothing at Colchester. And in fact, a few days later, the boy was found. He was dead. They had lost any chance of finding him alive by going off on a wild goose chase. He'd been dumped in a pond on a golf club in Billericay. Not a castle in sight. Not for miles.'

Claire swallowed a sore feeling in her throat. She still didn't turn her head.

'And do you know what else? Do you know who the medium's so-called spirit guide actually is?'

'Sophie,' said Alex. 'She... it's Sophie. It's just Sophie. Come on, Uncle B, we know them!'

'But do you know who Sophie *is*?' Basher read off his phone: '"Sophie Watson, missing, last seen in 2007 in Oxford after a day-trip, wearing a blue tracksuit and white trainers, would be thirty-two now." That's from a bulletin from eight months ago. She's still missing. Claire was her best friend at school. Claire went to *vigils* for her. She made a big stir at the time, giving interviews to local press about how much she missed Sophie – how she hoped Sophie would come home. And when that wore off, guess who suddenly had visions of her friend? Had to be pulled out of school?' He turned on Claire. 'It is beyond belief that, even this many years later, you would still be trying to make a missing girl all about *you*. Seeking. This. Much. Attention! Sophie's parents are waiting for her to come home. The police have kept the case open. They think there's a chance Sophie is still alive somewhere! But I suppose that's not as important as you making a name for yourself, is it, Claire?'

Claire wanted to protest: *Oh yes*, she wanted to say, *I'm doing great. I'm rolling in it. Just look at this palace. Look at my glamorous lifestyle, my legions of admirers, my completely normal therapy record.* But she knew from experience that it wouldn't help. This was it; this was the other shoe dropping, like it always did eventually. Best to let it fall, and then wait for everyone to pick up their respective footwear and leave.

'So what was it?' Basher went on. 'Naked opportunism? When you happened to be close by when Nana died, you thought you would take us for all you could get? We can't trust a single thing you say! You attached yourself to us like a fucking leech. Living in my flat. Eating my ham. Convincing us that our family were killers! Well, it ends now, you fucking *parasite.*'

There was a ringing silence.

'Is that true, Claire?' asked Alex in a small voice. 'Was… Did you know Sophie? Is Sophie a missing person?'

Claire tried to speak, and failed again. So she settled for nodding. She felt a tear slide down to the end of her nose and brushed it off.

Alex stood up and walked over to stand behind Basher, facing the door. They wouldn't look at Claire, either.

'But I don't think…' they said haltingly. 'I mean, Claire isn't a bad person.'

'She is. We're going.' Basher looked back at Claire as he started to walk away, and it seemed as if he was pleading with her to say something, to refute everything, to prove him wrong.

'The castle was a poster. The boy, he was already dead when I spoke to him,' she tried, her voice cracking. 'He was being held in a house, and he looked out of a window and saw a poster on a bus stop near that golf course. It was advertising a weekend break in Colchester. It had a picture of a castle on it, so he thought he was near the castle. He got confused, that's all. He was already dead. He was confused and scared and wanted to go home. They couldn't have saved him. I tried to tell them. He was already dead.'

But she was talking to a slammed door.

Sophie removed her hand from Claire and did not put it back.

Claire had a hot shower and scrubbed the red skin of her shoulder until it was no longer cold to the touch, but she felt the shiver in her bones.

She tried to watch an old episode of *Murder Profile*, but it only made her think about what had just happened. It had happened before, when whoever she met eventually googled her name and gradually – or abruptly – ghosted her, or else confronted her, as Basher had. Yelled at her about being a sick attention-seeker. So this wasn't special. She and Sophie simply had to ride it out, like normal.

Claire often wondered how people felt after shouting at her. Was it cathartic?

Sophie hovered around, looking blank and stroppy. 'Can we watch something else?' she asked.

'No. I want to watch this,' lied Claire.

'You've seen it before.'

'So?'

'Ohmigod. Don't be a child, C.'

'I'm not a fucking child. And don't call me "C" – since when do you call me "C"?' snapped Claire. 'You're never going to be as interesting as Alex, you know that?'

Soph flinched. 'Yeah, duh. I'll never get the chance. So what's your excuse?'

Claire ignored her, but Sophie walked around to stand in front of the TV.

'No, I'm serious, Claire. What *is* your excuse? You're alive, you have a life to do things with, and you... you don't do *anything* except watch this stupid fucking show over and over again. And drive people away. I'd have fucked off by now, if I could.'

Claire was genuinely open-mouthed. 'Are you serious? What's my excuse?' She felt her voice rising. 'You! You are – you stupid… fucking… *cow*. My entire existence is about you. I can't have anything else, because you're always, always here!'

'Like you could survive without me – like you could do anything without me. You need me. You wouldn't even have a job without me.'

'I only need you because you exist, idiot!' Claire was full-on yelling now, tears that she wasn't even aware of streaming down her face. 'I could have a normal job if it wasn't for you, I could have friends. I wouldn't have had four years of pointless fucking therapy.'

'We *had* friends, stupid. Basher and Alex knew about me and they liked me. I'm so fucking sick of *you*.'

'Yeah? Join the club. It's not like they left because of me. They left because of you – you're the package deal that nobody wants to buy, dickhead. You're the one that fucked up, talking to that missing kid. There wouldn't even *be* anything to look up about me, otherwise! How are you not getting this?'

Claire became aware that she was standing and they were both shouting at each other; the thought floated through her brain, mostly unobserved, that she hoped her neighbours assumed she was on the phone. Her face and neck were hot and wet, from the rage and shame and tears and guilt.

Sophie couldn't cry. Her eyes were like bowls of water that you could drop copper pennies in: the water seemed to swell and swell, but no matter how many coins you threw in, the surface tension wouldn't break, it would never overflow. But the air was horribly chill. The condensation on the windows was sparkling, little white ferns were tracing their way across the corners of the TV screen, and even the ceiling leak had stopped, becoming a tiny, grimy icicle that gave the impression time had stood still. Claire did not pause to take a breath.

'I have to be responsible for your fuck-ups, but you don't have to be responsible for anything. You have genuinely ruined my life.' The totality of the silence that followed this was so frightening that Claire felt like she had ripped a black hole in the world and was about to disappear into it.

Then Sophie broke it, and her voice was more than speech, it was an expression of force. It was like the terrible, sunken toll of the church bell in a flooded town. Claire felt it reverberate in her chest as if it were empty, as if she herself were hollow.

'It's not my fucking fault I'm dead!' Sophie screamed.

And because all Claire had left was the truth: '*It's not mine, either. But maybe you fucking deserve it!*'

PART III

I have been bent and broken, but – I hope – into a better shape.

Charles Dickens, *Great Expectations*

15

Cold Comfort

It was Monday morning again. Claire was lying in bed in the foetal position. Her toes and knees were braced against the wall, so she couldn't move. Her phone was playing through back-episodes of a podcast in which three loud Americans made fun of conspiracy theories, but she wasn't listening to it.

She and Soph were still not speaking to each other. Claire was starting to wonder if she would eventually lose the ability to speak. If she thought about it too hard, she couldn't remember what her voice sounded like. Sometimes she would whisper something to herself to check. 'Hello. Hello, Claire. Hello, hello, stop, go, goodbye.'

She felt hollow. Hollow and brittle. Like a chocolate rabbit. Absurd.

She lay with Sophie's butterfly hair-claw held loosely in her fist. Sometimes she woke up and it was gone, and she scrabbled around until she found it tangled somewhere in the sheets. It looked like the metal spring was coming loose on one side.

Sometimes she felt like she was chained to the bottom of a vast sea, and a storm was raging above the surface and she was being pushed by great swells that she could not see: it would relent for a moment, or even for hours, and then another huge invisible wave would overcome her and push her, and strain her limbs against restraints that would not snap. It hurt so terribly, but all she could do was cry out into her pillow. Each time she felt she could not bear it, but, alas, it seemed she had no choice.

Sometimes she felt the air grow cold and she knew that Soph was looking at her. Claire woke up in the night and Sophie was there, watching. Other times, Sophie went out to stand on the street, as if trying to get as far away from Claire as possible.

In between lying in bed, Claire had mostly been watching *Murder Profile* and listening to podcasts. She was eating a lot of sliced bread, straight from the bag. Her mouth was getting very yeasty. And she was running out of bread.

That afternoon she reached into the bag and found it was empty. And for some reason it was this, more than anything else, that motivated her to get up and make motions towards re-joining her life. She needed bread. She would have to go out to buy more bread.

Claire did this, and noted that buying bread had made her go overdrawn again. She had transferred the money that Hugh had sent her into a savings account, ring-fenced away from the rest of her life. Blood-money that she felt weird about touching.

The shop assistant's haunted expression was enough to make Claire think she needed to get out and talk to more people. Her regular customers were safe – people who wouldn't shout at her. And they would give her money. A two-birds sort of situation.

Her life seemed like a sort of slow-moving train that she had hopped off and now merely needed to jog a bit, in order to hop back on. It was a bit of effort, but fundamentally not much had changed. This, too, was somewhat depressing. Even her own life could function pretty well without her.

She had postponed or cancelled her regulars while she was investigating The Case, so she decided to call Donna, who always cheered her up and had a need for her services.

Donna was a woman in her seventies who combined pragmatism with a streak of delightful hedonism; as long as she wasn't hurting anyone else, she did whatever she felt would make her happy – and this included hiring a medium every few months to bicker with her dead older sister, Michelle, about TV soaps. They were both still hanging around in the two-up, two-down house that had belonged to their parents before them and Claire liked going to see them, especially because Donna always provided a hearty, but slightly grim old-person meal, like faggots in gravy, followed by prunes in custard. Technically, she did shout at Claire. But not in that way.

'HELLO!' said the profoundly deaf Donna, as she answered the phone. It was a crackly old house phone and Donna frequently blew out the line with her volume. Claire usually found her own volume rising, in sympathy.

'Hello. Donna! It's Claire!'

'OOOOH, CLAIRE...'

After two minutes' worth of small talk that took about ten minutes of mutual loud talking, and then a much more confusing conversation while they found a date and time that suited Donna (who had to look up her engagements in an honest-to-goodness paper diary), they were able to pin down a time for a seance the following week. Sophie's involvement would have to be a cross-that-bridge situation. Claire scribbled down the appointment on the first thing she found in her pocket, which happened to be the ticket from Brighton to London.

'WE'LL HAVE LIVER AND ONIONS!' said Donna in delight. 'THE BUTCHER SAYS HE'S GOING TO KEEP A NICE BIT OF BACON FOR ME!'

'What was that – sorry?'

'BACK BACON! WHO'S YOUR BUTCHER? YOU SHOULD TAKE MEAT CUTS SERIOUSLY. BACON!'

Claire froze. She suddenly had a strange feeling, like a bubble was floating down from the ceiling somewhere and she had to catch it, before it hit the table and exploded in very small violence. But if she moved too fast, it would also pop into nothing.

'Thank you, Donna. I'll have to call you back,' she said, suddenly almost whispering. She hung up. Possibly Donna would be completely unaware that she had done so and would continue shouting about bacon for several minutes.

What had she been doing? She had been looking at the train ticket, and Donna had been talking about lunch. Claire looked at the ticket again. It had several things scrawled on it: a swirly doodle, half a phone number, the name 'Arrowhead Beacon', Donna's appointment.

There it was again. Her mind snagged. Something about what Donna had said, and the name Arrowhead Beacon, was making her brain sluggishly try to fire off something – it was just very bad at it. This was the bit Sophie was good at: the logical connections. Claire did the emotion and the flights of fancy. She felt like a cat trying to walk in socks.

She tried out combinations, like rotating jigsaw pieces side-by-side.

Who's your butcher? Arrowhead Beacon.

Arrowhead Beacon. Meat cuts seriously.

Back bacon. Arrowhead Beacon.

Arrowhead bacon.

Arrowhead bacon? Bacon seriously.

Seriously bacon.

Beacon. Bacon.

'Oh my God. Oh my God!' Claire yelled out loud, jumping to her feet. '"I'm serious about *Beacon*!" Ohmigod, Soph – oh.'

Sophie wasn't there.

Claire dropped her triumphantly raised arms back down to her sides. Shit! Shitshitshit. Right. She decided to have a shower first, because the smell of her own hair was quite distracting and it was at least a *decision* that she could make *decisively*.

Then she got a pen and made a list of the top twenty accounting firms in the City. She made this list very neatly on the first page of a fresh notebook that she found under the Ikea table. Claire then spent an hour and a half ringing each of them, asking if they had any employees called Michael who matched Michael's brief description, and if he could please call her back, if so.

Then she remembered the printout she had nicked from the things Michael had left in Monty's office. Hope blazed strong in her chest that it would be a smoking gun – an email from Hugh to Monty saying, 'What should we do about that person we murdered and buried on our property?' perhaps.

Claire was quite disappointed that it turned out to be an apparently insignificant email from Michael to Monty, sent in July last year:

Hi Monty,

Just wanted to flag up some irregularities I've noticed in one of the shell accounts. I'm sure it's nothing, but it would be good to check some of the transactions going to one of the shells – Arrowhead Beacon. It's my job to be thorough, after all!

Thanks,

Michael

It was disappointingly boring.

No, that was the wrong way to think about it. Though Claire was loath to admit it, she needed to think about it like she would if Sophie was here to talk it through with her. So...

'Okay. Michael kept it – the email was important enough that he wanted to have a copy of it. Why a physical copy, though? Maybe because...' And here Claire resisted theorizing that Michael was going to pass it to a secret third party, or that it was part of a larger cache of documents that he had been smuggling, one page per day, out of the office. She forced her mind onto a less made-for-TV track. 'Because he wanted to show it to someone, but Monty's company can check the emails that their employees send.'

Talking out loud seemed to be helping. That, at least, was accurate from TV.

'So he couldn't forward it outside without the company maybe seeing. So he printed it off. And... and it was in the back of a notepad because he didn't want anyone else to see it accidentally. So that means... Hmm. I suppose it means Michael printed it off just before he left the company, when he knew something really was up, as double proof that he wasn't in on it. But then he probably forgot about it.'

Although it would be good if he'd written a message on it in lemon juice or some other invisible ink, she added internally. You check that with heat, don't you? Her oven had gas hobs, and she wasn't sure that would work.

Claire put a pin in that idea and started ringing the accounting firms on the list from the top down again, this time asking for Michael Brewin, because the email had revealed his last name.

Firm twelve recognized the name and promised to pass the message on. In a flash of inspiration, Claire added that it was 'about Beacon', reckoning that it was likely to get a faster response.

She was right. Michael called back to ask what she wanted, and when Claire said she needed to talk about the Wellington-Forge family and their accounts, Michael gave an extremely deep, long sigh.

'Okay. I'm sick to death of the lot of them. I'll tell you everything, as long as nobody ever mentions that family to me again. What do you want to know?'

This was easier than Claire had expected. 'Not over the phone,' she said. 'Someone could be listening.'

'What? Who?'

'I dunno – whoever. It's sensitive information.'

'This is... All right, fine, but after today I am never thinking or speaking about Monty and his dad ever again.'

They agreed to meet, after Michael had finished work, for coffee in Battersea. Which Claire supposed counted as neutral ground for both of them.

As the time got closer to the moment when she had to leave, Claire began to worry. There was still no sign of Sophie. She hadn't been anywhere without Sophie for most of her life. But she didn't technically have to wait for her... Claire paced around like a nervous dog for a bit, then put on a scarf, a long-sleeved top, a hoodie and a jacket. She zipped everything up and pulled up her hood before she left.

After she'd been walking for a few minutes she felt the little pull that meant Sophie was being tugged after her. It didn't happen often, because they were rarely apart, but whenever the connection was tested there was a sensation. Not unpleasant, merely an awareness. Almost as if Claire could feel the bump of an ingrown hair, but in her whole body. By the time she entered the Tube she could tell, without looking, that Sophie was closer behind her. *It Follows*, but with a noughties teenager in a shitty mood.

By the time they got to Battersea it was clear that Sophie was curious, but still too proud to get involved. As Claire went into a small local café, Sophie followed and stayed in one corner, just on the edge of earshot. Claire kept her hood up, so that she wouldn't have to look at her out of the corner of her eye. A bargain-bucket Banquo.

Michael came in a few minutes later. He was as obtrusively handsome and tall as the others had said, but he was also, Claire noticed, slightly hunched over and stooping, as if trying to make himself look smaller. He came over to Claire – one of the only other people in there, and definitely the only one wearing a hood up and ugly shades indoors – and asked very politely if she was waiting for him.

He sat down and they looked at each other. Inevitably Claire blinked first, but she still wanted to be cool, professional and mysterious, so she got out the email and slid it across the table towards him. Michael's face was expressionless, but in the way it is when a face is trying really hard not to have any expression.

'How did you get this?' he asked, taking it. Claire noticed how clean and neat his nails were. Michael frowned. 'And why is it a bit burnt?'

'How I got it isn't important,' said Claire seriously. 'It was burnt in the course of... er, classified investigations.'

The interview technique of being outwardly inept seemed to relax Michael. 'Okay then, we'll ignore that for now,' he said. 'Who are you? You're clearly not in finance, and obviously not police.'

'Yeah, *all right*. Jesus!' Claire decided to drop the terrible, short-lived act. 'I'm sort of a family friend of the Wellington-Forges. Well, I'm a friend of some of the family. Actually, maybe none of them.'

'So you're... a family enemy?' Michael looked confused, but also like he was trying not to laugh at her.

'I went to university with Figgy.'

'The waspy daughter?'

'Yeah. Anyway, not this weekend just gone, but the one before I was invited to The Cloisters...'

Claire told him the truncated version of the story that she was now used to giving, without the ghosts and, in this case, replacing 'There was an 'orrible murder' with a vague impartation that some illegal shit was possibly going down.

'And I don't really care about this Arrowhead Beacon thing, but I think it has something to do with that. Because Basher heard you arguing and he thought you were talking about breakfast, but you weren't, were you? You were saying you were serious about Beacon.'

'Well spotted. I'd have said you're probably right about Beacon being the cause, except that it turns out it doesn't really matter.'

Michael sighed heavily again, as if steeling himself to continue.

'Arrowhead Beacon is a pretty standard shell company attached to Monty's firm. Most places have more than one; it's maybe a bit weird for a legal firm, but they're corporate lawyers. Good for moving money around, I suppose. I was seconded to PP&R – sorry, Parker, Parker and Renwick – to do a general wash and brush-up of their accounts, make sure they won't get stung with a whopping tax bill, check that nobody had stolen anything from the pension pot. That sort of thing.'

'An MOT, but for office finances?'

'Exactly. But a few months in, I find Beacon. And it's... fishy. Being a conscientious accountant, I sent Monty that email straight away because, as a conscientious manager, he'd want to know. Except that he gets cross and starts putting pressure on me *not* to look into it. Which makes me want to keep looking into it. Eventually Monty invites me to his family home to work through a heap of files and receipts. That's unusual, obviously, but I decided to go, because by this stage I'm pretty convinced that the family business is something to do with it.'

Claire was genuinely on the edge of her seat. 'Go on,' she prompted. Sophie had edged closer, with practised nonchalance.

'I managed to sneak some time in their office, with help from their estate manager lady – Maude or Mary, or something – and even just a quick glance through their paper files confirmed it. Monty is skimming... embezzling, basically, and using The Cloisters to do so.'

'*WHOA!*' said Claire.

'Yes, that's what I thought,' said Michael drily. 'They've not been that clever about it really. PP&R books a couple of legitimate events at The Cloisters every year, so if you're skimming the account and see the transactions coming up, there's cover for it. But there are way more transactions than are reasonably legitimate, so if you look into it in any depth whatsoever, it becomes very obvious. Plus, it's only one step removed. Monty is not the Machiavelli of financial crime.'

'Yeah, his dad paid me directly from that account actually,' said Claire. Michael snorted at this.

'I think it's probably a family slush fund at this point,' he said. 'The Cloisters looked like it was running at a hefty loss, otherwise. Anyway after the weekend I was down there, I decided to back off, but to keep having a look discreetly, work the rest of my time at PP&R and then report everything to my boss at my firm, when I was out. I'd already got in touch with HMRC.' He sighed again. 'Except it doesn't matter. My boss told me to leave it, and HMRC never did a full investigation themselves.'

'What, really?' Claire was incredulous.

'Apparently, as crimes go, it's not really important or sexy enough. No money-laundering for the Mob, no millions in import and export scamming, just regular greed. It was implied to me that most executives everywhere are feathering their own nests, and if we report one of them, we have to report all of them – and then we wouldn't have any clients, and London wouldn't have any corporate offices. So there you go. Whole lot of stress and bother for nothing.'

'Hmm.'

Claire took a big sip of her tea, as cover to think. She had not expected this to be such a dead end.

'Did you see anything weird at all that weekend?' she asked, feeling a bit deflated. But in for a penny.

'Well, I didn't know there was going to be a police officer there. That scared me a bit. I avoided her the whole time.'

This seemed fair.

Michael paused. 'Also, the family themselves are awful,' he said, having decided that a family enemy was safe enough for this. 'The mum kept saying, "Oh, good for *you!*" to me, about any personal or professional achievements that I mentioned.'

'Oh, actually,' Claire said, suddenly remembering another important issue, 'where did you go? You said you were going to make a call, but you never came back and the timings don't match up.'

'Yes, I am afraid I did what we City professionals call "a lie",' said Michael. 'I asked that other man – the boyfriend, Kevin – to drop me at the station instead and not tell anyone; and to tell them that he drove me to make a phone call. So that I could leave. I trusted that everyone would be too self-involved to really notice or care.'

Claire leaned her face in one hand and drummed her fingers with the other. That did make sense: Kevin got back sooner, because he hadn't actually driven as far as they'd thought. This, too, was disappointingly mundane.

'In fact,' said Michael, after draining the last of his coffee, 'I was a bit indiscreet with him. I say "indiscreet". I was angry and told him almost everything during the car ride. I felt like I had to give him a reason to cover for me, I suppose. I was asking him to lie to his girlfriend and her family, after all. Kevin got really annoyed about the whole thing, though. More annoyed than I was. Started slapping the steering wheel and going on about the bourgeoisie and hypocrisy, and how borders are just lines in the sand. Called me "brother".'

'Hmm,' said Claire again, still tapping her fingers and almost forgetting Michael was there.

'So I'm going to go now,' he said eventually. 'And I'm going to take this,' he said, wafting the printed email.

'Huh? Oh. Er... yes, fine. Thank you,' replied Claire, her mind elsewhere. 'Glad you're not dead.'

'Sorry?'

'Oh, nothing,' she said.

She waited until the bell over the door clanged as he left, then turned to look at Sophie. She was standing a lot closer, but she still glanced away when their eyes met, like a drunk man on a train pretending he wasn't looking the whole time. Claire's heart sank a little more into the hollow in her chest. She thought she'd at least earned a bit of acknowledgement for a successful lone interview, and for some bloody good detecting.

After some hesitation, Claire sent Alex a text explaining that she had met Michael, and maybe there was more to Kevin than they'd thought, but that Mattie was still the number-one vic option. And that she was sorry and missed them, and hoped they were okay. Pressing Send made her sunken heart thud.

When they got home, she had a voicemail. Alex had tried to call while she was on the Tube. 'Hello, C. And S? Maybe? I dunno. I dunno why I'm calling really. Except to say maybe you should let it go? It's Nana's funeral on Thursday. Just feels like a place to end. You shouldn't come. Sorry.' They did actually sound apologetic. 'Okay. Bye.'

Claire spent the rest of the afternoon lying in bed crying, either big racking sobs that seemed to come from nowhere or the baby-sniffles of a sad, unhugged puppy. By the time the sun had set she'd exhausted herself, but lay there in the dark, unable to sleep.

After a while – Claire didn't know how long – Sophie came in and sat on the bed.

'That was good, working out the Beacon thing. I'm impressed.'

'Thanks. Hey, why were you so sure it wasn't Michael who had died?'

'The skeleton had long hair. Michael's bald.'

'Oh. You're right; it was stupid that none of the rest of us noticed that.'

'Yeah. I was being petty, though.'

'Yeah.'

They stayed there in silence for another while.

'Can't sleep?' said Sophie.

'Naw.'

Sophie lay down next to her. 'I'm sorry,' she said.

'Me too.'

After a few moments, Soph took Claire's hand. She actually held it, like it was a seance. They used to do this when Claire was younger and couldn't sleep, before exams or after a bad date, or because of the relentless prodding and poking and questions about why she thought she could talk to her dead friend.

Claire felt the battery *zip* and didn't fight it. After a couple of minutes she was very cold and very sleepy, and then after a few seconds more she was very warm and fuzzy, even though she could tell the sheets and the room, and her skin, were all the same smooth coldness as one carved block of marble.

Her eyelids drooped and Claire wondered, as they finally closed, if this was what it was like to freeze to death. It wouldn't be so bad, she thought.

16

Family Values

That Wednesday, Claire and Sophie were on a bus. Claire loved public transport, but did not like buses. Trains had to stick to where they were going, whereas buses could decide to pull wild-card moves, and frequently did. Also, people on buses seemed to be much more given to getting up and gobbing on the floor, or doing weird shit like shredding an umbrella to pieces or sicking up in coffee cups. When you got on a bus there was a 50 per cent chance you were stepping into a holding cell for the damned. That didn't seem entirely inappropriate for her and Sophie. But luckily they were the only people on the bus. It was that sort of route, winding through scrubby grass fields and bare hedgerows that seemed, to Claire, to be indistinguishable from each other, or from the hedgerows of any country lane she had ever seen. They could have been on the roads to The Cloisters, except that they were quite a long way from there.

They had come on a strange sort of Hail Mary mission. Even though Alex had advised them to drop it, Claire and Sophie had spent most of Tuesday talking about it and decided that neither of them wanted to yet. It would be like leaving an unsolved jigsaw all over your coffee table, even though you'd just started to fit the weird-shaped pieces together. Sophie had also said that maybe, if they could figure out what had really happened, it would be a reason to talk to Alex and Basher and they could maybe, possibly, be friends again. If Claire examined this idea for too long, it became the vain hope of some desperate, lonely children, so she kept it in her peripheral vision, where it was the noble hope of brave heroes. Because the other thing was that Claire kept remembering the agony of that ghost in the library. Their unending pain. And she and Soph had agreed that it would be good to help them, if possible.

Also, she kept remembering times when Basher had given her an awkward side hug or when their knees had touched on the sofa, and the feel of the skinny heat of his body under his hoodie. It was nice to believe that he might think well of her again. Sometimes she would type out a message to him on her phone and imagine that he had their conversation open as well and could see the 'CLAIRE IS TYPING' ellipsis. But she never sent anything.

The problem was that they were running out of trails to follow. Michael was clearly alive, so he could be crossed off the list as 'not dead' for absolute definite

314

(although a radical defence lawyer might argue that Claire speaking to someone wasn't cast-iron proof in her specific case, obviously). Mattie was less of a sure thing: she'd been betraying the family to the Du Lotte Hotels chain, so Clem and Hugh had a motive to bump her off, plus her husband was being paid off for doing something, and her son was upset at the family. But while Claire had no definitive proof that she was alive, there wasn't really any evidence she was dead, either, so Mattie was a bit of a dead end, without help from Alex and Basher.

But there was one thin, tenuous lead that hadn't been explored and that Claire could follow by herself: Kevin's parents.

After a lot of back and forth, Sophie had agreed that the logical thing to do was to verify that Kevin was definitely, 100 per cent alive, because when they thought about it, they realized they hadn't spoken to him in person, either. And if he was alive, then they could try and definitively find Mattie and then, if necessary, widen the pool of potential victims and go back to the drawing board. Usually one's parents will know whether or not you're alive. Not in every case, obviously, but it would be insensitive to mention that to Sophie.

Back at The Cloisters, in what now seemed about a decade ago rather just over a week, Figgy had mentioned that Kevin's parents were 'Sue and Jeremy, lovely little cottage in South Withemswall'. So now, in a reckless move, they were on the way to find Sue and Jeremy and their lovely little cottage in South Withemswall. Since these were the only directions they had, they were just... on a bus to South Withemswall.

After almost an hour they arrived at their stop. Claire checked the time. It was already nearly 4 p.m. She didn't want to get back home at 2 a.m., but she was now concerned that she wouldn't be able to get back home at all. She hadn't packed any clothes, simply grabbed her backpack and headed out, and she also hadn't checked if there was anywhere to stay in South Withemswall. But she wasn't voicing these concerns to Sophie. She felt that her successful locating and interrogation of Michael had set a precedent of competence.

South Withemswall was halfway between a town and a village. The houses had red-tiled roofs and visible beams. In the summer there would probably be rambling dog roses and apple trees full of ripening green fruit. The bus stop was next to a red phone box that didn't seem to have been used as a toilet. She could see a village shop, and a pub further down the road. It looked like there was even a school as well. There was bunting.

'This,' observed Sophie, 'is bucolic as *fuck*.'

Claire's vague plan had been to ask people where Sue and Jeremy lived, but because it was cold and damp here too, there was a dearth of people visiting each other with baskets of preserves, or helpful kids playing with skipping ropes. Sophie meandered down the road, scuffing her heels as she went.

'Where are you going?' asked Claire.

In answer, Sophie pointed: rising above the big green cloud of a yew tree was a squat church spire. Claire dropped her head and groaned like a teenager. *Gaaauuuuuuuud! UGH!*

She wasn't in the mood for the particularly self-involved, depressive brand of spook that hung around graveyards and churches. It wasn't their fault, really. If she had to spend eternity arguing with other dead people over what was basically a parking space, and listening to 'All Things Bright and Beautiful' every weekend, she'd probably not be a laugh a minute, either.

On the other hand, graveyard ghosts tended to be less starved for attention, since they had more people to talk to. And Sophie's logic, as far as she could guess it, was sound: they needed to ask locals for directions, and there was nobody more local than an elderly churchyard ghost.

Withemswall church's permanent congregation was a Just William-esque schoolboy cheerfully wellying a ghostly football around the yard; an old woman in black Edwardian dress and veil, who was watching him with grandmotherly affection; a man with a big moustache and sideburns, wearing a suit with very flared trousers (who was sitting against his own headstone in a carefully despondent manner); and a younger woman in a black poodle-skirted dress, who was looking at him with undisguised disdain. She was holding a lit cigarette that curled smoke into the air, but never burned down. Claire lit a cigarette of her own and let Sophie go ahead of her. It usually went better that way.

'Hello,' she said. 'I'm Sophie. This is my friend Claire. What's going on?'

The man seemed quite surprised, but recovered quickly and went back to looking tortured and interesting. 'Oh, what a question!' he lamented. 'What a world! Nothing's going on, and everything.'

The girl rolled her eyes. 'First new people he's been able to speak to in ages. Howard, baby, I'm pretty sure the sad poet act won't work on them.' She took a deep drag on the cigarette and muttered, *sotto voce*, 'Especially if you recite any of your poems.'

The older woman, who was keeping count of success-ful keepy-ups for the boy, chimed in to say that they were both being very rude. 'I'm Miss Pinkett, this boisterous young man is Luke, and that's Maisie and Howard,' she said.

Maisie pointed to each of them in turn: 'Old age, flu, coughing up a lung, writing poetry so terrible that he died to spare the world.'

'Drowning,' corrected Howard.

'Sorry, drowning.'

'I always get those two mixed up as well,' said Claire.

Maisie laughed and clapped her hands together. 'Oh, you are just a gas!' she said. 'What brings you here anyway?'

'We're looking for a couple called Sue and Jeremy, who live in a cottage somewhere around here,' said Sophie.

'Now there's a coincidence,' said Miss Pinkett. Claire was immediately suspicious. She didn't think there were such things as coincidences in murder investigations, because Smitty on *Murder Profile* said as much at least every other episode.

'Now, Luke – now, calm down and come here to talk to these nice ladies. They're looking for your old house. Jeremy is Luke's grand-nephew – isn't he, Luke?'

Luke stopped kicking the football and stood fidgeting in front of them. He had ruddy cheeks and radiated big-paper-bag-full-of-aniseed-balls energy.

'So what if he is?' he said, with the attitude of someone who treated all new grown-ups as if they were his headmaster. 'Those lot are boring. They used to come and visit me and my brother's graves, but now they barely ever do.'

'Is your brother around?' asked Soph.

'No. I'm glad, though; he was about a thousand years old when he died. He wasn't fun any more, either. Old people aren't fun. Well,' he added kindly, 'apart from ol' Pinko. You're all right, aren't you, Miss Pinkett?'

'Have you ever met your great-grand-nephew, Luke? His name's Kevin,' asked Claire.

'Dunno if that's what his name is, but he came here once, ages ago, and ol' Rogers, the vicar, got cross and chucked him out for talking about pagan religions and saying God wasn't a proper God, or something.'

'Well, that definitely sounds like Kevin,' said Claire. 'Can you give us directions to your old house, please, Luke?'

He did, very importantly. It turned out to only be about five minutes' walk away. 'Why d'you want to see them anyway?' Luke asked. He was starting to lose interest, though, and was fiddling with his football.

'Your great-grand-nephew is a friend of mine and I wanted to stop in and say hello to his parents while we were here,' said Claire, who was impressed by how good she was getting at lying on the spot.

'Huh. All right then.' Luke paused. 'Can you go and check on what they've done to my room, and come back and say?'

'I'll try,' said Claire. 'But we should probably be off now. It's nearly teatime already.'

'I miss having tea. All right. Bye!' He ran off and booted his football at a statue of a cherub.

'So, Sophie,' said Maisie. 'What was it that got you?'

Sophie looked straight at her. 'I don't know,' she said. The ghosts shared a moment of understanding and made sympathetic noises. 'It's all right. It doesn't seem to matter that much any more.'

'Tragedy, death, dinner – so many rich primal urges, now sloughing off us like so much... like... like gravy off a duck's back,' said Howard, his voice as thick with melancholy as, presumably, the gravy.

'Oh, do shut the fuck up, Howard dear,' said Miss Pinkett.

Claire and Sophie left as Maisie's roaring laughter filled the churchyard.

'It occurs to me,' mused Sophie, 'that we have not taken much advantage of our special talents during this investigation. Like – ohmigod, babes. I can walk through walls. We can talk to dead people. We should have been doing that the whole time.'

It took a little longer than expected to find Sue and Jeremy's cottage because it was getting dark, and because South Withemswall had changed a little in the last hundred years, so Luke's directions were not quite accurate. After a bit of backtracking, they ended up at a likely cottage and knocked at the door, and were then directed by Sue and Jeremy's neighbour to the house opposite.

Kevin's parents' house was a whitewashed thatched cottage that was long and squat, with little windows deep in the straw eaves. There was a horseshoe on the door. Claire was about to knock when Sophie declared, 'Go hard or go home!' and strode straight through it.

Claire loitered on the doorstep, unsure what to do, until she heard a muffled yell from Sophie.

'They're in. They're watching a recording of *The Chase*. I'm going to look around.'

Claire raised her hand to knock, momentarily panicked about knocking in a weird or suspicious way, and in a spasm of terror ended up doing 'Shave and a Haircut'. Soph's head and shoulders appeared from an upstairs window. 'LOL. Although I bet loads of people do that around here.'

Eventually the door was opened by a short woman with very freckly skin and wispy hair that looked as if it had once been chestnut-coloured. She was wearing a calf-length denim skirt, fluffy slippers and a big cable-knit jumper. A blast of heat and savoury cooking smells came with her. She smiled and waited.

'Yes, hello?' she said eventually.

'Oh, right. Er, sorry. Is it, um – it's Sue, right? My name's Claire, I'm a friend of Kevin's. We met whilst travelling in, er, India.'

'Gosh, I didn't think he'd been there.'

'Europe. Probably Europe actually. I've just been around so much that I get mixed up. But Kevin always said how nice this part of the world was for, er, things, and I thought I would drop in and say hello while I was passing through. I hope that's all right.'

'Oh, right! Well, yes. Do come in for a cup of tea, I suppose. Yes, that's lovely.' Sue seemed even more unsure than Claire was, but in the battle between ingrained politeness and feeling uncomfortable with strangers, politeness won. In fairness, it had awkwardness on its side, to deliver a flanking attack.

Claire was briskly introduced to Jeremy, who was wearing a similar jumper but in a different colour (Claire was later told that they were hand-made by Sue). He seemed mostly to want to be left alone to finish watching *The Chase*, so Sue took her into a slate-flagged kitchen to make her a cup of tea. The mug said 'PUG OF TEA' and had a pug on it. Claire took it in red fingers and noticed, as she often did, that she had grown very cold without realizing it. Sue noticed too and asked Claire if she wanted hand-warmers. It was the most mothered Claire had felt for years. No wonder the Wellington-Forges had been so upsetting for Kevin.

He was an only child, it seemed. There were pictures of him everywhere: bouncing baby, chubby toddler, crusty student, crustier adult.

'So you met him while he was Interrailing?' Sue asked.

'Yeah,' said Claire. 'It was... wow, can't even remember when now. Ha-ha! Just such a... er, wild time, you know, everyone gets thrown in together. Kevin was so, um, passionate. And knowledgeable. He had so many interesting thoughts about things.'

Sue nodded and smiled; Claire's furious inventing obviously sounded true to life.

'We've fallen out of touch recently, though,' she added.

Sue rolled her eyes. 'You and me both! Goodness, yes. Kevin texts us every so often from South America, but we haven't seen him for a whole year. Imagine! And coming up on Christmas again.' She lowered her voice. 'I think he's having a bit of a – whatdyoucallit? Like the Mormons.'

'Rumspringa,' said Sophie, walking in.

'Rumspringa!' said Sue, finding the word. 'A late one. He had a bad break-up, you see, and he sent a text to say he was going back to South America, because he'd found himself there before and wanted to do it again. I do miss him, though! And Jeremy misses him too, of course,' she added, clearly being the person who had to write all the birthday cards.

She topped up their mugs of tea again, just as a kitchen timer in the shape of a red pepper buzzed on the side.

Sue cried, 'The casserole!' and pulled a big orange dish out of the oven. It was pheasant in rich brown gravy, with carrots and potatoes and celery and thick suet dumplings. Claire had a brief flashback to the Red Line, and to the soft, beautiful birds hanging by the back door at The Cloisters.

'You... you should stay for dinner!' Sue said, after only a moment's hesitation. 'I'd love to hear stories about your travels and adventures.'

'This should be good,' said Sophie. 'Actually, no, it'll be fine. Sorry. You'll be fine. I can help – I've been in Kevin's room and looked around. Relax.'

'Thank you,' said Claire, looking at nobody in particular. 'That's nice of you.'

In fact dinner *was* mostly fine. Jeremy bore with stoicism the surprise appearance of a stranger. The only wobble came when he asked what brought her to the area, and Claire – a woman wearing a thin wool coat, unlined hoodie and canvas trainers, and carrying only a small fashion-brand rucksack – said 'hiking'. Jeremy raised his eyebrows, but said nothing. Sue sometimes tried to winkle out an anecdote about her son, but with Sophie's help, Claire was able to fob her off, or say something about *Chicken Soup for the Soul* (which, it transpired, Kevin had bought for his mum as well).

When her dish was clean, Claire excused herself to go to the toilet and, on the way back, Sophie directed her to Kevin's room.

'I think this was probably Luke's as well,' she said. 'But it has a big Kev vibe now.'

It was quite small, with white walls and black exposed beams like the rest of the house, and it was neat – but neat in a way that suggested Sue had tidied up a bit, not that Kevin kept it neat. There were a lot of books about meditation written by singers from punk bands, and some glow-in-the-dark stars stuck on the wall by the head of the bed. They'd clearly been stuck up by seven-year-old Kevin and left up by adult Kevin, and Claire suddenly felt a lump form in her throat. Kevin was a bit of a little boy, really.

There was a knot of necklaces and bracelets hanging off one of the bedposts. A lot of them featured the same design of a bright blue eye shape on a royal-blue background. Claire was sure she'd seen it somewhere.

'That's the *evil eye*,' said Sophie mysteriously. 'He must collect them or something.'

'Do you know that because the dead have a connection to all – you know – mystical symbols or whatever?'

'No, I know that because all the tourist shops were selling them that time we went on a school trip to Greece. *Ohmigod*, do you ever pay attention to anyfuckingthing?'

One wall had a cork board covered in printed-out photos, each carefully labelled in the margin. Kevin was in all of them – raising glasses in blurry focus with a whole group in a French bar, with his arm around a couple in a hostel in Vietnam, riding bikes in front of Swiss mountains – and always with people. Never alone, never only him in front of a landmark. There were lots in airports and train stations, too. Claire stretched out a finger towards one.

'Sue's behind you,' said Sophie.

It was very useful to have a talking alarm system. Claire made sure she didn't pause, and touched the photo like she would have if there was nobody else there. It was a selfie, of Kevin with another man about the same age, sitting on a plane. It looked like they'd just taken their seats, because Kevin was still holding his boarding pass. He looked happy.

'You can have it, if you like,' said Sue. 'I'm sure he wouldn't mind. He loved taking photos with people.'

Claire hoped Sue didn't notice that she herself featured in none of them. 'Oh I wouldn't... I can't...'

'It's all right, Claire. I can tell from how you talk about him... You miss him too, don't you?'

'Oh-ho!' yelled Sophie. 'Ohmigod, plot twist! She thinks you had the hots for Kevin.'

Claire curled her toes in her shoes. 'Yes,' she said, looking at this very kind middle-aged lady who had given her dinner. 'I, uh, I'm afraid I do... carry a torch for Kevin.'

'Don't be embarrassed,' said Sue.

Claire realized she was blushing.

'You know, I did think it was funny, you calling him Kevin.'

'What do you mean?' Claire asked.

'Well, it's not his name of course.'

'It... it isn't?' Claire went from blushing to blanched. It was possible that any semblance of cover was about to be blown. 'I'm sorry, I only ever knew him as Kevin.'

'No-o-o, he's not Kevin really. He's Jeremy too, after his dad, but we all called him Jerry. I don't know where "Kevin" came from. I thought he'd only really been called

326

that the past couple of years by his girlfriend – well, his ex, don't worry – and that set of London friends.'

'Oh. I don't know what to say – he's always been Kevin to me,' said Claire, stammering a bit. She was shocked.

'Goodness me, don't give it a second thought. But you go ahead and take that photo. I expect you'll want to be off soon. Not hanging around with a pair of boring old fuddy-duddies like me and Jeremy!'

'Yes, of course, you're right – I mean, no, you're not fuddy-duddies at all. Thank you so much for dinner.'

Claire smiled brightly as she bid Sue and Jeremy Senior goodbye, zipped up her hoodie, shouldered her pathetically small backpack and tried to stride off into the night like a confident and experienced hiker who definitely had a tent.

When they were around the corner, Claire paused to comment on how awkward the entire exchange had been.

'Probably some good clues, though, eh? Chin up,' said Soph.

They walked on in silence for a while, until Claire registered that she was colder than normal again. It was now dark, she realized. She had no extra clothes to put on, nothing to sleep in or on or under, a very low phone battery and, after using some of that battery to check, no bus home. She looked up. There were few street lights around, but unlike at The Cloisters, she couldn't see any stars. So, logically, that meant clouds, which meant there was a chance of rain.

She staggered a couple of steps, leaning all the way forward and then all the way back as she exhaled slowly.

327

'It's okay,' she said, as if she were reassuring Sophie, not herself. 'We'll just... we'll go back towards the pub we saw, right? That'll be open, probably.'

'That's... sensible of you.'

'I know,' said Claire proudly. 'So. Did you see anything in there?'

'Not more than you, really. Kevin's an only child, and they miss him. He really likes people. He makes friends easily.'

'Which is weird, because he is clearly quite annoying – from everything else we've heard,' added Claire. 'But... I hope it's not him. I mean, I hope it's not anyone. But I hope it's not him, for his mum's sake. Kevin's a spoilt "citizen of the world" type, but he's not, like, the *worst*. And Sue gave me hand-warmers.'

'LOL. In need of some motherly love, my little flower?' Sophie pretended to tickle her. Claire did not react, and stared into the dark.

'Well, it's got to be Mattie, right?' Sophie went on. 'Kevin is still in touch with his parents. I mean, I say "Kevin". The name thing is weird.'

'Not really,' said Claire. 'People get nicknames for loads of random reasons. I bet it went: Jerry, to Kevin & Jerry – like *Kevin & Perry Go Large* – to just Kevin. Rich kids like Figgy and Tris do that sort of shit all the time. "Eoooh, his name is Martin, but we all call him Jack, because once he puked up a whole bottle of Jack Daniel's at my sister's wedding, the fucking *ledge*." Don't you remember that guy everyone called Beard because one time he grew a beard for a bit? Or at uni, the kid called David, who got everyone to call him Michael because—'

'Because he really liked R.E.M. Ohmigod, yes. What a loser. On many levels.'

'Yeah. But yeah, you're right. Which means... that it's definitely Mattie, I suppose.'

'The one person we have almost no clues about. Fucksake.'

'Back to the drawing board.'

'Back to The Cloisters probably, if we really want to figure this all out.'

'I'm never going back there again,' said Claire, with some feeling. 'I'd either get shanked by Clem or disappeared by assassins that Monty hires through an offshore account.'

The pub was still open, but it didn't have rooms. Claire drank mulled cider until closing at eleven, mindful that the first few hours in a cold, unfeeling world would go more quickly if she was a bit pissed. She considered dipping into the blood-money that Hugh had sent, with every drink she bought, but couldn't quite bring herself to do it yet.

'Well,' said Sophie, as they left the pub and watched the other customers disappear back to their probably fully central-heated homes, 'since you're having all the good ideas today: where are we going to go now?'

17

Old-Time Religion

When she thought back on the totality of events, Claire would never be able to pinpoint exactly when she decided to try and break into a church – only that it seemed like a good idea at the time. But she was also drunk, so many things seemed like a good idea.

She had, for example, sort of forgotten that she didn't know how to pick locks, and had straightened a single hairpin and was trying to open the church door by sticking it in the lock and wiggling it around. She had definitely seen someone do this on *Murder Profile* and was feeling confident that she was actually quite good at it and was definitely catching at least one of the key pins inside the lock.

She had one ear pressed against the wood of the door, listening intently. There were several minutes of industrious silence.

'I think,' Soph said at last, as if talking to an animal she didn't want to spook – a rabbit, or an Englishman on holiday in Spain – 'that might be for cracking safes.'

'Think 's the wrong kind of lock anyway,' said Claire, unperturbed. 'I'm going to... gonna slice it with one of my cards. Where's my bag?'

'Let's maybe leave the bank cards as a back-up option,' said Soph.

Claire's idea to return to the church *had* been another good one, because the main entrance had a solid sort of porch that was paved and deep enough to have a stone alcove on either side of the door, with an inbuilt bench. It was enough for a medium-sized medium and/or an unprepared idiot to shelter in, for a few hours.

The problem was that the rain clouds had broken while they were still walking back. At first it was the kind of hesitant spit-spotting that made Claire wrap her coat a little closer around herself. But soon it became a proper deluge, the kind of rain that came down with a noise like the sea and shimmered across you in flapping curtains like billowing silk, but that stung when they whipped you in the face. By the time they got to the church, Claire was soaked to the skin, although she almost didn't notice.

Sophie had decided that it was best to get her inside as soon as possible. 'I bet someone comes in to help sometimes,' she said aloud. 'Some old lady doing the flower-arranging or, like, dusting the pulpit. There must be a spare key somewhere.'

Claire judged this to be sound. She bent over to look under the doormat, half fell over the weight of her own head and tumbled sideways into the door. She sat down, sneezed and started laughing.

Sophie scratched her head. 'Good impulse, weirdo. Lacking in execution. Stay there a second.'

Claire watched as Sophie walked through the door. She reached up and stroked the wood where her friend had disappeared. It was cold, but very solid. There were iron studs in it and everything.

Then she turned her head and looked out into the graveyard. It was very dark. She could barely see any-thing past the entrance to the porch. She was in a little lifeboat, she thought, or on a small island. And out there was the rain, her enemy. Sometimes it got in a bit, but it couldn't get in all the way. She'd been too clever for it. Ha-ha.

She became aware that the rain was flashing off some-thing, out in the darkness. It was a little smudge of chalk on a blank slate. Claire beckoned at it, and it came closer and resolved into Luke, the little ghost boy from earlier.

''Lo,' she said.

''Lo,' he replied. 'I've been watching you.'

'Rude of you. Big rude-o.' She slumped her head back and closed her eyes, but that was bad, because everything was going a bit spinny. 'Where've you lot been?' she asked him. He shrugged in reply: they were around, or gone, or everywhere and nowhere. Where did they go when they weren't here? Who knew? Claire didn't. Maybe they went into the memory of the stones, in the graves, in the grass, in the ground.

'What's wrong with you then?' he asked.

'I had too much to drink.'

'Huh!' Luke managed to convey, in one syllable, the full force of an eleven-year-old's contempt for the adult condition. 'Did you go to my house then?'

Claire nodded and described what the upstairs bedroom looked like now.

Luke was stout of heart. 'S'pose lots of things have changed,' he said. 'S'pose the whole place is different now.'

'Footballs are better,' said Claire. 'All made of... something – something special for making good footballs anyway. And... and England won the World Cup in 1966.'

This visibly cheered Luke up. 'Well,' he said, 'Howard didn't say that. That's all right.'

Claire asked if there were spare keys to the church, and if he knew where they were. Luke considered the question, which Claire decided meant he *did* know. She waited.

'I s'pose it's all right if you go in,' he said eventually. 'If I go with you. You won't do anything to get me into trouble?' Claire pointed out that he was probably past the point of getting into trouble. Luke nodded and gestured to the eaves of the porch. 'Up there.'

Claire stood and felt along the ledge under the roof. Yes, keys! Excellent. There was one for the big old impressive lock, and one for the smaller modern one. The door was heavy. The creak when it opened and the clunk as she pushed it closed again was an alarm that surely alerted everyone within a five-mile radius.

Inside, the church smelled of cold stone and old wood. Claire could make out the first few pews and the pillars shooting up to the distant ceiling. She whistled into the space in front of her, but there was no echo, as if the sound was absorbed by an unseen listener. Sophie loomed out of the dark like the top tenth of an iceberg.

Claire realized she was shivering. The ghosts led her to a side room near the pulpit, where she guessed the vicar got psyched up before doing his sermons; she imagined him shadow-boxing like Rocky, and started laughing again. There was a wire-fronted electric heater and she turned it on. The filaments started glowing like a baleful eye, pumpkin-orange and with a demonic flavour that struck Claire as vaguely transgressive in a church. In its dim light she found two brass candlesticks and a box of sensible, white Church of England-compliant candles in a cupboard, and after some fumbling with her lighter she was holding one aloft like a trembling Edwardian widow. The trembling was literal, since the shivers had now completely overtaken her and she stood there in her soggy clothes, a little forlorn, in that delicate way people did when they were trying not to touch any part of themselves with any other part of themselves.

'Here, look,' said Sophie, pointing at a dark mass hanging on the back of the door. 'It's a robe-thingy. A cassock.' She made Luke turn round and encouraged Claire to change into it, arguing that if the vicar had been here, he would have insisted, because it was the most Christian thing to do; and if he hadn't insisted, then he wasn't a proper Christian and was actually a massive shit.

Claire peeled off her wet clothes. They stuck to her, especially her jeans, and she felt as if she was pulling off an old skin. She hung them off the back of a chair and, hands clumsy with cold and cider, positioned the heater so that maybe it would get the worst of the damp out of them.

Standing almost naked in a church made her feel sort of *extra* naked. It took a while getting the cassock on, because she kept mixing up the arm holes and the head hole. It was black and much too big for her, and she felt like a child dressing up. The material was some kind of scratchy polyester, but it was, to her benefit, completely dry. She did the universal 'Look how big this thing is on me' T-pose.

Sophie laughed affectionately at her. 'It's a good look,' she said. 'Strong look.'

Claire fished around in her bag. She found, to her dismay, that many of her Case Notes were soggy, because cheap canvas bags are not known for their waterproof qualities. With the exaggerated care of the drunk, she tipped most of them out and peeled apart some of the more damaged pages, laying them out flat on the floor with some reverence. She also located a lone cigarette rattling around in a fag packet, and got down a couple of grateful gasps of hot smoke before Soph started going on about fire alarms. *Yeah, yeah. It's fine. It's all made out of stone anyway.*

'D'you think God is cross?' Claire asked, her tongue feeling very thick in her mouth.

'If he exists, he's probably got enough complaints about you at this point,' said Sophie. 'I shouldn't worry.'

'I reckon he does exist,' Luke chipped in. 'Or why would we still be here?'

'Can't argue with that,' said Claire. 'S'logical. Although fingers crossed now that he doesn't, cos we've done like, *well* a blasphemy.'

Luke nodded, taking her quite seriously. He was sitting on top of the cupboard that she had previously relieved of candles, and was kicking his heels. It seemed he was determined to keep watch on her all night, to make sure she didn't vandalize his church.

Claire stumbled back out into the main bit – the big main part, with the sitting and standing and singing and all that: whatchacallit? She regarded the altar and the cross on it. It looked quite spooky in the dark.

'Wh-what's this all about then, eh? Why me? Why us? Whaddid we ever do to you?' she shouted, suddenly irritable. There was no response. 'Ha! But the ol' religion keeps her secrets, eh? Typical.'

She hadn't properly unpacked her bag for the whole week, so it still had all her seance kit inside it. After some thought, she went and retrieved her ornate old Bible, and put it with the others on the back of one of the pews. It was a lot bigger than all the rest. This pleased her. She put her candlestick in the cupboard in the vestry. Vestry! Good word. Well done for remembering it.

'You're going to regret that tomorrow,' said Sophie, who had been following Claire as she made her erratic, giggling progress around the church, to make sure she didn't break anything. 'You're going to have to buy some new ones now.'

Claire was now sitting on the floor and had wedged herself up against the bench, feet in front of the heater. It was actually doing a pretty good job of warming the room. She located her phone and was dimly pleased it wasn't wet. She swiped through some of the photos Alex had sent her from the party a year ago, until she came to one where Alex and Basher were smiling together in the foreground, and she smiled back at them. *Ah, Alex and Basher are nice.* It was the photo where Michael was in the background. He was talking to a dark-haired woman she didn't recognize.

'Hey. HEY! Sophie,' she said, holding the phone out unsteadily. 'Whozat?'

'Hold still... oh. That's Mattie, I think. Why?'

'She's wearing Tuppence's cardigan.'

'Hmm? Oh yes, she is. That's weird.'

Claire thought about this. The facts: Mattie had been selling family secrets. Then she disappeared. Her husband is embarrassed, and her son is weirded out, but nobody has reported her missing. Tuppence disappears in the house for unexplained stretches of time, is sharing a cardigan with Mattie and has filed for divorce. Claire started laughing very hard. She picked through her Case Notes with an idle finger and retrieved her newest piece of evidence: the photo of Kevin – except not Kevin, but Jerry.

'Hey, Luke,' she asked, head flopping back against the cushion on the bench. 'Hey, Luke. Luke. What's your last name?'

'Maguire,' he said.

'Ha-ha-ha! Fuck off. It is not.'

''Tis so.'

'Ha-ha-ha. Jerry Maguire!'

Sophie was watching her carefully.

Claire sat wiggling her toes at the evil eye of the heater. The rain was still hammering at the walls and windows, but she was inside now. In a big fort. Ha-ha. There was a broken gutter on the outside somewhere, and Claire could hear the violent splatter from where it was overflowing. It was rhythmical and comforting. It was out there, all wet. And she was in here, warming up her toesies, all full of cider and pheasant. Pheasant – like the dead ones. Argh. She could feel herself slipping into unconsciousness and forced her eyes open to look at the photo in her hand.

'Jerry Maguire,' she snorted. Why would he have such a stupid nickname when his name was already literally Jerry Maguire? That's a built-in joke! Some kind of 'you had me at hello' thing made more sense than a *Kevin & Perry* reference. Someone else had been talking about that, hadn't they? Hmm. She was very tired.

She looked at Kevin's smiling face. He looked so happy. She wondered where he was going. But something else in the picture was trying to get her attention. Her head was jangling at her again, like it had for beacon and bacon. What was it about the picture? It wasn't the guy Kevin was with. Who cared about him? Nobody. Never seen him before. Loser. Get out of the way, loser man. Not important.

Kevin was happy. He was about to fly somewhere. He was holding all his flying stuff – he'd printed out his boarding pass. He probably kept all of them, for some kind of boring scrapbook. But he was holding something else too, only the boarding pass was covering most of it. Something bright blue.

And suddenly she realized. She understood it all. It was all so clear and obvious.

'Soph! Sophie!' she shouted. At least she tried to shout, but it came out as a slur. She had to make Sophie understand. But her eyes had fallen shut again and they were so heavy. Ugh! 'Soph. Look. S'blue.'

'What?'

'Blue. The thing. He can't be gone.'

'Ohmigod, you weirdo. What are you talking about?'

'Ugh! *Listen*. The blue. *The blue!* Like the heater!' Why wasn't Sophie listening?

'The heater? The heater's orange, Claire. Look, explain again in the morning.'

Claire was frustrated. Why didn't Sophie understand? It wasn't that complicated. Her thoughts were getting crossed over, and she was very, very sleepy. But it was important that Soph understood. She tried one last time. 'We have to... We've got to go back, Soph. Got to... go.'

She couldn't hold on any longer. The photo dropped from her hand onto the floor. She could just about hear Sophie and Luke as she slipped into unconsciousness.

'To be honest, she wasn't making much less sense there than she does when she's sober,' Sophie remarked to Luke.

The two of them sat there, talking quietly as the candles burned down. After a few minutes Claire started snoring. Under the cold gaze of two dead children, she slept the unrestful sleep of the blackout.

18

Breakin' the Law

The next day started poorly and went downhill from there. Inasmuch as one can sleep in, while passed out in a church that one has broken into while drunk, Claire accidentally slept in. She woke with an almost entirely numb arse, curled up on the floor. She was woken by Sophie, who had progressed from talking in her ear, up through shouting, standing in her, and the last resort of actually shoving Claire a bit, which she wasn't supposed to do without permission.

'Don't panic,' said Sophie, causing Claire to panic immediately.

She found she was wrapped in great swathes of cassock, to such an extent that she fell over three times just trying to stand up. At some point in the night she had pulled all of her limbs inside it, like the world's saddest, yet most devout tortoise.

'I said *don't* panic, weirdo. Maybe a small amount of panic. There's a woman coming through the graves

– she'll be in the doorway in a couple of minutes. Go-go-go.'

'Go *where*?' hissed Claire. 'Oh Christ,' she said suddenly, as her movement caught up with her, 'Christ, I'm going to be sick.' The cider hangover was worse than the one she'd got from the group rager with Tris, or the second rager with Alex. She vaguely remembered shouting at God the night before and regretted it.

'Do *not* be sick,' ordered Sophie. 'There's a side door behind that curtain.'

Claire stuffed all her errant bits of paper and mostly dry clothes into her bag, shoved the burnt-out candles in their holders back into the cupboard, and was flicking the off-switch on the heater just as the clanking sound of the main door echoed into the nave. She slipped out of the promised side door, which, luckily, had a latch lock. She caught it at the last second, remembering to leave the keys on the side table, and closed it as silently as possible. It was the worst Indiana Jones moment of all time.

Sophie walked along at a sedate pace as Claire crouch-ran through the graves, clutching her half-zipped rucksack to her front, and did a kind of lopsided attempt at a barrel roll into the bushes at the back of the graveyard. She poked her head out cautiously and noted that she had an audience. The church ghosts were watching. Maisie paused long enough to make it clear she was taking the piss and then waved. Sophie stopped to chat to them for a moment, and then sauntered over with a distinct lack of urgency.

Claire ducked down and was extremely sick onto the ground. *Vintage teenage vomming,* she thought. *Throwing up in a graveyard after drinking too much cider: absolute classic.* Could only be improved if it had been cans of Strongbow. She wondered if the police had vom experts, like they did for fingerprints. Could this puke tie her to the scene of her crime? It wasn't much of a crime, though. She hadn't technically broken in, and had only lightly used some candles.

Oh, she'd stolen a spare cassock, hadn't she? But stealing clothes off washing lines and what-have-you was, like, a cheery lovable crime, such as someone like Billy Elliot would do. Claire flopped back onto the dirt, still somehow exhausted.

'Why didn't you wake me sooner?' she grumbled, as Sophie finally arrived.

'*Ohmigod.* I don't have a watch, do I? Don't have anything. How do I know what time it is? Anyway it seemed like you needed to sleep it off.' Sophie surveyed her with a critical eye. 'I think you might be sick, you know. Did that feel like a hangover yak-up or, like, an "I'm actually dying" yak-up?'

'Dunno. I suppose only time will tell.' Claire put her hand to her forehead. It felt hot, but she was not sure if this was because her hand was cold or not. She remembered her mum putting her hand on her forehead when she'd been sick as a child, but she wasn't sure what kind of arcane knowledge was divined from this. It wasn't like she or her mum had thermometers instead of fingers.

By half crouching, half crab-crawling through the sparse hedgerows, Claire (who now thought of herself as being on the run, at least until she made it back to civilization, i.e. somewhere with colour-coded train lines) remained inconspicuous on the way back to the bus stop – although really because it was after 8 a.m. on a weekday and nobody was looking. Aware that she was still cosplaying a vicar, and because it was starting to spit rain again, she stood inside the phone box, breathing slowly and concentrating on not being sick again.

She looked at the phone and remembered something.

'Soph?' she asked, trying not to move in case it dislodged more hangover.

'Mmm?'

'You know when you asked if Monty's firm used Samsungs? Why did you ask that?'

'Because Tristan has two iPhones.'

'Yeah. Hmm.'

'Is this something to do with what you were on about last night? The blue and the heater?'

'What? Oh. *OH!*' Claire suddenly remembered. The rudeness and the urgency of the remembrance made her snap her head up, and she whacked the back of it against one of the panes of the phone box. 'OW! Fucksticks!'

'LOL. That knock anything loose?'

'Yes! Sort of. I figured it out, Sophie! I know what happened. Or...' she faltered, 'I *knew*. I definitely *did*. I can't remember all of it right now, but I saw it all last night. Argh.' She rubbed her head. Her brain was now being assaulted by pain from without and within. 'Shit! If I just had an hour to myself I could remember it all. I'm sure I could.'

Sophie looked sceptical. 'Do you remember the main thrust?'

'Yes. I think so. We need to go back to The Cloisters. Like, right now.'

'That seems like a bad idea. You said you never wanted to go back.'

'I don't. But – not to be mean – it's not like you can stop me, is it?'

'The funeral is today,' Soph pointed out, in a tone that indicated this was another reason to stay away.

'Yeah, but that means they'll be out of the house most of the day,' said Claire. 'Plus, Bash and Alex will definitely be there, so if we get caught, they can, like… stop me being murdered.'

'Caught,' asked Soph, responding perfectly to her feed-line, 'doing what?'

Claire took a deep breath. 'Caught breaking into The Cloisters.'

'And why are we going to do that?'

'Because I know who the ghost is. And I know how we can prove it.'

She was disappointed that the bus to the train station didn't round the corner at that very moment. They were waiting for another twenty minutes.

*

To get to Wilbourne Major they had to catch the bus back to Swindon and then the train into London, only to get a train back out again immediately from the other side of town. It was one of the most hellish tests of moral fibre that Claire had ever gone through. Each awkward turn on the bus was a fresh assault of nausea. Sophie was peppering her with questions, but she screwed her eyes shut and retreated into herself to find any atoms – any molecules within the entity that was Claire – that did not feel unwell, and tried to become them entirely.

At Swindon she took out some cash, and bought a phone charger and a bottle of sugary iced tea. The train tickets would take her almost to her overdraft limit, but she thought it would be worth it. On the train to London she plugged her phone in and looked up a couple of Instagram accounts. She nodded to herself in satisfaction. Sophie was growing impatient and stroppy, but Claire told her she needed to think. She got out some of the Case Notes and put them on the table in front of her. She tried to fit the pieces together as clearly as she had seen them the night before, but she felt them shimmering and changing shape if she looked at them too closely.

She would not remember getting across London. Sophie blew into her hot face and pressed her hands close, helped steer Claire through the thick, sticky veins of the Underground. On the train from London, Claire slept, and the fever set in, in earnest.

She had strange dreams. Dead pheasants with lolling heads and bright blue-and-white eyes. Monty and Ted the gardener were turning over potatoes with garden forks, but when she looked in the ground, they were burying Sophie. She tried to get them to stop, but Sophie opened her eyes and said it was all right. Claire looked up, and Ted and Monty had been replaced by the monk, who was still pointing. She ran into the house and saw Basher seated in front of the fire in the kitchen. He turned into an octopus and squeezed underneath the kitchen door, except that she knew it was the door to the library and she didn't want to go in, because she knew what was in there.

In the end, it was Sophie who roused her.

They had reached Wilbourne Major. It was early afternoon. Claire wasn't sure how long they'd have. She staggered down onto the platform and saw a sticker with a taxi company's number on the station sign. She tried calling it and then remembered there was no signal. Obviously. But a less-confused Claire had prepared for this at Swindon. She walked until she found a pay phone, this time at an intersection, and used some of the change from her iced tea and asked for someone to take her to the Red Line.

The driver, when he arrived, was alarmed. By this point, so was Sophie. Claire was pale and covered in cold sweat, but there was a strange glint in her eye that was terrible to behold. For her part, Claire was possessed of a kind of certainty that she had never felt before in her entire life.

'Why're we going to the pub instead of the house?' Sophie asked. 'That would be way easier.'

'Want to be as low-key as possible, though,' said Claire. 'Sneaky. Turning up at their front door in a taxi isn't very incognito. The house is only over the fields that way. Can easily walk.'

'I see the logic, but you wanting to walk anywhere is very out of character.'

The Red Line was full of people. Smokers were spilling out of the front door. They were all in black, so Claire, who had not bothered to change out of her cassock (although she had put her jeans on underneath, and her black hoodie on over the top) would at least fit in.

Oh, wait. Oh dear.

Peering through the window revealed people eating tiny cheese quiches, limp salad and tiny pieces of meat on tiny pieces of toast. Claire had hoped that if she ended up crashing the funeral, it would have been at the actual funeral, and she would have been standing in the graveyard at a distance, in mysterious Audrey Hepburn sunglasses rather than a second-hand stolen clerical robe. Tuppence was in the corner with Alex and Basher, who were standing close to one another, talking with their heads together. Her wasted heart thudded, and she almost lost grip of the iron rod of certainty that she would imminently use to batter down the door to the truth. So Claire turned away from the window. She put her hood up, in case any of the other Wellington-Forges were nearby.

Near the door she saw a familiar dog being held by a familiar figure. After a moment of hesitation, and with

348

Sophie hissing, 'What are you *doing?*' in her ear, Claire went over and bent down to stroke it. It was unbelievably soft. She buried her face in the fur and then stood up, unsteadily.

'Hello, Alf. I don't know if you remember me. I just wanted to say: I'm sorry. Like, I'm really fucking sorry. I was very rude to you before. I didn't mean to be.'

Alf assessed her, then nodded. 'Hmph. No harm done.'

'So,' said Claire, checking another hunch, 'Hugh's son once said that he isn't a good shot. Is he?'

Alf chuckled, despite himself. 'I'd say not, no.'

'And yet he always manages to hit loads of pheasants on shoots?'

Alf looked at her out of the corner of his eye and smiled in an almost bashful way, but didn't say anything.

'Say no more, Alf, say no more,' said Claire, as Sophie made an '*oh*' of understanding. 'Anyway, we must be off! Got a bit of a walk.' And she cheerily waved goodbye.

They hiked over the fields to The Cloisters, keeping off the road and the long drive, in case any of the family returned to the house unexpectedly. It was starting to rain again, but Claire couldn't feel it; in fact it felt like she was impervious to her old enemy, the sky-water, as if it hissed when it hit her skin. Sophie orbited Claire like a nervous moon. Claire tried to reassure her.

'It's okay, Soph. I know what I'm doing. This is really good actually. A finale! On the day of a fucking funeral! Just like on TV, like you said.'

Sophie didn't seem reassured.

Claire began to get tired. She started chanting Sophie's misremembered Spice Girls lyrics like a kind of incantation: Ham your shoddy clown and wipe it up and down. Over again, in march step. One foot in front of the other. Ham your shoddy clown and wipe it up and down. Eventually Sophie joined in. When the house came into view, it was getting dark and she looked more relieved than Claire.

Claire felt her knees begin to buckle, but she knew she could not stop, not for a moment. There could be no pause. It had to be as smooth as possible, because if she snagged on anything, she would unravel.

There were no lights on, and no signs of movement. They went round the back of the house, which was totally silent. Claire rattled the kitchen door as she passed, but it was locked. 'Key under the mat?' said Sophie hopefully – but Claire had already moved on, stalking to the other end of the building and the damp, sad rose garden. Ted was sitting there.

'Hello, Ted,' said Claire. She scooped up a big flinty stone from one of the flower beds.

'Miss Claire, is it? And Miss Sophie! Blimey. What're you two doing back here? I was just sitting here remembering Miss Janey.'

'That's nice, Ted,' said Claire dreamily. Then she turned and hoofed the stone as hard as she could at the library window.

Sophie threw up her hands. '*Ohmigod!* She's lost it, Ted! I can't stop her. This is it. Endgame. We're going to go to prison.'

The little panes shattered beautifully, all bulging inwards. Claire used her backpack to push as much of the rest of the glass through as possible, before hauling herself inside – she didn't want to be unsafe, after all. But she was mostly shrouded by the fabric of the cassock anyway. She dropped into the dark room like a crow with two broken wings and shook herself down. Ted and Sophie followed closely.

The ghost was there, on its hands and knees, crawling pathetically and mewling, scrabbling at the floor. A whole year spent like this.

Strangely, this time she felt no fear. Only sadness. And anger.

Claire dropped to her knees and reached out to the bony shoulders. She could feel a strange solidity, as if ghostly flesh still covered them, though her eyes could only see a few decaying wet ribbons of muscle and sinew. But she could feel the *zip* like she did with Sophie, and it was twice the drain now, because she had half the strength. 'But I have enough,' she whispered to herself. She made herself look the ghost in the face, as she forced it to experience her presence.

'I'm going to help you,' she said. 'I'm going to find you. Hold on, okay? Just a little bit more. Fuck, I know it's hard. But you can do it. Just a little more. We can do it.'

This seemed to calm the ghost. Claire hauled herself to her feet and it stood as well. It was still. She felt the ghost's gaze on her as she walked as quickly as she could out of the library and into the strange maze of the house.

351

'Which way is the office?' she asked.

'This way,' said Sophie and Ted together.

The office door was unlocked. Claire did not have a plan, physically or mentally, for if it had been locked. She went straight to the desk drawer and pulled it open.

'Oh, thank God.' She nearly wept with relief. 'It's still here. It's still here. They didn't get rid of it.' She reached in and picked up the thin notebook, with the blue cover decorated with what she now knew was the evil eye.

'Oh,' said Sophie. A light of understanding was starting to bloom in her face. 'Oh no.'

Claire opened it and turned to the last page. She nodded to herself once more. At that moment there was the slippery crunch of a car braking hard on wet gravel. 'Ah yes,' said Claire cheerily, as if she had factored this in. 'Probably a silent alarm.' She tucked the little booklet into her pocket as Sophie began directing her: the quickest way out is via the kitchen, so out to the kitchen we go, my girl.

There was a plate of drumsticks under cling film on the side.

'Why is it always fucking chicken?' murmured Claire. She paused to unwrap the plate and take a huge bite. *Ha-ha-ha, I am the chicken weirdo now, Clementine*, she thought; *I have cucked you in your own kitchen. Clucked you. Because, chicken.*

This lame standup bit to the inside of her own head proved to be Claire's undoing. The door onto the lawns swung open and the light flicked on, blinding her for a moment. She raised an arm to block the light, and in that same split second there was a blood-curdling scream of 'The monk! The *mooooonk!*' and a crash.

Claire realized that whoever had just opened the door had seen, in broad strokes, a figure in a black-hooded robe on the day of their grandmother's funeral. As the family legend foretold, a ghostly monk would appear to whomever of the family was next to die. That the detail in this case included sick-stains and a chicken drumstick was immaterial.

'It's Figgy!' Sophie yelled. 'She's keeled over in the doorway. Some others are with her. Let's go-go-*go!* This way.'

Claire obeyed instinctively; it was a voice she had been following almost all her life. She scrambled back the way she had come, following the bright jewel colours of Sophie's hair and clothes through the dark house. Behind them, she heard Figgy shouting something panicky.

'It was *not* the monk, Figgy,' came Monty's voice, deep and cold and dangerous as a glacial spring. 'It had trainers on.'

Sophie brought Claire back to the library and suddenly jinked to one side. Claire dived after her without pause and crashed straight into a bookshelf. She cracked her knees on the floor and grazed a hand, and suddenly everything was awful. It was like something had been uncorked in her throat and she started crying.

Sophie reappeared. 'Shhh,' she cooed. 'Shh, come on, love, it's okay. It's the priest-hole. Come on, quickly.'

Claire scrabbled to locate the button, and then crawled inside to the safety of the darkness. She clapped a hand over her mouth, so that she was crying in silence. Sophie went out to look.

Several pairs of footsteps thundered across the wooden floor, then came to a halt.

'Oh *no*, look. The window!' It was Clementine.

'It was her. I'm sure it was her.' There was Monty, spitting venom. 'That *bloody* woman.'

'D'you think she knows?' That was Tristan.

'Of course she bloody knows!' exploded Monty. 'Why else would she be here? For fuck's sake!'

'Don't worry, darling,' purred Clementine. 'Monty knows it was an accident, don't you, Monty?'

'It was that bloody ha-ha thing.' Tristan sounded like a petulant teenager who'd been asked why his homework wasn't finished. 'It's basically *your* fault, Mum. I told you and Dad there should be more lights out there.'

More facts slotted into place as Claire listened, fixed points in the churning, confused maelstrom of her thoughts.

The floorboards creaked as the footsteps moved around the room.

'She must have gone out into the grounds,' said Monty. '*You* need to get out there and find her – this whole thing is because of you.'

'I'm not going out there without a mac and some wellies,' moaned Tristan. The footsteps came closer to the priest-hole. She could hear someone breathing.

'Stay very still,' came Sophie's voice.

354

Then, very suddenly, there was a long, low wail, a scream, a crash and the sound of running feet. Then, silence.

'Quick! They've gone! The button works from the inside.'

Claire fell out of the priest-hole and lay on the floor, sobbing dry, ragged sobs. She raised her head and saw that the skeleton was lying on the floor too, giving a long, wordless moan. It must have appeared to the Wellington-Forges in order to save her. It had clearly cost a lot.

'Come on, get up,' said Sophie.

'I can't, I can't,' she cried.

'They're coming back, Claire!'

'It hurts,' Claire said, rolling over pathetically.

'Yeah, well, they say life is pain. Maybe that's how you know you're alive.'

'That's the stupidest fucking thing I've ever heard,' said Claire.

She looked at the skeleton again. She got up.

19

Grave Business

Claire had never understood the phrase 'my soul is about to leave my body' before, but as she sprinted across the lawn with the very last screed of energy within her, she did begin to feel strangely weightless. The icy air seemed to be forming cold diamonds in her lungs, so she was drawing less and less breath with every gasp. And now it was raining properly too, so her face was wet and the cassock was cloying, wrapping around her legs. It was like drowning on dry land.

The burning of the lungs in her chest was matched by the burning of the lactic acid in her thighs and the bile rising in her throat. She was either going to pass out or throw up – except she could not do either, because the echoing shouts behind her were a reminder that she was being chased.

She laughed at the absurdity, but no sound came out, because she was already heaving air in and out of her lungs like a bellowing racehorse – albeit one with reduced lung capacity, from an entrenched smoking habit and what she was now realizing was probably the flu. Her heart was hammering too fast; it would surely explode. *This is how I die*, she thought. Record scratch. Freeze-frame. Yup, that's me.

Her rucksack was thumping against her arse in a very annoying way. It shouldn't have been important, but in that moment it really felt like it was.

It was almost pitch-black outside. Sophie was in front of Claire, calling out which way to go. Ted was beside her, pushing her forward with his usual unceasing muttering, though now it was gently encouraging: 'Come on, Miss Claire, nearly there – them toffs won't catch us, don't you worry...'

Suddenly Sophie yelled, 'Stop!' and they screeched to a halt, which was almost as painful as it would have been to keep running. 'It's the bloody pissing fucking ha-ha,' she said. 'It's just in front of you.'

Claire began to inch forward with some caution, having a wary respect for the ha-ha, but suddenly Ted shouted too. 'The lights!' he said. 'Miss, they're turnin' on the lawn lights.'

She spun round and saw that The Cloisters was now eerily lit by blueish floodlights pointing upwards from the ground, angled at the walls – the sort of thing to make the grey stone look good in wedding photos. The next step, then, would be floodlights on the building and the roof, angled at the grounds...

Claire panicked and took a blind running jump into the dark void in front of her.

It wasn't quite far enough. One foot clipped the top edge of the ha-ha's wall and pitched her forward. Something in her ankle *crunched*. She fell awkwardly at the bottom of the ditch and curled over like a child, biting her own hand to stop herself crying out at the pain, the white-hot red feeling blooming from her foot. She would have been winded if she wasn't already almost completely out of breath.

But she'd dropped out of sight before the lights hit her. The bright white of the lawn floodlights was blaring out over the top of the ha-ha, a big fanfare of the Wellington-Forges' reach. It cast a long shadow onto the rough grass beyond the lawn. But in the lee of the ha-ha, she was safe and hidden. They had no idea where she was. Claire took some satisfaction from that. Where once the rain and the dark were her enemies, now they were allies against the light. *Yes*, she thought to herself, as she began to hop along the length of the ditch, leaning on the rough bricks in lieu of a crutch, *I must become the dark...*

The ghosts followed her. Ted was walking along the top of the wall, keeping an eye out. 'Why's she doing a funny voice?' he asked Sophie eventually.

'Er...' said Sophie, who was walking alongside Claire, and apparently could not think of a way to explain the memetic qualities of certain movie characters to a long-dead gardener.

'You merely *adopted* the darkness...' mumbled Claire, unaware that they were talking at all, much less about her. They hobbled on for a few more minutes, although her perception of time was beginning to rubber-band in and out. It stretched to a point of agony, where each step felt like an hour, and then snapped back to her, so that she was aware she did not have enough of it and that every second was precious. If she could get to the far edge of the grass, she'd be in with a chance. From there, she thought, trying to remember the old blueprints, she could crawl along and make it around the hook-shaped bit of grass that reached to the back of the copse, where the old monastery ruins were. Claire was convinced that was where the body was. And if not, she could hide there. It'd be all right. She was quite warm now, really.

They were in sight of the bushes and scrubby trees that marked the right-hand boundary when Ted flapped his hands and indicated for them to be quiet. He even started whispering, which Claire thought was quite sweet. Sophie made a zip-yer-mouth-shut motion at Claire, because she was still muttering things like 'I didn't see the light until I was already a man.'

Footsteps were slipping over the wet grass. Claire pressed up flat against the wall, trying to disappear into it, if at all possible. Her breathing was still ragged and she tried to hold it in, but she was pretty sure it wouldn't matter, because they'd hear the pounding of her heart and the thunderous rushing of her blood.

The lights of a couple of powerful torches were tracking back and forth across the distant trees of the copse, but without much enthusiasm. And they were very narrow beams, lighting up only what they were shining on directly. That was good to know.

'I don't... I don't fucking like it, Monty,' said Tristan, who now sounded like he was, or was about to start, crying. 'It's fucked – the whole thing is fucking fucked.'

'Everything will be *fine* once we find her,' replied Monty, doing a very good job of sounding confident. They were both half shouting over the rising wind.

'You saw it too, Monters. What the fuck was that – it wasn't a fucking monk, it's after me, Monty, what are we going to do?'

'Shut up. Just shut up. We didn't see anything.'

The torches flicked off. Footsteps turned away, back towards the house.

'Don't say anything in front of Alex or Basher, you bloody idiot, you know that they'll...' But then they trailed out of earshot.

Ha-ha, thought Claire. I was right under their noses, and they didn't even know. Good ol' cassock. Good ol' darkness.

After a moment Ted indicated they should move again. 'You all right, Miss Claire?' he asked.

Claire smiled cheerfully at him. '"The shadows betray *you*, because they belong to me!"'

'I think that's a yes,' said Sophie critically. 'I don't think we have a choice any more, anyway.'

'My foot hurts,' Claire added. 'This thing is a health-and-safety nightmare. Tristan *did* fall over and ruin his suit, and he *did* get in a fight, but that's not the whole story, you see? If you want to lie well, you tell a bit of the truth.'

'That's making more sense. Attagirl.'

360

'Oh yes, that's exactly what happened. I saw the whole thing,' said Ted, as if he wasn't saying anything at all. Claire stopped and looked at him incredulously.

'You saw the whole thing? This whole time?'

'The fight last year, and the body and that? Of course. Lot of us did. Not much interesting goes on round here. Someone gets killed, we all has a look. You would too.' Claire started laughing uncontrollably, until Sophie shushed her.

'Ohmigod, Ted,' said Soph, turning on the old man. 'Why didn't you *say*?'

'You never asked!' said Ted, sounding affronted. 'How'm I s'posed to know what you want to know and what you don't, of everything that happens here? And you all buggered off after a day.'

'Bloody hell,' grumbled Sophie as they reached the end of the ha-ha.

Claire got on all fours and crawled into the bushes and leaf mould. It already smelled of death. Also, of what she suspected was sheep shit. She fumbled into her pocket for Sophie's hair-clip to rub at, for comfort, but it wasn't there. She started thrusting her hands into the dead leaves and dirt in a panic, trying to find it, but she was mindful that Tristan would soon be back out, with his torch and his wellies.

'What are you doing, idiot?' said Sophie. 'Come on – come the fuck on!'

Claire got up and started to limp/hop/run towards the ruins. She glanced back towards The Cloisters and saw pale figures drifting across the lawn. Evidently Ted was right. The local ghosts turned out for anything exciting. But as she looked, the kitchen door opened again and disgorged a hunting party of Wellington-Forges. Claire didn't pause to count them, but hobbled off into the darkness once more. The wet slick of leaves made a terrible noise as she dragged her feet through them, but she couldn't be sure that it wasn't lost in the wind anyway.

With directions from Ted, they made it to the ruins. These were suddenly cast into sharp monochrome relief by a crackle of lightning – the first appropriately dramatic moment of the night. Claire approved.

She hadn't expected the ruins to be so... ruinous. The tallest point was the shell of a two-storey building, but it clearly was no more than that – it had no guts or roof left. There were vestiges of walls for other structures, and two and a half rows of columns forming part of a square, some of them broken and sticking up like jagged teeth. The titular cloisters.

'Come on,' Sophie encouraged her. 'In here.' She pointed Claire to the building.

As she got close, she could make out that it was made of stone in all different sizes, no nice clean uniform bricks. It was almost like it was formed of a single lump of clay. As Claire stepped towards the blank gap of the doorway, a tall figure loomed into it.

'Argh! Christ! Don't do that!' she exclaimed.

It was the monk. *The* Monk. Simeon, Ted had called him. She'd seen him the very first day, but far off. Up close,

362

Claire could see why he would frighten a lot of people, possibly to death. He was very tall, and all you could see under his cowl was a stern mouth and a long, thin nose, the same colour as his cloudy grey habit. He stood there, looking imposing, sizing her up. Around him the rain pounded on the walls of his home, yet he stood implacable. Calm as the stones. Claire felt small and ashamed, and wanted to apologize that anyone had ever mistaken her for him, even if only for a second. And for all the blasphemy.

When Simeon spoke, his voice was deep and rich, and he had no need to shout against the wind.

''Sup,' he intoned.

'I... Sorry, what?'

'It is a traditional greeting, is it not?'

'LOL!' said Sophie.

It was her first LOL in a while, and hearing it calmed Claire down a bit. Her foot was throbbing in a way that indicated rubbing it and going 'ooooh, owwww' for a bit wasn't going to cut it; her skin was sizzling; her thoughts were flying into all corners of her head like frozen peas sliding under the cooker, and she was very, very afraid. But Sophie could still do a LOL. So it wasn't all bad.

'This way, child,' said Simeon, stepping aside and sweeping out a proprietary arm. 'He is here.'

Claire staggered into the shadow of the building. The rain still swept in, but the sound and fury of the wind were immediately less. She decided to chance the torch on her phone. 'Can't see fuck all otherwise,' she explained out loud.

Simeon coughed in disapproval, but otherwise stayed silent.

It was a sad little room. The floor was bare mud, with puddles here and there and leaves building up in drifts in the corners. There was a patchy carpet of sickly green moss and little stones, but Claire thought – perhaps imagined – that one area was disturbed and wasn't as weathered as the rest. She noticed a spade, starting to grow rusty, discarded to one side. Immaterial. Doesn't matter. Leave it all here.

'You tried to show me, didn't you?' she said suddenly, looking up at Simeon. In reply, he only spread his hands in mute appeal. 'Bloody ghosts! Why can't you ever *say* what you want. It's all cryptic this, and pink shepherdesses that! Oh don't mind me, I'll just pick up the shovel, will I? Yes, I will. Fucksake. Can't even hold the torch for me. Go and keep a lookout, Ted.'

'You're sounding more lucid,' remarked Sophie.

'Well, I'm narked off, aren't I?' she replied.

Claire began to dig. It was very hard because the earth was cold, and she couldn't put her weight on her bad foot either, to leverage the shovel, or to push down on it. She started jumping awkwardly on the blade with her good foot and levering it with her whole body. Clods of earth began to come up. Claire was exhausted. Her arms were like noodles.

More ghosts were seeping through the walls as she worked. All ages, all epochs, shapes and sizes. The air grew unbearably cold. The rain falling inside the walls turned to sleet and then snow. It was, Claire thought, almost beautiful. She fell to her knees and started using the shovel with her hands, holding it near the top of the blade and dragging and scraping away at the ground. Her fingers were numb. The exertion was throwing iron rings around her heart and chest again. She could not breathe deeply enough. She was sobbing out loud in rage and pain and fear, but she couldn't feel the tears.

At last the point of the blade hooked on something. A loop of plasticky canvas material. It wasn't really very deep after all. Of course it wasn't. They didn't even care *that* much. Claire grabbed it and pulled, and the ground disgorged it, almost vomited it up like it knew it shouldn't be there. It was a backpack. A proper one. Covered in patches and badges. COEXIST. She set it to one side and saw that it had brought something else with it.

It was still half buried, but it gleamed yellowish-brown in the light of her phone: an almost skeletonized arm, from the elbow down. Claire was dimly aware that if she'd been in a normal state of mind she would have been horrified. But now she felt only relief. She reached out shakily and clasped the hand.

'Hey, Jerry,' she said. 'I've got you. Your mum misses you. I've got you.'

Several things happened. First, Claire heard someone shouting. Second, she felt the lifting of a great oppressive weight that she hadn't even realized was pushing down on her. This was tempered a bit by the third event, which was an explosion of agony from her injured foot, because someone was using it to pull her back.

She slid over the muddy ground. Her rucksack was pulled off her back, twisting her arms round as it went. She screamed a gargling, unwilling scream of pure pain and kicked out instinctively with the other leg. It caught someone in the arm and they fell back: Tristan, who dropped his torch. It lit him from below and he looked haggard and scared. His face was streaked with tears.

'Tris!' Claire cried desperately. 'Please, Tris, it's okay. I know it wasn't your fault.' He hesitated and looked confused. Claire pressed on. The wind was quieter in here, so she lowered her voice and talked calmly. 'It's okay. You'd just fought about the Arrowhead Beacon thing, right? You were trying to protect the firm – to make Monty proud. And Kevin fell off the wall in the dark. You weren't to know. He hit his head on a rock – you didn't kill him. It could have happened to anyone.'

Tristan nodded almost involuntarily and picked up his torch slowly. Sophie nodded too. 'You've got him Claire, you've got his number. Exactly like a seance. You know what to do.'

'That's what I thought. I bet it was your mum who made you cover it up, wasn't it? They put so much pressure on you, but it's not your fault—'

Other people were shouting in the distance now, and Tristan's head snapped round.

'No, Tristan, wait, please, you don't have to... aa*arrghaaaaa*!'

He pulled on her foot again and shouted, 'Here! She's here! I've got her for you, Monty!'

Sophie stepped forward so that she was occupying the same space as Tristan. He did an involuntary full-body spasm, and Claire managed to kick out with her good leg again. She cracked him across the face as he bent over; he landed with a thump and did not immediately get up again. His torch fell and winked out.

Claire scrabbled to her feet, but her phone had skittered off and the light was gone. There was only the wild disco-swinging of someone else's torch, and she couldn't see – she couldn't see! Someone slapped her across the face, hard, and she fell down again.

'Sophie!' she screamed. 'Sophie, where are you?' She was so afraid. She had never been alone. She started crying again, but in a desperate way, like a child.

'You're mad,' said a familiar, cruel voice, full of contempt. 'But at least that means nobody will believe you.'

Stupid, stupid Claire. What was the plan, anyway? Dig up a dead body in the middle of the night, and then what? Hike back towards the pub and die in the field on the way there? Ask the Wellington-Forges, very nicely, if she could use their phone to snitch on them? She rolled over, mewling.

Ted was raging at Monty. 'Bastard! You toffee-nosed bastard! You're a disgrace.' He was flailing and punching right through Monty's face, but all it did was cause Monty to shiver and twitch his nose. Claire could see the other ghosts watching. The Monk was bending over to look at Tristan.

'Sophie?' she whispered.

At last: 'I'm here. I'm right here. I'm not going anywhere.'

'Sophie, I can't get up,' Claire sobbed.

'You will,' said Sophie firmly. 'You fucking *will*. You will, because nobody else here can. I can't. I'm not strong enough. I need you to do it for me. Please, Claire. You were always stronger than me.'

'I can't, Soph, I can't. I'm not strong. I don't have anything left. Please tell me it's okay to stop.'

'If that's what you really want, you can stop. I'll hold your hand and you can go to sleep. But I don't think you want that yet.'

'But I'm so tired. It hurts. I lost your hair-clip, Sophie. I dropped it somewhere out there.'

'That doesn't matter. It's only a thing. It's not real. It doesn't matter,' said Sophie. 'I'm not real, Claire. It doesn't matter.'

Claire realized that Sophie was crying too. She hadn't ever seen Sophie cry. Her tears disappeared before they hit the ground. 'I can't do it alone,' she whispered.

'You're not alone. Let's do it all together, Miss Claire,' said Ted, stepping away from Monty. His voice was quiet and firm, like he knew exactly what to do. 'All of us together, eh, Miss Sophie?'

'I don't know how,' said Sophie, equally quietly. 'It only takes. When I hold her it only takes from her.'

'Ah, it won't be that hard. Don't take, Miss Sophie. Push the other way. We can help you give.' He reached out his hand to Sophie and she, after some hesitation, took it.

And, smiling and kind, with his other hand Ted beckoned to the other ghosts. 'Don't just stand there looking, you useless buggers.'

Slowly, but then with more confidence, the dead of The Cloisters linked hands. Simeon first, and then the old lady and the little Frenchman, still bickering. A girl in a sailor dress and a straw boater. A serious-looking butler. On and on through the centuries, a daisy chain of the dead. Claire could not understand what was happening.

Monty, without the distraction of a cold ghost slapping him in the face, was advancing on Claire. He looked wild. His hair was askew, his suit was torn. He was, she was sure, probably going to kill her. Claire heard more shouting, saw more flickering light in the distance. She hauled herself back a few feet, met her rucksack, scrabbled in it for her candlestick to use as a weapon and then realized she no longer had it. Monty laughed at her, and she saw how pathetic she must look in his eyes.

Then Sophie took her hand.

A river of warmth flowed into Claire. Strength flowed down hundreds of years, from one memory of life to the next and the next, pouring their existence through Sophie, and through Sophie into Claire.

'Get up, weirdo. Get up one last time. *Get. Up.*'

Claire rose like an avenging angel. There was no pain. There was no fog clouding her mind. Even if she wasn't actually glowing, she *felt* like she was. She felt like stars sparkled in the wake of her every movement. She felt like death astride a pale horse. And she did have a weapon.

Her arm swung in a graceful parabolic arc as she strode forward, backed by the vengeful dead of every generation. She hit Monty with great and terrible force, full across the face, with a big purple dildo.

He spun. He frowned. He dropped. Cold-cocked.

Claire let go of Sophie's hand and stood, swaying, as she lost herself again. One by one, the ghosts were disappearing. The snow was turning back into rain. Soon it would all be gone, like nothing had happened. She saw Ted smile and blow a kiss as he faded away, and she tried, groggily, to reach out to him. Her vision dimmed and she staggered sideways as she began, at last, to faint. It was probably long overdue. The last thing she saw as she fell was Basher sprinting towards her, and the last thing she heard was Sophie screaming.

'Help her. Fucking *help her*!'

20

After the Funeral

The next thing Claire knew was a white ceiling. There was pain in her foot, but it was remote. She observed the sensation objectively, like it was happening to someone else. Mmm. That was a hurty ankle all right.

Good deduction. Back on track.

She turned her head to one side and further observed that she could only blink very slowly. There was a machine bleeping at her, and a drip-thingy. Stuck in her arm. Furthermore, the wall was a curtain, and Sophie wasn't there.

'Sfr?' she said.

'LOL. This side, weirdo.'

She rolled her head to the other side. Sophie was lolling in a chair that had wooden arms and upholstery that looked easy to wipe down. A nurse in an old-time sixties uniform was standing next to her.

'Whermy?'

Sophie opened her mouth, but was cut off.

'You're in the Royal Bournemouth Hospital,' said the nurse. 'And you gave everyone a fright, I'm sure. Now, you just go back to sleep. We've got you on plenty of fluids and a good whack of painkillers. You need to rest up and let your body heal. Keep you in for a week, I shouldn't wonder! Now I must do the rest of my rounds.'

She breezed through the other dividing curtain in a chilly gust. Soph jerked her head after her. 'Ohmigod. Thought she'd never leave. Barrel of laughs, her. And FYI, I heard a more this-century nurse say they'd probably hoof you out tomorrow, if not later today. NHS cutbacks, mate. They need the beds, and you've been sleeping it off for a night already. I'm very bored, by the way.'

'Wzappen?' Claire insisted.

Sophie told her that everything was okay; people had been arrested, nobody extra had died, the wake had been ruined, and so on. So Claire went back to sleep.

When she opened her eyes again, no time had passed, except that it definitely had. Claire could think quite clearly and her foot hurt quite a bit, and Sophie definitely wasn't on either side of her. She also desperately needed a wee. This was her main concern.

A solid, fleshy nurse with warm hands was taking her vitals. He smiled and told her that her temperature had gone down loads. He said it with such approval that Claire replied, 'Oh, thank you', as if she'd done it on purpose.

A young doctor came round and made eye contact almost exclusively with the file about her. He told her that her foot wasn't broken, just badly sprained, but she had also given herself flu and had almost killed herself by not eating or drinking and by gallivanting about the countryside digging up skeletons, which was very silly of her – although Claire was obviously the talk of the ward. Anyway, now that her fever was under control, she could go home with her friends and rest for a while and keep off that foot. But if she got bad again, she was to go straight back to hospital. Was that clear?

'Everything but the going-home bit,' said Claire. 'I live in London. That's ages away. How am I supposed to get back? Is there a train or something?'

'Well, I don't know about that. There are trains, but you'd have to look up the timetable. I was told that someone is filling out your forms at the ward desk and is taking you home. That's why you're being discharged.'

The curtains around Claire's bed were thrown violently apart. 'Hello, C!' cried Alex, a vision in a silver catsuit. The doctor beat a hasty retreat in the face of a hurricane that had ripped through a haberdasher's on its way to the hospital. At some point they had changed their hair from blue to bright pink. 'We're getting you out of here, *Cuckoo's Nest*-style!'

'You're going to throw a sink through a window and I'm going to be lobotomized?'

'Very funny. At what point does deliberate pedantry cease being a defence mechanism and start being you... being a dick? Here, eat this.' They thrust a hot sausage bap into Claire's hand. It was the most delicious thing she had ever eaten in her whole entire life.

373

'They look an extra from, like, a budget *Star Trek: TOS* cosplay group,' observed Sophie, strolling up behind them.

Alex had also brought Claire some clothes, since she had been admitted in a large men's-size cassock covered in mud, and possibly with trace particles of dead body – and, even if she'd wanted it back, the cassock had been taken as evidence. They waited while Claire went to the toilet and changed into a nice snuggly oversized jumper and leggings, and some fuzzy slipper-socks. She was also able to address the need for a wee, which made her feel less anxious about the world in general.

Basher was the one filling out her forms, it turned out. He smiled at Claire as Alex helped her over to the desk so that she could sign the paperwork.

'Come back, strange ghost-talking girl,' he murmured, giving her a brief hug. 'All is forgiven.'

'What he means is that *we* are very sorry and hope you forgive *us*,' said Alex, rolling their eyes.

They weren't given a wheelchair, but were allowed a hospital-issue crutch. Claire leaned heavily on it, but slightly more heavily on Basher, who was helping her. He felt strong but wiry, like he was made of Twiglets and muscle. Sophie noticed what she was doing and told Claire that she was a creep, but had probably earned it for now.

Alex was carrying her things – at least the ones that hadn't been impounded – along with the cassock (black) and dildo (purple). Claire was vaguely worried about the cassock. Was she going to be arrested for stealing it? Surely the police had bigger fish to fry than cassock-thieves? She also felt it was very important to explain to someone that the dildo was not in fact for personal use. This information needed to reach the CPS.

Unresisting, she was bundled into the front of Basher's car and covered in a blanket. Sophie sat behind her and kept leaning forward to check on her, like a family dog worried about the new baby. Alex slid into the back next to Sophie.

'Thanks for taking me home,' Claire said as they set off.

'We-e-e-ell,' said Alex, 'what else could we do? You clearly can't look after yourself. Not that Uncle B can, either, obviously.'

'Can too look after myself,' said Claire, snuggling into her blanket. Alex was pulling bits of embroidery out of their bag, and Basher was whistling tunelessly through his teeth. Alex started to explain the finer points of advanced embroidery techniques out loud for Sophie, pointing out how they formed different stitches to create different effects. It felt familiar. Claire promptly fell asleep again.

When Alex shook her awake, they were not in London. They were on the street outside the flat in Brighton. Claire voiced her confusion.

'What did you think we meant when we said "take you home"? You didn't think we'd leave you in that shithole flat, did you?' replied Alex, somewhat incredulously.

'In fairness, if we'd have gone back there you would have been found dead three weeks later, covered in bread-crumbs and fag ash,' said Soph.

Claire thought she would probably quit smoking. She was soon safely ensconced on the sofa, wrapped in a new layer of blanket, and had ibuprofen and Lucozade liberally administered. Basher put her foot up on a chair, on a cushion of frozen peas.

'You look like a cross between a mummified queen and a fat baby,' said Sophie. 'Actually, you know when Princess Margaret used to get wheeled around in a chair with big sunglasses on? That vibe.'

'I thought you were going to be nicer to me.'

'That is nicer, I said you look like a princess. It's a work in progress. Oh, all right. You did well, weirdo, and I'm glad you're not dead.'

Claire looked up and realized that Basher and Alex had, as best they could as a two-person group, gathered around her and were looking at her expectantly.

'G'wan then,' prompted Alex.

'What?'

'Come on, we all know you're dying to do a summing-up.'

'You even tried to do a summing-up while we were waiting for the ambulance at The Cloisters,' added Basher. 'I am afraid I did not appreciate how funny it was at the time.'

'Yeah, you tried to stand up and went, "I suppose you're wondering why I gathered you all here" and everything. Uncle B just went, "NO-O-O-O!" and you instantly passed out again. It was brilliant.'

'Oh,' said Claire. 'I don't remember any of that.' She was too tired to be embarrassed. Physically tired, not mentally. She was feeling quite awake and alert now, but if someone had demanded that she lift her arm an inch or they'd have to kill her, she'd have had to dictate her last will and testament.

Basher and Alex took turns explaining their side of the story. Alex had spotted Claire's ghastly visage peering through the pub windows, on account of the fact that she had done nothing to hide herself, but when they went to look, she'd already gone. Then later, when they heard that the rest of the family had hightailed it back to the house after the alarm had been tripped, Basher and Alex realized who must have tripped it. They had arrived just in time to restrain a distraught Clem, and to see Claire knock out Monty with a sex toy.

And they had also seen the ghosts. Only for a moment. A strange mist that, in one bright flash of lightning, looked for a second like a crowd of people. And then it was mist again, already thinning. Already never there. But it was enough.

'Pretty sure you're not a fraud any more, C,' said Alex, looking at their feet. 'Er, sorry again, about all of that.' They were uncharacteristically embarrassed. It made them sound like the rest of their family: posh and a bit stilted.

'I, too, am very sorry, and now believe in ghosts,' said Basher, nodding. 'Although *for the record*, not believing in ghosts would not make me the strange one.'

All of the rest of the Wellington-Forges – bar Figgy, who genuinely had no idea about any of it; Tuppence, who was likewise completely innocent and visibly relieved to see her soon-to-be ex-husband carted away; and Tristan, who had a broken nose and was under observation after hitting his head – were in custody in St Leonards police station. Bail was being arranged. Claire would need to be interviewed. It was, Basher said, probably a bit naughty of them to have spirited her away from the hospital without telling the police, and someone would be told off, but it would be him, so that was all right.

'So,' he said. 'The stage is yours. Let the summing-up commence.'

'Wait, though,' said Sophie. 'Are you two... all right?'

'Oh, fuck no, of course not,' said Basher, laughing. 'This is all awful. I also found out that Nana left me everything, but nobody told me, because they were planning to dispute it! Fabulous stuff.'

'He's been letting me smoke indoors and everything,' said Alex, lighting up as evidence. 'I am gravely concerned. Anyway. Off you go, Claire.'

'Oh. Right. Er.' She found that, having never actually done a murder summary before, she wasn't quite sure where to start. It looked easier on television. 'Right, so, it wasn't really murder. It was an accident. Michael told Kevin – Jerry, his real name was Jerry – about Arrowhead Beacon, a shell company that Monty and Hugh were using to embezzle funds from—'

'No, no, we know all that.' Basher cut her off, flapping a hand dismissively.

'Uncle T crumbled like a soggy biscuit as soon as a police officer, like, *looked* at him,' said Alex. 'Buckled

378

like a cheap belt. Tumbled like a badly-built Jenga tower. It was honestly a bit embarrassing.'

'I want to know how you figured it out,' said Bash. 'I didn't figure it out, and it was my job to figure things like that out. It is a point of some personal pride.'

'Well, a lot of it was luck really,' said Claire. She was trying to sound humble. The great detective. 'I spoke to Michael, see, about the accounts, and he told me he'd spoken to Kevin about it. So I started to think we might have got things mixed up. It wasn't really about what we *thought* it was about. Kevin got angry about something else, which is why we didn't see it, d'you see? It was the wrong... thingy. Motive. The motive didn't match the victim. Kevin accidentally stole Michael's motive.'

Claire realized she was not putting things very clearly.

'Ohmigod. Just lie about the order that you thought of stuff,' said Sophie. 'Go on. Say, "My first clue came when..."'

Claire smiled.

'Really,' she said, 'my first clue came when I found the blue notebook in your parents' office, but of course I didn't realize it at the time. But we'll come back to that. The second clue – of *vital* importance – was Basher hearing the boys arguing about breakfast. What he actually heard was Michael saying, "I'm serious about Beacon." Arrowhead Beacon! But the mind plays little tricks, and Basher thought he'd heard "bacon", and a year later all he could remember was that it was something about breakfast...'

She paused, and Alex went '*Ooooh*' in a very satisfactory way.

Claire explained how her conversation with Michael had started her thinking about Kevin's state of mind. He was already angry about how he'd been treated by the family, especially by Tristan and Monty, and now he had a way to pick a fight with them that wasn't about Figgy. And that, more importantly, gave him leverage.

That didn't prove that Kevin – or Jerry really, as she was trying to think of him now – was actually the victim. And she hadn't thought he was really, until she'd seen all the evil-eye charms in his room, and later had been looking at the picture of him on the plane and saw that he was holding something bright blue behind his boarding pass.

'And what do you hold alongside your boarding pass when you've just got on a plane?' she asked.

'Your passport!' exclaimed Basher.

'*Précisément*. I remembered seeing a blue notebook, the same bright blue with that evil-eye design on the cover, in the desk in the office at The Cloisters. I didn't realize it was a passport at first, because he had it in a protective passport cover, but when I saw all the evil-eye decorations in Jerry's bedroom I started to realize. I had to come back to the Cloisters to check, but I was pretty sure it wasn't a notebook by then. And if Jerry didn't have his passport...'

'He couldn't have left the country,' finished Basher.

'Exactly. From there, everything else started to make sense. Tristan and Jerry got into a shoving match, and

Jerry fell off the ha-ha and hit his head, and of course the first thing Tristan did was run to get his mum. That's what Tuppence and Alex heard in the kitchen – Tristan ruining his suit happened during the fight. Then Clem took control of the cover-up. She got the lads to carry Jerry inside, but upright. I was right about what The Clefs saw: not some brothers carrying one of their own inside, after a fight, but a family sneaking a body past them. They counted on the fact that The Clefs wouldn't have kept tabs on everyone there.'

And there was more.

'They stashed Jerry in the priest-hole for a day until they could bury him on Sunday night, and got Tristan away from you all, in case he broke down in front of you and Sami. That's why he went on the shoot with Hugh. And Sophie noticed that Tristan had two iPhones, when the company phones are Samsungs, so that second iPhone couldn't have been a company phone. Well, one of them was actually Jerry's. The messages that Figgy got were ones he tried to send on Saturday after the argument, but they only went through when Tristan and Monty left the area and the phone got a signal again. So they all arrived at exactly the same time.'

Later Tristan had used the phone to set up an Instagram account for Kevin, posting old photos that he found in the gallery. He, like the rest of the family, didn't know or could not remember Kevin's real name, and so he didn't find the Instagram that already existed under Jerry Maguire. But Claire did.

'How did you know it was Tris?' asked Basher.

'The *Kevin & Perry Go Large* references. He kept making them on the fake account. And he couldn't help it in real life, either.'

Alex raised a hand. 'Sorry to stop you mid-flow,' they said, 'but I have no idea what any of this means. Please remember I'm not old, like the rest of you.'

Claire snorted, then sneezed. '*Kevin & Perry Go Large* is a film, based on a sketch from a sketch-show, about two grown adults playing stereotypical teenagers. They go on a bender in Ibiza and try to have sex and become famous, that kind of thing. It came out when we were, like, ten or eleven, but people latched on to it. All that Eyeball Paul stuff – that you get more drunk if you do shots through your eyes. That was all around my school for years after.'

'I remember that,' said Soph. 'People stopped trying after a while, because it really stings. I bet Tristan was trying to use his initiative with the Instagram, because there's no way Clem or Monty is stupid enough to think that was a good idea. Like, the minute anyone went looking for Jerry, they'd be pinging his phone off whatever BT tower was next to Tristan.'

'Yeah, if Dad had known, he would have been furious, I bet,' said Alex. 'Poor old Uncle T.'

'Feels like we got lucky with the passport, too,' said Claire. 'Keeping that was a massive liability. I bet it fell out of Jerry's bag before they buried him, and then Clem found it and kept meaning to do something about it, but

382

just shoved it in that drawer and half forgot about it. It was definitely Clementine who organized the cover-up, though. Moving the body, getting all her boys in line. She's... formidable.'

'One word for it!' snorted Soph.

'All right, so what about Alf and Grandad Hugh and the drug-smuggling?' asked Alex.

'Oh, that's easy, I can do that one,' broke in Soph. 'Hugh is a massive loser – no offence – and simply wants to fit in and be respected, like at the pheasant shoots. But he's a terrible shot – you told us that, Basher – and the only way he knows how to fix problems is with money. He was paying Alf to keep back pheasants that someone else shot and then pass them on to Hugh, to try and make it look like he bagged loads. I don't think he was fooling anyone. It was nothing to do with Mattie.'

'So the only thing that doesn't really fit is the crystal button,' said Basher, sounding almost wistful.

'I, er... I worked that one out too,' said Claire. She looked at Alex and was a bit shocked to see that they had started giggling.

'You *did*?' said Sophie in an incredulous tone.

Alex raised a hand like they were in class. 'I actually found out this one yesterday. Mum has left Dad. Not a moment too soon, as it turned out. I'm very pleased for her. But, um, as it happens, that is also the answer to the Mattie mystery, and the where-Mum-was-always-sneaking-off-to mystery. Because that is who Mum has left Dad for.'

'*Ohmigod. Amazing.*' Sophie looked positively thrilled.

'You mean...?' said Basher.

Alex rolled their eyes. 'Yes, panto cast-member, I mean that Mum and Mattie have done an elope. Well, half of one. Mattie has spent the last year setting herself up in a cottage in Cornwall for them both, partly using her ill-gotten Du Lotte Hotels gains. I'm told there is a herb garden, a collection of novelty teapots and two cats. Most middle-aged lesbian idyll ever.'

'And they share cardigans,' added Claire. 'I think the priest-hole was where they sometimes went for a secret daytime snog.'

Basher cracked his hands on his thighs. 'Well! Is that the wrap-up wrapped up then?' he said. 'Because life is going to get quite complicated, for a while.'

'Yeah, I suppose,' said Claire, suddenly gloomy again. 'It just all seems so... pointless. Michael said that when he told his boss, nobody cared about Arrowhead Beacon. There was no need for Monty to be scared, or for Tristan and Jerry to get into a fight. It was all for no reason.'

'It definitely was an accident, though?' asked Alex. 'I mean, the family name remains not a murderers' name?'

'Oh yes. Turns out Ted the gardener saw the whole thing,' said Claire.

'Making, basically, *all* of this pointless, if we'd only thought to ask him. LOL,' added Soph.

'I am *so* glad we are technically not murderers that I am not going to enquire about Ted the gardener,' commented Basher. 'Although I will be grappling with how absolutely cold-blooded my mum is, for a long time. You don't expect that, you know. She's… well, she's my *mum*. And I do not think the police believe it was an accident. There's going to be some kind of inquest, and it'll delay burying poor Kevin… Jerry. Possibly for months.'

'Well, from their point of view, I suppose that "Honestly, Officer, we've been hiding a body on our property for a year because of an accident, not a murder" isn't very convincing,' said Claire. 'Also, Monty did sort of try to do a light murder on me. A murderette.'

'A little bit of bodily harm, as a treat,' said Basher. 'In either case, I am choosing not to think too far into the future just at the moment. That's a problem for later. Come on, invalid. We should put you to bed. To be spoon-fed any soup other than chicken, and so on.' He bent over and actually picked Claire up, bride-over-the-threshold style. 'Oh, this was a foolhardy idea,' he murmured, almost instantly. 'Please get the doors, Nibling.'

Claire looked feebly at his peachy-fuzz jawline, because if she looked into his eyes she felt she might start crying. She caught the scent of sweet soap and clean laundry, and a little bit of sweat.

Basher carried her carefully, politely disguising the effort it took, down to his bedroom. The secret sanctum. It was airy, but smelled of paper. There were books stacked everywhere, in teetering piles up against the white walls. For some reason, Basher eschewed shelves. The double bed had been dressed in clean slate-blue sheets, like a wide, welcoming sea.

He turned his head down to look at her and smiled. Claire was struck by a sudden kind of madness. It was the knowledge that she had a future at all, that there would be people in it, that she was alive, and that Sophie was here and things would keep happening, one after the other. She flung her arms around Basher's neck and pressed her face towards his.

He went, 'Erk, what are you doing?' and reflexively dropped her.

Claire landed on the bed and bounced.

'Sorry! Sorry, are you all right? Oh dear. Sorry,' said Bash, looking guilty. 'Claire, I'm sorry, I'm gay. I assumed you knew!'

'Oh,' said Claire, going extremely red.

A million miles apart, but right next to each other, Alex and Sophie leaned against the wall and both laughed and laughed and laughed.

Epilogue

Weeks later there was another funeral, in a church that Sophie and Claire already knew. They stood a little apart from the other mourners, but Sue came up and said thank you for helping to find Jerry. She looked like her life was already over.

Sophie observed this with some curiosity, and asked Claire if she thought that was what her mum was like now, or if Sophie technically being missing allowed her to pretend things were going to be all right again. They talked about, maybe, going to visit her. One day. Eventually.

They loitered in the graveyard for a while after Jerry was buried, waiting for everyone else to leave. They stood by his graveside for a bit, but it stayed quiet. That made Claire happy.

Before they left, Claire put a clean cassock wrapped in brown paper by the door of the church. Then she went round the back of the building and took a brand-new football out of her bag. She looked around carefully, took out a knife and stabbed the football violently for several seconds.

'Cor!' said Luke, in disbelief, bouncing his new toy. 'Thanks!'

Sophie smiled. '*Ohmigod*, I really didn't think that was going to work,' she said. 'Trust you to murder a football, weirdo.'

'We've got to get going. Basher says he's having to physically restrain Alex from filling out the paperwork to start a kind of Mystery Inc., but for ghosts.'

'I think that's a good idea. You'd be brilliant at that. Anyway, Mystery Inc. for ghosts is just regular Mystery Inc.'

'No, it's not. The whole point of Mystery Inc. is that when they pull the sheet off the ghost, it's just a normal old man.'

'Ohmigod, why are you like this?'

So they went home. To Brighton.

Acknowledgements

Writing acknowledgements is immediately giving me anxiety because I'm going to forget someone. And, like, are they too long? How long are they supposed to be? Can you get acknowledgements *wrong...?*

I'll thank my family, *I guess,* particularly for leaving me alone when I was reading books I probably shouldn't have been at age 13.

Eternal and most important, thanks to Colm Ahern for being proud of every small piece of progress I ever made.

To Jay Wood: the burner of ships; bright-eyed; the first and most wonderful of readers.

Mega cheers to the other early readers: Chris Durston, Brendy Caldwell, Graham Smith, Hirun Cryer, Dean Rogers, Harry Scoble (also for being cool that I got a book published before him), and Johnny 'Rules' Chiodini, who didn't read but is generally lovely and supportive. To Chris Wallace for always texting me when I'm busy: fuck you pal x

Not many agents will put in the effort to help with edits and rewrites, and the intersection of those who will with those who provide lovely dog pictures is surely just Stevie Finegan at Zeno, a wonderful person who totally *gets it.*

Likewise, thank you to Sarah Hodgson at Atlantic and Anna Kaufman at PRH for being fabulous editors, especially to Sarah for looking after me at my first literary festival and Anna for often asking me to make bits sadder and, essentially, *make them kiss*.

Thank you so much to Felice McKeown, Kirsty Doole and Kate Straker for making me and my book both seem competent and cool and exciting – no mean feat, especially in the case of the 'me' bit. Thank you, too, to Hanna Kenne, Niccolò De Bianchi and Beth O'Rafferty for making sure this book physically exists, Ed Pickford for making it look like an actual book, and to Dave Woodhouse, Gemma Davis and Isabel Bogod for doing the tough bit of actually selling the thing.

A thank you and an apology to Art Director Richard Evans and my brilliant cover designer Lisa Horton, both for creating a cover that I love and putting up with me giving extremely vague vibes-based feedback, and then asking to move the broken window to a specific ground-floor window because it was very important to me for some reason.

Thank you Mandy Greenfield for the excellent copy-edit that caught how much I say 'actually', and putting up with me explaining, shame-facedly, when things are misspelled on purpose because I think it's funny. Thanks to Jan Adkins for proof reading at a time when I didn't think I had the strength to read this *again*.

I have nothing but pathetic gratitude to all the Irish writers who have immediately reached out and made me feel welcome.

Shout out to Coffee Cove, where almost all the edits on this book were finished with the help of vegetable soup, toasties, and massive scones.

Whoever it was who wrote an account of going to a WWE show and taking mushrooms on Reddit: it is one of my favourite pieces of writing and I think about you at least once a week.

And to any video game developers, writers, musicians, directors, artists and dream-weavers who ever made something I loved: thank you, thank you, thank you.